Praise for *Solaris Rising*

"One of the three or four best SF anthologies published this year... there's nothing here that isn't at least good, and some that's outstanding."
Gardner Dozois, *Locus* Magazine

"★★★★ The literary equivalent of a well-presented buffet of tasty snacks."
***SFX* Magazine**

"This anthology of new short stories is essential reading."
***BBC Focus* Magazine**

"A+, highly recommended... A very strong, eclectic anthology with something to please any lover of contemporary sf."
Fantasy Book Critic

"An excellent collection... In my review of *Engineering Infinity*, I pondered 'I'd be surprised if there's a stronger anthology in 2011.' Well, the same publisher has now produced another anthology that is right up there with it."
BestSF

"Believe me, it's a journey well worth taking. Science fiction storytelling at its finest..."
***Mass Movement* Magazine**

THE NEW SOLARIS BOOK
OF SCIENCE FICTION

SOLARIS
RISING 3

EDITED BY
IAN WHATES

SOLARIS RISING 3

THE NEW SOLARIS BOOK OF SCIENCE FICTION

EDITED BY
IAN WHATES

INCLUDING STORIES BY

Benjanun Sriduangkaew

Chris Beckett

Ken Liu

Julie E. Czerneda

Tony Ballantyne

Sean Williams

Aliette de Bodard

Alex Dally MacFarlane

Gareth L. Powell

Laura Lam

Ian Watson

Adam Roberts

George Zebrowski

Cat Sparks

Benjamin Rosenbaum

Ian R. MacLeod & Martin Sketchley

Nina Allan

Rachel Swirsky

SOLARIS

First published 2014 by Solaris
an imprint of Rebellion Publishing Ltd,
Riverside House, Osney Mead,
Oxford, OX2 0ES, UK

www.solarisbooks.com

ISBN: 978 1 78108 208 9

Cover Art by Pye Parr

A CIP catalogue record for this book is available from the British Library.

Designed & typeset by Rebellion Publishing

Printed in Denmark

CONTENTS

Introduction, Ian Whates   9

When We Harvested the Nacre-Rice, Benjanun Sriduangkaew   13

The Goblin Hunter, Chris Beckett   29

Homo Floresiensis, Ken Liu   45

A Taste for Murder, Julie E. Czerneda   61

Double Blind, Tony Ballantyne   83

The Mashup, Sean Williams   99

The Frost on Jade Buds, Aliette de Bodard   105

Popular Images from the First Manned Mission to Enceladus,   127
Alex Dally MacFarlane

Red Lights, and Rain, Gareth L. Powell   141

They Swim Through Sunset Seas, Laura Lam   157

Faith Without Teeth, Ian Watson   169

Thing and Sick, Adam Roberts   181

The Sullen Engines, George Zebrowski   205

Dark Harvest, Cat Sparks   223

Fift and Shria, Benjamin Rosenbaum   243

The Howl, Ian R. MacLeod & Martin Sketchley   253

The Science of Chance, Nina Allan   275

Endless, Rachel Swirsky   303

INTRODUCTION

IAN WHATES

I STILL HAVE to pinch myself when realising that this is now the third volume of *Solaris Rising* (the fourth if you include the e-book only *SR1.5*). I can't thank the folk at Solaris/Rebellion enough for inviting me to compile and edit this series and for allowing me such a free rein. The appearance of *Solaris Rising 2* on the 2014 shortlist for the Philip K Dick Award came as a complete though very welcome surprise, suggesting that I must be doing something right.

As stated in previous introductions, what I've been attempting is to showcase the rich variety that modern science fiction has to offer, without placing any restraints on the authors' imagination by imposing a theme, and that remains the guiding principal.

The first two submissions I received for *Solaris Rising 3* were from Gareth L. Powell and Aliette de Bodard. Both contributed to the *SR1.5* mini-anthology, which was intended as a bridge between the first book and future volumes. Neither writer has disappointed, with Gareth providing a typically odd but action-packed piece and Aliette a new story set in her highly successful Xuya universe: surely one of the most interesting alternative/future histories currently being written.

I owe Tricia Sullivan a debt of thanks for suggesting I check out the work of Benjanun Sriduangkaew and Alex Dally MacFarlane. I did, and was suitably impressed. Both authors have contributed stories to recent NewCon Press anthologies and it's a pleasure to work with them again here. Alex seems to enjoy playing around with unusual narrative structures, while Benjanun brings a refreshing perspective to her writing as well as genuine depth. As Tricia suggested, here are two writers that definitely merit watching.

No one needs to introduce me to either Adam Roberts or Ian Watson: award-winning authors who appeared in the first volume of the series and return here with typically clever tales. Ian's is surreal and bristling with toothy wordplay, while Adam's is thought-provoking and intense. It was Ian who introduced me to George Zebrowski, a writer whose short fiction I've admired for decades but never dreamed I would have the opportunity to work with (I suppose that's another drink I'll owe Ian at some point).

Best Opening Line Award has to go to Laura Lam. How could anyone resist a tale that begins: "I thought I would write and tell you what happened after you died."? Thankfully, what follows lives up to that initial promise. The darkest contribution comes from Tony Ballantyne, whose claustrophobic story shows an all too plausible near future that's likely to induce an involuntary shiver, while the oddest is probably from Swiss resident Benjamin Rosenbaum. I met Benjamin by chance at World Fantasycon in Brighton, and instantly recalled his entertaining 'Biographical Notes To "A Discourse On The Nature Of Causality, With Air-Planes" By Benjamin Rosenbaum' (it's difficult *not* to remember a novelette with a title like that), which was shortlisted for a Hugo award a few years back. Of course I had to invite him to submit.

Ken Liu and Sean Williams are two authors whose work has long impressed me. I've been seeking stories from both since the very first book, but each has invariably been too busy. This time around, Solaris gave me a considerably longer submission window and I was delighted when both Ken and Sean found the time in their busy schedules to write something; even more so when I received the stories and realised how good they were.

Ian R. MacLeod is another writer I've been gently badgering since volume 1. Ian doesn't write many shorts, but those he does are always of a high quality – every short story he was responsible for in 2013 made it into a *Year's Best* anthology, for example. I was expecting the usual polite brush-off (Ian is ever the gentleman) and so was pleasantly surprised when he said, "You know, I might just have something for you this time." It turned out that Ian was planning a collaborative story with mutual friend Martin Sketchley (who appeared in volume 2).

The remaining contributors fall into two categories: authors whose work I admire and have long hoped to work with, and those I *have* worked with and am always eager to do so again.

The latter include Nina Allan and Chris Beckett, two of the most exciting writers of intelligent, modern SF working in Britain today. Nina gets under the skin of a protagonist as effectively as any writer I know, and her story here, a police procedural in an alternative Russia, is no exception. Chris manages to instil a sense of social commentary into his work without ever obstructing the narrative. 'The Goblin Hunter' is set on the strange colony world of Lutania, one of my favourite Beckett milieus – I'm fortunate enough to have published two previous Lutanian stories in the collection *The Peacock Cloak*.

Julie Czerneda, Cat Sparks, and Rachel Swirsky fall into the former category. Oceans separate me from all three, which means that our paths have never yet crossed at conventions, we've never nattered at the bar, shared panels or lively debate... Only the quality of their fiction has brought them to my attention, but how better to meet a writer? These are busy, multiple award-winning authors and as ever in such instances I'm extremely grateful that they have found the time to write me such cracking stories. Another dip into the murky world of police and crime, Julie's contribution is very different in style and texture from Nina's, while Cat provides the closest to traditional military SF you'll find in the book, though the story is far from straightforward. Rachel's submission arrived at the very last minute but was worth the wait; its punchy high-tempo narrative proved an ideal closing word for the book.

So there we have it: eighteen stories from nineteen authors, providing a cross-section of the genre which, hopefully, will entertain and satisfy, and might just tempt you to explore some of the contributors' work further. Happy reading.

Ian Whates
Cambridgeshire
May 2014

WHEN WE HARVESTED THE NACRE-RICE

BENJANUN SRIDUANGKAEW

Benjanun Sriduangkaew writes soldiers, strange cities, and space opera. A finalist for the Campbell Award for Best New Writer, her fiction has appeared in Clarkesworld, Beneath Ceaseless Skies, Phantasm Japan, Dangerous Games, *the* NewCon Press *anthology* La Femme, *and has been reprinted in best of the year collections. Her contemporary fantasy novella "Scale-Bright" is forthcoming from Immersion Press.*

THE UN-WAR between Jiratar and Sujari is fought by madness and ballistic allegory, by trojan-fire aimed at collective memory. The sky flashes not with ammunition charges but perceptive warp, fractures in shared consciousness.

History blisters apart. Recall gains the property of liquids and flows to fit its vessel. No one remembers.

Under this climate, everyone is a combatant.

THAT PARTICULAR DAY Pahayal is wading out to the Amraste, her secondskin mottled with sweat and river silt. The trap-drones nibble at her ankles, the sun's glare rough as grit in her eyes.

She finds the stranger floating among catfish that swirl belly-up and engine drift like mourning-weeds: a face dressed in soot and bruises, eyes tight shut against a day too bright. Dead, Pahayal thinks as her shadow falls across; alive, her datasphere insists. Almost she expects the body to dissipate, another figment of hallucinatory sync, another leftover from an illogic burst.

Clenching her teeth against the weight and the wet she pulls the body out. Her grip slips and slides, but she perseveres until they are both on muddy banks and then on solid ground. Readings indicate eighty-six kilos and steady vital signs. She doesn't bother requesting an ambulance; an overview of hospitals in the area shows her staff shortage and overtaxed equipment. For a patient in non-critical condition there will never be a slot.

Pahayal looks up at a sky so clear, so true. There's no interference buzzing and scratching at her mind. She doesn't want to return to the city and she has no time or energy. But in the end she summons her carrier.

On the way home she takes a second look. The stranger is phenotypically local, the mode of dress off-world: too cosmopolitan and sleek by far. An aggressive jawline, a sharp nose, and eyelashes voluminous enough for two. With profile metadata offline she doesn't assume a gender but feels certain this is no enemy. Elsewise she would have a duty – but she doesn't think of that; she's long ago given up the luxury of what-ifs.

She sets the house replicant to clean and monitor her good deed. These days only basic units, none too clever, can be relied on. Advanced intelligences have shattered long ago, victims of their own heuristics. Pahayal imagines humans will follow someday until Jiratar is a country of lesser replicants cycling through their default routines, cooking for the dead, cleaning empty houses.

She goes to sleep lucid; holds out the hope she will wake up the same.

The next day arrives with dawn gone and midday imminent. Ten hours of sleep, all of them bad: a throb in her temples, an itch under her skin. She unfilters a window and kneels dazed in a pool of sunlight. Listening to birds and feeling ill, but grateful that she is not seeing what isn't there. The noon is calm, a promise of normalcy. Allusion-coded channels give no warning of imminent attacks.

She's halfway dressed in mismatched lehenga choli when she realizes that the first-aid subroutines have gone silent. One glance at the wardrobe and she decides she doesn't care.

The kitchen is on, simmering pots and toggled cookers. The stranger presides over them, datasphere online and profile broadcasting female. Pahayal judges her build. Exceptionally dense and, though earlier scans haven't revealed implants, almost certainly augmented. An athlete, or – "Are you a soldier?" The proper kind, trained and ranked.

"Am I?" Enunciation precise and angular, the perfect Costeya only found on Hegemonic cradle worlds. "If you honestly wanted to know you could have gene-matched me. Since you didn't, I'll have to assume that's a conversation starter more than a real question. You could've just said hello."

"Where are you from?" Pahayal means to ask more but the smell of blue-rice steam distracts. The cooker has been working for fifteen minutes. Garlic and ginger sit in saucers by the side; stains on the stranger's hand tells her the dicing has been done manually. "Look, the replicant could've done that."

"A friend of mine doesn't let replicants cook. Bad influence." She drops the ginger and garlic into the pot, adding dollops of shark-eel concentrate. "I'm Etiesse Hari-tem-Nakhet, from Imral. A mouthful, I know."

"Pahayal Rukhim. And half *your* name is local." Though Etiesse is as Costeya a name as she's ever heard, carved-ice syllables, elegant and aristocratic.

"Some great-great-such-and-such were from this planet, yes. That's why I'm here – I've never been to Jiratar before and my parents insist it's past time I connect with our heritage." Etiesse stirs the pot. A hiss of oil; a bouquet of spices. "This is Tiansong food, as close as I can approximate it. You'll have to let me know if the taste disagrees with you."

It doesn't, though the absence of chargrilled bread and pickles for breakfast is unusual. More unusual is a person cooking for her. Pahayal can't remember the last time that happened. When she lived with her family? Years ago, a decade at least. "How did you end up in the Amraste?"

"An engine failure." The off-worlder touches a chrome shark at her throat as if to ward off bad luck. "A really stupid way to die. I owe you a hell of a lot. Is there anything I can do for you?"

Take me away from here. Pahayal does not say that. "Not much. I'll get you to the tourist board."

THERE WAS A time when they weren't at war.

Pahayal likes to imagine that electors in their gold-threaded brocade and commanders in their fire-kissed gauntlets remember the cause, what shape the conclusion might take, whether they have hope for victory. She likes to imagine there will come a time when every child doesn't become de facto combat personnel the instant they receive their first neural implant linking them to the public sync. The nature of their conflict with Sujari makes everyone a target, erasing distinctions between civilian and not.

No weapons are deployed beyond the rare low-grade disease, the occasional supply sabotage. Instead the grid is the battlefield, neural paths the besieged infrastructure, data synapses the entry points. Over the decade casualties have been low – theirs is a war by treaty, governed by strict terms – to avoid Hegemonic attention, but the effects of constant fact-fluxes and contradiction strikes have shown. Pahayal's work includes rudimentary media-processing, turning figures into readable reports, and she's lost count of the suicides. There have been rapid advances in adaptive partitioning and grid filters, but they can't keep up with Sujari ballistic glitches. It's easier to accelerate weapons development than defensive measures, a military friend told her once.

The same friend succumbed to an attempt to rip out all her network nodes without a surgeon's help. Pahayal is only surprised it doesn't happen more often; she has felt the urge, might have tried it if she weren't so squeamish about her own blood.

Near the city, data streams are haunted by echoes of scattershot assault. In her peripheral sight Pahayal glimpses cascading cilia, twitching barbs. On better days there is no sensory load – sight without tactility or smell is easier to dismiss – but sometimes they can be so solid she's nearly convinced she's facing foreign replicants, bristling limbs and eyes full of black light.

"Is my imagination overactive or do they look alarming?" Etiesse shades her eyes and leans close to the silver-web window. "Like they could be anti-infantry units."

For a moment Pahayal thinks the off-worlder has been infiltrated too, that Etiesse is seeing a trembling world, thin surface tension a whisper from collapse. She follows the Imraal's gaze to the harvesters in their fields of nacre-rice. They cut and collect, eight legs keeping rhythm ballet-precise over nutrient and water pipes. Reaping the riches of Jiratar to be distilled into pearl perfume and opal tea.

She wipes her hand on her hip, sweat-smear quickly absorbed. "If you're an arachnophobe." Anti-infantry is precisely what they are, multipurpose. "What do you do for a living?"

"Security contractor – civilian sector strictly, since the other one is, ah, fussy to work with. Duller job than most think and I hardly ever get time off."

Their visit to the Immigration and Tourism Bureau is quick, though Etiesse is scandalized when she discovers that a tourist visa lets her stay no more than a week and doesn't apply system-wide. "So if I wanted to visit Sujari, which is all of *next door* away, I'd have to apply for a different one?"

"Just how it works." Pahayal shrugs. An Imraal rarely requires a visa to travel anywhere. "You're used to getting your own way, aren't you?"

The off-worlder makes a soft, unamused noise: "It's just – never mind. Can't I repay you in some way? Pick a place or twenty. My treat."

Pahayal chooses the most exclusive, most remote attractions. A performance of Lijaj Enmu sculpting herself in live obsidian, the new aviary where replicant crane-serpents evolve by the minute to lay unique flower zygotes, a lunch at the most fashionable desert restaurant where they are served fennec roe, pepper lychee, and glacier seal curries. Unfazed, Etiesse pays for every item and admittance.

During dessert, a glistening tadpole with a newborn's features climbs out of her opal tea. Pahayal sets the cup down carefully. It is not real, she knows, but this one reeks of mud and rot. Even after routine data purges, there are always some vestiges left behind. "Just what kind of salary do security contractors make?"

The Imraal sips from her cup, evidently seeing and scenting nothing more extraordinary than nacre-rice essence. "Hey, that's indelicate to ask."

"Not exact numbers. On a ratio of risk to reward?"

"Much too little. My work takes me places but most of the time I spend hours at grid-dead conferences, site inspections, and eating *dreadful* food." Etiesse smirks, a flash of perfect dental care. "You don't ask; you interrogate. What do you do?"

"Journalist. My investigative phase is long past." In the grid a report flashes by. Wind plant explosion. Two workers attacking each other, a third engaging a pressure valve.

"Hah, I knew it'd be something like that. And thank you, you've been a wonderful host."

Come evening, Pahayal sees Etiesse off to a hotel as furiously expensive as anything else they have sampled that day. A beehive of resin walkways and soft hexagon windows, the lobby lined with military-grade network disruptors. Guests never have to feel the slightest ripple of Sujari viruses.

She doesn't expect to see Etiesse again.

THE FOLLOWING WEEK something changes. Commander Indoma falls. Captain Daharej, after that. From all reports, though such information is always inexact, Pahayal doesn't think either ate their own guns. It was something more, a virus that overloads cardiovascular implants, turning heartbeat to heart attack.

Defensive sub-grids, Mazael's Apiary and Seven-Teeth Stream, shudder to fragments. Their adjuncts stagger. Both officers were in charge of primary countermeasures, and while they did prepare subordinates the integration process is arduous.

Pahayal doesn't dwell on the news too much. The glitches become worse and she has to fight harder to separate what's real from what isn't, to ignore the stabs of nonexistent pain, the pinpricks of fictive memory. Someday, Jiratar and Sujari will be a subject for anthropologists and historians. Abstract and endlessly fascinating.

Inexplicably, Etiesse invites her out again; just as inexplicably Pahayal says yes and books them a visit to frost orchards on Mount Ushol. For the occasion she dresses better than usual, gleaming sari over thermal secondskin, beads in her hair. Makes her feel almost human.

For their first destination Etiesse selects a weapon gallery. When they arrive she races ahead, kicking up snow, all the graceless haste of an excited child. Pahayal follows without trying to keep up, her gaze on the shimmering peaks, her senses and sync quiet for once.

In the gallery she finds Etiesse bright-eyed and grinning over a fanfare of winter blades patterned on the lace of ice crystals, the softness of frost-laden branches, the entropy of thawing leaves.

"These are gorgeous." The Imraal holds up a talwar, turning its serrated edges sidewise. Shadow matrices refract through them. "I didn't know Jiratar made anything like this. You should export them, collectors would pay a fortune."

"There are monsoon and summer blades too, but none of them is really functional."

"With the right specifications they could be. And the forms are so unique! Is this a rime orchid?"

Pahayal rolls the texture and shape of tact across her tongue, decides to advance without. "You don't know much about Jiratar, do you? Or speak any of our languages? Lahili, Sepaan, even Jiresh?"

Etiesse gives her a look, eyebrow raised. "Cut a tourist some slack, will you? My parents have ideas, but I'm just here to sightsee."

"Your family a few generations back –"

"What belongs to my ancestors doesn't necessarily belong to me." A small smile, held steady, not tense or brittle: this is a challenge Etiesse has met before, an argument she must have subdued many times. "Mind, my genealogy is all Jiratar, so obviously my parents and theirs disagree. They'd be frantic if I pick a partner outside our stock. Awfully traditional, my family."

"What would you prefer then?" Pahayal knows she is testing an edged limit. "A Costeya? Pale, with eyes like ice?"

"Imral is full of devastatingly clever people to marry, if you like that sort of thing." Etiesse picks up an urumi and runs a gloved finger along its whip-curl. "These overlapping veins are so pretty. They are hand-generated too, aren't they? Anyway, why are you so offended that I don't wish to claim my forebears' heritage?"

"Because aren't you saying Jiratar isn't good enough; that you have all you need from being Imraal?"

"To be properly Imraal I would have to be Costeya." The smile widens. "Even if I get surgery to *seem* like one and never go within spitting distance of a sari or sherwani, my ancestry records would still be evident. So I don't do that. I'm content with what I am."

Pahayal steps close – for what, she isn't sure. What point to prove if one even exists, what confrontation to force if she's even that brave.

A shadow closes over them, proboscis and legs arranged like wheels. The shriek of rivets coming loose and metal beams snapping under impact, the tinkle as pieces of roof splinter and fall – soft – on bright arctic tiles.

Gunfire; a smell of scorched glass. Pahayal thinks dispassionately that of course Etiesse is armed. Then she realizes that this isn't a glitch-missile or malware manifesting. What she sees is not optical augmens.

When she takes the off-worlder's arm she feels the warmth and throb of recoil. "This way," she says through her teeth.

Etiesse doesn't holster her pistol as they join the thin flow of staff.

The panic shelter seals. Pahayal counts twenty shell-shocked faces: like everywhere else the gallery is phasing people out for replicants, minimizing human employees. Looking from one stricken expression to the next she knows none of them can believe this is real, a physical attack at last, a seismic shift in Sujari tactics.

She tries to open an outbound channel for distress calls. Finds she cannot.

"They disrupted communications on a civilian target? For pity's sake, have some fucking *principles*." Etiesse's voice is low and harsh, chipping at the quiet. "Is this facility armed?"

"Yes." A thin man brings up an overlay. His hands shake. "Explosive drones. I'll just – automatic."

"Make it manual and turn control over to me. And pray, since remote warfare isn't my forte."

A rumble of architecture coming apart. Pahayal stares as Etiesse switches on auxiliary lenses, feeds of churning legs and razor tails pearled with detonation beads. Pahayal has seen Sujari locusts in simulation, because every Jiratar citizen must be prepared. The genuine articles are so much more, so much worse.

She will think back on this moment, often. Jaundiced light falling on them. Etiesse settling into a distant calm as her hands move across the input panel, painting rapid ruin.

It is impossible for defensive drones to dismantle and decimate Sujari flyers. Etiesse makes them.

Silence stretches. The overlay gives a close, explicit view of shattered mouthparts, splayed legs, broken pinions. All targets neutralized.

"We are at war," Pahayal says on the train back, "with Sujari."

There has never been a penalty for giving the secret away. Hegemonic discovery would mean punishment of both planets; in the face of that, convicting individuals for the breach is pointless. Sheer mad tribalism has silenced them all. Or their ragged minds forgetting that salvation can be had at the price of treason.

"Ah," Etiesse murmurs. "That explains."

They have the carriage to themselves. Jiratar trains are segmented vehicles, each made to detach and seek an individual destination as required. The idea appeals to Pahayal more than ever. Perhaps she can catch the first ship off-world, out-system. Perhaps she can step forward and taste the weightless relief of free fall.

"Pahayal." The way her name is spoken makes her look up. "Whatever happens I want you to know that you weren't the first to tell. We've had agents on Sujari for a year. You can't blame yourself, not for anything. And you probably knew this would happen sooner or later."

"What are you saying?" She can't breathe.

"That I am sorry."

"Who *are* you?"

"I never gave an alias. Colonel Etiesse Hari-tem-Nakhet, currently assigned to – no, that doesn't matter. It's not as if what command I'm associated with is relevant."

Pahayal's throat closes. "You're Hegemony."

"When you're non-Costeya, you have to be twice as Hegemonic to stand a chance, and what better way than to serve as a soldier?" The off-worlder shakes her head. "Our tactician projected Sujari would be the first to escalate, but not this soon. Our presence must've made them panic."

Pahayal checks. There have been other strikes. "They attacked because you're here. *You* are why five thousand died and counting. Intervention is –" The Hegemony has no right, they have always agreed. The one point of consensus: neither planet would appeal to a higher authority. Jiratar and Sujari have long been Hegemonic constituents, but they would not surrender this final shred of dignity.

Etiesse's shoulders tense. "Do you want this to continue?"

"It's not for me to decide. You can't just..."

"Who do you trust to decide? I don't mean who has the power. I mean who you believe has the competence, the sense." The soldier – the *soldier* – has the grace to avert her eyes. "The moral code, if you will."

"To best collaborate with you and hand over the last pretense we have of sovereignty?"

"To stop the bloody war!" Etiesse exhales sharply, too loud.

"Ministry of Education," Pahayal says, her fingers twisted into a hard whitened knot. "Second Magistrate Shahari Udha."

"Thank you." Etiesse tugs her shark pendant free and sets it in Pahayal's lap. "Stay safe. I'll do what I can to make this no uglier than it has to be." She leaves the carriage. Soon the vibration of a unit uncoupling resonates down the train's connectors.

Pahayal stares at the pendant. She unlocks a window, but in the end cannot find the courage to throw either it or herself out.

IN THE PRIVACY of her home Pahayal scans the pendant for malware, a tracking signal, anything. But it's just a piece of jewelry, an antique crafted in a Tiansong city. The price it would fetch at auctions is criminal.

She climbs to her roof, searching the sky for silhouettes of Mahing scythes and Sujari locusts. Wings like monsoons, mandibles like hail.

She uncovers more about Colonel Etiesse. An officer from a rich family, gifted with copious talent and ambition to match. Piecing together publicity and administrative rhetoric, Pahayal judges that if Etiesse succeeds here, her advancement will be as good as given.

Shahari messages her, effusive. *This way we'll gain everything Sujari stands to lose. Our weight in Hegemonic regard will change.* Pahayal never responds.

It doesn't escape Pahayal that this is the best outcome for Jiratar. Waiting for Sujari to make the first move, sacrificing Commander Indoma and Captain Daharej, the five to six thousand casualties. So Jiratar can claim victimhood to Sujari aggression – previous grid warfare will be accounted as nothing compared to the unleashing of physical weapons. And the Hegemony has known for some time, Etiesse said as much. A year. A year ago, many more people were alive. Hundreds of thousand. Half a million.

Through reports she follows the colonel's progress, a chart of tidy skirmishes on the ground, efficient battles in orbit. "I should have brought a gun," Pahayal whispers to herself, to an empty room, just to hear it aloud. "I should've drowned her."

The replicant warns that she is receiving less social stimuli than is advisable, that her nutritional intake is dipping below acceptable threshold. She extinguishes its voice.

She leaves the house once for the municipal disposal, where the pendant will be crushed and turned to raw material. Probably for armament fabricators. That thought turns her around and back to the relative security of her rooms. It's no longer safe to be out.

MIDDLE OF THE night she wakes up suffocated in nacre-rice. When she opens her mouth for breath more rushes in, pouring down her throat thick and blue and precious. Her muscles clench and her joints quiver in their sockets as she struggles upright, hard brittle grains pressing down like burial.

The illogic burst ends. She retches over her bed, bile and saliva, dry-heaving. A little longer and her body would have been fooled into asphyxiating.

She turns on the news. One of the feeds shows harvesters tearing each other apart. Stalks and collected grains are scorched under the fire of unsheathed weapons and the thunder of percussive webs. Paddies grow viscous with machine blood.

Entire minutes pass before she understands the real damage. A glance at some stills on the wall, a few tokens from her family – conch shells, costume jewelry – but she can't recognize any of them. If they've ever existed... but they must have. Everything frays.

When the silence of her house can be borne no longer, she takes what essentials will fit into her carrier, short-circuits safety protocols, and has her house burn itself down. The fire doesn't last, but it is thorough – she stays to witness the walls char and the windows crisp. The entire time she can't stop shaking.

She goes to the river whose name lurks under her tongue but doesn't emerge, parks her carrier by a dense jasmine bush, and sits at the bank watching trap-drones.

A call from Etiesse, the first since they parted on the train. She takes it, too hungry for another human voice to refuse.

"Cut off from the local grid," the colonel says, no preamble: all business, precisely a soldier. "They've deployed logic bombs. From the look of it they seeded those in the rice fields a month ago."

"You're too late. Didn't you anticipate this?"

"Logic bombs are proscribed." Etiesse's voice is leaden. "You've an offline census archive, haven't you? Integrate that, initiate a population-wide sync, and the damage will be... not all reversed. But mostly."

"I'm seeing –" She feels nothing at all. "Medical channels are lousy with distress calls. Cerebral hemorrhage, cardiac arrest, more. Is that reversible? Of course not."

"It's proscribed for a reason. May I visit you? I want to give you short-term partitioning to proof you against further impact. Not something I can just transmit."

"Fine."

The colonel doesn't ask for a location; she turns up within the hour. In a glance her mouth tightens. "You haven't eaten or slept enough. You look like hell and smell like burnt plastic. When I said stay safe I also meant stay *alive*."

"What's my name again? I must've told you."

Etiesse's expression contorts. In another person it might have looked as if she might cry. "Pahayal Rukhim. You'll remember that in a moment. Come on, we have to establish a link."

They peel back their secondskin, connect their tertiary sockets. The click of joining, an unpleasant brush of dataspheres pulsing each to the other.

"I can't imagine what living with this has been like. Exposure to repeated grid stress, abstract trauma, and barely any conditioning to soften it. You've held up well." Etiesse smooths shut her port. "The partitioning expires in a month. By then everything should be resolved."

"Sujari's surprised you twice." Pahayal fingers her own socket. The world is so silent, her sight so clear. No interference, not a whisper of signal that doesn't belong. She's grown so accustomed to the mental fog, the instability of her own perception. "You sound very confident."

"Logic bombs don't affect our personnel. We've been dealing with a light hand and that's made the Chariot of Sujari cocky. The Wheel and the Lotus tried to steer him away from open warfare, but he consolidated his power a long time ago."

"Did they send you because you look Jiratar?"

"Did they now?" Etiesse sits down among the grass rising high and glinting like swords between them. "I wonder. There are officers better suited to this, but I do blend in at a glance."

Pahayal reaches across, sliding her fingers through the colonel's hair, a gesture as calculated as it is desperate. "This is your forebears' world; this is the soil you could've called your own. Tell me you feel something."

For half a minute Etiesse cants her cheek into Pahayal's palm. Then she gently pulls away. "When your system falls under a unified government led by Jiratar, you'll find doors opening that were always shut. Opportunities you never even thought of. Eligibility as officer candidates."

"Provided we comply with the Hegemony on every point."

The colonel's mouth twists. "Shahari is a pragmatic person."

Shahari as the planetary governor: her reward for collaboration. They will need a whole new title for her. Perhaps they can crown her empress or goddess. Pahayal almost laughs. "You've known for a year what was happening in this system. You delayed taking action because you wanted us to surrender our sovereignty willingly, to ask for Hegemonic intervention."

"I can't confirm any of that." Etiesse passes a hand over her face. "You'd think it wouldn't get to me."

"I should have drowned you."

"I know."

"I'll never forgive you."

"Yes." The colonel stands. "I know that too."

AFTERMATH CELEBRATIONS ARE immediate and ubiquitous. Pahayal eschews them all and keeps to the funerals, drifting from one to the next until her mouth tastes of nothing but mourning dishes.

They are mass affairs, too many dead for individual rites. As a sign of newfound unity Jiratar and Sujari bodies lie in state side by side. Hegemonic personnel stand guard in chitin-plated ranks, faces hidden behind helms.

Elector Shahari Udha officiates along with the Wheel and Lotus of Sujari. She wears severe clothes, sharp stiff lines and unpatterned fabrics. Next to the platinum- and gold-threaded robes, Shahari could have been from anywhere, a cultural chameleon. In public addresses, on her own or jointly, she never speaks of Colonel Etiesse.

Despite that omission Etiesse attends, her dress uniform scarab-dark, rank insignia a cold star over her heart. She doesn't draw attention to herself, doesn't impose her company. Just one more officer among dozens.

In the end Pahayal makes herself approach the colonel at the pyres. They watch smoke thicken over the bodies and their funeral silks.

"One day," Pahayal says, "that'll be you."

Etiesse inclines her head. "Eventually that will be all of us."

"Got your promotion?"

"Not yet. After everything settles, I'll be made brigadier-general."

"Congratulations." Pahayal unclinches a twist of cloth from her throat, holding out the shark pendant. "A gift from an important friend, unless I'm wrong. You shouldn't just pass it around."

"Keep it."

They rise, follow the priests down to the riverbank, a gray small procession: too few come to the funerals. The trap-drones and their detritus have been swept away, leaving the Amraste a stark blazing path.

"Keep it." Etiesse nods at the priests floating ashes down fistful by fistful. "You can be the one to put me in a pyre. Burn the pendant with me, that's all I ask."

"I'm not going to tend to your funeral rites. That'll be the duty of your family and spouses."

"Oh, no. I was hoping you'd shoot me. You can even pick the gun; tell me the specs and I'll bring or custom-order one. It's important for the balance and grip to be just right."

Her fingers clench over the shark, its edges biting into skin. "I won't be your absolution."

The colonel turns to her. River-light seethes gold on the black of armor, gold on a face like sculpted teak. "One day," Etiesse says, laughing as if imparting a wonderful joke, "I'll be sick of what I do; I'll tire of life and what I am. It won't be soon, perhaps in a hundred years or hundred fifty, but it's inevitable. When that day comes I'll catch a ship here and look for you. I'll bring a weapon of your choice and you can have, if not justice, then a little satisfaction."

"And to abet your suicide I'll have to wait more than a century?"

"What with the implants I will see two hundred plus, and I didn't say I was in a hurry. Still, a fair enough deal, wouldn't you agree? I'll make sure you are provided for – the best medical care, so you can last as long as I do. My life I'm afraid you can't have, but my death is all yours." Etiesse's smile is quick and mischievous, a shared secret. Just like the war.

But this one would be trivial. By any standards, two casualties hardly signify.

"I'll wait," Pahayal says. "And I will not forgive you. Not in the next ten years, or fifty, or hundred."

In the river, the ashes have turned the water gray, a murk of dead eddying toward the sea. Quartz cicadas shine and sing among the whispering grass, the music of a perfect spring day.

"Good." Etiesse laughs again and fastens the pendant around Pahayal's neck. "I look forward to it."

THE GOBLIN HUNTER

CHRIS BECKETT

First published in Interzone *in 1990, Chris Beckett's stories have since appeared regularly in magazines and anthologies on both sides of the Atlantic, as well as in two single-author collections,* The Turing Test *(winner of the Edge Hill Short Fiction Award in 2009) and* The Peacock Cloak. *He has also published four novels:* The Holy Machine, Marcher *(now available in a new revised edition from NewCon Press),* Dark Eden, *winner of the Arthur C. Clarke Award, and its sequel,* Mother of Eden *(November 2014). Chris lives in Cambridge, England.*

SHE WAS ON the far side of the abyss. She was in a truly alien world. She was in Lutania. Here it was, in front of her now, as solid and real as her own hand, trees like giant mushrooms, without the smallest trace of green.

"It's *so* quiet!"

Sergei smiled.

"I know. It takes some getting used to. But none of the creatures here use sound to communicate. They don't need to because…"

"Because of telepathy."

"Exactly, because of that strange capacity they have that we don't yet understand. And they don't come out much in the daytime in any case."

"So right now, they're…"

"They're underneath us. We're standing on a million years-worth of matted lateral roots, and a metre below is a sea. Look, I'll show you."

"Oh it's *so* lovely of you to take the time to show me around like this, Sergei," Janet suddenly gushed, as he led her through the trees.

Everything in this world was wonderful, it seemed to her, even her new boss, who was about her own age and surely the most beautiful man she had ever met.

Sergei gave her a little tight smile which told her rather plainly that she was pushing things further than they were ever really going to go. But her enthusiasm was only dampened for a moment. How could she feel anything other than excitement, with this all around her? This silence. This otherness.

"We call these ponds," Sergei said. "You find them at regular intervals pretty much throughout the forest. Of course they aren't really ponds at all, they're openings into the ocean. It's from them that the creatures emerge every night."

The pond was an oasis of light. All round it, clumps of fleshy, lichen-like vegetation shone pink and white in the sunshine. The water itself was about five metres deep. She saw a shoal of tiny creatures – they were too small for her to be able to tell if they were anything like terrestrial fish – and then, just for a moment, she spotted something larger moving down at the bottom. It shot away under the roots of the trees before she could get a proper look at it.

"That wasn't an…"

"An indigene?" Sergei smiled. "No it wasn't. You'd know, believe me, if it had been. I think that was probably a biggish water dragon, but I really only caught a glimpse."

"A water dragon. Wow."

Janet stared down into water.

"I can't wait to see my first real indigene," she said.

Her boss straightened up and looked at her.

"Yes, well, you need to bear in mind that it's not usually a very pleasant experience."

"Oh I know they mess with your head, Sergei. Of course I do. But I'm well prepared for that, and I'm sure…"

"Prepared for it or not, Janet, the fact remains that when you get close to an indigene, you're confronted with your own darkness. It's not a nice feeling, not for most people, and not something you ever get used to: it works at too basic a level. Of course it's really only a defensive mechanism that they've evolved, the telepathic equivalent of a skunk's smell, but I can sort of understand why the Luto…"

"Oh wow, look at that!"

A strange object was drifting among the shadows of the trees about three metres above the forest floor. It looked a little like a balloon and a little like a jellyfish, with long tendrils trailing beneath. From time to time it bumped against a mushroomy trunk and bounced off again.

Sergei laughed.

"That's just a floater. You'll soon get used to those."

THE SHACK WAS beside a pond, a kilometre or so from the rest of the village. On the far side of the pond was the silent forest, pink and yellow and grey, but here, round the dilapidated shack with its single smoking flue, there were bedraggled plots of maize, a few rows of tobacco plants and some poorly tended beans climbing up ramshackle poles. From the air, Luto settlements resembled patches of green mould.

Anna was sitting on the steps of the rickety veranda. She was a young woman of twenty-three, but a stranger might easily have mistaken her for a ten-year-old boy, for she was less than five foot tall, wore boy's clothes, and had her hair cropped to within a few millimetres of her scalp. Right now, she was clearly not happy. She was holding her face in her hands, rocking back and forth, and softly muttering to herself.

"Shut up, shut up, shut up."

She was shivering slightly too, even though the air was warm: the caramel air of the Lutanian forest, with its faint hint of decay.

THE FIRST INDIGENES Janet saw were dead ones; two grey half-dried things, like decapitated frogs, nailed to a gibbet beside a forest track.

"Oh, that's awful. Who does such a thing? Who could possibly bring themselves to kill an intelligent being that's lived here peacefully for millions of years? It's not as if they're a danger of any kind."

"I'm afraid that's not how the locals see things," said Sergei as he stopped the truck.

There was another protection officer with them called Tom, a quiet man, a generation older than Janet and Sergei, who'd been on Lutania for some years, and it was him that pulled out the nails.

Janet tried not to retch as Tom and Sergei pushed the thin shrunken things into plastic body bags.

"They don't seem to have bones at all."

"No, they don't," Tom said, as they climbed back into the truck. "Their bodies work with hydraulics."

The truck was painted yellow, the same colour as their uniforms, and had black writing on the side.

Lutanian Development Agency: Indigenous Protection it said, and then the same thing in Luto.

"Well I suppose we have to ask about this in the nearest village," Sergei said. "God knows they've had enough input from us round here about how goblins are harmless and protected by law, but, all the same, I'll happily give you each a whole week of my pay if anyone admits to knowing the slightest thing about this."

He looked out for a moment through the silent forest at the ponds shining in the distance, then pressed the starter button. The truck rolled forward with a faint electric whine.

"Our informers tell us that a lot of village councils are paying a bounty on goblin heads these days," he said. "It seems to be a whole new campaign."

"Some people think the Agency's efforts to protect the indigenes have made things worse," Tom observed. "We've tinkered with a balance we didn't understand, and made the locals think they need to wipe them out altogether while they've got the chance, rather than just keep them at bay like they always used to do."

"'Some people' meaning you of course," Sergei observed acidly. "What do you want us to do? Stand by while the intelligent race of another planet is treated like vermin to be hunted down?"

Tom raised his hands.

"I'm not a policy-maker, Sergei. Don't ask me. I don't have that kind of brain, and I don't get that kind of pay either. I'm just saying that the bounty-hunting is a new thing, and it began soon after we started prosecuting goblin killers."

"I'd put it down to the fact that we also started paying out development grants to village councils. That's put a lot more cash into their hands. The intention was to encourage investment in skills, but instead it's created a market for specialist goblin-killers."

"It has," Tom agreed. "Some of them make enough to support a whole family, by all accounts."

"I don't see how they can bring themselves to do it," Janet said. "Okay, I know indigenes make people feel weird when they get too near, but they never kill, they never steal, they don't stop the settlers from doing anything they want."

Sergei shrugged.

"Goblins take over your mind, if you let them, that's what the Luto people think. Give them a chance to get into your head, and before you know it you'll be a goblin too. Not really human at all, not really even an individual. More like some kind of fungal growth."

"Weird thing is," Tom observed, "most of these goblin hunters are young girls."

"Yes, and social misfits," Sergei said. "Unmarriageable girls. The lowest of the low. Villagers keep their distance from them because they're seen as half goblin themselves, but they get a certain amount of respect because of what they do, which they might otherwise not have had."

"Poor things," murmured Janet. "How awful they have to commit murder to gain acceptance from their community."

UP THE STEPS of the shack came Anna's uncle Paulo. He was a big pear-shaped man with a thick tobacco-stained moustache and eyes that looked in two different directions, almost at right angles to one another. Now his left eye regarded his niece and took in her agitated state while his right gazed out accusingly at the mushroomy forest.

He squatted down beside her. Absently, he slipped his left hand under her shirt and began to stroke the skin of her back.

"They're out there again, are they?" he asked. "You can hear them in your head?"

He spoke in Luto. Neither of them had any English.

Anna took her hands away from her face, and nodded. It was a funny little face, wrinkled like an old woman's.

"Telling you all those bad things again?" Paulo asked, his left hand still stroking his niece's skin.

Anna, shivering, nodded.

"Well we know what to do about that, don't we?" said Paulo.

He turned towards the shack and gave a loud whistle.

*   *   *

SERGEI'S MONEY WAS safe. No one in the village knew the slightest thing about the gibbet, and certainly not the headman, Feliso, with his leathery skin, his sparkly eyes and his enormous black moustache.

"I am desolated not to be of more help," he told them, expressing his regret not only in words but with an expansive gesture that seemed to include not only his arms and his face, but every part of his body.

Sergei had introduced Janet as a new arrival from Earth and now Feliso leaned towards her, so close that she received the full blast of his garlicky breath, and spoke to her personally, as if confiding to her alone an unfortunate episode in his family history, which he'd rather the others didn't hear.

"We regard the Agency as an older brother, you see, my dear. We'd been all on our own here in Lutania for so long, generations, toiling away with our rough wooden spades in our little plots, and then suddenly – *pouf!* – the Agency arrives from the home planet we thought had forgotten us. Almost like an angel from heaven. They bring us knowledge, tools, medicines. They bring us roads and schools. How could we not be grateful? How could we not wish to help you? But, alas, we know nothing about these dead goblins. There are so many strangers in these woods these days, you see, since you brought us trucks and cars. They can come from far away and be gone again the next day."

"Lying bastard," Sergei commented as they drove off. "That Feliso's up to his neck in it. All our informers tell us the same. Not only is he involved in it, but he may well be one of the principal movers behind this whole head-hunting business."

Janet was quite shaken by this. She'd liked the headman – he'd conformed to all her preconceptions about wise, earthy peasant folk – and it troubled her greatly to think that all his garlicky charm had been a calculated performance.

"So why can't we just bust him then?"

"Intelligence isn't the same thing as evidence, unfortunately. We need to catch these people red-handed, and that's quite hard to do. This is a *big* forest. There are almost a million settlers, and they're spread out over an area as big as the Eurasian landmass."

*   *   *

RESPONDING TO HIS uncle's whistle, Caledon came ambling out of the shack. He was the youngest of Anna's brothers, in his middle twenties and, like his uncle, a big man, both in height and girth. Now he stood on the veranda, meditatively watching his uncle's hand as it moved under his sister's shirt.

"Girl having one of her turns again?"

"Don't call it a turn, boy. It's a gift our girl's got, to sense them out there, to sense them and hear them, when we don't feel anything at all. Go and get the others."

"Dad's over in the village."

"Well go and get him! Only don't shout off your mouth like Felipe did last time, or someone will cheat us of what we're due."

Caledon nodded, but didn't move.

"So what are they telling you then, eh, Anna?" he asked his sister.

"Leave our girl alone," said Paulo, gently stroking the soft skin of Anna's waist. "Go and get your dad like I told you."

Caledon scratched his groin.

"How many do you reckon there are out there, Anna?"

"I said leave her alone."

Caledon nodded and began to roll a cigarette.

"Headman pays ten dollars a head these days," he observed.

"Where are your brothers?" his uncle asked.

Caledon tucked his cigarette under his moustache, drew in the moist rich smoke and slowly savoured it.

"Felipe's inside sleeping, the great slob," he said when he finally exhaled. "The other two are with Dad."

"Well go and get them then."

One of his eyes looked at Caledon, the other at a floater drifting over the pond, trailing its wispy tendrils.

Caledon turned and called into the shack.

"Felipe, you tub of lard. Wake up and get the guns ready. Girl's hearing goblins again."

"Tub of lard yourself," Uncle Paulo said to him, as he caressed his niece's skin. "Get your arse over to the village and fetch your dad and your brothers."

*   *   *

35

THAT NIGHT JANET found it hard to sleep. She kept thinking about those decapitated indigenes, and about Headman Feliso and that colourful and exotic charm of his that had turned out to be a cold and cynical ruse. She imagined some girl coming in with a sackful of goblin heads just as she and Sergei and Tom were leaving the village, and the headman shaking with laughter as she tipped them all out at his feet.

She climbed out of bed and walked to the window. There was a little yard at the back of her bungalow and beyond that, more bungalows, but she could just glimpse between two of them the shapes of mushroomy trees in the forest that lay beyond. She pulled on some clothes and slipped outside into the warm caramel air. The forest was still silent but there was a sense of energy, of presence, that hadn't been there in the day. The ground had a faint pinkish glow and the ponds shone with phosphorescence, illuminating the tree trunks around them.

"It's beautiful," Janet whispered. "It's absolutely beautiful."

Suddenly she saw a line of pale animal shapes moving rapidly through the trees in the distance. And almost in the same moment they finally disappeared, she heard a loud splash from a nearby pond. Janet began to walk out into the forest. There was another splash as she did so, and she saw a pale and slender creature rising from the water of a pond and bounding away until it was hidden by the forest: completely alien life, sharing no common ancestor with the life of Earth other than primal matter itself, and the fertile nothingness from which it emerged. Janet was enchanted.

"Tall, and thin, with sort of… glittery wing-things," she said to herself, trying to memorise the animal so she could ask Sergei about it in the morning.

Then she noticed how much she was looking forward to talking to Sergei, and all her elation vanished.

"You are *pathetic*," said a familiar voice inside her head. "You are utterly pathetic. You work yourself up into these artificial little moments of excitement, you develop these little crushes, but you are nothing but a pathetic, desperate lump of neediness that nice people are willing to tolerate, but no one will ever really want."

That was when she saw the indigenes, two of them, no more than twenty metres away, watching her through the trees with their black button eyes, and smiling their V-shaped smiles.

*   *   *

Anna covered her face with her hands again and began to rock back and forth.

"Shut up!" she whispered. "Shut up, shut up, shut up!"

"Look at the state she's in, Caledon!" her uncle said. "Why can't you just go down and get your dad? It's not like it's far!"

"Okay, okay, keep your hair on! I'm going, aren't I?"

He squeezed down the steps past the two of them, but even now he didn't just head straight to the village, but turned again to Anna.

"About four or five, do you reckon?"

"We'll find out soon enough, for the love of God!" Paulo exclaimed. "Just get your dad and your brothers and we'll find out."

"Only it's always at least four or five of them when you get as bad as that," he went on, as if his uncle hadn't spoken. "That's unless one of them has got right up close, of course, but then we'd *all* feel it, wouldn't we?"

He regarded his sister with an appraising eye.

"And I don't feel anything at all now. Nothing. So I figure it must be a whole bunch of them, but some way off. Four or five at least. Not bad. Forty or fifty dollars-worth."

"Go!" commanded Uncle Paulo.

Anna rocked and moaned.

"You ready for a raid, Janet?" Sergei asked.

"A *raid*?"

"That's right. A proper raid. Joint operation between us and the police. We've finally got some witnesses who are willing to testify in court. Things can get a bit ugly on a raid, and you're still very new here, so don't feel you have to come, but if you're up for it you'd be most welcome."

"Well of course I'm up for it, Sergei! This is what I've trained for! This is why I came to Lutania!"

"Let's go then. We've a whole day's drive ahead of us."

They grabbed backpacks and headed to the truck. The Agency Police were waiting outside in two vehicles of their own.

"This is exciting," said Janet as they headed off.

The night had drained her, but this felt good and strong.

"I'll say," Sergei agreed. "It's great to be able to finally *do* something. And apparently, this woman's one of the deadliest goblin hunters in the business, with scores of kills to her name. It seems her family have made a few enemies in the local community, though, offended a few proprieties, and that's what's given us this chance. Just once in a while, Luto village politics work in our favour, and this is one of those occasions."

IT WAS GETTING towards evening when they set out, Anna, her father, her uncle and her four brothers, every one of them armed. The five big men walked behind, the tiny woman in front. She was no taller than a goblin herself.

"Come on now, girl," her dad called out reproachfully to her. "Don't forget to keep *us* in the picture. Are we getting near?"

He was a slightly shorter and balder version of his brother Paulo. In fact he had no hair at all, except for one single tuft that stuck out like a brush from the left hand side of his head.

"Yeah, we're near," muttered Anna, her hands tightening round a gun that was almost as big as she was.

The sun was setting. The pink moss under the trees was starting to glow, and so were the ponds that dotted through the forest all around them. Soon the animals would start to come up out of the water.

"Don't listen to what they tell you, girl," her father reminded her. "You know what..."

"Oh shit, I can hear them now," his son Felipe interrupted him. "Time to stop, eh guys? Let's let the girl go on ahead. It's her job, after all."

"So what are they telling you then, Felipe?" demanded his oldest brother George, with a sneer. "What are the goblin voices saying?"

"That he's a tub of lard," said the second brother, Stephan, the most ordinary-looking of the three.

"Oh crap," muttered Caledon, "I've got them now too. No way am I going any further."

Anna was muttering rapidly and constantly, like people do when they're trying very hard to blot something out from their minds.

"Shut up, shut up, shut up, shut up..."

"You keep going, girl," her dad instructed, sitting himself down with a sigh. "We blokes would only scare them away."

Anna carried on into the forest, muttering all the while.

"WE'LL LET THE police deal with the actual arrest," Sergei said as they drew nearer to their destination. "We're not trained for shoot-outs. But since her family are all blokes and the hunter's a woman, the police suggested you ride back with her in one of their cars, and they'll take the men in the other. From what I've heard she'd been the victim of a few crimes herself. Makes sense to separate her from them."

"Yes, of course," said Janet enthusiastically.

Sergei had said that goblin hunters tended to be outsiders. Well, she was an outsider too. She'd been teased at school. She'd found it hard to make friends. Once she'd driven a needle right though her own hand in response to a dare. She'd hoped to earn some respect for her courage. In fact the other girls had laughed at her for rising to their bait.

She looked at the forest outside the window, the trees, the ponds, the floaters nudging along in the distance, and imagined a meeting of minds in the police car. She would reach out to the poor young goblin hunter, the girl would realise she wasn't alone any more, and she would no longer need to kill.

"FORTY OR FIFTY dollars, eh?" chuckled Caledon. "Forty or fifty dollars! So what are we going to spend it on?"

Anna was far off in the distance now, a shadow against the softly glowing moss.

Felipe pulled a flask from his pocket.

"Drink anyone?"

"Don't mind if I do," said Uncle Paulo, opening his knapsack. "And here's something to go with it."

He took out bread and a large sausage.

"Now that's a bit more like it," said Dad.

The young men laughed and rubbed their bellies, and Caledon opened his tobacco pouch and began to roll a fat cigarette.

"You going to pass that round, Cal," demanded his brother Stephan, "or are you going to keep it to yourself?"

"I'll pass it round right enough, Steph, when you stop guzzling Felipe's rum, and Dad stops hanging on to that sausage like it's his precious cock."

Stephan made a lunge for the tobacco pouch. Caledon snatched at the flask. And then all six men were pushing and shoving for the various treats, laughing and yelling at each other, so as to drown out the whispering in their heads.

"VERY NEARLY THERE," said Sergei. "She lives just outside the village, I gather, beside a pond. Have a look at the satellite image, will you, and see if you can figure out the way."

FAR OFF THROUGH the forest to her right, a delicate little hart emerged from a pond and looked round at the dimming forest with its shiny black eyes. Anna moved slowly through the mushroomy trees.

"Shut up! Shut up! Shut up!" she muttered to the voices inside her head.

They were identical to her own voice, but they were speaking words she hadn't chosen and didn't want to hear.

"What kind of father does those things to his own little daughter? What kind of brother? Look at them now, letting you do the work. And then tonight they'll come to you one by one, stinking of meat and booze...'

"Shut up!" she hissed.

She peered through the trees. They were rapidly losing their colour as night fell and the glowing moss and the ponds became the only source of light. A golden water-dragon, the size of a stoat, peered at her from behind a grey trunk, its scales quivering.

"Kiss my arse!" came George's bellowing voice from the distance behind her. "Kiss my arse!

Her men were horsing around while they waited for her, making lots of noise as they always did.

"I wouldn't kiss your hairy arse if you give me two hundred dollars," she heard Felipe shouting back.

The voices in her head were quieter, but they were much, much nearer.

"No one likes you, do they? No one wants you for a friend even, let alone a wife."

She tried not to react. She needed to make them feel that she was holding out against them, so as to make them come closer.

"They all know what goes on back there in the shack, don't they? And who wants spoiled goods?"

She could see them now ahead of her. There were four of them, thin grey creatures, hand-in-hand, smiling their V-shaped smiles.

"They don't even let you keep the money, do they? They gamble it on cards and go to whorehouses, or buy themselves new boots, while your feet stay bare."

There were three full-sized ones, about the same height as Anna, and a single smaller one on the left-hand end of the row. Their hose-like penises dangled down. The little one was clutching a pebble of quartz that it had brought up from the water. Now it held the thing out to her, as if offering a present.

"If you had any guts you'd run away and leave them, wouldn't you?" said the voices in her head. "But you don't dare. It's much easier to lie to yourself."

"*Shut up!*" snarled Anna, lifting the heavy gun and blasting a hole right through the chest of the little goblin.

Grey strands of flesh splattered onto the pale tree trunk behind it as it crumpled to the ground, smiling all the while. The other goblins went on smiling too, and the voices kept speaking inside her head.

"And anyway, you know quite well that no one but them would ever want you."

She fired at the one on the right. It fell open sideways, as if hinged, so that its grinning face ended up next to its feet, from where it carried on watching her as the whole creature toppled slowly to the ground. The other two turned and bounded away with the strange skipping motion that was the goblin equivalent of a run.

She fired twice more. One of them fell twitching to the ground. She missed the other – it was further off – but she blasted away at it until it dropped, then ran after it to finish it off.

"That'll teach you," she hissed, as she emptied two more rounds into its grey, fibrous flesh, taking care not to shoot the head.

"I THINK IT'S just down that track there."

"Never mind that, Janet! Look over there through the trees!"

* * *

"WELL DONE, OUR girl!"

"Good good girlie!"

Coy as they had been about approaching the goblins when they were alive, the men came bounding eagerly through the forest with their machetes at the ready. Four times they sliced through the grey and boneless flesh, then Paulo slung the sack of grinning heads onto his back, while George picked Anna up like a little doll and hoisted her onto his shoulders.

"Good girlie!" they all told her.

She felt like the happiest person alive.

"You're better now, aren't you, girl?" said Uncle Paulo. "No more rocking and trembling, eh?"

Anna giggled happily, like a little child.

"That's more like it," said Uncle Paulo. "No more muttering under…"

Suddenly a new, heavily accented voice called out through the trees, and powerful beams of light flared out through the trees.

"Halt right there! This is the Agency Police! Stop where you are and put down your guns!"

JANET FOLLOWED SERGEI and the four armed police officers as they surrounded the little group. They were pathetic, misshapen, malnourished-looking creatures all of them. The men made her think of lumps of clay which some sculptor had begun to mould into human form and then changed his mind. The tiny, flat-chested girl managed to look both much older and much younger than her real age: a wizened ancient child.

One of the policemen walked forward and collected the guns and machetes, while Sergei fetched the sack and emptied the four heads onto the ground. They lay there grinning, each with its long dark shadow stretching away over the pink moss.

"The girl did it, officer," said the man called Paulo. One of his eyes looked at the agency people, the other at the young woman who her brother had lifted down from his shoulders. "She's not right in the head, you see, sir. We all came out to try and stop her. Well, it's not right is it? Everyone knows that shooting goblins is wrong and against the law."

* * *

"Why do you do it, Anna?" asked Janet gently in the best Luto she could manage. "They never harm people. They never steal. They never stop people taking whatever they want from the forest. And, after all, they were here long before human beings."

Anna pressed her face to the window of the police vehicle and said nothing.

"We're not saying those horrible feelings they give us aren't real," Janet persisted, "but that's not a reason for killing them, is it?"

Still looking out into the forest, Anna lifted her small thin hand to her mouth and chewed at a broken nail.

"I'll tell you something about indigenes, though," Janet tried again. "They can't tell us stuff that isn't already in our heads. How could they? How could a goblin know anything about us?'

Anna still looked out of the window, and her voice was so quiet that Janet could hardly make out the words she spoke

"You're goblin-lovers," she said, "all of you Agency people, and we hate you for it. You never take our side, do you, even though we're people like you? No, you always take theirs.'

HOMO FLORESIENSIS

KEN LIU

Ken Liu (http://kenliu.name) is an author and translator of speculative fiction, as well as a lawyer and programmer. His fiction has appeared in Fantasy & Science Fiction, Asimov's, Analog, Clarkesworld, Lightspeed, *and* Strange Horizons *among other places. He is a winner of the Nebula, Hugo, and World Fantasy awards. He lives with his family near Boston, Massachusetts. Ken's debut novel,* The Grace of Kings, *first in a fantasy series, will be published by Saga Press, Simon & Schuster's new imprint, in 2015. Saga will also publish a collection of his short stories.*

BENJAMIN DUCKED INTO the bar reluctantly. It was loud, stuffy, full of gaudy decorations for the tourists, and he didn't like the idea of having to buy a drink when he didn't want to. But it was that or getting drenched in the thunderstorm.

He cursed his own lack of preparation. Here in Maluku Province, the heart of the Spice Islands, it was always hot and humid and rain a possibility every day.

While he sipped his beer (watery and overpriced) and waited for the rain to stop, two locals approached him.

"I don't need a guide," he said preemptively. Each day, he got several such offers.

"No problem," one of the men said in English. He was burly, squat, with a grin that seemed to stretch across the entirety of his wide face. "On vacation?"

"No," Benjamin said. "I'm a grad student." He figured that giving the honest answer was the best policy. If he made it clear that he wasn't some wealthy Westerner looking for exotic local mementos, maybe they'd find someone else to fleece. To emphasize his uselessness as a source of foreign currency, he pointed to the heavy, muddy backpack on the ground next to his foot. "I study birds. I'm going to be camping most of the time."

Unfortunately, this failed to have the anticipated effect. If anything, the two men's eyes lit up.

"You are a scientist then?" the squat man asked. "You'll like these."

He took out a thick photo album and flipped it open in front of Benjamin. It was full of pictures of parrots, their iridescent plumage like costumes at some convention for superheroes, none alike.

"We can get you anything you see in here. Fair prices. Dead, alive, stuffed, whatever you want. Some of these no one outside of this island knows about. I know you scientist like that."

Benjamin looked at the pictures, stunned. He recognized at least three species that were thought to be on the verge of extinction.

"This is illegal," he muttered.

The man misunderstood his tone. "If you're worried about customs, we'll show you how to hide them. We have a good system." The other man said something in Ambonese, and the squat man added, "You can always slip the agent a few bills. It won't be very expensive."

Rage gradually rose in Benjamin as he recovered from the shock. *Who knows how many species have been hunted to death because these men wanted to make a few extra dollars from the collectors? And to think that they actually thought scientists would be a good niche market!*

"I'm going to the police with this," he said, taking the photo album from the man. Righteous disgust made him feel brave. "I'm here to study them, not kill them. Don't you have any respect for life?"

The ingratiating grins on the men's faces froze. They looked at each other, and then back at Benjamin. Now their gazes were cold, and the air seemed to solidify with tension. The squat man reached behind him. *For a weapon?*

Benjamin looked around the bar: the tourists were oblivious; the locals and the bartender studiously avoided looking this way.

Benjamin tensed his body and tightened his fists. He had thought he would be a good visitor, someone who respected local traditions, not an ugly American. But here he was, about to get into a violent confrontation with poachers.

"I see you've already met," said a voice to the side. The accent was American.

Three heads turned at the same time. The speaker was a woman, older, maybe in her late forties. She was wiry, compact, her face leathery from years spent in the tropics.

Benjamin had no idea who she was.

"I thought you weren't going to arrive for another day," she said, coming up to Benjamin and giving him a hug as though they were old friends. "I was going to introduce you to my two favorite suppliers, but they are, as usual, more proactive."

She turned to the two locals and spoke to them in Ambonese, glancing at Benjamin from time to time. The two men looked from her to Benjamin and back again, and their expressions gradually relaxed. The squat man's hand came out from behind his back, empty. The woman spoke some more, and she and the two men laughed.

Benjamin was utterly baffled, but he decided to wait and see what the strange woman had in mind. Now that the rush of adrenaline was over, his body was trembling uncontrollably. He was not a violent man, and he deeply regretted his earlier rashness. *Maybe it's best to just let it go.*

She turned to him. "I explained you were just testing them to be sure they weren't working with the authorities to entrap you. Your act was very convincing, maybe a bit too convincing." While she continued to laugh, her eyes locked gaze with his.

He decided to play along. "You have to be careful of strangers."

"Of course," she said as she looked back at the two locals, spreading her hands in a *you see?* gesture. The men nodded and relaxed some more.

She spoke more to the men in Ambonese, asking a question at the end. The two men looked at each other. The squat one said, "Sure. But you have to come along. We don't have them here."

They turned and left the bar, and the woman followed, pulling Benjamin along.

"What is this about?" he hissed at her, keeping his voice low so that the men wouldn't hear. "And who *are* you?"

"I'm Lydia. I told them that you're really interested in fossils. So they're going to show you some. You're going to have to buy something."

"It's illegal to trade fossils, too."

She looked askance at him as they walked, a smirk on her face. "Fossils are already dead. Unlike the birds, they're not going to kill anything for your patronage. I figured it's the best compromise."

"That's not the point."

"Would you like to spend some time in a local jail? You've really pissed off Loy and Thias with that holier-than-thou display. If you don't buy something from them, they'll go to the police and report you as a smuggler."

Benjamin stumbled. "That's –"

"– how things are done here," said Lydia. "Is this your first time doing field work?"

"I've been in the field every summer for three years," Benjamin said indignantly.

"Let me guess, you worked only on permitted expeditions with official support," Lydia said. "It's not quite the same when you're on your own, is it?"

Benjamin said nothing, which gave her all the answer she needed.

They arrived at a small house, barely more than a storage shed. The squat man, Loy, looked around to be sure the street was clear, then he opened the padlock and swung the door open. The four of them ducked and entered.

It was hot and stuffy inside, the space harshly illuminated by a single lightbulb dangling from a wire.

Benjamin looked around. The walls of the shed were filled with shelves from floor to ceiling. Fossils and bones lining the shelves cast long shadows. There were also trussed-up, feathered bundles.

"What do you want to see? Bird fossils? Primates? Lizards?" Loy asked.

"Birds," Benjamin said.

Loy went to one of the walls and came back with a shoebox. He opened it to show Benjamin. "We got these from the field by the hill west of the town. I can get you the exact coordinates and even some pictures of where we dug them up. I know you guys like that."

Giving the contents a cursory glance, Benjamin asked the only question that he cared about: "How much?"

Loy held up five fingers.

"Five hundred?"

Loy and Thias laughed and shook their heads in disbelief. The shoebox was snatched away and put back on the shelf. "You better be serious," Loy said, looking at Lydia.

Lydia shrugged. "He's just a lowly grad student. He has to file all expenses with his professor and the grant committee. Not a whole lot of room to hide things in the budget. He just wants something to show he hasn't been lazy on this trip, you understand. But he might become a big deal in a few years, and then he'll come back with the big bucks. You have to build the business."

Loy and Thias were visibly disappointed. But they tried to make the best of it. Loy thought about it for a while, went to another wall, and came back with a brown paper bag. He emptied the contents onto a small table.

Benjamin examined the bones. They looked like curved pieces of a skull and segments of arm or leg bones: maybe a monkey or something similarly sized. He had taken classes on primates as part of his program, of course, but he wasn't an expert.

Lydia came over and looked at the bones as well. She picked one up and held it under the lightbulb to examine it closely. Then she put it back on the table, apparently bored.

"I can let you have these for a thousand," Loy said.

Benjamin was about to refuse again and ask for something still cheaper, but Lydia spoke up first. "Come on, Loy, these aren't even fossils. They're just bones. Maybe from something you killed last week. Who are you trying to fool?"

Loy chuckled. "Can't blame a guy for trying."

"Where did you get these?" Lydia asked.

Loy looked to Thias, who answered by telling some long story in Ambonese. He made exaggerated gestures, and Lydia listened, rapt.

"What did he say?" Benjamin asked.

"He says he got it out of the stomach of a dead shark." She turned back to Loy and Thias. "Maybe he can do something with it. But you have to be reasonable."

"Five hundred then," Loy said, resigned.

Lydia looked at Benjamin, and he understood that this was as good a deal as he was going to get. It was still a lot of money, but it was better than going to jail.

Reluctantly, he nodded.

*   *   *

"So you've just been living here since you didn't get tenure?" Benjamin asked.

"Why not? It's cheap here, and I get to help my fellow scientists with acquiring research materials from the locals. I'm still doing science."

They were back at the bar. While they sipped warm, watery beer, Lydia continued to examine the bones Benjamin had bought. She had explained that she used to be a specialist in lizards, but these days, she was a sort of jack-of-all-trades, learning a little about everything so she could arrange meetings between Western fossil collectors, scientists, resellers, and the locals who had the goods they wanted.

"This isn't the 19th century any more," Benjamin said. "We shouldn't be acting like colonial explorers. You're encouraging them to break the laws designed to protect Indonesia's natural heritage."

"The laws? You mean the rules those bureaucrats made up in Jakarta to show how they're in charge? What do they know about the livelihoods of the people here? Besides preserving scientific evidence, I'm also helping the poor make a few bucks from rocks they dig up from the fields and the animals they catch for food. My conscience is clear."

"You're just making excuses. Because of you, the poachers end up killing already endangered species for money."

"You think poachers are the problem? You do understand that the real threat is habitat destruction, right? People here have to clear the jungle to make fields so they can feed more mouths, or else they have to turn the land into resorts for tourists. The poachers are the only chance for us to get any specimens before they're all gone."

"Then you should be working at helping the locals manage development more responsibly."

"Listen to you. Who are you to tell these people how to live their lives? And you think I'm the one with the 'colonial' attitude here?"

Benjamin wanted to argue some more, but Lydia shushed him. "These bones aren't from a black macaque, as I thought. I don't know what kind of animal it's from. It may be a new primate species in Maluku."

Benjamin was skeptical. "How likely is that? New species of birds or lizards, maybe, but an unknown primate coming out of the stomach of a shark?"

"Why not? Plenty of new species have been discovered when some scientist ordered a new dish in a restaurant in the tropics. There's plenty we don't know in the world."

"Well, you can have the bones if you want them," Benjamin said. "I'll be leaving for other islands tomorrow. Thanks... for stepping in."

"Good luck," Lydia said.

STILL GROGGY, BENJAMIN rolled out of bed. The pounding on his door was loud and continuous. *The police? Have Loy and Thias decided to carry through their threat despite the bribe?*

But it was only Lydia at the door. Without waiting to be invited, she pushed past him into the room.

"What is this about?" Benjamin asked. Dressed only in his underwear, he felt vulnerable, embarrassed.

"I took some pictures of those bones and sent them to a colleague who I thought might know more. And I got the answers back this morning."

"And?"

Lydia handed a stack of papers to him. "Read these."

Benjamin flipped through the papers: *A New Cranial Capacity Estimate for* H. floresiensis; *Proposed Skeletal Reconstruction of* H. floresiensis; *A Meta-Analysis of Latest Survival Date of Hominid Species...*

He looked at some of the photographs in the papers: old bones, tens of thousands of years old, not quite fossils yet; small skulls, like children.

Lydia kept on talking, but Benjamin only caught the end of what she said. "... I want you to come with me. Are you awake enough to understand what I'm telling you?"

Benjamin desperately wished for coffee. His mind felt sluggish, not working at full speed. He remembered hearing something about the 'Flores Men' a few years ago. The media had dubbed them 'hobbits': a new hominid species that might have been alive as recently as 12,000 years ago. Our cousins, of a sort, kind of like the Neanderthals.

Here in Indonesia.

"No, it can't be," he said, finally understanding. "You must be wrong."

"I could be," Lydia said. "But do you want to miss risk missing the discovery of a lifetime if I'm right?"

"I study birds! What do I know about... extinct hominid species with fantasy names?"

"So? My thesis was on lizards. But the anthropology department didn't turn me down back when I applied to join the expedition to make contact with uncontacted tribes in Brazil. Field experience is field experience. I can use someone who can carry a heavy bag and won't complain." She appraised him some more and added, "It even helps that you're impulsive. Shows that you still have a sense of adventure."

"And someone you can boss around because you think he's young and raw."

Lydia grinned. "I prefer to think of it as sharing my wisdom with the next generation."

"But the terms of my grant only cover bird surveys."

"Look, I know what's on your mind as a grad student. I've been there. What do you think is going to put you in a better position for a teaching job: more bird specimens, or confirmation of the survival into modern times of a hominid species?"

Benjamin rolled his eyes. But he didn't say no.

AFTER INTERROGATING LOY and Thias to find out where, exactly, the shark that yielded up the strange bones had been caught, Lydia badgered her shark specialist friends until they gave her their best guesses as to the shark's likely migration path. Like bloodhounds on a trail, Lydia and Benjamin set off to hunt down the source of the bones.

Everywhere they went, they asked the inhabitants about rumors of a tribe whose members were unusually small in stature. Some shook their heads and laughed at the strange scientists. Others told them long, fantastic tales that turned out to be elaborate jokes at the visitors' expense.

Benjamin found that he enjoyed hiking through the jungle and island-hopping with Lydia. He knew some of his professors and colleagues back home would disapprove of her methods – she had no compunction about paying bribes or lying when it suited her – but he had to admit she was effective.

They switched from planes to ferries to rented speedboats. They moved further from the conveniences of modern life, and each island they set foot on was more sparsely populated than the last. This archipelago of more than 18,000 islands held one of the most diverse biospheres in the entire world. There were many far-flung isles that had never been explored.

Finally, on Beliwan, a tiny isle in the Banda Sea, a local elder brought up legends of the 'little people' on a nameless, jungle-covered isle to the north, which did not appear on the charts. "They speak, and do not speak."

"Are you talking about some kind of monkey or parrot?" Lydia asked. A reasonable question, considering they had been fooled too many times.

The elder shook his head. It was clear he was not joking this time. His voice sounded full of awe and fear. "No one had gone there in many generations."

He showed them two skulls in a shrine-cave. They looked just like the one Benjamin had bought.

LYDIA AND BENJAMIN held their breath as they watched the dance in the clearing.

The biologists were well camouflaged in their treetop perch some three hundred meters away, and the rain forest in between was filled with the noise of chittering birds, scurrying lizards, skittering insects, and dripping water. Still, it was best to stay as quiet as possible.

Through their binoculars, they could see that the tribe, numbering about thirty, stood in a semicircle. They chanted tunelessly and knocked coconut shells together without rhythm. To the accompaniment of this not-quite-music, an old man with fuzzy white hair performed in the middle. He jumped, ducked, waved a stone axe above his head against imaginary enemies.

They got a good look at his face as he turned to face their direction: protruding jaw, dark and wrinkled skin, strong bony ridges around the eye sockets, a flat nose. Though he knew the image was technically wrong, Benjamin couldn't help thinking of it as halfway between a human and an ape.

The old man continued to dance, his grapefruit-sized head bobbing above his three-foot tall body.

"I KIND OF wish we had champagne."

"Oh, when we get back, you'll have all the champagne you can stomach."

THE YOUNG MAN attacked suddenly with a stone-tipped cudgel. He meant to kill.

But the old man was experienced. He dodged out of the way and kicked the cudgel out of his opponent's hand. Then he wrestled the youth to the ground. It was a brutal fight, teeth were bared, ears torn, blood flowed.

"What's the fight about?" Benjamin whispered.

Lydia shrugged. Dominance? A female? Or was it something more abstract and human: vengeance, justice, a moral stance?

Through the binoculars, the old man bit into the young man's neck. The biologists flinched.

BENJAMIN FOUND IT hard to interpret the behaviors of the subjects he was observing. If he assumed they were 'people,' it looked like they held conversations, enjoyed friendships and family time, sat around the fire as they cooked and daydreamed. How was the flavor of their thought, the qualia of their experience, Benjamin wondered, different from ours?

But if he assumed that they were 'not people,' it looked like they shared brief vocalizations, were rigidly hierarchical in their social interactions, and sat still in the midday heat to conserve energy. They groomed each other sometimes, and they made primitive tools not much more advanced than those made by the great apes.

Am I seeing them? Benjamin wondered. *Or only a shadow of us in them?*

They were clearly not as intelligent as humans, different, alien. Benjamin imagined how the footage would play on TV.

* * *

"WHEN DO YOU want to make first contact?" Benjamin asked.

He had been daydreaming about the hero's welcome he'd receive when he got home with the discovery. *Professor Mair will surely be a little more polite now that Benjamin is a celebrity for grant committees.*

"We're not prepped for that," said Lydia. "It's not as easy as just walking in there to say 'we come in peace'."

"So what's involved?"

"Well, for one thing, you and I are carrying millions of germs which the Flores Men have never encountered. If they're closely related to us, they're likely susceptible to them as well."

Benjamin sobered. In the history of first contacts, disease had caused many more deaths than ill will. "What else?"

"I'm certain they'll react to us with hostility. We'll need to be prepared to protect ourselves. Can't say I blame them. Imagine if you saw a couple of odd-looking giants stumping into your backyard."

Benjamin nodded reluctantly. "Didn't you say you worked with an uncontacted tribe back in the Amazon? How did you manage that?"

At first, Lydia was reluctant to discuss it, but Benjamin persisted. She said, "The professor planned it for years. He designed decontamination procedures, drew up possible nonverbal communication protocols, and investigated nonlethal weapons that could be used to protect us without killing or injuring them. The summer I signed on was supposed to be the big year, when we finally put everything into practice. But it was all for nothing."

"What happened?"

"To get funding, he had to do quite a bit of publicity. A few enterprising Brazilian companies heard about it and decided that they'd run adventure tours and bring wealthy American and European tourists into the jungle to make their own first contact with the tribe."

"Oh." Benjamin tried to imagine the chaos.

"Yeah. It was a circus. They had news helicopters flying in to film the people throwing spears at the cameras. A few of the tourists were injured, and then the guides brought out their guns. Lots of diplomatic protests and finger pointing followed. The professor's life's work was ruined."

Benjamin noticed that Lydia didn't mention what happened to the tribe after that.

"MAYBE..." BENJAMIN LOOKED at Lydia across the camp lamp, shaded so the light wouldn't be seen from a distance. "... we shouldn't speak of this when we get back."

"You want us to keep mum until you publish?"

"No," he said. "Can we just... say nothing, forever?"

"What are you talking about? This is the find of the century. Living fossils! These people will be the very poster children for human evolution. There will be bestselling books, documentaries, movies!"

"Are you sure that they'll be seen as people? The 'little people' are not human. That's the point. The adventure tours, they'll come. So will trophy hunters and poachers."

"They'll be protected. They're too valuable scientifically."

"Then they'll be taken from their home to be bred in captivity in research labs. That's not a life for people." He paused, and fidgeted with a length of rope. "But I think they are people, just a little different from us."

"Believe it or not," Lydia said, "it's not riches or fame that I care about. There are easier ways to get both. You and I are both here because we're scientists. We're obsessed about finding out things, but we're not the source of evil."

"No matter what, when our world finds out about them, their world will be gone. We've never been able to co-exist peacefully with a species so close to us and yet so alien. Wherever modern humans arrived, other hominid species disappeared."

Lydia narrowed her eyes at him, but she kept her tone even. "I know very well how ugly it can get when people justify barbarism in the name of science. My great grandfather was one of the subjects in the Australian Aboriginal IQ studies that declared a whole people inferior. But it's not right to keep this discovery a secret out of fear."

Benjamin blew out a held breath and shook his head. He gazed into the woods, where the Flores Men were hidden. "This will be even worse. We and they don't belong to the same species. There will be no moral prohibition against treating them as inferior, as not human. It's not about fear. It's about responsibility."

"So you preach ignorance. You think the responsible thing to do is to leave them here and pretend that they don't exist? I know you have these romantic notions about not interfering with the 'natives,' but what makes you think you get to decide for *them*? The world is changing. Sooner or later, our poisons and diseases will arrive here on floating garbage or on migratory birds. Maybe the sea level will rise and flood their home, at the rate things are going. There's no place on this planet free from our influence. Do you want to see them die from causes that we have solutions for? Can't you hear the arrogance in what you're proposing?"

Benjamin looked around helplessly, unable to decide if the dense jungle was innocent or savage, knowing that both words were wrong.

Is THERE A *way to make sure that the Flores Men will be seen as human?*

Benjamin decided to look for something specific.

He searched for and found abandoned tools: the stones were chipped roughly, the handles smoothed for easy grip. There were no decorative carvings or flourishes.

He examined their clothing through the binoculars: sun-shielding head coverings woven from leafy branches and pelts draped over the shoulder to carry food and tools. All very functional.

He squinted at their fire pits: circular and lined with bare stones. He thought about their almost-dance and close-to-music: was it just an expression of excitement or were there deliberate patterns that served no purpose but to be pleasing to the ear and eye?

He looked for anything that could be called *art*, and found nothing definitive.

THROUGH THE MIST, the biologists could make out the tribe huddling by the shore.

They settled the young man onto the raft and pushed it into the water. Half-hidden in a nest woven from branches, the lifeless body seemed even smaller, more fragile.

The old man stood on the beach and watched as the raft bobbed up and down in the waves, until the current seized it and pulled it out to sea. Behind him, the other members of the tribe waited, silently keeping watch over the sea burial like stone statues.

Then, one of the women collapsed to the ground and howled. Tears and mucus covered her face as she wrapped her arms around herself and rocked back and forth.

The old man turned around and walked to stand before her. Then he knelt and lowered his face to the ground.

Without speaking to each other, Lydia and Benjamin lowered their binoculars at the same time and turned their faces away. It was too intimate a moment: simultaneously older than the Trojan War and newer than the puddles left by the morning thunderstorm.

STRIKING CAMP DIDN'T take very long. They had been careful about keeping their footprint small.

As they continued to pack supplies into the boat, Lydia said, apropos of nothing, "That summer, one of the men in the tribe was killed. They filmed the whole burial with a tree-top camera, and then had commentators dissect it in slow motion, picking over every frame on TV. Someone later decided it was a good idea to try to dig up the body and try to sell it to scientists. I'd never been so disgusted."

Benjamin nodded. There was no need to say anything. This was as close as Lydia was going to get to *maybe you're right*.

They scoured over the campsite, picking up trash, processed food, anything else that might harm the inhabitants of the island.

"But you know this is only temporary," Lydia said. She was now sitting in the boat, hand on the tiller. "People are always looking for virgin beaches to develop, to build new resorts. The Flores Men can't hide forever."

Benjamin huffed as he pushed the boat away from shore, wading into the sea up to his knees. "Not forever. We'll come back in a few years and check on them."

"We will?" Lydia's eyebrows lifted. "And what do you hope to find in a few years?"

"Signs." Benjamin jumped into the boat. He pointed up the shore, at a small pile of objects piled some distance away from the waterline.

In that pile were some photographs he had taken in Jakarta: the skyscrapers and the street vendors, the bright lights at night and the busy colors during the day, the ten million inhabitants of all races and faiths in a worldly capital. He also left behind the binoculars and his Swiss Army knife. Added to that were a few buttons, coins, and a set of stainless steel dining utensils. He had chosen objects that he could sterilize with their field kit.

On top of the pile, he had also left his sketchbook. In it was a hand-drawn map of the island and many sketches he had made of the Flores Men. He wasn't much of an artist, but he had tried to capture what he had felt: the fluidity of motion as the old man had danced; the explosive force and power of the fight; the calming camaraderie of two friends in conversation; the gut-wrenching pain in the presence of unspeakable grief.

"Why?"

"These are signs of a world beyond what they can see. Perhaps they'll be inspired to leave home and explore beyond the horizon. Perhaps they'll come up with new tools and new uses. But no matter what, when they finally see us, they'll be more prepared than they are now."

What he didn't voice was a secret hope. He hoped that they would take up art based on his examples. Once the Flores Men could produce their own art, it would be much harder for others to deny that they were people.

"But maybe they'll start a religion based on these objects. Or they'll fight a war over them. You can't predict what will happen, Benjamin."

"Maybe not," he conceded. "But contact or not, it shouldn't be only our decision. You're right that it's arrogant to decide for them. I want to give them a few signs so that they can at least decide on their own time, on their own terms, whether they want to come and seek us out."

"And if we come back and find that they wanted nothing to do with your gifts?"

"Then we should respect their decision to want no contact at all."

They felt the current tugging the boat away from the island. Benjamin took from his backpack the skull pieces he had purchased from Loy and reverently dropped them into the sea. The two of them observed a moment of silence.

Lydia let out a held breath. "I wonder how many others before have done what we're doing. We often celebrate the discoverers. But maybe it's the undiscoverers that we should be proud of."

"Just because we think the story will end inevitably a certain way doesn't mean that we have to tell it that way. We have a choice." Benjamin gazed back at the island as the current sped up, and the boat accelerated. The jungle, he saw now, was neither Eden nor the heart of darkness. "And now, so do they."

A TASTE FOR MURDER

JULIE E. CZERNEDA

Since 1997, Canadian author/editor Julie E. Czerneda has poured her love of biology into SF novels published by DAW Books NY. Her latest work is the fantasy A Turn of Light. *Coming fall 2014:* Species Imperative, *the 10th anniversary omnibus edition of her acclaimed trilogy, and* A Play of Shadow, *sequel to* Turn. *After that, she's back to SF with* Reunification. *Visit her at www.czerneda.com for more.*

THURSDAY WAS DIALLED warm and sunny, with a soft breeze aimed straight over the rose arbours. Perfect for a funeral.

I should know, I'd been to more than my share this week. Before you ask, that's because I'm sitting a homicide desk while Ortmer adapts to his clin-mod – stupid blighter's regrowing fingers – and the newest face always gets stuck in a suit to attend funerals. Not any or all, mind you. Just those of particular interest to the department.

Judging by the glitter of media eyes amid the branches of the nicely groomed trees edging the high-class section of *Glendale's Forever Gardens*, we weren't alone in wondering about the untimely death of Marie-Jeanne Baptiste, tastemaker.

Me? The name's Martin. Denny Rashid Martin. Probably the only one unawed by present company. Back when I was a street cop, as in last week, the Fashion District was my beat, making Baptiste's funeral like being home. Most of the celebs here I'd watched slink from the synth clinics through back doors or after hours, desperate to avoid the paparazzi until their friv-mods had taken hold and they could show off the result. They'd spot me and demand to know where their limo or taxi was waiting, as if I was someone who gave a shit. I'd tell them to take the first available right turn, while trying not to look too close. Trust me, you don't want to see skin ripple as it changes colour or texture – or facial bones melt and reform – and as for horns bursting from boils? Then there's the screaming when the drugs wear off...

No thanks.

Perishing chance any of them would recognize me out of my blues. A uniform's better than an invisibility cloak.

I recognized them, as I'm sure they'd expect, and could make a good guess as to the clinic responsible for their mods, which they wouldn't.

Scuttlebutt claimed a senior investigator wanted this assignment and was refused. A fan, I suppose. I wasn't. The District is pure theatre. The ground floor clinics are fronted by gorgeous facades and glamorous lounges, with staff who are oh so professional and smooth and reassuring. All have booths where you can preview your perfectly modified self. Oh, and every one discreetly offers credit, if you can't afford the fee, at interest rates to make a loan-shark blush. Get you coming and going, they do.

Gag a maggot.

Their back doors opened on the truth. Cramped incursion rooms, illegal biowaste digesters, poorly-trained techs. Dreams forced into unwilling flesh; nightmares, often as not, the result. The alleys crawl with drooling, mindless addicts hooked on whatever they'd been given to shut them up when their mods went wrong; late night deliveries of questionable supplies send them scurrying into the dark, but they always come back. So do the gangs sneaking in new members for tag-mods because, hey, nothing says you belong – and keeps you belonging – like the same bargain-basement fangs or claws.

No hint of cheap here. Or failure. To ogle high-end friv-mods like those on display at Baptiste's funeral, you'd have to pay a fortune for a seat by the runways at Fashion Week, when mod developers reveal their latest wares.

My maternal grandfather once told me: "you can't teach an old dog new tricks." Maybe then. These days, dogs don't age mentally any more than people. It's coming up with new tricks for them that's troublesome. They get bored.

So do we. Which explains quite a bit, in my opinion.

Right around the time clin-mods became the cure-all everyone had hoped, with genetic tweaking leading the way and biotech taking up any slack, synth clinics like Star Power Inc. sprang up to offer custom career-enhancing modifications. Not so essential to health, but popular. Society barely gasped for breath before true friv-mods appeared – guaranteed safe, mind you, as if... – the results sweeping like a contagion across the world. Want a new skin colour? Different eyes? Sex? Nostril hair? DIYbio kits offered anyone the chance to create the next must-have mod. Anything seemed possible.

Maybe it was, but possible didn't translate to prudent in any way, shape, or form.

Regulations couldn't begin to keep up with the inventiveness of people who could now change themselves. Wasn't long before clin-mods were necessary to reduce the harm done by poorly planned friv-mods. Changes piled up like garbage during a strike.

Case in point? Well before my time, synth clinics advertised a friv-mod to remake feverish young fans into the 'type' reportedly preferred by their teen idol. Enough took the plunge that there was a bump in honey-toned skin and round dark eyes in the populations of every city.

No one knew – or rather no one paid attention to those who did – that some of those 'tweaks' would prove epigenetic and express themselves happily, or not so much, in their children.

And grandchildren. Within two generations of such modifications, human diversity had blown the old racial distinctions away. Newborns still had their genomes tagged and registered at birth and clinics were supposed to update records with any mods. Right. These days, who could prove they had 100% virgin DNA, or be sure it would express as it had in their ancestors?

I'm fond of my grandfather. We look alike simply because we're related and that's not only old-fashioned, it's rare. My other half, Daisie, insists on carrying a dige of him in his forties in her grab to flash any doubters. A sweetheart, Daisie, and the light of my life. She's also 60 kilos of pure genius, spiked with enough drive to power one of those starships she's busy designing, which goes to prove love don't always make sense.

'Cause me? I'm the definition of bland in a world gone to extremes. Unlike my to-the-future-and-beyond darling, the only drive I've got is to do the job and make it home at the end of my shift – oh, and to retire with my original parts. That'll be in eleven years, five months, and twenty-two days. I plan to sit on a dock with a keg of beer, watching folks with more money than sense struggle with boat ties and sails.

Till then? Well, being a cop is one of the professions that keeps going no matter how the world changes around us. Easy to see why. Mods or not, people don't change. Not in the ways that make them bump into each other or into walls. Stupid is what keeps us employed. I see that more than most, being a beat cop. Never wanted a desk. I like my streets. My people – decent, dregs, something between – and I have an understanding. This, I might put up with; that, the hell I won't. Good days, some need an ear; others to be told where to go. And how.

The bad days? All I'll say is mine end better than theirs.

I go home.

So long as it stays that way – and they, meaning most everybody, stays out of my way – I'm as happy as can be. Daisie claims I'm a throwback to a time before we – the civilization 'we' – began moving faster than we could parse our course. That's how she talks; I don't always get it. Me, I go by what I see. Her smile. The look in her eyes when I come through the door.

Yup, I've a good life.

Life had been good to Marie-Jeanne Baptiste too, until its end. That had been nasty.

I stood in rose-scented shade, close enough to the cluster of funeral staff to be mistaken for one of them, and watched the Who's Who of synthetic graft and genetic transfection mill around the open grave. I knew these phonies. Those gawking at their neighbour's mod were the ones strutting their first extremes in public. Those who'd missed the trend boat did their pathetic best not to appear envious or dismayed, though I was amused to see the hornies edge almost by instinct away from one another. Too late, I'd have told them. Antlers were over. It was all about skin this season. The pleasant weather arranged for Baptiste's graveside service meant most of that skin was exposed.

I got looks because mine wasn't. What was different about him, they wondered, certain something was. Who didn't have a mod of some kind, if only to avoid wearing sunglasses or having to – shudder – carry a cell?

Oh, I'd my share. They just weren't flesh. Department-issue ceramic soles on my feet, department-issue liner in my gut, swallowed this morning. I could walk forever and my body exist on any combo of fast food and caffeine without harm. More importantly, calls of nature waited till I was off the clock. Basic cop tech. The union paid for it. If I wanted the homicide desk for good, they'd haul me in for scene analyzer implants, truth serum spit, and who knew what other nonsense.

Not that I needed any of it today. There were department eyes among the media for the routine record. Me? Try as they might, despite union protest, nothing performed an on-the-fly analysis of human behaviour better or cheaper than another human. My report would be more impression than detail, but it mattered. A quick scan of the crowd gave me the faces I'd flag later. My gut – the real one – told me which of those to keep watching now.

Like Kamea Hale, Baptiste's former boss. The Hales had started in cattle – not that she owned any now. Free range animals were scarce and pricey, not to mention the idea of consuming parts of one nauseated the majority. Instead, Hale owned All Your Favourite Strains, the world's largest producer of vat-meat, patent-protected and available in any flavour of fish, fowl, or mammal desired. A success due in large part, according to the background, to the infallible taste buds of Marie-Jeanne Baptiste.

Baptiste was – had been – an epicure. Made her rep as a food critic, then moved on to become premiere taster for 'Strains. Their slogan was 'We feed you too' and it wasn't a boast. After fifty plus years in uniform not much surprised me, but I'd whistled at the company's size and scope, then again at Baptiste's reported salary. Before perks.

Hale's mods were tame for this group. Enlarged eyes, purple feathers on her head. Her skin – more likely its hairs – had grown overlapping scales that sparkled like the side of a dying fish on a sunny dock.

Was she here to mourn Baptiste or her valuable mouth?

Another A-lister, Sir Bolivar Walczak of Star Power Inc, stood nearby, his none-too-subtle security a step behind and glowering. His presence accounted for most of the crowd and all of the media. Walczak was the prime mover behind Star Power Inc's latest 'We Can Make You A Star' campaign: part reality show contest and part re-makeover; he was rumoured to have single-handedly created the current skin-mod craze. Me, I like my DNA as it is, thanks. Okay, as a teen I'd kept Star Power brochures under my pillow and dreamed about becoming a superhero. Or taller. Who hadn't? But my family was too poor – or too sane – to mod me. Once I gained some years and smarts of my own, most notably Daisie's, I was fine with the existing me.

Walczak was a virgin himself – or had everyone believing it. In this crowd, his bald head and ample girth looked more exotic than Hale's feathers and scales. A busy man and a notoriously media-shy one.

Until today. What was he doing here?

Despite the circus atmosphere – helped along by the vintage calliope being played quietly but with a snappy beat – there were a few sincere mourners graveside. I'd done my checks during the sermon. Baptiste left two daughters, both in their teens, and two husbands, only one in his teens, the other possibly my age or more. The older man had gone for blond and stalwart – or was it elf? – with pointed ears and sweeping eyebrows. The younger looked to be a trope – one of the unfortunates who continued to express their grandmother's idol choice. Or round dark eyes and honey skin were making a comeback. Odder things happened.

Dual spouses weren't odd. Marriage had come to accommodate any combination who wanted a lifelong commitment. Many did. According to my Daisie, when what was human began to change almost daily, relationships had to expand as well. As a cop, let me tell you domestic violence went along for the ride. Don't get me started on families torn apart by one partner's mod-addiction, which they'd want me to fix in a ten minute visit. As if.

Among other minor mods, the daughters' arms and legs were in different primary colours, which made them look like poorly assembled dolls. All four seemed appropriately unhappy and uncomfortable.

Other than the human scenery, Baptiste's funeral was as dull as any of the others I'd attended until the unicorn showed up.

HE WAS LATE, in a rush, and I knew him. Who didn't? All-star goalie Kris Rebane had been fans' MVP pick when a stick took out his mask and most of his face in game seven of the playoffs. Instead of regrowing what he'd had, he'd taken a buy-out and opted for full unicorn, complete with horse nostrils, goat beard, and the trademarked spiral horn erupting between now-violet eyes. His skin was covered in fine white hair, what showed beyond the kilt, and he'd added a mane since I'd seen him last. A gold, sparkly one. Heroic as hell.

Ridiculous on a lesser man; Kris had the shoulders and bearing to make it work. Not to mention attitude.

He was one of mine. Grew up in a tiny apartment below the clinic where his mom worked as night sterilizer. Hot-headed, impulsive, with a heart bigger than his brain, he'd find trouble faster than any kid I knew. Won't say I got him into hockey, but I helped make sure he stayed there.

Unicorn. I'd told his mother it was better than bull.

He spotted me and changed direction, charging through a trio of bunny boys who scattered, then regrouped, noses atwitch with interest.

"Constable Martin, sir." When a unicorn comes to attention, it causes a stir.

A stir I didn't need. I didn't bother mentioning I was 'Inspector Martin' for the funeral. I glowered up at him. "Piss off."

"But... M.J..."

Belatedly, I realized the mauve streaks down his cheeks had to be from tears. How his path crossed Baptiste's I didn't know; celebs had their own circles. "Sorryforyourloss," I grumbled.

"I'm just glad to see you," Kris assured me a little too happily. "I didn't think anyone took me seriously."

That couldn't be good. One of the daughters looked our way, a green hand drifting to her purple throat in almost theatrical dismay. I gave her my "move along" glare and she glanced away quickly. "No one's taking you seriously yet," I warned Kris. "What's this about?"

"M.J. was murdered." The whites of his eyes fluoresced. It didn't look like grief, but that was the problem with many mods: the unexpected extras. "Isn't that why you're here?"

No, I was here because Ortmer hadn't kept his fingers out of a drunk's mouth. "You didn't file a statement." It wasn't a question. If he had, and it'd reached homicide, I wouldn't have been sent.

"They wouldn't listen!" He snorted like a horse.

Which wouldn't have helped the be-taken-seriously part. I sighed. Even before growing a horn with a sharp point, Kris in full righteous rage had never been good for those around him. And he was, as I said, one of mine.

Maybe all he needed was to vent. I resigned myself to the inevitable. "Thirty seconds. Don't waste them."

"However they said M.J. died, it's a lie."

I'd seen the autopsy report. The term was CMF. Catastrophic Modification Failure. In other words, the unexpected. Techs from the synth clinic responsible had been questioned and her DNA examined; nothing culpable, concluded the department biotechs before moving to the next case. Between the ever-present risk of a new change interacting with something previously unexpressed, and the simple reality that we still didn't know everything about our own coding, it was no wonder the waivers required before any mod were the tightest legalese known to humanity.

"CMFs happen, Kris. You know that."

"Not like this. It was murder."

It was gruesome, I'd admit, which didn't make it murder but did make me question the competence of the clinic. Baptiste had wanted to enhance her ability to taste – maybe someone was on her heels for the same job – and had ordered a forked tongue with a greater surface area for tastebuds.

What they'd done was ciliate her tongue, using the portion of her DNA that coded cilia for the inner ear and many other parts. Vid from the clinic, a cheery voiceover describing the design features, showed a tongue made of separate thickened threads able to spread apart during tasting, then to collapse into a normal-looking tongue once done. Handy.

Unfortunately for Baptiste, her cilia abruptly grew past their intended design limit. They'd filled her mouth, sinuses, and throat then punched through to her brain. The younger husband had found her when he'd gone to her bed that morning. His screams had set off the building alarm.

"CMFs don't happen weeks after the mod's settled. Not without some warning. Someone did this to her," Kris insisted.

So much for the details of Baptiste's death being kept to immediate family, the department, and... "The clinic." I nodded to myself, putting it together. "It was one of yours." His mother had insisted he invest; she hadn't foreseen the unicorn.

Kris shuddered, mane sparkling in the sun. "Yes. I asked to see the – they showed me –" Beneath the white hair, he turned green. His throat worked convulsively, jiggling the goat beard.

Baby. The funeral staff came to the alert, presumably ready with a bucket. I waved them off and, grabbing his arm, marched my unsettled unicorn to the chapel building. We weren't alone. Media drones now hovered over the arched door, hunting tears as the mass of funeral goers were cued to retire to the waiting reception. Serve them right if Kris vomited on the marble steps. Then again, he'd probably hit my boots.

Murder?

They'd have sent someone else – anyone else – if that'd been remotely on the radar. My job was to observe the people drawn to this death. Who talked to whom. Who wouldn't and why. Gossip was grist for the department info mill; funerals made for easy pickings. The most private of people would talk to a stranger, given a sympathetic look. I wasn't great at sympathetic. The look I could fake.

I was bored. I was curious. Okay, and Ortmer'd been a pain in my ass since his promotion to almighty inspector. The notion of asking a few questions of my own was irresistible.

Should have known better.

GLENDALE'S FOREVER GARDENS' chapel lay within a sprawling edifice of reused stone, glass, metal, and wood, each and every component labelled with its source. Maybe they meant to be respectful. Historic, even. Ask me, it was a nuisance. When I finally located the restroom for Kris, it was unhelpfully labelled the 'Old Montrose Railway Depot.' Though I did like the coat check. Its long polished counter had once graced 'Darby's Fine Meats.' Nice.

The reception was in the main hall, named the 'Bradley Greenhouse No.6,' presumably for the glass ceiling. The hall itself was a maze of tables covered in soon-to-be-compost flowers and unrecognizable food. Beverage fountains tinkled gloomily. Windows, curtained in dark velvet, were set deep within semiprivate alcoves for those overcome. I'd have said by grief but it was doubtful most of those here had met Baptiste or her family. Eaten food she'd tasted for them, yes.

Eat the food here, definitely. Hungry work, a funeral. And thirsty, by the swarm around each fountain. Other means of dealing with sadness were changing hands or whatever in the Railway Depot. I wished them luck. Sex-mods were no more reliable than the basic model and some required a manual to even rev up.

I'd parked my unicorn with two of the bunny boys. Turned out they were hockey fans and Kris, rightly figuring I didn't want him underfoot, resigned himself to adulation.

I walked around, listening more than watching. Most conversations, predictably, were about anything but the woman now dead. The few of interest to the department I noted as I passed, feeling more ridiculous by the moment. Kris had no motive or suspects, just his guilt and an overblown desire for justice. The same desire had got his face rearranged, truth be told. Unicorn.

After half an hour. I'd made one circuit of the tables and alcoves and was starting my next when,

"– you know it's your fault she's dead."

I feigned a craving for some green goo and crackers on the nearest table. Whatever was in it, my gut liner could manage. I hoped.

Who'd spoken?

"Don't be ridiculous. I never blamed M.J."

That voice I recognized. Kamea Hale had given a short eulogy at the service. She was holding court in the alcove behind and to my left.

"What'd you lose – billions? You couldn't afford another mistake."

Male, older. I reached for a napkin, managing to avoid the red-dappled ribcage of the nearly naked lady doing the same. Skin-mods. The air was cooler in the hall – for the food and flowers, I assumed – and gooseflesh marred most of her pattern. Still, it was prettier than some. Almost like rose petals.

As we exchanged the requisite tight-lipped nods of funeral-goers, I got the glimpse I was after.

Hale was sitting with Walczak. His security, stationed on either side of the alcove opening, noticed my interest and gave me the eye. Three each.

Morons. I lifted a green-smeared cracker at them and popped it in my mouth before turning away again.

The taste curdled my toes in their ceramic soles. Wishing I could spit, I swallowed hastily, then helped myself to something bubbly from the closest fountain.

From the mouthful, it had a good kick to it, if I hadn't already guessed from the rising volume of voices to every side. Oh, I wasn't drinking on duty. You kidding? Another so-called perk of my cop's gut. Alcohol's just another source of hydration.

I smelled unicorn – cloves and day-old armpit, I kid you not – before I glanced sideways to confirm that yes, Kris had run out of patience and found me.

His eyes glowed white around the violet again. Not a sign of calm. "He could have done it." Which 'he' wasn't in question, given the swing of that wickedly pointed horn towards Walczak.

Security tensed as security is paid to do. I grabbed Kris by one thick arm, again, and shoved him behind the fountain. "A dozen designers are here. Why him?"

"He was M.J.'s."

A tidbit not in any report I'd seen. Had I gone for ears able to prick up, mine would have stood on end. Means and opportunity. If, I reminded myself, it'd been murder and not error. Still, an error this big wouldn't help the next season of 'We Can Make You a Star.'

Who was I kidding? Of course it would. The risk was the draw. New question. Why the secrecy? "Keep your voice down," I grumbled. I shouldn't encourage this; my mouth kept going anyway. "Walczak could buy a middling country. Why bother with a career mod?" Something else niggled at me. "And why did Baptiste? Was someone after her job?"

"Don't you remember? The Veggie Turkey."

Right. Last year's Xmas dinner had cooked up more like broccoli than fowl. Consumers had howled. 'Strains had released a statement about a mix-up with their vegan option ordering and given credit for a month's supply to any affected family.

Whose wasn't? Billions lost.

Hale had claimed not to blame her. "Think the company insisted on the mod?" I asked. Insisting was illegal; hiring based on a desired mod wasn't.

Kris looked offended. Unicorns did that exceptionally well, which gained us a modicum of privacy as people edged away. "M.J.'s – she was – their best. Besides, it wasn't her fault. Production had rushed ahead for the holiday." A huff, then he unwound a little. "Sure, she worried about missing the next mistake. She was like that, wanting to be better. Someone could have talked her into the mod and then used it to –" He closed his wide lips over the rest.

"Or maybe" – I used my let's-be-reasonable voice, the one before don't-give-me-that-crap – "the mod failed, as many of them do. Murder takes motive, Kris." This homicide stuff wasn't so hard.

"You're right." His nostrils flared thoughtfully. Then, "What if we have it wrong? What if she was murdered because of her mod?"

Judging by conversations I'd overheard, there were plenty of people in this room willing to murder to keep whatever they'd painstakingly built into their flesh exclusive. Didn't mean they would. Still...

My pause let Kris keep on thinking. Not good. Sure enough, he ducked to bring his face next to mine, horn passing alarmingly close to my nose, and whispered hoarsely, "What if 'Strains is putting something it shouldn't into the food stream? Something M.J. would have tasted with her new tongue. They'd have to be rid of her!" He straightened and tossed his mane in triumph. "It was a plot!"

First murder; now conspiracy? I was done here. I pulled out my compassionate voice. "Look, Kris. I get it. A person you knew – you respected – died at the hands of people you employ. It shouldn't have happened – to her or to anyone. You need to make your" – At his now-stricken expression, I changed 'peace' to – "need to think of those still alive. You don't want to upset the family." With a nod to our people-filled surroundings. "Or anyone else."

I was reaching him. Maybe. Then he grumbled, "Why would they be upset? None of them care. I don't even know why they're here."

"For the media –"

I'd forgotten who I was talking to; Kris Rebane made the news when he ordered a multi-grain bagel at Tims. He shook his head. "Not one posed for a feature grab or waited on a personal. They came in here, where there's no coverage at all."

Not even the department's eyes, this being the private part of the function. The more we watched ourselves, Daisie'd said once, the more important surveillance-free space became. I'd laughed and called it nuisance-space.

What I'd meant was scary-space, but I wouldn't say that to her. No watcher meant no backup, no record, just me.

Like now.

The unicorn looked as uneasy as I felt, so I put on my best everything's-fine face. "Free food and drink, then."

"That's the other thing." Kris lifted his head to gaze around the room, something easy from his height, then his eyes came back to me. They glowed. "Skin-mods show every gram."

And the crowd was gorging itself, not to mention draining the beverage fountains.

My street-sense twitched. Not that I was an expert on celebs when they let their figurative hair or feathers down, but something wasn't right in this room.

Fine. There was someone left to question; someone who'd know all about this crowd, as well as Baptiste's death.

After all, he'd had a hand in creating both.

Sir Bolivar Walczak.

FUNERAL HOMES HAVE their egalitarian side. Coffins might range from minimal to ridiculous but, no matter who you were, eventually the food and drink would send you to the Train Depot.

Unless you were a cop with a liner, but I could fake that when necessary too.

It became necessary when Walczak finally made his excuses to Hale and stood. I made sure to leave promptly enough to be inside the restroom before his security. No chance they could clear the public facility for their boss, not with Baptiste's former husbands cuddled in mutual misery on the anteroom couch.

I judged the private Sir Bolivar Walczak would have had his fill of the crowd outside. Right I was. I heard him order his protectors to stay with the husbands.

I delayed in the stall till I heard the sterilizer field hum. As I approached, he turned his head and fixed me with a blue-eyed stare as cool and collected as any I'd seen. "Cop."

Two kinds of people greet us like that. Those with experience avoiding us and those who've hired those with experience avoiding us.

Interesting.

"Homicide," I returned agreeably. "Inspector Martin. Sorryforyourloss. Were you a friend of the deceased?"

"Her designer."

I didn't pretend to clean my hands. "So your mod killed her."

"Far from it." Walczak paused to suck some rinse and spit. Why the stuff always smelled of mint, I don't know. "I recommended against any mod. M.J.'s job was to taste new products the way any of us – any unmod – would. What was the point of her becoming a living chemoanalyzer when it was her discrimination and sense of taste that mattered?" He ran a towelette over his sweaty head and nodded to his reflection. "She listened. Seemed to like what I said and agree." Tossing the crumpled towelette at the disposal, he turned back to me. "Then... this tragedy."

My bullshit detector flaring into the red zone, I smiled nicely. "What changed her mind?"

"Who," he replied without hesitation. "That's why you're here, isn't it? To uncover the truth about her death."

I was here because Ortmer – I gave up making the excuse to myself. I'd blown my original assignment the moment I'd listened to the unicorn. "There've been – questions – raised."

"You think she was murdered." Walczak smiled. "A CMF would be the perfect weapon, wouldn't it? Talk someone into a cutting edge mod – untried, exciting, risky – and design it to be fatal. Not right away, of course."

"Why not?" Was I hearing a confession? Maybe homicide wasn't as hard as I'd thought.

Maybe dogs could learn to juggle geese.

"The clinic would be accused of a poor incursion. There'd be an inquest. No, the mod would have to settle in and work as promised first. Anything goes wrong after that, well, it's a skeleton in the code." At my frown – who doesn't hate jargon? – he went on, "An undetected conflict within the client's genome."

"What are the odds of that?" Though how Baptiste died wasn't going to clear anything up. To be murder, someone had to want her dead.

"Higher than we like to tell clients, but slim." Walczak took one of the two easy chairs at one end of the restroom. There were such paired conversation spots everywhere in the Forever Gardens, each with its small table bearing a box of tissue and bowl of candy. He waved me to the other chair, clearly in no hurry to return to the funeral.

I obliged, well aware he wasn't trying to be helpful. This was no unicorn. This was a highly intelligent, self-assured villain. If he'd frequented my streets I've have ordered up all the surveillance the department could muster. Surveillance that wasn't in this both public and very private space.

For some reason – maybe for that reason – Walczak smiled again. Then, as if he'd pulled the thought from my head, he commented, "The real question is why."

I didn't smile back. "Any ideas on that, sir?"

"If I were to speculate…" He leaned back – his belly testing the buttons of a suit that likely cost more than I made in two years – closed his eyes and worked his lips in and out.

More bullshit. I stood to go.

His eyes shot open, anticipation gleaming in their depths. "You really should speak to Kamea, Inspector. Mention the Ministry of Health and – oh yes – do ask her about using the consumer food stream as a delivery mechanism, will you? And what M.J. thought of it. If you're any good at your job, you might find your reason. If it was murder. These things do happen, you know."

My words to Kris, back in my face.

I didn't bother to respond.

As I pushed my way past Walczak's waiting security, I caught myself hoping that, if it had been murder, I'd be able to nail their boss with it.

So I turned at the door, looked the nearest goon in all three eyes, and snapped, "Walczak stays available."

"Sir Walczak."

As if.

People killed each other every day for the simplest of reasons. *You smell funny. You're in my way. You have what I want. You took what I had. You don't love me. You love me too much.*

Baptiste?

Maybe one of the husbands decided to do in a rival. Who the rival was remained moot, considering I'd last seen the two in a tight embrace, but they could have worked together. Then there were the daughters. Not an uncommon motive, impatience to gain an inheritance, but it didn't wash here. Both had substantial trusts tied to their ages, not their mother's life.

Which took me back to what was way past my pay grade: Kris' notion of a conspiracy by All Your Favourite Strains to be rid of their top taster because of something they intended to put in our food.

I really hated that idea.

For one thing, it'd mean recalls and shortages and nothing got the streets uglier than shortages – real or imagined. For another, Daisie didn't have a cop liner in her gut to protect her. If there was something wrong with the food on our table, if something might have harmed my family...?

I stopped myself there. We'd have to know. That was what mattered. Again above my pay grade.

Give me an angry guy with a bat standing over a still-twitching body any day. For an instant I considered calling Ortmer. No. New fingers? Probably out working on his golf swing.

I could take Kris to the station, unicorn head and all, sit him at my pretend desk in homicide, and start a file. They could stick me with it. More likely, they'd hand it to someone who didn't know him or the District.

For a moment I thought of begging off, of reminding Kris I wasn't his cop any more.

But I was. I'd wiped his bloody nose after a fight behind the arena. Gone to a game or two or ten when his mother couldn't be there. Taken him to a synth clinic where they wouldn't ask questions when he'd gotten himself twisted about trying to get back his game during the strike.

I'd helped his mother find polish for his stupid horn. If that wasn't being a fucking hero, I don't know what is.

Kris, who'd met me outside the Train Depot, gave me a bright-eyed hopeful look that meant all my thinking had shown on my face and I was toast. "I want to talk to Kamea Hale," I said, giving in.

"Great. I'll come with you. She knows me," this rather urgently.

I recognized the light of battle in his eyes, despite their lilac. If I didn't let him tag along, he'd start asking his own questions. Great. "You," I told him, grabbing the horn and using it as a handle to shake his head in emphasis, "will leave the talking to me. Got it?"

You'd have thought he'd won the Cup. "Yes, sir!"

* * *

ALL I HAD was a dead taster, a unicorn, and a villain. Not even a murder, not for sure. Yet I trusted my instincts. Something was off in the reception hall. The crowd of brave new humans – or crazy fashion extremists, take your pick – had gathered for another reason than a funeral.

Kamea Hale? Her scaled hands trembled as she lifted her glass to her lips. Her huge eyes were haunted. As Kris and I sat across from her in the alcove, the couch creaking under his weight, she sipped and swallowed and looked as guilty as anyone I'd ever seen.

I showed her the palm of my hand, activating my badge with a tap of my ring finger, then shut it off again. "I'm sorry for your loss –"

"Kamea, did you kill M.J.?"

What part of –? Using the tissue table for cover, I tromped on Kris' bare foot, ceramic soles being good for that. He shut up, giving me a hurt look. Unicorns.

"There've been some questions raised," I said smoothly, ignoring their source. "Sir Walczak suggested you could be of assistance. If you have a moment."

"Bolivar?" Up close, the scales of her skin-mod didn't touch one another, letting me watch her cheeks go ash white. She set her cup down without taking her eyes from mine. Kris quickly saved it from missing the table; I doubt she noticed. "This doesn't – I don't see –" Her voice firmed. "This is hardly the time or place, Inspector."

Couldn't argue with that. "You'll come to the station, then," I said cheerfully. "Thank you."

Hale collected herself, a glint of what helped her successfully run an international megacorporation in the lift of her head. She looked at me, not Kris, but her first words were to him. "I most certainly did not kill Marie-Jeanne. She was one of my dearest friends as well as a valued employee." To me. "As for questions about her death? It was a horrible way to die and a tragic waste of a life. What else could you want to know?"

Walczak thought he was using me. The difference between us was that I didn't care. "What did the deceased think of the government using 'Strains' consumer food stream?"

"M.J. hated it," Hale replied without so much as a blink. Good or honest or both. I reserved my opinion. "Not the reason – who could argue with testing our ability to deliver emergency rations in a crisis? – but how it interfered with her work. She didn't like any strain being released to the public without being tasted. She was a proud person. Responsible." She dabbed her eyes with a tissue. "Irreplaceable."

Kris' horn dipped and rose as he nodded.

"Her sense of taste was that good?"

"Better than any analyzer money could buy, Inspector. Raw components don't matter. M.J. infallibly predicted consumer mouth response to any food we dreamed up. She guided the research responsible for putting strains into almost every home. Including yours." Hale frowned and leaned forward. "Bolivar told you about the ministry. That bastard." She pointed a scaled forefinger at me. "There's your suspect, Inspector."

"What's Star Power got to do with food production?" Kris asked, looking as puzzled as I felt.

"I've no idea," Hale admitted, sitting back in her seat. The frown, I noticed, remained. "Bolivar tried to hire M.J. away from us. When she refused, he bribed someone in production to discredit her. He denied it, but I have" – another glint – "a very efficient security staff."

"What else did they learn?" Her hesitation was as good as an admission. "Your friend suffered, Kamea. No one should die like that."

"No." A long pause. "Nothing concrete," she said at last. "A rumour at best. They could be using grey source DNA to shortcut their mod development."

Great. Now vice would start sniffing around. "How grey?" Used to be grey meant corpses. Now it could be anything from trafficked children to some test tube concoction.

Her lips twisted. "Animal."

On the face of it, using DNA from other species wasn't a big deal. We shared most of ours with everything from bananas to whales. But the devil, as my grandfather would say, was in the details. In some instances, our cells didn't use interspecies DNA in the same way, or to the same results. The earliest animal mod attempts – because oh, yes, they tried – had been so horrific the entire world had agreed to ban them.

It hadn't slowed the synth clinics; our own DNA has virtually no end of possibilities. Turn on the right gene and you've a penis to your knees.

"You blackmailed him," I concluded with admiration.

"I didn't need to," Hale replied primly. "I planned to put M.J. in charge of the overhaul of our production staff, with full authority to fire anyone she suspected might be involved with Walczak or Star Power. If only she'd –" Her eyes went past me and widened impossibly. "What's Belle doing with him?!"

I stood and turned to look, Kris looming like a golden-maned monolith beside me.

Sir Bolivar Walczak stood in the doorway to the reception hall, one of M.J.'s daughters – the elder – snug at his side. As my thoughts immediately turned to a less complex and time-honoured motive for murder, namely a mother with better taste, the air above the couple filled with incoming media eyes.

Then the lights went out.

THE UNICORN'S EYES glowed in the dark. That, I'd expected. The glowing horn, not so much.

The skin of everyone in the room emitting light?

Okay, not mine. Yes, I checked.

We seemed the only ones shocked. Chants of "Star Power! Star Power!" mingled with cheers and the joyful smashing of glassware.

I looked over my shoulder at Hale. I'd been wrong to think it a glow. Her skin pulsed with fluorescence, greenish light marking her every vein. No, moving through her every vein. She stared at her bare arms, her face a ghastly mask, then her mouth opened and she screamed.

Kris moved faster than I did – or could – easing her down, taking her hands in his. He looked up at me. His skin, I realized numbly, hadn't changed like the others'. He said something I couldn't hear over the bedlam.

Not that I needed to.

Walczak.

Maybe he'd murdered Baptiste. Maybe he hadn't. But this stunt at her funeral?

This he'd planned.

* * *

Finding Walczak was easy. He'd stayed by the doors, surrounded by adoring masses and the media. I found myself more invisible than usual, being the only one not generating a personal circle of light, and moved close enough to Belle Baptiste to smell her perfume.

I resisted the temptation to whisper "nice funeral" in her ear. Besides, Walczak was holding forth.

"– permanent? Yes, of course. 'Bright Skin' is Star Power's latest friv-mod, guaranteed to last until the owner wishes a new look. And that, my friends, will be as easy as drinking your morning coffee, won't it?"

Cheers and whistles drowned out the broadcaster's next question.

"– all volunteers. And why not? This will go down in history" – Walczak paused, as if savouring the words – "as the first flash-mod in history. Won't be the last, will it?"

"Nooo!!!!!"

They were all certifiable. Certifiable and drunk.

"I didn't agree to this!" Media eyes zoomed close as Hale staggered forward, hands grabbing for arms and shoulders, sliding over glowing skin. "You'd no right to mod me!"

The unicorn was beside her, horn lowered. I was amazed at his restraint. Wouldn't last.

"I warned you not to drink, my dear Kamea."

Walczak had put his 'Bright Skin' mod in the fountains?

Daisie'd said there'd be a breakthrough one day, something to take the sting – literally – out of mods. She'd called it a world-changer.

Then, I'd chuckled. The urge to vomit almost overwhelmed me. What if I hadn't used the liner today?

I'd be glowing. And look ridiculous.

And unable to do my job. A glowing cop?

More importantly – far more importantly – if so, he'd done what everyone said was years away: to deliver a mod into a body through ingestion.

There must have been another question. "– being available through regular retailers is the long-term goal, but for now we're giving 'Bright Skin' away. This is the future. Mods without pain. It's the end of expensive synth clinics. Drink up to be what you want. Whatever you want! The essential precursors went out in the latest shipments from 'Strains."

Shipments Baptiste hadn't tasted, being dead. By a staff she hadn't purged of Walczak's influence, being dead.

I had him.

No, I realized a sickening heartbeat later.

He had us.

Silence spread through the darkened hall as even the drunks realized something more was happening here. Something dreadful. Hale whimpered. She wasn't alone.

"The precursor transinfects the DNA of every cell in your body, ready to accept whatever mod-code you ingest. No need for nanovectors. Total efficiency. Mods activate the moment they enter cells." Walczak chuckled. "Unless stopped. The real market will be for what I call 'code-glue.' If you want to stay as you are, simply take code-glue to suppress the precursor. Elegant, isn't it?"

Hale was speaking frantically to her elbow – shutting down distribution centres, flushing tanks, trying to stop this.

Too little, too late. "First you had to murder Baptiste," I said, the words echoing. Media eyes whirled to focus on me, but it was the department I hoped heard. The department, and one other. "M.J. was on to you, wasn't she? Your little plan to own the world." The murder weapon hadn't been Baptiste's mod; it had been whatever Walczak – or her daughter – had put into her food or drink. How didn't matter. It never had. This was why. "Aren't you rich enough?"

Walczak's laugh drew back the eyes and sent cold fingers down my spine. "Let there be light!" he ordered.

The hall lights came on, washing away the glow, turning everyone back to a semblance of normal. But no one was. They held out their arms, bunnies and pseudo-fish and elves. Black words strutted in their skin. A name. 'Bolivar Walczak.'

"Wealth doesn't go to the grave, Inspector. I've rewritten humanity and signed my name in every one of your cells. I will live forev –"

Blood, not another word, spurted from his mouth as the unicorn's horn went through him.

IT WAS MURDER and I solved it. After a reprimand, I was back on my beat. Kris? He's a fucking folk hero.

The rest of us? Life's about change, my Daisie says. Humanity's been changed, again, this time at one man's whim, this time in a way that accelerates the pace of our evolution.

No one's willing to say what we'll become.

My guess?

I'll still have a job.

DOUBLE BLIND

TONY BALLANTYNE

Tony Ballantyne is the author of the Penrose and Recursion series of novels as well as many acclaimed short stories that have appeared in magazines and anthologies around the world. He has been nominated for the BSFA and Philip K Dick awards. His latest novel, Dream London, *was published in October 2013. He is currently working on the follow up,* Dream Paris, *due for publication in September 2015.*

AFTER THE COLD swab and the smell of antiseptic, after the prick in the arm, after the masked medics folded up their cases and filed from the room and the door was locked, after that, we were left to wait.

Five people, five seats, five beds, one table. A little kitchen, a little cubicle for the chemical toilet, another for the shower. A long mirror set in one wall.

We sat around the table. Five people, fingers clasped together, fingers laid flat on the table, fingers tapping nervously. Five people looking at each other, wondering.

"What are you thinking about, Paul?"

I smiled at Liza. She was the youngest of us, barely out of her teenage years, not quite filled into her body, with the gaunt, half-starved look of someone who had been born in a town far from the employment zones.

"I was wondering if this was itching," I said, rubbing my arm.

"It's all in your mind," said Solomon. "You just relax, young man. Five days and we'll all be out of here. You'll see." I didn't buy his wise old man act. If he knew so much, what was he doing in here?

"It's not in your mind," exclaimed Groone, nervously. "Look Paul, it's flaring up red beneath the sticking plaster." He looked at his own arm. "Just like mine! Oh shit!"

He stood up suddenly, sending his chair clattering backwards across the glazed tiles.

"Now, Groone, stay calm." That was Solomon's voice. I was too busy looking at my own arm, now itching like crazy. Could I see a rash?

"Stay calm?" Groone gave a laugh that was completely without humour. "Hell, it's getting worse!"

"That's because you're scratching it," said Milly, plump and complacent. Her own arm was smooth beneath the plaster, I noticed.

"No, I've not touched it! Hell, it itches!" Groone's voice was shrill with panic. He walked around the table, twisting our forearms around so that he could get a better look at them. "Look, Liza has the mark, too. Look at us, Paul. You can see it growing."

He placed his arm next to mine. We watched the blistering red rash spreading.

"See?" he shouted. "But mine is worse! Much, much worse! And it's spreading faster, it's spreading faster!" The panic in Groone's voice was contagious. Solomon and I were on our feet now, dancing back and forth. Liza was licking her lips, looking from her arm to Groone's.

"Who was injected first?" asked Solomon. His face betrayed the assumed calm of his voice. "That would make a difference, wouldn't it?"

"We were all done at the same time," said Liza. "I'm sure we were."

"No," said Groone. "The doctor had trouble with the seal on my syringe. I was done last. My rash really is spreading the fastest! I got the strongest dose!"

"Now," said Solomon. "You heard what they said. There isn't necessarily a strongest dose. They don't always work that way…"

They had this time, I thought. Groone's arm was burning red now. Liza was pulling at her fingers.

"Take off your rings!" she called. "Take them off whilst you still can!"

I didn't have any rings, but both Groone and Liza were festooned with jewellery. The fingers on Groone's left hand were already swollen like red sausages. He was pulling at the silver knot ring on his middle finger.

"It won't come off!" he said. Solomon took hold of it.

"Don't yank it!" called Milly. "You'll make it worse. Here, use this." Milly had a handful of white soap. She rubbed his hand, lubricating it. Liza's rings clattered to the floor. Silver and indian gold, black metacarbon and verdigised copper bouncing on the floor.

"I think my arm is swelling up too," said Solomon, matter-of-factly. Mine definitely was. I sat down and breathed deeply, tried to remain calm. Groone grabbed at my shoulder, his eyes were wide. I could smell the acetone hunger of his breath.

"Too hot!" said Groone. "Too hot!"

I could feel the heat coming from his skin. Liza was undressing, pulling off her loose top, stepping out of her pants, quite unselfconscious.

"Stay still!" said Milly, pulling Groone's hand free from my shoulder. "You need to get those rings off more than you need to undress." She was rubbing soap over his fingers, her plump pink hands massaging them, raising thin bubbles. "There we go," she said, easing the heavy silver knot over his knuckle.

"I feel sick," said Groone. "I'm going to throw. Need to get undressed…"

I felt sick too. I was itching all over. Solomon pulled off his shirt. The skin of his chest was raising up in bumps.

"I've got all the rings," said Milly. "Strip off, Groone!"

"My head hurts," said Groone, to the room in general. "Have you got that too?"

Liza moaned something in reply. She was feeling her way over to one of the beds. She collapsed on it, face down.

"Liza! Are you okay?"

"Headache. Don't shout."

Milly hadn't shouted, though her voice echoed around in my skull. A headache charged in behind my eyes.

Groone screamed.

"My head! My head! It's going to explode!"

Solomon was scratching his chest. Liza was writhing on the bed. Only Milly seemed untouched by the symptoms. I tried to raise myself up, to make my way to the bed. The room moved with me.

Groone fell thrashing to the floor.

"You okay, Paul?" That was Solomon.

"I think I need to lie down. I don't think I can get there."

"Let me help you," said Milly.

"No, get Groone onto the bed."

"He'll fall off," said Milly. "I'll pull the chairs away. He can't bang into anything."

Groone's arm swept across the floor, sending the discarded rings scattering in flashes of silver and gold.

Milly scraped the chairs back behind the table. Groone was screaming now. I was itching like crazy. My head was pounding. I lay down on the bed. I could hear Liza whimpering on the next bed, her long dark body twitching.

A retching noise. The sharp smell of vomit. More retching, more vomit. That was me.

I AWOKE TO see Liza gazing down at me with bloodshot eyes.

"How are you?" she asked.

I touched my head. It felt like a bell. Tap it and it would resonate.

"I ache all over, but I'll be okay, I think."

She nodded. "Groone's dead."

I nodded, and my head rang with the movement. Her words didn't surprise me. I felt half dead myself, and Groone had clearly got the highest dose.

"Poor bastard," I said. "How are you?"

"Not too good. I've got a splitting headache, but they say that I'm okay." She jerked her head towards the one way mirror that stretched along the wall. "They say that my brain didn't swell in my skull like Groone's did."

I sat up. Milly was standing in the little kitchen, making scrambled eggs. Solomon sat on his bed, watching her.

"We're still going ahead, then?"

"What do you think?"

That was the deal. Why waste time arguing about it?

"I'm the last one awake," I said. "Where's Groone's body?"

"Milly and I put him in the storage locker."

"You should have let me do it. You had a worse dose than I did."

"I'm younger than you. Besides, it's not just about the dose. It's how it affects you. I might get it worse next time. You can clear up then."

I gazed at her, wondering. *Next time?* I was thinking. *They were really prepared to do this again?* Of course they were. That was the deal.

"Come to the table," said Milly. "Breakfast is almost ready."

Solomon got up from his bed and sat down at the little table. Liza busied herself setting out the cutlery.

"Hey, let me," I said.

"You can barely stand up," said Liza.

She was right. Whatever had been in the first dose had affected my balance. The walk to the dining table was a seasick, roller coaster ride that took me on the waltzers around the little room.

Milly moved around the table, spooning scrambled eggs onto our plates.

"I don't feel hungry," I said.

"They said we should all eat," said Milly. "They said we'd feel better faster."

"Isn't there any toast?" asked Solomon.

I opened my mouth to tell him to get it himself, but Milly silenced me with a look.

"It's coming right up," she said.

Liza carried a big jug of coffee to the table, then returned to the little kitchen to fetch four mugs.

"Next dose is tonight at six," Liza announced.

"So soon?" I said. "Bastards!"

"It's supposed to be a kindness," said Liza. "The waiting is the worst part."

"It's the most cost effective, I bet," said Solomon.

"Not at the breakfast table," said Milly, taking her place. "Let's enjoy the meal."

"Amen to that, Sister," said Solomon, picking up his fork and scooping up a fluffy pile. "Mmmm! These are good."

They were. I couldn't remember the last time I'd had real eggs. I scraped creamy butter all over my toast, watched it melt into an oily yellow pool in the middle of the brown toast, saw the little seeds in the bread float up.

"It's almost worth dying, just to taste these," said Solomon.

"Groone never got to taste them," I said.

"Not at the breakfast table," repeated Milly. "Liza, will you pour the coffee?"

"Let me," I said. I lifted the heavy jug and splashed hot brown liquid onto the table.

Liza gently took the jug from my hand.

THE DAY PASSED slowly. Solomon seemed quite happy just to watch the video feeds they pumped into the room, occasionally tapping out his thoughts on his console. The tip tapping of his fingers on the plastic screen irritated me, and I bit my lip and tried to ignore it. We all had to keep personal logs as part of the testing process; *they* wanted to be able to examine our mental as well as our physical state.

Milly had brought a reader. She tapped its screen in counterpoint to Solomon, flicking through the pages of glossy magazines one by one. Tip tap tip tap tip tap.

I chatted with Liza. Partly to distract myself, partly because she was so pretty in her half-starved way.

"Are you really going to take the second dose tonight?" I asked her.

"Why not?" she replied. "What's changed from when we first came in here?"

"You almost died," I said. She was a young woman. I was just a little too old. That didn't stop me worrying about her. "Didn't you?" I said. "You must have got the second strongest dose."

"You got it worse. We both lived. Anyway, I've had my bad dose. If anything, the odds are more in my favour next time."

"It doesn't work that way," I said. "The coin doesn't have a memory. Flip heads ten times, there's still a 50% probability of it coming up heads on the eleventh go."

"Don't tell me that." Liza put her hands to her ears. "I don't want to hear it."

She was silent, thinking. I looked at her face, her green eyes. Give her a good diet and the chance for regular exercise and she would be a real looker. Match that to her quiet confidence and she would have been incredible.

"Anyway," she continued, "what would be the point of me stopping the doses now? My family wouldn't get paid, there'd have been no point in me coming in here in the first place. Last night would have been for nothing."

It was a fair point, I suppose.

"You came in because of your family?" I said.

"My mother was killed by gangrene. My father died of blood poisoning. I'm the oldest. Someone has to earn some money." She nodded to herself. "What about you? Why are you in here?"

"Something similar." I wonder if she read something in my eyes. I guessed that she didn't believe me.

Milly put down her reader and came to sit with us.

"How are you feeling?" she asked me.

"Much better. I wish you wouldn't fuss."

"Why are you here, Milly?" Liza asked, and I was grateful to her for changing the subject.

"I'm earning some money for the grandchildren. You've got to put away a little bit for them, haven't you? Especially these days."

Liza was open-mouthed with wonder.

"Is that it?" she said. "You mean you don't have to be in here?"

"Well, I like to think that I'm doing my civic duty. We need to find new cures for old illnesses, don't we?"

"Well, yes, but you're risking your life for money for your grandchildren?"

Milly smiled.

"It's not that bad. This is the sixth time I've done this. Groone is the first fatality I've ever seen."

"But you hear stories," said Liza. "The strong batches. What if that's what they've given us?"

"They're just stories," said Milly. "Besides, there's no problem if you live your life right."

"Live your life right?" I said. "What does that mean?"

Milly took my hand in hers. She was plump and comfortable, she had the air of someone who'd figured everything out a long time ago.

"Live your life right, Paul. If you do good things to others, then good things will happen to you. Now, who'd like some more coffee?"

"Me, please," said Solomon, laying down his console on the next bed.

Milly was already heading to the kitchen.

"Why are you here, Solomon?" asked Liza.

"Free medical care," replied Solomon. "I need an operation. I don't have the money to pay for it. *They'll* do it as part of the package" – he jerked a thumb towards the one way mirror – "and even throw in some reserved antibiotics to help with the recovery. Can I have two sugars in that coffee, Milly?"

AT SIX O'CLOCK, Milly brought pack number 2 from the fridge. She placed it on the dining table. We all sat around, looking at it. There were five syringes.

The video feed flashed at us.

Disregard syringe number 2.

"Is that the control?" asked Solomon.

We looked at the video feed. No other message was forthcoming.

Milly reached out and took the syringe marked 1.

"You really don't care, do you?" said Solomon.

"I take care of people. I have good karma." She peeled the seal from the syringe.

"And we don't, I suppose?" said Solomon.

"This isn't a zero sum game."

Liza picked up the syringe marked 2. There was a buzzing noise, a low raspberry. The video feed had changed.

You were told to disregard that syringe. If you fail to follow instructions once more, your pay will be docked.

"I'm sorry," said Liza. "It was an honest mistake." She dropped the syringe, moved her hand to the one marked 3.

"Hey, that's my lucky number!" said Solomon.

"You take it," said Liza. Her hand moved to the one marked 4. I took the one marked 5. It made no difference, of course. It was a purely random choice. One of them may have been deadly, one of them may have not. We had no way of predicting which.

I held syringe 5 in my hand. There was no way of me knowing, but did the universe know? Was it already written somewhere whether I lived or died? Was that what Milly believed? She thought that her actions influenced the future. Did I?

Plastic wrapping flickered to the floor.

Go ahead.

Milly did so without hesitation. Liza was watching her.

"Go ahead," said Milly. "You did a good thing."

Solomon hesitated. You could see what he was thinking. What would be the cost of Liza handing him syringe number 3?

"You want to swap back?" asked Liza. They looked at each other, and they both laughed.

Solomon's hand shook as he injected himself. Liza and I looked at each other, gaining courage, and then we injected ourselves together.

"Well, that wasn't so bad," said Milly.

We sat, waiting. My arm was itching, I felt as if something burning was spreading through my body, but maybe that was just psychosomatic.

"Nothing's happening," said Solomon.

We didn't answer. We didn't want to tempt fate.

"Who wants some coffee?" said Solomon. "I'll make it. Shall I do dinner as well? Who wants a chicken salad sandwich?"

Liza and I couldn't meet each other's eyes. Solomon had expected the women to wait on him since he had arrived here. The talk of karma had spurred him into action.

"DOES ANYONE ELSE think this sandwich tastes funny?" asked Liza. "Or rather, that it doesn't taste of anything? I feel like I'm chewing plastic."

"I didn't want to say," said Solomon, miserably.

It tasted fine to me. I could taste chicken, I could taste fresh lettuce. There was the tang of tomato in each bite. I don't know how long it was since I'd last tasted tomato.

"What do you think, Milly?" I said.

"It seems a waste," she said, dropping her sandwich on her plate. "Real, proper food and I can't taste it."

"It will pass," I said. "I'm sure it will pass."

"You're okay, aren't you?" guessed Milly. There was no hiding the reproach in her voice.

"Sorry," I said. "I must have got the control dose."

"Don't apologize," said Liza. "It's nothing to be ashamed of. You got lucky this time. Oh dear…"

She closed her eyes and died. Just died, just like that. She didn't fall unconscious, she simply rolled her eyes up in her head and slumped down in her chair, slowly slid to the floor. You could almost see her life evaporating from her.

Solomon was on his feet, his eyes wide.

"What the hell is going on!" he said. His voice was shaking. "What the HELL is going on? What are you doing to us?"

Milly had her eyes closed, her hands were pressed together over her plate, she was muttering something under her breath.

Solomon was over by the video feed bending over it, shouting.

"This is a heavy dose batch! You've given us a heavy dose batch!"

Milly's eyes were open now. She was looking at Liza's body, slumped out on the floor. Poor old Liza. There was a flake of chicken at the corner of her mouth, her thin wrist emerging from her cuff, her fork on the floor just beyond her hand. Milly touched her hand to her throat.

"You're killing us off, one by one!" A rattling, banging noise. I watched Solomon hammering on the screen of the feed. Words appeared there, fuchsia words.

This was not planned. Something has gone wrong.

I felt the fear grip my heart, I saw Milly touch her hand to her throat again.

"What do you mean, something's gone wrong?" shouted Solomon. "What the HELL do you mean, something's gone wrong?"

The words took a moment to appear. Someone was typing those words in a room somewhere, I guessed. Someone was being told what to say.

This was not planned. This is an unforeseen reaction. This is a...

The words paused on the screen for a moment, and then they vanished. Then new words marched across.

We are analysing the initial batch of injections now. We're testing a new course of antibiotics...

Of course they were. They were always testing a new course of antibiotics.

"To hell with your course of antibiotics!" shouted Solomon. "This test is over. Let us out of here!"

"Paul, I feel so..." Milly coughed. She sounded hoarse, she was still touching her throat.

I took her arm. "Sit down, Milly. I'll get you a drink." I filled a glass with water. Milly sat at the table with her head in her hands.

"Why can't you let us out?" Solomon was pounding at the hard plastic of the screen. I looked to see the last message being overwritten by marching fuchsia letters.

We can't let you out until we know what's gone wrong. What if you are infectious?

"What if we die in here?"

That was the risk you took when you entered the room. The words hesitated, someone's conscience must have been pricked. *I'm sorry.*

"You're sorry!" Solomon didn't seem to have noticed that Milly was shivering. I put my arm around her and I felt the heat she was giving off.

"Solomon," I said. "Ask them what I should do about Milly."

There was no need for him to ask. The words were already scrolling across the screen.

Keep her calm. Keep her cool. Drink plenty of fluids. The next injection may cure her.

"The next injection?" Solomon laughed. "No way are we taking the next injection! And don't even think of trying to stiff us on payment. You messed up! You owe us in compensation."

You will be well compensated. But you don't understand. The remaining three injections must be taken, for your own good.

"For our own good? Why?"

Because you have introduced the antibiotic strain into your body, and left unchecked it will eat you up from the inside. The remaining three injections are intended to bring the course to termination.

Solomon looked at me. I shook my head. I didn't believe the words, either.

"Bullshit!" shouted Solomon.

It's true. You know we have to tell you the truth. It's in the contract. We can keep secrets for the sake of the double blind test, but we cannot tell lies. That would be unethical.

"Unethical? Two dead and you're worried about being unethical!"

This is not unethical. Farming is not unethical.

"Farming? What do you mean, farming?"

You read the contract. Farming. Agriculture. The cultivation of animals, plants, fungi, and other life forms for food, fibre, biofuel and other products used to sustain human life.

He stared at the screen, absorbing the words. People were dying due to a lack of working antibiotics, and now we farmed humans in order to sustain human life. I never thought of that before. I suppose that, according to the definition, what was happening to us was a form of agriculture.

"Am I dying?" asked Milly. She was shivering now, her whole body shaking with the cold.

"You're all right," I said. "You're going to be all right."

"We're not cattle!" said Solomon. "You can't treat us like this."

We're not treating you like cattle. We're trying to save you!

"I won't take the next injections."

Then you'll die.

"Which syringes are the safe ones? Which have the lowest doses?"

They're all the same.

"You say that now! Before you said that everything was random!"

This is a double blind experiment. We're only just finding out the full facts ourselves.

"Will we come to any harm if we take the next injections?"

There was no answer.

"Will we come to any harm from injecting ourselves again?"

No reply.

I DIDN'T SLEEP that night. Neither did Solomon. I could hear him shifting in his bed, I could hear him muttering under his breath. Swear words, words of hate directed at the people beyond the mirror, directed at the life that had left him here.

I could hear the soft snoring of Milly. Her earlier illness hadn't shaken her faith in karma.

"Hey, Paul."

I pretended to be asleep.

"Hey, Paul. I know you're awake."

"I don't want to wake Milly," I whispered back.

"She'll sleep through anything," said Solomon. "Paul. Are you going to take the dose in the morning?"

"Probably. Why not?" I said.

"Because they're lying to us. You know what I think, Paul? I think we've got a death batch."

I shivered at those words. That's what my cellmates had said to me, when I told them what I'd done. I put their words down to jealousy. In a few days I would be free. They would remain locked in prison...

"You hear what I said, Paul? It's a death batch!"

"No way, Solomon. There's no such thing. Why would there be a death batch? What would they gain by killing us?"

"Don't you get it? They use human bodies to grow things in. They inject us with diseases and then they use us as farmland to cultivate white blood cells. All those white blood cells your body used to fight the diseases. Okay, maybe you die, but they still get to harvest those cells, those strong ones that fought the disease and almost won... They can use those cells in other people. You think we're farm animals, Paul? No way! They're not that interested in us. We're not the farm animals, we're the farm!"

"Shut up, Solomon," I said. "Go to sleep."

"You hear what I'm saying, Paul. You know I'm right."

I WOKE UP next morning to the smell of coffee and bacon and good karma. Solomon had laid the table, Milly was frying breakfast. Solomon handed me a cup of steaming coffee as I sat up.

"Next dose at 9," he said.

I didn't taste my breakfast. Only Milly seemed to enjoy the meal, chewing at her food with a plump complacency. Soon enough it was nine o'clock. Milly brought the next pack of syringes to the table.

Disregard packs 2 and 4.

Solomon swore when he read the message on the screen.

"I thought they were all meant to be the same," he said.

The remaining three are.

"They're lying," said Milly. Even she didn't believe them now. She reached out for a syringe and then paused.

"I was going to choose number three," she said, looking at Solomon. "Do you want it?"

"It makes no difference," I said. "It makes no difference if this is random."

"It worked for Liza," said Solomon. "Or it would have done if I hadn't taken it from her. You have number three, Milly. Paul, you go next."

I took syringe number one. It didn't make any difference, did it? Solomon took number five.

"I've got grandchildren as well," he said. "I've never seen them." He looked towards the wall. "If anything happens to me, I want the money to go to them. Not to my idle, no good daughters."

He took a deep breath, placed the needle on his arm. He didn't push it in.

I looked at syringe number one. What was in there? In a couple of minutes I'd know.

"I don't want to do this," I said.

Milly took a deep breath and injected herself. Solomon did the same.

"Come on, Paul," he said.

I looked at him.

"Take it, Paul. Come on."

"Take it."

The needle felt cold as it went in.

"That feels different," I said.

We all looked at each other, examining each other's faces for clues.

"I feel okay..." said Solomon, carefully.

"Me too."

"I feel okay."

We waited.

"Perhaps they're telling the truth," I said. "There is no death batch."

"Do you feel cold?" asked Solomon.

"The room's cold," said Milly. "You're being paranoid. Everything's okay. We're on wind down now. Everything will be fine. Why are you staring at me like that?"

Solomon looked at me.

"What!" said Milly. "What! Why are you staring at me? Tell me! There's nothing the matter with me! I feel fine!"

Solomon spoke first.

"You're drooling, Milly. Wipe your mouth."

"Drooling? I'm not drooling. I'm..." She touched her mouth, felt the saliva there. Her eyes erupted with tears.

"I'm not crying," she said, saliva spilling from her mouth. She was sweating now, sweating profusely.

"I'll get a towel," said Solomon.

"I'll be fine!" shouted Milly. "I'm a good person. I've got credit."

She spat the last words out. She was blushing now, crying and blushing and drooling.

"I... Oh hell... I... I... oh... oh..."

"Paul. You're drooling too."

I wiped my mouth and looked at my hand. Silver saliva trailed in strands.

"I feel fine otherwise," I said, my eyes filling with tears. Solomon looked okay.

"Milly got the strong dose," I said. "I got the middle. You got the placebo."

Milly's clothes were soaking with perspiration. She pulled off her top, dropped it to the floor with a wet squelch.

"Cattle," said Solomon, looking at her.

"We're not the cattle," I dribbled. "You're right, Solomon. We're the farms. They try planting different crops in us, and some of the crops thrive, and some of them ruin the soil."

I looked at Milly, pink and naked and dripping with sweat and saliva. She was moaning softly to herself in the middle of the floor. My clothes felt disgusting. Wet and heavy. I began to strip off.

I felt so odd.

"Solomon," I said. "If anything happens to me…"

"PAUL'S DEAD," SAID Milly.

Solomon lay back on the bed.

"I know. I heard him go."

"Why didn't you move his body? You've just left him lying there on the floor."

"What's the point?" said Solomon. "We'll all be dead by the morning. This is a death batch, isn't it?"

"There's no such thing."

"Why are you really in here, Milly? I don't believe it's for your grandchildren. You're in here for the same reason I am, for the same reason he was."

He pointed to Paul's body, naked and glistening on the floor.

"I didn't kill them," said Milly. "I'd never harm them. It was an accident. My grandchildren were my world."

"I believe you," said Solomon, tapping at his console.

"I chose to come in here because I knew I'd be safe. I'm a good person. This will prove it."

"It's certainly been the case so far."

She frowned.

"Isn't that Paul's console you're writing on?" she said.

"It is. Paul asked me to take over his log if anything happened to him."

"Why?"

"I guess he just wanted *them* to see the end of his story. I guess he wanted them to see him as a person and not just a container for their diseases."

Solomon bit his lip.

"I hope I get to finish it."

He looked at Milly.

"If I don't, will you write this up? For me and for Paul?"

"I can't promise that," said Milly. "I'm not much of a writer."

Next dose said the screen.

"Are you coming?" asked Milly.

"Just finishing this sentence."

THE MASHUP

SEAN WILLIAMS

Sean Williams writes for children, young adults and adults. The author of forty novels, ninety short stories and the odd odd poem, his work has won awards, debuted at #1 on the New York Times bestseller list, and been translated into numerous languages. His latest novel is Twinmaker, *the first in a new series that takes his love affair with the matter transmitter to a whole new level.*

THE VENUE THE next morning was still a little funky, in both senses of the word. There was mess everywhere – someone had put the CEO's cardboard standee headfirst into the chocolate fountain, which was a waste of good wake-up juice as far as I was concerned, particularly on the publisher's dime – while at the same time music still thudded away in the smaller party room, accompanied by the occasional slurred whoop.

I had a cab waiting outside. The plan wasn't to stay long.

"Hey, James." My friend the DJ was nursing a coffee in a corner with the most beautiful woman I've ever seen. Knowing him, though, she was for show, and somewhere under the skintight dress was a cock the size of an eggplant. "Just came by to get the name of that track you were playing earlier. Yazoo meets jungle – who knew?"

"Yeah, you love a good mashup." He seemed more curious than peeved at the interruption. "I was going to send you the link, honest."

"Network's down, and this is on the way. Thought I could download it en route." If the network got its shit together first.

"Sure. Right." James looked for a piece of paper and a pen. It took a while. He jotted a name and held the slip of paper under the light to make sure I was reading it correctly.

"Moyët," he said, pointing at the umlaut. "Devil, details."

I patted him on the cheek and left him to his conquest.

"Hey," he called after me. "You got one too, huh?"

"Got what?"

He indicated the ceiling above my head, where a small black sphere was clinging to a halogen lamp fixture like a surveillance camera that had popped free of its mounting. The thing wobbled and backed up when my eyes locked on it.

"What the hell?"

"They started showing up an hour ago," James said. "Now they're everywhere."

There were two watching him and his conquest, and another studied the guy asleep in the corner. One trailed after an intern who passed through, an empty garbage bag dangling limp from her left hand. Her sphere rolled across the ceiling as if gravity didn't work for it the normal way, hopping and jumping to get past obstacles.

"They don't do anything," said the girl as she left the room.

"All they do is watch," James' date added in a contralto that sent shivers up my spine.

"Safe flight," James said with a wink.

Outside the taxi was gone, but I could afford to be philosophical: the only luggage I had was in my jacket, and if I missed the flight I could always get another one. Besides, the sphere had followed me out, which was more interesting than getting home in a hurry. It had zipped through the door before it shut behind me and now clung to the wall of the building. The space between my shoulder blades tingled. It was watching me, I knew it.

"I'm going to find a cab," I told it. "You coming?"

The sphere made no sound or sign of understanding, just followed in a series of zippy leaps and bounds. Once, I caught it hovering in the air like a drone, as though deciding where to set down next. I ducked left. It kicked off empty air to follow me.

They were everywhere, now I knew to look, and I wasn't the only one noticing them. We all had one – man, woman and kid. Some people tried to swat them away with brooms or bats. Some tried to outrun them. I passed a guy staring his down, to no avail, and a woman cursing hers in a steady stream. In the distance I heard shouts, gunshots, sirens. A motorbike roared by, driven by a teenager who was paying more attention to what was behind him than what lay ahead. His sphere slewed and skidded in his wake, but kept pace without faltering. They screeched in tandem around a corner. The crash I heard moments later might have been related.

"You enjoying this?" I asked mine. It didn't respond.

I found a queue of people waiting for cabs and joined the end of the line, although I wasn't hopeful. The streets were sludging up like the arteries of a fat man in a sauna.

"What do you think?" asked the woman next to me in the queue. She was huddled with three guys, all of them nursing hot drinks that stank of sugar and spice and everything that definitely wasn't supposed to be in coffee. Four spheres watched from a nearby tree, fat attentive grapes that were soon joined by a fifth, mine. "Is it some kind of stunt?"

"Apple," said one of the three guys before I could answer. "Or a start-up. Maybe something to do with life-logging."

"I think it's aliens," said the guy next to him. "We're at war, and we don't even know it."

"Seriously?" I said.

He shrugged. "Why not? Makes as much sense as anything else."

"It's the Singularity," offered the third guy. "The Internet plus AI plus 3-D printers plus reality TV. Had to happen eventually."

I didn't know what to think, but I doubted it was a robot uprising, or aliens, or some stunt gone wrong. Truthfully, I was less worried about being watched than about where they all came from. I'm a numbers guy. There's no such thing as a free drone. So who was paying for all this? How many Chinese workers were soldering their fingers to the bone to make them?

My phone was still dead, and no wonder given the bandwidth those things were gobbling up. I couldn't call home or check the news, but it seemed safe to assume they were everywhere. After an hour of hopeless waiting and speculating I abandoned the cab plan and decided to walk back to the hotel. I didn't really want to, but there was nowhere else to go. By then, weirdly, the watchers appeared to have watchers of their own, smaller red spheres that trailed the ones trailing us, and soon there were green ones too, and yellow, in descending order of size. The air was full of simplistic atomic models, the kind you saw in class as a kid. Spheres spun, swooped, and whizzed around the city's human inhabitants, who looked increasingly perplexed and desperate as the morning wore on.

Add to that the holes that were appearing in buildings, lampposts and cars, like Swiss cheese. This explained where the spheres were coming from, I guessed: material was being sucked out of the environment to make more of the things, somehow. So maybe the Singularity guy was right, after all. The Internet plus whatever plus nanotechnology as well. It was as if we'd put all the ingredients out on the table and they'd assembled themselves while our backs were turned.

AT THE HOTEL, the concierge had gone but the clerk who'd checked me out was still behind the desk. She gave my key back to me and didn't re-swipe my credit card. Two multicoloured constellations watched the transaction from several dozen angles at once, orbiting around our heads. I asked about breakfast and she said there might only be soup available now, since the kitchen had pretty much shut down. She said she'd find someone to send it right up.

I took the stairs in case the power went out and let myself back into the room, feeling like I was looping back on a life I had left behind. The air smelt stale. Feeling faintly hungover for the first time that day, I fell onto the unmade bed and pulled the sheet across me. A pair of mesh stockings slithered out.

I rolled away from the memory with a groan. She had seemed great, and we had got on fine, and it was an open question as to who picked up who, which always worked for me. Things had only gone wrong when we had come back to the hotel and started making out.

"Bite me," she'd said. "Go on. You know you want to."

"Why would I want to do that? I *like* you."

"Yeah, and you like steak too, right?"

"Actually, I'm a vegetarian."

"Really? Well, shit. Pretend I'm tofu. It might still work out."

"You want to be tofu?"

"Uh, yeah... maybe not."

I rolled over and closed my eyes. I didn't need to see the spheres to know they were there, occupying all the niches and cracks of the room, watching, always watching. Their eyes didn't close. Thank god, I thought, they were a recent phenomenon.

I slept and had a nightmare about M&Ms.

When I jerked awake an unknown time later there were spheres everywhere. All sizes and colours, they stretched in filaments across the ceiling, down the walls, and pooled in the corner behind the lamp. They were all the colours of the rainbow and every imaginable shade. The smallest looked like fine grains of talcum powder, only visible when they moved.

I sat up and they rustled, forming new shapes and structures, revealing new holes where they had eaten into the walls and fixtures. I looked around the room in numb amazement, feeling an emptiness in my stomach that hadn't been there before. If the soup had come, the watchers had eaten it, along with the bowl, cutlery and tray. The porter too, for all I knew.

"Am I next?" I asked the assembly of spheres, thinking of the OMG *aliens* guy in the street earlier. Was this some cosmic demolition crew, devouring all we built and all we were while the cameras kept running, like *This Old House* in space?

A thought slid into my head that wasn't really a thought. It was a certainty, and it didn't originate with me.

Moyët.

It took me a second to place the name of the track James had played the previous night. Yazoo and jungle; champagne and Alison Moyet. The note was still in my pocket.

I sat up to address the spheres properly.

"Was that you? Did you just talk to me?"

What is 'you'? What is 'me'?

I rubbed my eyes and felt something that hadn't been there before. That got me out of moving. In the bathroom mirror I saw one black sphere and a multicoloured cluster growing out of my forehead like alien acne.

"Get it out," I said, breaking into a sweat. "I don't want this in me."

What is 'out'? What is 'in'?

"Stop saying shit like that! Why are you doing this? What do you want?"

There was a whisper as all the other watchers swarmed into the bathroom with me.

This isn't an either/or situation.

The thought was urgent in my mind, and although it had the strangest flavour it felt like one of my own. Humans had believed themselves removed from nature ever since we became civilised, but we never had been, really. Global warming showed us that. Yet somehow we still thought we were removed from technology, whether it was made by us or someone else. Weren't we machines as well as animals? And weren't we also works of art, swimming in a soup of cultural context? My thing wasn't James' thing wasn't tofu girl's thing, but all those things coexisted and sometimes they rubbed off on each other. Sometimes they blended.

I was feeling dizzy. Whatever this was, it wasn't an invasion or a robot uprising or anything simple like that – or maybe it was, but it was all of them at once, instead of just one. The possibility throbbed like a tumour in my thoughts, turning me, twisting me. It was then I realised.

I was part of the biggest mashup in history. How could I possibly miss that?

I opened my arms and held them out Christlike, minus the cross. My hands shook just a little. The spheres rushed in, bringing new senses, new feelings. The watchers became the watched. It was all so very meta. I opened my mind and let it happen.

THE FROST ON
JADE BUDS

ALIETTE DE BODARD

Aliette de Bodard lives and works in Paris, where she has a day job as a computer engineer. In her spare time, she writes speculative fiction: her stories have appeared in markets such as Clarkesworld, Asimov's *and numerous Year's Best. Her Aztec noir trilogy Obsidian and Blood is published by Angry Robot, worldwide. Visit http:// www.aliettedebodard.com for book reviews, writing process and Vietnamese recipes.*

ON THE COMMS-IMAGE, Chi looked much as Thuy remembered her: tall and thin and dour, almost skeletal, as if what had happened to her in her youth still stifled her metabolism – and, in truth, perhaps it did. Neither Thuy nor any of the family – nor, indeed, any inhabitant of the Scattered Pearls Belt – really knew the full extent of what happened to her, or how to reverse it.

"You look well, elder sister," Chi said. The words would have suited the Imperial Court; would have been appropriate for an elder of Chi's generation. There were other, more familiar ones, more suitable for the sister of one's blood; and Chi could have used them. She could have pretended to care. But of course she no longer bothered.

Thuy couldn't bring herself to lie. "You don't."

Chi laughed, but it didn't reach her eyes – and even the makeup and the plucked eyebrows couldn't distract from the red, burst blood vessels in her corneas. "You never could lie."

"Not to family," Thuy said, simply. She wondered where Sixth Aunt had got to; she'd left the ship a bi-hour ago, saying she needed to find something in the Apricot Blossom Ho orbital, and hadn't come back. Staring into her sister's eyes, Thuy wished she could have counted on Sixth Aunt's biting wisdom and overbearing presence; on her reassurance that she was handling this the proper way; for anything that would have taken away that feeling of baiting a tiger with nothing but her wit to save her – and ancestors knew wit had never been her strength.

On Thuy's implants-feed, the signal from *The Dragons in the Peach Garden* flowed like a meditation prayer – the ship's trackers were attempting to trace the call, hopping from node to node in the network, discarding the more remote planets of the Black Tiger solar system, moving in closer to the centre...

Let them find something; anything that would help them. Let them track Chi down before it was too late.

"You shouldn't be here," Chi said.

"Did you expect me to stay away after I got your message?"

"What, that I was coming back to the orbital of my childhood?" Chi's voice was slightly ironic; as if already detached from the conversation. Of course it would be.

"You know what I mean," Thuy said.

The trackers were narrowing it further; to the middle band between the large space stations and the stunted, burnt planets; to the Scattered Pearls Belt itself...

Please please please...

"I know exactly what you mean. You have this pathetic notion that you can stop me, that you can make me change my mind." Chi's face was closed again – as serene, as enigmatic as the statue of Quan Am in the temples. "You're free to try, elder sister. But you'll never succeed."

And with that, the comms cut off. Thuy remained standing for a while, staring at the emptiness in front of her eyes – the ship's network superimposed the images directly on her field of vision – and tried to banish her sister's image from her thoughts.

The Dragons in the Peach Garden spoke up. "I tracked the signal to the vicinity of this orbital, and then I lost it. I'm sorry, child."

Thuy sighed. "Not your fault, great-aunt." The mindship was old; old enough to have seen her mother and grandmother as children – old enough to remember everything about Chi before... the incident. "How close a vicinity?"

The calligraphy scrolling on the walls flickered, turning from red to pale pink for a barely perceptible moment – the mindship was a proud one, and not easily embarrassed. "A neighbourhood of at least three orbitals, including this one."

Anywhere, in other words.

Thuy stared at the walls, hoping to find some distraction, some wisdom in them. But her eyes were drawn inexorably to the intricate, etched pattern of chemical burn-marks – back from a time before the war, when *The Dragons in the Peach Garden* had been a transport ship for Galactic factories; when her overseer had cared little about acid damage from burst boxes – cheaper to hire a new ship than to bother spending money on repairs. No solace to be found there; only painful scars.

Thuy sighed. With a flick of her fingers she called up Chi's previous message, and stared at the vision that coalesced in front of her, as translucent and insubstantial as the Courts of Hell.

It was a mindship – one that bore as much resemblance to *The Dragons in the Peach Garden* as the calligraphy of a child did to a New Year's welcome scroll painted by a master. Lines that should have been effortlessly flowing were crooked and jagged; the hull was a jumble of metals haphazardly joined, much as though everything had melted together in the furnace of the workshops.

Thuy moved her fingers, turning the image of the mindship back and forth – every new point of view revealing fresh details – exhausts bursting at sharp, impossible angles from the hull; rivets and connectors spread like fungi on the pitted surface; protruding fins and wings, cancerous growths in a tumultuous, nausea-inducing pattern that was impossible to take in all at once. It was hard to tell how much was the original Galactic ship and how much was Chi's painstaking reconstruction work, but Thuy suspected that even brand-new the mindship would have been an eyesore; and an abomination in more ways than one.

There had been only one line in the message; a handful of words that had chilled Thuy to the core of her being.

Is she not beautiful, elder sister?

She didn't know what the ship was called, but she knew who had made it; and for what purpose; and some of Chi's purpose in putting it back together.

For years she'd hoped that Chi's absence at New Year's Eves and family death anniversaries meant that she was somewhere else, whether in Galactic or in Dai Viet space; that she'd found a place where she could fit, where she could be happy. The message had proved otherwise.

She brought her fingers together; and let the ship vanish from her field of vision. "We're too late," she said, aloud.

The Dragons in the Peach Garden was silent for a while. "By those standards we've been too late for ten years, child."

"I guess so," Thuy said.

"I know what you're thinking," the mindship said. "It wasn't your fault."

"I know," Thuy said, but she didn't. She kept telling herself that, when she woke up in the grip of shadowy nightmares; when she remembered hanging in the void of space, bathed in the merciless light of the stars – hearing Chi's heavy breathing and knowing it was too late – that even if her thrusters came online now she would never reach her sister in time...

It wasn't her fault. She had to keep thinking that; or she'd fall, and ancestors only knew how far she'd fall.

Thuy found Sixth Aunt at one of the stalls in the Scavenge Market, sipping lotus tea – by the smell that wafted up to her, the expensive, delicate kind grown only in the light of the Black Tiger star. An uneaten plate of cakes lay at her right hand.

"Sit down, child," Sixth Aunt said, with a graceful move of her sleeves. "Have a cake. They're not the best, but Madam Second makes a very good pandanus and durian filling."

"There's no time for that," Thuy protested. On her newsfeed, the Galactic delegation was being welcomed by the President of the Forest of Brushes; something flashed at the bottom of the image, a schedule that involved visiting the Hall of Supreme Harmony in the Central orbital, and then the orbitals of the most powerful families in the Scattered Pearls Belt. The Apricot Blossom Ho, the orbital where they were, was second on the list.

"Pfah," Sixth Aunt said. "There's always time. The Galactics will put their hands on the pulse of power, and try to see where it flows from. That's what they did, after all, when they first took us over as a colony. It'll take time."

Thuy shook her head. "My younger sister is here." But the habit of obedience won out; she picked a cake and bit into it – letting the rich tang spread in her mouth, a heavy burst of flavours on her palate.

"Of course she's here. Where else would she be?" Sixth Aunt was a small, plump woman with uncanny eyes – they were brown like most Rong, but in some types of light they shone green, as sharp and as deep as imperial jade.

"In Central," Thuy said, more sharply than she'd meant. Sixth Aunt had that effect on people.

This close to the edge of the Scavenge Market, it was quiet. The only people in Thuy's field of vision were a group of elderly men and women sitting at a table: ex-workers from the Galactic factories, their bone-atrophied arms flexed like lengths of tubing, their eyes covered with a bluish film sprouting hairs as fine as insect feelers; their faces prematurely aged, skin sagging like molten plastic on their cheeks and chins. They were all too common on the orbitals: the last remnant of those who'd handled Peters' Blue in colonial times, in places where the safety of the workers had been an afterthought to the lure of easy money – an unsettling sight, with the Galactics negotiating for the re-establishment of factories in the Scattered Pearls Belt.

Sixth Aunt, oblivious to her surroundings, sipped her tea, as daintily as if she'd been in her own quarters – her eyes closed in something approaching bliss. "Ah. One should always take the time for proper tea."

"Younger aunt..." Thuy started; and stopped, for any word she could have added would have been disrespectful.

Sixth Aunt laid her cup back on the table, as carefully as she'd have put down a winning hand of *mat chuoc*. "Finish your cake, child, and we'll go see a friend."

As they walked through the Scavenge Market, Thuy felt as though she were ten years back – as though she were one of the kids in the market, proudly showing vendors what they'd salvaged from the floating mass of debris in the Belt – kids borrowing the shuttles of their families' mindships, playing soldiers and immortals in the vast jumble of leftover junk from the Galactic War – picking up shiny things, bringing them back, never considering what might happen to them; as if the debris zone were just another playground.

"Takes you back," Sixth Aunt said – of course she could always tell what Thuy was thinking. In Mother's absence she'd practically raised her and Chi.

Three kids ran past Thuy, laughing. She caught a glimpse of what they were carrying – cracked, warped devices that hummed with threatening noises, and the blackened remnants of smart-mine swarms – one wrong word, one wrong gesture and they would not only expel paralysing gas but cause their swarm-mates to do the same.

She opened her mouth; but Sixth Aunt forestalled her, shaking her head.

"They're spent. Harmless."

And they both knew it was a lie; that she didn't know, that she *couldn't* know how damaged they were. They both knew how dangerous it could be, to be out there in the Belt debris, in what had once been the front line of the independence war against the Galactics. But the kids were gone, rushing ahead to sell their new toys; or to play in the nooks and crannies of the orbital. Thuy bit her lip, fighting an urge to run after them; but what would she have done? There were dozens of kids in the Scavenge Market, all of them carrying things that could be equally dangerous.

The market was quieter than usual; its customary ebullience gone. It hung almost... silenced, watching the screens; watching the Galactics. They'd been gone for forty years, longer than the lifetime of half the people of the orbital, but old habits die hard.

There'd be protests, of course; demonstrations against the return of their former masters – but the Imperial Court had planned for that. Security had trebled at all keypoints, and the Galactics would be moving in their very own bubble of quiet, deserted space. They would meet the leaders of the Scattered Pearls Belt; smile and discuss what they wanted, as if nothing had ever happened, as if the war was but distant, harmless memories.

No security, however, would ever protect them against Chi.

Sixth Aunt led Thuy to one of the smaller stalls at the back of the Scavenge Market; so small, in fact, that it seemed to be selling almost nothing but a few holo-displays. Then Thuy's eyes caught the holo-displays – and saw that the stall was empty, not because it sold small trinkets, but because its products were too large to be lined up on shelves.

The owner was a middle-aged woman with a few hints of white at her temples. She smiled at Sixth Aunt. "Your friend, yes?"

"My niece," Sixth Aunt said, nodding. "Child, this is Madam Anh."

"And she'd be the one looking for a ship?" Madam Anh nodded. Thuy looked at the holos.

"Mostly parts," *The Dragons in the Peach Garden* said, unexpectedly speaking up on her comms-link. "This is a helicoidal thruster, and this is a multi-input reconstructional antenna... And, oh, I wouldn't mind one of these..."

"We don't have the money," Thuy subvocalised. "Besides, it's all Galactic tech –"

"No sense in closing oneself to new things, I've always said."

Thuy tore herself from the conversation to find Madam Anh deep in talk with Sixth Aunt. "I'm afraid I can't help you, elder sister – you'll understand that my customers expect confidentiality..."

"Pfah." Sixth Aunt's lips pursed, in that all-too-familiar gesture. "What harm does it do to know who purchased what ship parts? We're no longer under the Galactics, and maintaining mindships is no longer frowned upon – there's no need to hoard your knowledge from us."

The Imperial Court probably kept a watch on ship parts, but in a desultory fashion: part of the Scattered Pearls Belt's attraction was the freedom to trade, and traders who got controlled too often moved to places without such restrictions.

Madam Anh grimaced. "With some customers, it's clear that they need... a little less attention in their direction."

"Of course," Sixth Aunt said "But I'm not interested in who they are." The lie slipped, smoothly, easily from her lips. "I just think they might have something else we need, based on what they bought here."

"She's my sister," Thuy said, ignoring the sharp look Sixth Aunt threw her. "We need to make sure that she's fine."

"What if I told you she was?" Madam Anh asked. Even though Thuy kept her eyes lowered as a sign of respect, she could feel the weight of Madam Anh's gaze. "Would you truly go away then?"

Thuy took a deep breath – and then, before Sixth Aunt could stop her for impertinence to an elder, she said, "If I believed you told the truth, yes."

A sharp inhalation of breath from Madam Anh – a moment which hung suspended like a knife – and Sixth Aunt, starting to say, "I apologise –"

Madam Anh made a small, sharp noise – a bark of amused laughter. "The young always challenge authority, do they not?"

"I'm sorry," Thuy said, feeling the heat of the blush spread to her cheeks. "She's my younger sister, and I'm the one responsible for her care."

"That is the role of parents," Madam Anh said, though her voice was a little less sharp.

Thuy waited for Sixth Aunt to speak up, but she didn't. It fell to her, then; because she'd spoken up and pulled the conversation towards her as inexorably as a star pulled its comets. "Mother and Father are dead."

"You're too young for them to have died in the war." Madam Anh's voice was flat.

Thuy shook her head. "It was afterwards. Fifteen years ago. Their ship was going from Central to the Eastern Sea Tran orbital, right next to here. It must have collided with some debris on the way back." She'd said it so many times now that the words came out on automatic, without any emotion; a mere fact of life that couldn't be budged or changed no matter how hard she beseeched her ancestors at night.

Madam Anh was silent, then. It wasn't as if this was an uncommon story; there was enough debris in the Scattered Pearls Belt to last over several lifetimes, ten thousand booby traps and ambush tools the Galactics had dropped as though there were no tomorrow. Most of the Independence Forces' weapons were inactive or easily avoided by now; after all, they hadn't wanted to lay waste to their own country. The Galactics, though, had been in their colonies, and hadn't much cared by the end whether they destroyed the entire Belt if it meant winning the war.

"So, yes, tell me she's fine and I'll go home," Thuy said, forging on even though the little voice at the back of her head told her she'd better remain silent, better let her words sink in. But she couldn't. There was no time. "But I doubt she is."

"Your sister was here," Madam Anh said at last. "Looks much like you – if you'd not eaten or slept for days on end. Bought a couple parts." She waved a gnarled hand; and one of the screens changed, rotating a handful of parts Thuy couldn't identify. "Those ones."

Thuy heard *The Dragons in the Peach Garden* stir on the comms-link, giving her the technical details on each part and the possible uses in language so dense she could hardly process it.

"That doesn't help," she subvocalised. And then, aloud to Madam Anh, "Did she say – anything?"

Madam Anh spread her hands. "No."

"But she was not well," Thuy insisted.

Madam Anh sighed. "If she'd been my daughter, I would have sent her home and fed her caramel pork and crab fritters until she got some fat on those bones." Before Thuy could speak up, she gestured, and the holo-screens shifted, to display a point blinking amidst the stars.

"That's where she asked me to deliver the parts," Madam Anh said. "Take a good look and memorise it, because I won't show it to you twice."

"Got it," *The Dragons in the Peach Garden* said.

The screen went black again. "May your ancestors send you good fortune to find her," Madam Anh said. "She needs guidance, that one."

You have no idea how much.

Thuy bowed to Madam Anh, and followed Sixth Aunt out of the market. Sixth Aunt's lips were pursed; she couldn't tell how much was disapproval, or scepticism. "You think she'll be gone," Thuy said.

"Of course. I didn't raise fools," Sixth Aunt said.

A noise tore through the din of the Scavenge Market – an explosion, soon swallowed again by the hubbub around them. What had –? Thuy couldn't see very clearly, but there was a crowd clustered around one of the stalls. A handful of medic-drones swerved past them, intent on getting to the wounded.

Text scrolled at the bottom of her field of vision, on the newsfeed for the market: *explosion near the Street of Calligraphers. Minor wounds: three victims. Major wounds: none. Precautions: none. Expect minor jams around stall 17573.* It wouldn't be more than a blip on people's feeds; an everyday occurrence in the Scavenge Market. People knew, after all, what risk they were taking by tinkering with Galactic debris. Everyone knew. Everyone had always known.

If only it were just explosions. If only it was just flesh wounds, easily closed, easily cured – limbs, easily regrown, shards and projectiles, easily extracted, though even that thought was trivialising other people's hurt.

But, of course, Galactic weapons had gone beyond that a long time ago; and Thuy and Chi and Sixth Aunt knew all about that, too.

"WELL, WE'RE HERE," *The Dragons in the Peach Garden* said. "No one will be too surprised if I detect a distinct absence of spaceships."

Thuy sighed, massaging her temples. "It was the best information we had. Are you sure –? A mindship would have many ways to conceal itself –"

"Yes," *The Dragons in the Peach Garden* said, patiently, as if to a small child. "But not this thoroughly."

They were in the middle of the debris field. The various objects lit up on the ship's sensor: mine swarms, acid traps, enhanced-gravity bombs, and the odd, twisted objects that couldn't be properly labelled by the ship's systems. Those were the best finds for kids; the chance of finding something new.

Thuy remembered a time, ten years ago, when the biggest debris of the swarm had lit up on their shuttle's scanner; the way Chi's eyes had lit up from the inside, the begging and pleading that they needed to go check the thing out, that it would be an experience to boast about to their cousins, that they might even bring something back, something pretty enough to outrank the holo-projector that Cousin Hieu had salvaged from the ruin of a Galactic shuttle. She'd always been curious; and Thuy had never been able to refuse her anything.

"She was here," Thuy said, aloud.

"Quite obviously. Equally obviously, she's not here anymore." Sixth Aunt was sitting at the table, staring at a map of the square quadrant. Underneath, in transparency, the table showed the Galactic delegation exiting the Hall of Supreme Harmony. They were smiling, their teeth as white and as sharp as those of tigers on the prowl. No doubt they'd got what they wanted – perhaps even the military bases they'd been angling for, the 'buffer zone' between the Scattered Pearls Belt and the much larger Dai Viet Empire. "You remember colonial times," she said to *The Dragons in the Peach Garden.*

The ship sniffed. "When they thought it fitting to send mindships on extended delivery runs throughout the galaxy – treating us no better than beasts of burden, and caring little as to whether we saw our families again at New Year's Eve? Yes, of course." She didn't sound pleased.

"Everyone in the family ended up working for them," Sixth Aunt said, thoughtfully – and, to Thuy, "You weren't born, of course. But their soldiers drove customers away from the restaurant with their rowdiness and arrogance, and paid like misers. Your grandfather had no choice but to take work at the barracks – and not be paid much more than an errand boy."

"Is this really the time?" Thuy asked. She knew about the Galactics – about the slow, orchestrated ruin of their family – but that wasn't the point. The point was that they couldn't afford another war with them; and that was what would happen if Chi had her way.

Sixth Aunt stared at the table and its image of the Galactic delegation – her face as unreadable as Chi's had been. "Perhaps. Perhaps not. Who knows what the future might hold?"

"It's the past I have no interest in conjuring up again," *The Dragons in the Peach Garden* said, stiffly.

Thuy tuned them both out. She stared at the wall – at the projected images of space, with the stars and debris helpfully labelled by *The Dragons in the Peach Garden*'s sensors. She thought of Chi – of her sister, alone in the room of her rebuilt mindship, making her plans with the same ruthless clarity she'd applied to everything since the accident.

"Can you show me the projected path of the Galactics' shuttle?" she asked the ship.

The view zoomed out; a thin line of green threaded its way through the debris – a zigzag course through some of the less cluttered areas. "My best guess," *The Dragons in the Peach Garden* said.

"That's assuming they'll take the obvious path," Sixth Aunt said, her eyes still on the map.

"Security reasons?" Thuy asked. "They'll assume there isn't a ship that can touch them; and ordinarily they'd be right." She stared at the map again, willing the truth to emerge from the jumble of debris

– but the only truth that would come was the same Chi already knew; that nothing was fair or equitable in life.

"What would you do if you were Chi?" Sixth Aunt asked.

Thuy shook her head. "I can't tell what she would do. Not anymore."

Sixth Aunt said nothing. Chi had stayed a while, after the accident. At first, she'd tried to act normal; to pay her respects every morning to her other elders, to bring fruit fresh from the orchard to Sixth Aunt, to pretend that everything was fine. But the change that had come over her – the magnitude of what had happened to her while she'd hung alone in the carcass of the ship with her spacesuit's thrusters disabled – was like a wound in the family's everyday life, like a swarm-mine ejecting shards long after it had detonated, like smart bullets still worming their way through a body years and years after the impact.

The parts. Thuy blinked, and said aloud, "Can you tell me what the parts would be used for?"

"I don't know Galactic mindships very well, especially not old models cobbled back together," *The Dragons in the Peach Garden* said, slowly. "But this one is a connector for a heartroom. And..." she paused; the scrolling calligraphy on the walls sped up, taking on an orange tinge. "Looks as if she had a thruster to fix, possibly one of the deep space ones."

"Deep spaces." Thuy said the words, tasting each syllable on her tongue. "There are no deep spaces involved in travelling from Central to the Apricot Blossom Ho orbital."

"No, there shouldn't be," Sixth Aunt said. "But she just wanted the mindship to be complete, didn't she?"

Deep spaces. Debris. Smart swarms. Too many ideas and images in Thuy's mind, overcrowding each other. "Could you..." she hesitated. "Could you remain in deep spaces and emerge just in time to fire your weapons?" Humans didn't like deep spaces; didn't go into them until they had to – the weird geometry and compressed timeline that enabled fast travel between the stars had strong, unpleasant side effects on humans, even more so when the mindship wasn't moving – it did something to your perceptions, twisting everything slightly out of shape until your brain and your body both felt equally sick. But Chi wasn't... She stopped herself in time before thinking 'not quite human', because she didn't know where that thought would lead – Chi wasn't like most humans anymore, was she?

"In theory..." *The Dragons in the Peach Garden* said. "Possible, but..."

"Chi would do it if it were possible," Thuy said.

Sixth Aunt sniffed. "She could be anywhere in deep spaces."

"She'll be close," Thuy said, with a growing certainty in her belly. "As close as possible to her exit point. She'll want to feel... connected to them." Even though she couldn't, strictly speaking – even though that feeling had been excised from her long ago, by the same mindship she now made her home. "Can you take us into deep spaces, and look for a ship?"

There was silence, for a while. *The Dragons in the Peach Garden* said, "You haven't taken any of the standard drugs or thought-dampeners. Child, I'm not sure..."

"There's no time," Thuy said. On the table, the Galactics were finishing the boarding of their shuttle; their escort was likewise on board their own ships, the squad in full military formation – what a show they were all putting on, smiling as if all sins and atrocities had been forgiven, as though the orphans and wounded and absences on the ancestral altars could really be wiped clean, given enough years; as though the debris of their weapons wasn't still harming children. "We have to –"

"As you wish, child." The world lurched, and contracted; and everything vanished in a blur of darkness.

EVERYTHING SEEMED BLURRED, twisted out of shape, every surface coated with an oily sheen; and, on the edge of hearing, there was a booming noise like the waves of the sea (the sea Thuy had only ever seen on holo reconstitutions of Dai Viet on Old Earth). Thuy moved – with an uneasy feeling that she was doing so through thick tar, a feeling that didn't seem rooted in anything – her body, her perceptions – but a nagging one that wouldn't go away, like a distant pain that had yet to bloom.

And there was a presence with her in the room – a huge pressure against her mind, the touch of the mindship she was in – something that should have been familiar but wasn't, was utterly alien and discomforting and a stark reminder of the gulf between her and *The*

Dragons in the Peach Garden. Her mind felt twisted and stretched and pulled in all directions, her thoughts running slow as honey and pressed against the confines of her skull.

Sixth Aunt still sat at the table, calmly talking to *The Dragons in the Peach Garden* as though nothing were wrong. "Anything, Great-great aunt?"

"It's not as easy as putting sensors online," *The Dragons in the Peach Garden* protested. "Give me a moment, child. I can't see anything –"

A screen-view appeared on the walls of the ship – before, it had opened up on stars, but now there was only oily darkness – and, swimming out of the swirls of odd, disjointed colours, Chi's hollow face. "Clever," she said. "Much cleverer than I expected of you."

"You're here, aren't you?" Thuy asked. "Waiting for their arrival? Younger sister, you don't have to do this –"

Chi's face twisted, in what might have been pain, or anger. "You want to dissuade me? Fine, elder sister. But we'll do it on my own terms. Come aboard."

On *that* ship? On that monstrosity, that mangled approximation of a mindship, the reconstruction of an entity that had already destroyed Chi and Thuy and the family –

Thuy looked at Chi – at the hollows in her cheeks; at the set expression in her eyes – remembered hanging in the void of space; remembered the heavy breathing in her comms-system, the background noises that still woke her up in her nightmares. Her mouth spoke before her brain caught up. "I'll do it."

"No," Sixth Aunt said. "You're a fool, child."

No. She'd been a fool ten years ago. She'd wasted time, racing after the past that could not be erased or changed. "I have to," she said. "Don't you see?"

Sixth Aunt sniffed. "I see I've lost one child, to all intents and purposes. I don't want to lose another one."

On the screen, Chi's face was frozen in that odd expression – in her eyes, that desperate need for help that could not, would not ever be met; because Thuy had failed her. "You haven't lost either of us," Thuy said, firmly. "Please, Younger Aunt."

"I'll return her unharmed, if that's what you're worried about," Chi said. "Unless you don't believe my word?"

It was a challenge – an unseemly one, made from younger to elder, on the borders of insolence – and Sixth Aunt stiffened. "Manners, child," she said. And then, realising the futility of it, "I don't doubt your word."

"Good," Chi said. "Then we can go ahead, can't we?"

Sixth Aunt's mouth set in a frown; she opened and closed her mouth – the first time Thuy had seen her at a loss. Then, finally, she said. "There isn't much time."

"All the more reason to hurry, then," Chi said, with a smile that was cold and without joy. "Tell your ship to synch to mine. I'm sending my deep-space referential."

IN PHYSICAL SPACE, a transfer from a mindship to another would have involved an access hatch, and a tube extended from one ship to another, a link that Thuy could have walked along.

Here, in deep spaces, none of that happened – *The Dragons in the Peach Garden* muttered under her breath while she sorted out some 'technical details', and cursed several times at obsolete code configurations – and there was a wrenching, and a subtle reconfiguration of space – the oily sheen on the walls taking on slightly different tinges, the table turning from metal to crystal, the sense of the ship's vast presence increasing tenfold for a moment before receding to scarcely bearable levels. And then, as Thuy was still struggling to comprehend what had happened, *The Dragons in the Peach Garden* spoke in a voice like thunder overhead, "You can go ahead."

There was a door in the wall, where Chi's image had been. It opened only on a well-lit corridor – white-washed walls that looked incongruously normal; a few pictures on them that showed towering buildings under a moon so large it seemed to crush them – a Galactic planet, had to be, because none of the architecture looked familiar.

The ship's presence in the air was dilute, like a hundred scattered droplets of water; a relief after *The Dragons in the Peach Garden.*

Or was it? Did she really need so much confirmation that this was no ordinary mindship?

"We're with you," Sixth Aunt's voice said in Thuy's ears; but it was faint, and fading away already – as Thuy walked deeper and deeper into the ship.

There were no fountains, or scrolling calligraphy on the walls; at most a few symbols, like the cross of the Christian God and the blue-and-red flags of countries from long-dead history, and here and there, the spiral-galaxy and bird silhouette insignia that were the old mark of the Galactic armed forces. Everything smelled – stale, like old books, like a well-scrubbed hospital block, too clean, too empty to be real. And there was the same oily sheen of deep spaces everywhere, curling on the pictures and on the white walls; and the flickering sense of something following her through the corridors, some vast cosmic attention turned her way, in that split-second moment before it turned from vaguely puzzled to hostile...

"Get a grip." Sixth Aunt's voice cut through the morass of her thoughts. "The Galactics' shuttle has left Central. You have half an hour before they reach our position."

Thuy said nothing. She followed the corridors, struggling to assert a sense of normalcy on something that had never been normal in the first place; followed the rising sense of dread within her until it was all she could do not to stop, not to retch on the crazily shifting floors.

At last, at long last, she reached what must have been the heartroom. There was nothing in it, save a huge rectangular box marked with a spiral-galaxy – masking the innards of the ship's Mind – and Chi, standing by the side of the box with one hand negligently trailing on its surface.

She wore a white *ao dai*. The traditional tunic hung loose on her frame, and in the freak geometry of deep spaces its colour seemed to have turned into the grimy hempen of mourning. "Elder sister. How pleasant of you to visit me. This is *The Frost on Jade Buds*."

A typically Rong name. "Not its original name," Thuy said.

"No," Chi said. "He had a Galactic name once, but it would have been... inappropriate, in the circumstances. Though" – she smiled, as if amused by a joke only she could understand – "his original name was *Despoiler*."

Thuy could feel the ship's Mind everywhere now – the unpleasant sharp tang of it; the pent-up aggressiveness coiled in the air, the eagerness. It *was* a war mindship, and Chi had rebuilt it. "You have to stop," she said, not knowing what other words to use. "Don't you see? You can't just target the Galactics –"

"Oh, but I can."

You're my younger sister, Thuy wanted to say. *I know you're not a murderer.* But she no longer knew what Chi was; what she'd been turned into.

"You don't understand," Thuy said. "I know you want your revenge, but what good would it do? The delegates aren't the ones who planted the mindship here; they're not the ones who... damaged you. What –?" *What do you want to achieve,* she wanted to ask, *what do you think you can do, start yet another war that will destroy us all?* But the words remained stuck in her throat.

"I don't know what you hoped to achieve, coming here." It was such a matter-of-fact declaration it chilled Thuy to the bone.

"Come home," Thuy said. "Please. Sixth Aunt and the rest of the family want you back. Please leave this ship; this breaker of families, this maker of the dead."

Chi laughed, bitterly. "I think it's already too late for this, isn't it?"

"It's never too late. One drop of blood is always heavier than a body of water."

"Received wisdom." Chi grimaced. "You should know the value of that."

"I *know* the value of that." Thuy rubbed her fingers, feeling the grit of the ship between them, like the ash from burnt incense sticks. "That's the only thing that kept us standing. What else but values and received wisdom do you have to guide you through bitter times?" She knew all about that: the platitudes said at her parents' funerals, at those of her elders, of her youngers – all the meaningless words she'd said to herself at night, to lull herself back to sleep after the nightmares.

"You know what else there is."

"Revenge?" Thuy said the word, letting it hang in the air like a blade. "You have to let go of this."

"Because I should forgive? Here's the thing, elder sister. It's easy to say this when you're the one receiving the forgiveness. Have *they* come here contrite, asking for reconciliation? Have they admitted what is it that they did – have they said they're sorry for the thousands of deaths and orphans, all the attempts to utterly own or destroy us, all the debris that's still polluting and shattering our families? No. Instead they've come here for their own gain, offering us their meaningless protection against the Dai Viet Empire. And we'll indulge them again, because we can't afford not to." It should have been an impassioned tirade; but Chi's voice was utterly emotionless.

"Lil' Sis," Thuy said. She didn't understand. She didn't see.

"Look at this ship." Chi swirled around, her hands spread out. "Look at what they built. A living weapon."

A weapon, Thuy thought, fighting against a bout of nausea. A weapon that took smiling, happy girls like Chi – and made them into... this. Something that removed... love, compassion, filial piety. Chi *knew*, intellectually, that Thuy was her sister, that Sixth Aunt was the woman who had raised her; but felt nothing more for them than she did for random strangers. And she never would. The capacity to build new connections had been excised from her as neatly as with a surgeon's knife, taken from her by the ship in which she stood.

A weapon that turned people themselves into weapons, that struck at the heart of a society built on kinship and respect for one's elders, leaving only ashes in its wake.

"You see," Chi said. She had gained a disturbing ability to read Thuy's thoughts; or perhaps her disgust was evident on her face.

"No," Thuy said. "Listen to me. If they die – if anything happens to them – we'll have another war. Is that what you want?"

"Is it what I want?" Chi shrugged. "Do I have a choice? Because they'll conquer us anyway, won't they? Trade is another way of waging war. We'll be seeing their holo-movies and their soldiers and their factories worm their way into the Scattered Pearls Belt once more – exactly as we did seventy years ago. Now," she said, in quite a different tone of voice.

Now. What –? Thuy opened her mouth to ask a question, and then realised that her sister hadn't been addressing her.

"As you wish," the mindship – *The Frost on Jade Buds* – said. His voice was low and cultured, that of a scholar, that of an official; the aggressiveness in the air almost incongruous by comparison.

The world spun and spun, and collapsed – Thuy reached for one of the walls – felt a slimy cold seize her, climbing into her heart, slowing down each of her heartbeats until they became a pain against her ribs – felt the entire ship lurch so hard the wall suddenly seemed to rise up against her, and she found her left cheek pressed against it, but it was normal once more, cold metal and polished plastic, nothing like the odd textures of deep spaces.

She pushed against the wall and turned to stare at Chi.

Her sister stood immobile – her hand had gone back on the box, trailing on it as if this were the most beautiful thing under Heaven. How could she –?

On one of the walls was a screen, showing the same trajectory *The Dragons in the Peach Garden* had shown Thuy – except that there was now a dark blue point, the position of the delegation's ship and its escort. And another point – their own position? Another image, side-by-side with the trajectory, was plugged in straight from the newsfeed, showing the same image Thuy had seen, the one with the Galactics walking down the stairs, smiling at the crowds as they wended their way to the shuttleport and their next destination.

"Please, Lil' Sis," Thuy said, making a last, desperate attempt. How could she find the words to convince Chi – how could she appeal to emotions Chi could no longer feel? "You're not a murderer. You –" Chi wouldn't survive this; not if the Galactics died. All their resources and firepower would go into tracking her down, into killing her; if their escort didn't manage to vaporise her here and now in retaliation for the attack.

"You know this is wrong," Chi said.

"I –" Thuy thought of the Galactics, smiling like sharks, like tigers as they strolled down the stairs of the Hall of Supreme Harmony.

"They'll settle here again; do what they did seventy years ago as if nothing had ever been wrong. Do you think that's fair?"

Thuy said, in the end, "Life is never fair. You should know that. It's one of the first lessons Sixth Aunt taught us."

Chi's hand tightened on the rectangle. "Arm systems, please."

Nothing changed perceptibly; but *The Frost on Jade Buds* said, "Systems ready. What weapon do you want to deploy, child?"

"Swarm-missiles," Chi said. "Or anything you think they won't counter."

The ship appeared to mull on this for a moment. "They're in an Immortal-model shuttle. They'll probably have lures against swarm-missiles. I believe a wide-radius electromagnetic blast would be more appropriate."

"As you wish." Chi shook her head. "As long as it blows them out of the Belt."

Thuy stood, struggling to take it all in, to make sense of this casual talk of death and destruction – coming from her own younger sister, from her own blood... It was the same as ten years ago: she hung in the darkness of space, powerless to do anything, to help her sister, to save Chi from herself.

She – she wished Sixth Aunt was there, but there was no sign of her or of *The Dragons in the Peach Garden*. They were probably still in deep spaces, with no easy way to determine whether Chi and Thuy were still with them. Now there were only the two dots, getting closer and closer to each other; and the voice of the ship going through the details of the weapons setup procedure in dry, technical language Thuy couldn't understand.

"They'll hunt you down," Thuy said. "They'll –" She thought of Chi, alone and unable to feel anything for anyone; thought of her single-mindedness, the sheer bloody obstinacy that had led to years and years of work, rebuilding the ship that had damaged her. And, for the first time, seeing the way her younger sister's hand clung to the Mind's resting place, Thuy thought of what *The Frost on Jade Buds* could mean, to someone who had nothing else to call hers in the whole of the world. "They'll destroy the ship," she said.

Chi's head jerked up.

"Piece by piece if they have to," Thuy said. "Do you think they'd let you steal their own technology and use it against them?"

"I'm no longer a Galactic ship," *The Frost on Jade Buds* said.

"You're a deserter," Thuy said, slowly – trying to remember that this was a mindship, one like any other – no different from *The Dragons in the Peach Garden* or *The Sea and Mulberry*, or any other of the ships she'd seen in the docks – and knowing, deep in her heart, that no mindship would have had that coiled aggressiveness, that general sharpness of metal shards. "And you know what they do to traitors."

"I'm no traitor," the mindship said, as calmly as if he had been discussing the solar flares forecast. "As far as I'm concerned, the Galactics left me wounded in the Belt, and never bothered to come back for me or even to communicate with me. I don't see how this makes me owe them any loyalty, if they won't even extend a thought in my direction."

"You're wrong," Chi said. "They won't catch us."

"Of course they will. You said it yourself – we just don't have their level of technology, and they wrote the book on war weapons. There's no place you can escape to where they won't find you. I know you don't mind dying" – and the thought was a shard of metal, lodged against Thuy's heart – "but are you going to drag the ship down with you?"

Chi didn't speak for a while; and the ship had fallen mercifully silent, as if he had clean forgotten about arming his weapons systems. At last, Chi said, and her voice was much smaller and more subdued than it had been. "Ship?"

"Yes, child?"

"You knew, didn't you?"

The whole room seemed to contract; the walls to become a little less bright for a fraction of a second. "Your elder sister is, technically, correct. I was made for war. Death is what happens to us all. Why should I mind dying?"

Chi was silent, again.

"Please," Thuy said. "There's no good way out of this, Lil' Sis."

"You're right." Chi's face was set. "Better take the honourable way. At least war is clean. Isn't this what they say?"

"You, of all people, should know that isn't true," Thuy said. War was messy and bloody; a mass of torn things, of torn connections that would never be repaired. It was absences at New Year's Eve and the other festivals, holos on the ancestral altar of men and women who looked barely old enough to have children; all the myriad details that hurt like twisted knives. "You know what war is. You've grown up in the ruins of it." She threw Chi's own words back at her, more viciously than she thought she'd ever do; but fear seemed to give everything a shrunken, sharp edge.

Chi's face didn't move. It seemed to be frozen with no expression, like the masks painted on theatre players.

"Please. Come home, Lil' Sis."

At last, at long last, Chi said, to the ship, "Stand down." And, to Thuy, "Fine. You win. But *The Frost on Jade Buds* comes home with me."

The ship? Thuy silenced the first reply that came to her lips. "Of course," she said, softly, smoothly. "That won't be a problem."

Chi smiled; and they both knew she knew about the lie. "Come on. Let's call Sixth Aunt, and go home."

Home. She wondered what place there would be, for the ship; for Chi – for the discarded weapons of war in a society that fought to cleanse the war from its history, that strove to rebuild itself into a peaceful, buoyant future.

Thuy caught a glimpse of the twin screens, one showing the trajectory of the delegation's shuttle moving away from them, towards the Apricot Blossom Ho orbital; the other the Galactics coming down the stairs with the smug, oblivious smile of the powerful. The scrolling text of the feed spoke of favoured trade agreement, of the re-establishment of factories and military bases in the Scattered Pearls Belt; the slow, inexorable re-encroachment of their former masters in their everyday life, with no apologies for the war, for the lives ruined, for the people irrevocably changed.

War would have been a cleaner way out of this, Chi had said; and Thuy had told her, with the utter certainty of the desperate, that it was a lie.

Except that now, in the cold light of reason, she wasn't so sure if she'd been right; or even where – with her family's home on the verge of the insidious, devastating upheaval Chi had foreseen – either of them could make a fitting stand.

POPULAR IMAGES FROM THE FIRST MANNED MISSION TO ENCELADUS

BY ALEX DALLY MACFARLANE
(for Dr. Leah-Nani Alconcel)

Alex Dally MacFarlane is a writer, editor and historian. When not researching narrative maps in the legendary traditions of Alexander III of Macedon, she writes stories, found in Clarkesworld, Interfictions Online, Strange Horizons, Beneath Ceaseless Skies, Phantasm Japan, Heiresses of Russ 2013: The Year's Best Lesbian Speculative Fiction, The Year's Best Science Fiction & Fantasy: 2014 *and other anthologies. Poetry can be found in* Stone Telling, The Moment of Change *and* Here, We Cross. *She is the editor of* Aliens: Recent Encounters *(2013) and* The Mammoth Book of SF Stories by Women *(2014).*

Be Proud, Scientists, You Will Be The First To See The Ice Plumes Of Enceladus! (2076)

THIS, THE MISSION'S first poster, was issued by the China Space Administration five years before the launch, concurrent with the announcement of the team's leaders. They stood together on the poster: Liu Gan, He Hongxia and Avapim Sannikorn, in dark blue spacesuits, helmet-less, gripping one another's hands, high in the airless star-patterned space above icy-pale Enceladus. A small red silhouette of their research station – which the team leaders later gave the name of *Liu Yang* – hung beneath their feet. All three leaders were pictured smiling: proud, joyous, as on the day of the public announcement.

The poster, displayed around the world in over five hundred languages, online and printed, remained one of the most iconic.

To go to Enceladus! To be the first to see its ice plumes – and the ice rings of Saturn, and the great planet itself, its yellow body banded with storms! In one of many interviews, Liu Gan sat across from a *Dainik Jagran* journalist, her eyes as wide as moons, saying, "I'm so! I can't believe! Enceladus!"

To Saturn! (2081)

PRODUCED BY THE European Space Agency in the year of the launch and painted on the side of the agency's headquarters in Paris.

The European Space Agency provided some key pieces of equipment for the mission: the analysis machines for samples taken from Enceladus' sea, the primary life support system, and several sensors, including the magnetometers and far-infrared spectrometers, as well as the chips and primary materials to construct instruments in situ.

This image showed all twelve members of the team, standing side-by-side. Each wore a dark blue spacesuit with the flag of their home nation on the left shoulder. At the bottom, a row of logos identified the main agencies funding and providing equipment for the project: the China Space Administration, the Indian Space Research Organisation, the Japan Aerospace Exploration Agency, the European Space Agency, the Space Technology Agency of Thailand, the Malaysian National Space Agency and the Philippine Space Agency.

Seven Years, Seven Hundred Dreams! (2081 - 2088)

A SERIES OF images created by the team.

The journey to the Saturn System took seven years. The team's dreams: arrival in 2088, deployment of the research station in Enceladus' orbit, beginning to take readings remotely and through the autonomous exploration unit – and, eventually, manned exploration.

* * *

Life In The Sea Of Enceladus! (2090)

THE SEA OF Enceladus dominated the poster: pale blue, full of enlarged creatures, microbes the size of mammals. The first life beyond our world! Above the ice of Enceladus' surface, the plumes – unceasing, essential – were cut off by the poster's edge, no longer the focus. The life! The artist revelled in it, rendering it in a level of detail so faithful that He Hongxia was alleged to have cried out in joy upon receiving a transmission of the poster. The thin black lines patterning the life forms' pale spherical shells! The feelers like fine braids of hair! The artist depicted these features with a precision impractical for a poster: from afar, the patterned shells looked grey, the feelers simply could not be seen. Copies of the poster often omitted these details.

What intricate life! Minutely complex! Each patterned shell unique!

He Hongxia quickly realised, on examining the collected specimens, that 'shell' was an inaccuracy, an Earth-inspired assumption. The hollow sphere did not protect a soft inner-body. The sphere – and its long feelers – was the life form. The processes of life occurred in that rigid structure.

On Earth, children in coastal countries imagined collecting one: a stray creature washed up from a distant world.

The first poster rapidly fell out of date. Other life was found in Enceladus' sea.

A Vast Reserve, Just Beyond Our Grasp! (2091)

SCRATCHED ONTO THE rock walls of asteroid interiors. Painted – at great expense – on the mining vessel *Venture 16* with the caption: No One Mining The Moons Of Saturn Will Go Thirsty!

There were many alternative captions. (Another, popular on several asteroid nets: So Good It's Teeming With Life!) But the basic image remained the same: Enceladus the canister of water, a tap on its side.

Planetary Resources sponsored the poster's wide distribution.

When it reached *Liu Yang*, He Hongxia denounced it in a statement sent in ten languages to the asteroids, the research station and young residential settlement on Mars, and across the countries of Earth: "Enceladus is not a sterile container of blue-painted metal, covered in Planetary Resources logos. This is a world, full of life, and we are so new to it; there is so much we do not yet understand. It is possible that we can use its water. It is possible that doing so would irreparably harm the life here – would kill it. We will not risk that. Our research is on-going. We will certainly consider how the water of Enceladus could support human industry and habitation of the Saturn System, but now is not the time to demand that we turn this sea over to anyone who wants to drink from it! It is far too soon!"

Liu Gan and Avapim Sannikorn did not make independent statements at this time. Their names, along with those of everyone on the research team, were simply appended to the transmission. In all probability, Liu Gan did not begin to disagree with He Hongxia until later.

Together We Will Understand The Lives of Enceladus' Creatures! (2092)

THE TEAM ON *Liu Yang* sent back a barrage of images. More details of the Shells. New images of the swilling sea. The single-celled organisms, primary producers in the sea's food chain. The unspecialised multicellular organisms. The tubular creatures, each a hundred micrometres long, their sides marked with dark lines that so many likened to writing. The flat, round life forms like microscopic rays, uncoloured. And there were clips of the scientists at work, readying the autonomous exploration unit for launch, examining data – and, most famously of all, the clip that inspired a state-created artwork in Thailand, distributed globally and on Mars: the three team leaders bent over a microscope together, so close they were touching, Liu Gan and He Hongxia clasping hands, Avapim Sannikorn's arm slung over their shoulders, all three women gazing down at a screen unseeable by anyone but them.

The artist added a screen at the bottom of the image. It displayed one of the tubular creatures, its side covered with the black lines of the caption.

Other, quieter news left *Liu Yang*. One of the modified species of rice was performing excellently in the lower gravity of the habitat. One of the species of onion had died out. One of the scientists had developed cancer – bad luck, not a sign that the radiation shielding was performing below expectation – and he was responding well to treatment. A storm had spread in a band around Saturn. Avapim Sannikorn and her wife, Cristina Tangco, an autonomous exploration unit technician, had decided to have a child. Following a successful implementation of the Kaguya parthenogenesis technique with the women's cells, Avapim reported a healthy pregnancy, the habitat's first: one of the mission's goals, if any team members consented to try.

Discoveries continued.

He Hongxia reportedly avoided sleep wherever possible, so excited by the research into the life processes of the Enceladus life forms – their genetic construction, their life cycles, their reproductive methods and rates, their diversity – and afraid of the asteroid miners, who continued to send out their own images: mining stations in orbit around Saturn and Titan, miners drinking from Enceladus-water while life continued to swim under the ice, miners cracking open the surface of Europa for its ice and lifeless water.

"We don't know if the water of Europa is lifeless!" He Hongxia broadcast. "Finding life on Enceladus has shown that we cannot assume anything about our solar system. Any manned mission to the Jupiter System must take the same care when exploring Europa as we are taking here on Enceladus!"

The images accumulated like a new ring around Saturn.

Defend Enceladus! (2092)

POPULAR OPINION ACROSS Earth cried out for action. We must send soldiers to defend the scientists from the miners! We must not let their work be wasted or lost! We must hurry!

On Earth, online, an image was created: large red font on a starry black background, above an Enceladus and small *Liu Yang* threatened by an army of mining vessels with weapons protruding from their fronts like the Shells' feelers. Fear rose. There were at least a hundred people living in the asteroid belt against *Liu Yang*'s twelve! *Liu Yang* had not been built to withstand continuous bombardment! Laser weaponry would slice it open like Enceladus' surface!

The team on *Liu Yang* and the asteroid miners worked, four years apart.

Treachery! (2092)

CONVERSATIONS CROSSED THE solar system slowly: an interruption for Liu Gan as she analysed visual light, infrared, radar and sample scoop data from the autonomous exploration unit. Such density of life throughout Enceladus' ocean! Preliminary indications of genetic diversity across species populations! Another message from Mason Ng of Psyche Corporation on Psyche in the main belt: one of three companies mining that metal-rich asteroid. Liu Gan briefly set aside her work.

Her reply took thirty minutes to reach Psyche.

It took months for Liu Gan and Mason Ng's conversation to be noticed among the busy signal traffic of the solar system.

Even He Hongxia – betrayed by her own wife – decried the images labelling Liu Gan a traitor.

"It is not treachery to have a different opinion!" He Hongxia said in her next update on the *Liu Yang*'s work. "I will not be confining Liu Gan, or restricting her research. Liu Gan is a valued member of the team."

Liu Gan, in her own update – her first – said, "I have been exploring – in words only – the possibility of using Enceladus' ocean as a source of water, hydrogen and oxygen for future habitation of the Saturn System. There are so many factors to be taken into consideration: the question of the stability (or fragility) of the life on Enceladus, the ease of acquisition compared to other potential sources on the many icy bodies of the Saturn System, the other resources necessary for human habitation and where they will need to be acquired. One of our missions is to assess the role of Enceladus in human habitation. I do not agree with He Hongxia that Enceladus must be ruled out because of the life found here. My research into the extent of the Enceladus life will continue."

The sea, so full of life!

*　*　*

Swimming In The Sea Of Enceladus! (2093)

AVAPIM SANNIKORN WALKED through the sea of Enceladus as if across a street or a field, with her recently born daughter bound to her back. In her hands, Avapim held an unspecific scientific instrument. Around her, the life of Enceladus floated, disproportionally large in black-and-white. Avapim stood out: the red and blue of her environment-suit, the brown of her face, the yellow, black and red tree-patterning of the fabric securing her daughter. Her face was joyous.

To be in Enceladus' ocean! To see its water, murky with life, pressed against her visor!

Her life nearly ended there.

Two weeks after the successful delivery of her daughter, Avapim and Module Technician and Pilot Ju Dimagiba embarked on the first manned mission into the sea of Enceladus in the *Roshini Muniam* exploration module. The first stages progressed successfully: the launch from the *Liu Yang*, the secure landing of the launcher at the edge of the designated fissure, the separation of the launcher and the module, the module's entry through the fissure and its fine spray of ice, down into the ocean of water. The *Roshini Muniam*'s controls operated smoothly. Ju steered the module on its predetermined route, with the tether to the launcher unspooling behind. Avapim examined the collected data. The life, swimming around them!

The ocean's tidal currents, so powerful and unpredictable!

Tidally pulled by the great mass of Saturn and the lesser masses of other moons, Enceladus' H_2O was made liquid: able to support life. It heaved under the crust of ice. It swilled with great currents, tentatively named by the *Liu Yang* team: the Great Polar, the Great Deep, the Song (for how it flowed up to the ice and made it creak and groan in a long, low voice), the Shell (for its shape, so like the Shells swimming within it). Mapping of the currents was ongoing, but the route of the *Roshini Muniam* went through well-charted water.

The Song, strong and sudden, flowed up and flung the *Roshini Muniam* against the ice. The uneven under-surface of the ice cracked the vessel open like a nut.

Alarms blared. Metal tore. The *Roshini Muniam* spun. The inner wall remained intact, but the pressures on the torn outer wall threatened it. Without an outer wall, they would not be able to return to the *Liu Yang*. Without an inner wall, they would die instantly.

Avapim went out into the sea: double-tethered to the *Roshini Muniam*, double-tanked, in constant communication with Ju.

The life is invisible to the naked eye, so Avapim saw only water: murky, dark, pierced by the *Roshini Muniam*'s beams of light. Avapim hauled herself along handrails on the module's outer wall – spinning, spinning – to the crack, where she pulled the pieces of metal towards one another and applied the sealant. It worked quickly. Avapim returned to the airlock and entered the module, and Ju activated the tether to pull the still-spinning *Roshini Muniam* – slower, slower – back to the fissure in the ice: mission over! Mission failed, mission accomplished. The reconnection with the launcher, the return to the *Liu Yang*: fraught, successful.

The technicians repairing the *Roshini Muniam* discovered a secret success in the water caught between the inner and outer walls: that the up-flow of the Song had brought a single specimen of a creature that lived at the bottom of the sea. A new form of life!

The Sunflower Seeds Carried on Song! (2093)

THE LIFE WAS a hundred cells, a circle: a head of sunflower seeds. Avapim Sannikorn, Ju Dimagiba, He Hongxia and Liu Gan surrounded it like petals. Circling them, the Song and the poster's words. What wonders in the deep waters of Enceladus! What else awaited us!

The life was a simple multicellular organism, its cells unspecialised. Dead.

The joy of finding it lifted the team's sadness at suspending the manned exploration schedule until the interactions of ocean's currents were better understood.

Oh Life, Tenaciously Anchored To The Ice! (2094)

LIFE! DISCOVERIES WITHOUT end!

A year's analysis of data collected in the *Roshini Muniam*'s cameras during its single mission revealed clues of another form of life: dimples, a millimetre in diameter, in the underside of the ice.

He Hongxia and Liu Gan announced the discovery together.

"We are fortunate that the *Roshini Muniam*, in its erratic spinning, cast a light on the ice and allowed our high resolution visual light spectrum camera to capture images at a far closer range than we would ever have risked," He Hongxia said. "It certainly proved the camera's auto-focus capabilities!"

Beside her, Liu Gan smiled and said, "The shutter rate ensured that sufficient images were not blurred by the module's spin speed. This enabled us to examine them very closely. What we have discovered are these."

The dimples, like circular footsteps!

"These," Liu Gan continued, "are the marks left behind by life forms no longer alive. The life forms would have been anchored in the ice: extending, we theorise, into the water to collect the nutrients carried on the currents. Each visible dimple represents a cluster of hundreds or thousands of these life forms. In common with all other life we have found on Enceladus, each individual would not be visible with the naked eye. However, in these clusters, it is probable that the life *would* be visible!"

"Although we do not yet know the rate of erosion on the underside of the ice," He Hongxia said, "we suspect that it is quite swift: the dimples must represent life forms that died recently. We hope, on future missions, to find live colonies."

A poster produced by a Vietnamese artist showed nine people – the technicians on the *Liu Yang* – in a glass-roofed vessel under the ice and the life, viewing it. Long, slender, a single form. Colourless like so much of Enceladus' life. Swaying in a current, plant-like (although no life on Enceladus was a plant). The life!

Saturn Has Become The Shore Of The Universe! (2095)

AN IMAGE CREATED by Psyche Corporation to celebrate the completion of phases one and two in their manned mining mission to the Saturn System: design and funding. It showed the final design for a pair of mining stations in the high atmosphere of Saturn, black against those bright bands of colour. Enceladus orbited in the bottom-right corner, its ice plumes spreading horizontally across the bottom of the image: a white space for the text.

Psyche Corporation predicted a 2105 launch date for the mission.

Building A Home At The Shore Of The Universe! (2095)

LIU GAN BORROWED the Psyche Corporation's slogan for an image that accompanied her preliminary report on the habitability of the Saturn System using Enceladus as one source of mineral resources. Saturn sat at the bottom, less than a hemisphere, and above it hung the rings and the moons Enceladus, Titan, Rhea and smaller, un-marked spheres and cratered shapes. Light grey against the space between the moons, space stations spelling the word 'future'.

Introducing her report, Liu Gan said: "One thing is inevitable: human populations will continue to grow. There are now eleven settlements and twenty scientific research stations on Mars. After their setbacks, the Lunar settlements are growing healthily. Five major corporations work in the asteroid belt, as well as an unknown small number of private contractors. While Psyche Corporation plans to begin mining activities in the Saturn System, Planetary Resources is looking at expanding its mining efforts within the asteroid belt and Acersecomic is developing plans for larger scale civilian habitation there. People want to live in space! The Psyche Corporation will come to the Saturn System! What I will do in my new role as Settlement Liaison is ensure that all habitation of the Saturn System prioritises the safety of the life on Enceladus and the possible life elsewhere, as well as human life."

To live alongside the Enceladus life!

"One other thing is true: we have been living in reduced gravity for fourteen years. Avapim Sannikorn and Cristina Tangco's daughter was borne and born in reduced gravity. The difficulties of returning to Earth for any of us would be immense. Perhaps a home could be found for us in the asteroid belt or on the Moon. Perhaps in special facilities on Earth. I want to live here! Seven years of travel, seven years of orbit, waking each day to the pale sphere, the plumes of ice! I can't imagine any other sight and neither can He Hongxia."

A fond smile at the thought of her wife. "With Mason Ng, I will ensure that the Saturn System is a home for all!"

Her relationship with Mason Ng received hostile reactions on Earth.

I Alone Hold Up *Liu Yang* For Scientific Discovery! (2095)

AN UNPOPULAR POSTER. He Hongxia stood alone on the surface of Enceladus, holding the *Liu Yang* in one hand high above her head. A banner trailed from the *Liu Yang* with the poster's caption written on it, black on red.

He Hongxia dismissed the poster, stating in a transmission sent to Earth and picked up at the places in-between: "I do not hold up the *Liu Yang* alone! There is Liu Gan, who works at my side, and Avapim Sannikorn, who will go under the ice again with Ju Dimagiba in the next twenty months now that our mapping is more extensive and the outer wall of the *Roshini Muniam* has been rebuilt, reinforced, and Li Fuquan and Cristina Tangco, who run the autonomous exploration unit – our primary source of data from under the ice! There are twelve of us living here, working every day to expand our knowledge of Enceladus and its life forms. Do not say that I work alone."

Seven Years, Seven Hundred Steps! (2088 - 2095)

THE CULMINATION OF seven years: a second series of images created by the team. How far they had come! Further than the hundreds of thousands of kilometres they had travelled to reach the Saturn System in the first seven years, further in knowledge, in understanding.

Imagine, the final image said in Enceladus-pale text, The Next Seven Years' Steps.

How far, how changed: the future!

A Live Map Of The Ocean Currents Of Enceladus! (2100)

THE ENCELADUS TEAM had been able to access this map since late 2096, but only in 2100 was it made available to the public: the live feed of the micro-machines mapping the currents across the main ocean body. Of course, on Earth it lagged by seventy minutes. On Enceladus it was fresh, used by Avapim Sannikorn and Ju Dimagiba to more safely survey the sea. The map spread across the nets in hundreds of stylised variants: true colour, line art, illustrated with oversized life forms, two-dimensional segments, an immersive game. To swim among the life! To feel the tidally-pulled water against your skin, tangling your hair with Shells and Lontar, tugging it up towards the Anchors swilling in the sea!

For some people, the map closed the astronomical units of distance between the inner system and the *Liu Yang*. For some, it showed how great that gap was.

Nineteen years since the team on the *Liu Yang* left Earth, twelve years since they arrived in the Saturn System. In 2100, An Tangco-Sannikorn turned seven years old! Discoveries continued – of multicellular, unspecialised life – enriching theories of the full ocean life cycle. The discovery in 2098 of live Anchors went un-illustrated. It had already been drawn in 2094! In 2100, the Moon reopened its borders to settlement. In 2100, the population of Mars tripled: primarily immigrants, but the percentage of births grew. Psyche Corporation's Saturn System mission launch date was pushed back to 2107.

"We are all part of the Solar System," Liu Gan said in a report. "We are all working together to learn, to make homes, to act responsibly. This is our future: Earth, the Moon, Mars, the asteroid belt, the Saturn System – where next?"

Oh, radiant Venus!

Distant stars!

"We have come so far from Earth," He Hongxia said to Liu Gan privately, as they lay in their bed looking out the window above: the ice plumes of Enceladus cascading into space!

Enceladus Is My Home! (2103)

DESIGNED BY AN Tangco-Sannikorn. The girl stood on the ice of Enceladus, wearing the dark blue spacesuit designed for her first mission outside the *Liu Yang*, her face beaming bright behind her helmet's visor. Excited. Successful. At her back, the ice plumes rising into the star-speckled sky, dominating the image, painted in subtle shifting hues. Shades only a person who walked on Enceladus would know!

To stand near Enceladus' plumes! To see, only five hundred metres away, what Cassini first detected in 2005!

To call it home.

RED LIGHTS, AND RAIN

GARETH L. POWELL

Gareth L. Powell is a novelist from the South West of England. Although he has written two well-received space opera novels and numerous short stories, he is probably best known for his Ack-Ack Macaque trilogy, published by Solaris Books, the first of which won the BSFA Award for best novel in 2014. He can be found online at: www.garethlpowell.com

IT'S RAINING IN Amsterdam. Paige stands in the oak-panelled front bar of a small corner pub. She has wet hair because she walked here from her hotel. Now she's standing by the open door, holding half a litre of Amstel, watching the rain stipple the surface of the canal across the street. For the fourth time in five minutes, she takes out her mobile and checks the screen for messages. From across the room, the barman looks at her. He has dark skin and gold dreads. Seeing the phone in her hand again, he smiles, obviously convinced she's waiting for a date.

Outside, damp tourists pass in the rain, looking for the Anne Frank house; open-topped pleasure boats seek shelter beneath humped-back bridges; and bare-headed boys cut past on scooters, cigarettes flaring, girlfriends clinging side-saddle to the parcel shelves, tyres going *bop-bop-bop* on the wet cobble stones. Paige sucks the froth from her beer. On the other side of the canal, a church bell clangs nine o'clock. As it happens, she *is* waiting for a man, but this won't be any sort of date, and she'll be lucky if she survives to see the sun come up tomorrow morning. She pockets the mobile, changes the beer glass from one hand to the other, and slips her fingers into the pocket of her coat, allowing them to brush the cold metal butt of the pistol. It's a lightweight coil

141

gun: a magnetic projectile accelerator, fifty years more advanced than anything else in this time zone, and capable of punching a titanium slug through a concrete wall. With luck, it will be enough.

She watches the barman lay out new beer mats on the zinc counter. He's just a boy, really. Paige should probably warn him to leave, but she doesn't want to attract too much attention, not just yet. She doesn't want the police to blunder in and complicate matters.

For a moment, her eyes are off the door, and that's when Josef arrives, heralded by the swish of his coat, the clack of his boots as they hit the step. She sees the barman's gaze flick past her shoulder, his eyes widen, and she turns to find Josef standing on the threshold, close enough to kiss.

"Hello, Paige." He's at least five inches taller than her; rake thin with pale lips and rain-slicked hair.

"Josef." She slides her right hand into her coat, sees him notice the movement.

"Are you here to kill me, Paige?"

"Yes."

"It's not going to be easy."

"I know."

He flicks his eyes in the direction of the bar, licks his bottom lip. "What about him?"

Paige takes a step back, placing herself between the 'vampire' and the boy with the golden dreadlocks. She curls the index finger of the hand still in her pocket around the trigger of the coil gun.

"Not tonight, Josef."

Josef shrugs and folds his arms, shifts his weight petulantly from one foot to the other.

"So, what?" he says. "You want to go at it right now, in here?"

Paige shakes her head. She's trying not to show emotion, but her heart's hammering and she's sure he can hear it.

"Outside," she says. Josef narrows his eyes. He looks her up and down, assessing her as an opponent. Despite his attenuated frame, she knows he can strike like a whip when he wants to. She tenses, ready for his attack and, for a moment, they're frozen like that: eyes locked, waiting for the other to make the first move. Then Josef laughs. He turns on his heel, flicks up the collar of his coat, and steps out into the rain.

Paige lets out a long breath. Her stomach's churning. She pulls the coil gun from her pocket and looks over at the barman.

"Stay here," she says.

SHE FOLLOWS JOSEF into a small concrete yard at the rear of the pub, surrounded by walls on all sides, and lit from above by the orange reflection of city lights on low cloud. Rusty dumpsters stand against one wall; a fire escape ladder hangs from the back of the pub; and metal trapdoors cover the cellar. Two storeys above, the gutters leak, spattering the concrete.

Josef says, "So, how do you want to do this?"

Paige lets the peeling wooden door to the street bang shut behind her, hiding them from passers-by. The coil gun feels heavy in her hand.

"Get over by the wall," she says.

Josef shakes his head.

She opens her mouth to insist but, before she can speak or raise the gun, he's closed the distance between them, his weight slamming her back against the wooden door. She feels his breath on her cheek, his hand clasping her throat. She tries to bring the gun to bear but he chops it away, sending the weapon clattering across the wet floor.

"You're pathetic," he growls, and lifts her by the throat. Her feet paw at empty air. She tries to prise his hand loose, but his fingers are like talons, and she can't breathe; she's choking. In desperation, she kicks his kneecap, making him stagger. With a snarl, he tosses her against one of the large wheeled dumpsters. She hits it with an echoing crash, and ends up on her hands and knees, coughing, struggling for air. Josef's boot catches her in the ribs, and rolls her onto her side. He stamps down once, twice, and something snaps in her left forearm. The pain fills her. She yelps, and curls herself around it. The coil gun rests on the concrete three or four metres away on the other side of the yard, and there's no way he'll let her reach it. He kicks her twice more, then leans down with his mouth open, letting her see his glistening ceramic incisors. They're fully extended now, locked in attack position, and ready to tear out her windpipe.

"Ha' enough?" he says, the fangs distorting his speech.

Paige coughs again. She's cradling her broken arm, and she still can't breathe properly. She's about to tell him to go to hell, when the back door of the pub swings open, and out steps the boy with the golden dreads, a sawn-off antique shotgun held at his hip.

"That's enough," the boy says. His eyes are wide and scared.

Josef looks up with a hiss, teeth bared. Startled, the barman pulls the trigger. The flash and bang fill the yard. Josef takes both barrels in the chest. It snatches him away like laundry in the wind, and he lands by the door to the street, flapping and yelling, drumming his boot heels on the concrete.

"Shoot him again," Paige gasps, but the young man stands frozen in place, transfixed by the thrashing vampire. He hasn't even reloaded. Paige uses her good arm to claw her way into a sitting position. The rain's soaked through her clothes.

"Shoot him!"

But it's too late. Still hollering, Josef claws his way through the wooden door, out onto the street. Paige pulls herself up and makes it to the pavement just in time to see him slip over the edge of the bank, into the canal, dropping noiselessly into the water between two tethered barges. She turns back to find the boy with the shotgun looking at her.

"Is he dead?"

She shakes her head. The air's tangy with gun smoke. "No, he'll be back." She scoops up her fallen coil gun and slides it back into her coat pocket. Her left arm's clutched against her chest. Every time she moves, she has to bite her lip against the pain.

The boy takes her by the shoulder, and she can feel his hands shake as he guides her into the pub kitchen, where she leans against the wall as he locks and bolts the back door.

When she asks, the boy tells her his name is Federico. He settles her on a bar stool, plonks a shot glass and a half-empty bottle of cognac on the counter, then goes to close the front door.

"I'm going to call the police," he says.

As he brushes past her, Paige catches his arm. "There's no time, we have to leave."

He looks down at her hand.

"I don't *have* to do anything," he says. "Not until you explain what the hell just happened."

She releases him. He's frightened, but the fear's manifesting as anger, and she's going to have to do something drastic to convince him.

"Okay." She puts her left arm on the bar, and rolls up the sleeve, letting him see the bloody contusions from Josef's boot, and the splinter of bone, like a shard of broken china, sticking up through the skin.

"What are you doing?"

"Shush." She takes hold of her wrist, forces the arm flat against the zinc counter, and twists. There's an audible click, and the two halves of broken bone snap back into place. When her eyes have stopped watering, she plucks out the loose shard and drops it with a clink into the ash tray. With it out of the way, the skin around the tear starts to heal. In less than a minute, only a red mark remains.

Ferderico takes a step back, eyes wide, hand pointing.

"That's not natural."

Paige lifts the half-empty bottle of cognac with her right hand, pulls the plastic-coated cork with her teeth, and spits it across the bar.

"Josef heals even faster than I do," she says. "You blew a hole in his chest, but he'll be as good as new in an hour, maybe less."

"W-what are you?"

Paige takes a solid nip of the brandy.

"I'm as human as you are," she says, and gets to her feet. The stiffness is fading from her limbs, the hurt evaporating from her ribs and arm. "But Josef's something quite different. And trust me, you *really* don't want to be here when he comes back."

"But the police –"

"Forget the police. You shot him, that makes it personal."

Federico puts his fists on his hips.

"I don't believe you."

Paige jerks a thumb at the back door. "Then believe what you saw out there." She stands and pats down her coat, making sure she still has everything she needs. Federico looks from her to the door, and then back again.

"Is he really that dangerous?"

"Oh yes."

"Then, what do you suggest?"

Paige rubs her face. She doesn't want to be saddled with a civilian, doesn't want to be responsible for anybody else's wellbeing; but this young man saved her life, and she owes him for that.

She sighs. "Your best bet's to come with me, right now. I'm the only one who knows what we're up against, the only one with even half a chance of being able to protect you."

"How do I know I can trust you?"

She looks him square in the eye.

"Because I'm not the one who's going to come back here and rip your throat out."

PAIGE LETS FEDERICO pull on a battered leather biker jacket two sizes too large, and they leave the pub and splash their way down the cobbled streets in the direction of the Red Light District, and her hotel. As they walk, she keeps her eye on the canal.

Federico says, "Is he really a... you know?"

"A vampire?" Paige shakes her head. "No. At least, not in the sense you're thinking. There's nothing supernatural or romantic about him. He's not afraid of crosses or garlic, or any of that bullshit."

"But I saw his teeth."

"Ceramic implants."

They cut across a square in the shadow of a medieval church. Federico has the shotgun under his jacket, and it makes him walk stiffly. The rain's still falling, and there's music from the bars and coffeehouses; but few people are out on the street.

"Then what is he? Some sort of psycho?"

Paige slows for a second, and turns to him. "He's a guerrilla."

"I don't understand."

She starts walking again. "I don't expect you to." Her right hand's in her coat pocket, gripping the coil gun. She leads him out of the square, across a footbridge, and then they're into the Red Light District, with its pink neon shop fronts and narrow alleys. Her hotel's close to Centraal Station. By the time they get there, they're both soaked and stand dripping together in the elevator that takes them up to her floor.

"In a thousand years' time, there's going to be a war," she says, watching the floor numbers count off. "And it's going to be a particularly nasty one, with atrocities on all sides."

The lift doors open and she leads him along the carpeted corridor to her room. Inside, the air smells stale. This has been her base of operations for nearly a month, and she hasn't let the cleaner touch it in all that time. She hasn't even opened the curtains.

"The vampires were bred to fight in the war," she says. "They were designed to operate behind enemy lines, terrorising civilians, sowing fear and confusion." She shrugs off her coat and drops it over the back of a chair. "They're trained to go to ground, blend in as best they can, then start killing people. They're strong and fast, and optimised for night combat."

Federico's standing in the doorway, shivering. She ushers him in and sits him on the bed. Gingerly, she takes the shotgun from his hands, and places it on the sheet beside him; she then drapes a blanket around his shoulders.

"After the war, some of them escaped, and they've been spreading backwards through time ever since." She crosses to the wardrobe, and pulls out a bottle. It's a litre of vodka. She takes two teacups off the side and pours a large measure for him, a smaller one for herself. "They're designed to survive for long durations without support. They can eat just about anything organic, and they're hard to kill. You can hurt them, but as long as their hearts are beating and their brains are intact, there's a chance they'll be able to repair themselves, given enough time."

She puts the bottle aside and flexes the fingers of her left hand – there's still an ache, deep in the bone.

"That's important," she says. She kneels down in front of Federico, and takes his hands in hers. "The next time we see Josef, we've got to kill him before he kills us. And the only way to do that is to do as much damage as possible. Stop his heart, destroy his brain, and he's dead."

She takes one of the teacups and presses it into Federico's hands.

"Sorry," he says, accepting the drink, "did you say that this war is *going* to take place?"

"A thousand years downstream, yes."

"So it hasn't happened yet?"

"No."

He frowns.

"Who are you?"

Paige reaches for her coat, and pulls out the coil gun. "I'm a fangbanger, a vampire killer."

"And you're from the future too?"

Paige stands.

"Look," she says. "All you need to know tonight is this: When you see Josef, shoot out his legs. That'll immobilise him, and give us time to kill him." She stops talking then. Federico's clearly had enough for one night. She slips a pill into his next drink and, within minutes, he's asleep, wrapped in the blanket, with the shotgun clasped protectively across his chest.

Alone with her thoughts, Paige moves quietly. She turns out the bedside light and crosses to the window, pulling aside the heavy curtain. It's after twelve now, and the trams have stopped for the night. The streets are quiet. She feels she should congratulate Josef on his choice of hiding place. Amsterdam is an easy city in which to be a stranger; there are so many tourists, so many distractions, that it's a simple matter to lose yourself in the crowd. If she hadn't known what to look for she might never have found him. But then, she's been a fangbanger for a long time, and she's learned to piece together seemingly unrelated deaths and unexplained crimes; to filter out the background noise of modern urban life in order to reveal the unmistakable MO of an active vampire. She leans her forehead against the window glass; heart pumping in her chest, knowing it won't take Josef long to track her down. She's been doing this job for enough years, waded through enough shit, to know how dangerous a wounded vampire can be.

AT 4AM, THE sky starts to grey in the east. Federico's still asleep, and Paige gives up her vigil. She tucks the coil gun into the back of her belt, pulls on a sweater to cover it, and wanders down to the hotel restaurant. She finds the place empty, although cooking sounds reach her from the kitchen as the staff gear up for the breakfast rush. She helps herself to a cup of coffee from the pot, and a large handful of sugar sachets, and takes it all over to a table by the window, where she stirs the contents of the little packets into her coffee. There are sixteen altogether, and she uses them all. Then, leaving the sticky mess to cool, she rests her left arm on the table and clenches and unclenches her fist. Everything seems in order. The tendons move as they should, and there's no trace of the break. It doesn't even ache now. Satisfied, she takes a sip of the lip-curlingly sweet coffee. It tastes disgusting, but she needs the sugar to refuel the tweaked macrophages and artificial fibroblasts that have enabled her to heal so quickly.

Outside the window, it's still raining. She watches the drops slither on the glass. It makes her think of Josef in better times, before he had his fangs implanted. She remembers him as bright and swift and clever; a sociopath, yes, but still her best student. And there it is, her dirty little secret, the inconvenient truth she's been hiding from Federico: the reason she makes such a good vampire hunter is that during the war, before the vampires were deployed against the enemy, it was she who trained them. She was a military psychologist at the time, an expert in guerrilla warfare. While combat instructors taught the vampires how to kill, she showed them a range of nasty tricks culled from a thousand hard-fought insurgencies; from the Scythians of Central Asia to the soldiers of the Viet Cong, and beyond.

She remembers her penultimate briefing in particular.

"The vampire's a powerful archetype," she said to the cadets. "It's an expression of our darker side, playing to our most primal anxieties, from the threat of rape to the fear of being eaten." It was a hot day, and the sun had blazed through the classroom windows. She walked up and down in front of her students, hands clasped behind her back. At the rear of the room, the surgeons waited with their trolleys, ready to wheel the young men and women down to the operating theatre, one-by-one, in order to implant their fangs and night-adapted eyes. "To complete your mission, you must be prepared to kill. You must become assassins – anonymous killers in the night, spreading panic and mistrust." She stopped pacing and turned to Josef. He sat in the front row of the classroom, chin on fist, eyes blazing, and she knew it would be the last time she'd see him before his transformation. "If you do your jobs correctly," she said, "each of you will be worth a hundred troops. You'll demoralise the enemy, eat out his fighting spirit from the inside. You'll have the soldiers worried about their families, the families suspicious of their neighbours. But in order to achieve this, you'll have to move like shadows, and show no mercy. Do anything that needs to be done, be ruthless, and be prepared to strike anywhere, at any time."

She had taught them every psychological trick she knew, and shown them how to exploit the power of myth, how to generate fear and horror from darkness and blood. From their test scores, she'd known they were intelligent. In fact, she'd personally overseen the original selection process, picking only those recruits with the right balance of brains and insanity – those clever enough to survive the mission, but also psychotic enough to become the monsters they'd need to be in order to succeed.

And then later, when the war went temporal, spilling into the surrounding decades, they came back and she briefed them again, only this time on the peculiarities of each of the time zones in which they were to operate, giving them the background they'd need in order to blend into each zone's civilian population.

Sometimes, she wonders if her history lessons inspired their eventual escape into this dim and distant past, far from even the outermost fringes of the conflict. One thing's for certain: since they mutinied and fled to these primitive times, she's had to travel all over the place to hunt them down. She's tracked individual vampires across half a dozen decades, in Los Angeles, Cairo, Warsaw, and London.

Now she's here, in Amsterdam.

And suddenly, there's Josef.

He's standing in the shadow of a doorway on the other side of the street, watching her through the glass. He has his hands in the pockets of his black raincoat. Their eyes meet for a second and Paige can't breathe. Then he's gone, moving fast. Between parked cars, she catches a glimpse of him crossing the street, heading for the back of the hotel. With a curse, she pushes herself to her feet. Josef will know which room she's staying in – a simple phone call will have furnished him with that information – and now he's after Federico, hoping to kill the boy before tackling her.

Paige bursts out into the foyer. Her room's on the fourth floor, so there's no time to take the stairs. However, luck's on her side; this early in the morning the elevators all stand ready, their doors open. She slams into the nearest and slaps the button for the fourth floor. Then, even as the doors are closing, she's pulling the coil gun from her belt and checking its magazine.

*   *   *

Paige kicks her shoes off in the elevator and pads along the corridor in her socks. As she nears her room, she hears the door splinter: Josef's kicked his way in.

"Damn."

She lifts the coil gun to her shoulder and risks a peek around the frame. The room's dark. She can see a faint glow from the curtains. There are shadows all over the place: chairs, desks, and suitcases. Any one of them could be a crouched vampire.

"Fuck."

She ducks back into the corridor and takes a few quick breaths. If Josef's still in there, he'll have heard her already – and there's a good possibility Federico's already dead. She flicks off the coil gun's safety catch. There's nothing beyond this room but window; the chances of civilian casualties are slight. Stepping back, she gives the trigger a squeeze. The gun whines. Holes appear in the door. Splinters flick out. The TV sparks. A chair blows apart.

And there, in the maelstrom: a shadow moves.

She tries to hose him down but he's moving too fast. He hits the wall and pushes off; hits the floor and rolls; and then he's running on all fours, leaping at her throat before she can draw a bead.

Paige rolls with the impact, still pressing the trigger. Scraps of material fly from Josef's overcoat. An overhead light explodes. Blood sprays. His ceramic teeth scrape her neck, grazing the skin. Then his momentum carries him over her head, and she uses a Judo throw to heave him into the corridor wall. He hits like an upside down starfish, arms and legs splayed, and then falls to the floor.

They both lie panting.

The carpet's soft. She rolls onto her side. Josef's lying on his front, looking sideways at her. His eyes are as blue as a gas flame. This is the first good look she's had at him since he left her class, and he looks older and harder than she remembers. His fangs are white and clean. Blood soaks into the carpet from a hole in his side.

He doesn't move as she elbows herself up into a sitting position; but, as soon as she lifts the coil gun, he twists. His wrist flicks out, and a pair of shiny throwing stars bite Paige's arm. She cries out and the gun drops from her fingers. Instinctively, she reaches for it with her left hand, but Josef's anticipated the move. He pushes himself towards her, delivering a kick to her cheek that shatters the bone.

Paige falls into the open doorway of her room. Black spots dapple her vision. She feels Josef grip her leg. His hands work their way up. He's climbing her, using his weight to keep her pinned down. She tries to fight back, but she's still dazed. He swats her hands away from his face.

Then he's on her, his thighs clamped across her hips, his knees pinning her arms. He wraps his fingers in her hair, and yanks her head back, exposing her throat. His fangs are fully deployed. She sees them through the hair hanging down over his face, and cringes, expecting him to lunge for her artery.

Instead, Josef clears his throat.

"I don't want to kill you," he says around his teeth. He pulls away, and his incisors slip back into their sheaths. He lets go of her hair and sits up, straddling her. Paige blinks up at him as he smooths back his wet hair. "I just want to talk."

THEY END UP slumped against opposite walls of the corridor. Josef's bleeding onto the carpet; Paige feels as if she's been hit by a fire truck. One side of her face throbs with pain, and the eye above her broken cheekbone won't focus properly.

"You've got me all wrong," Josef says.

She gives him a look.

"You're a killer."

"Not anymore." He lets his shoulders relax, but keeps one hand pressed to the bullet hole in his side.

"But Federico –"

"I haven't touched him."

"He's still alive?"

Josef shrugs. "I can't say for sure. You sprayed a lot of bullets in there."

And suddenly, they're falling back into their old pattern: teacher and student – and she *knows* there's something he's not telling her.

"What's going on, Josef? Why am I still alive?"

He tips his head back, resting it against the wall.

"Because things are different now. *I'm* different." He reaches into his coat and pulls out a photograph, which he Frisbees across to her.

"I wasn't trying to hurt you, you know? Not here, and not at the pub." He dips his chin and looks at her. "Just acting in self-defence, trying to stop you from killing me."

The picture shows Josef holding a child, maybe four or five years old.

"What's this?"

"It's my daughter."

The girl has Josef's blue eyes and blonde hair. She's wearing a red dress.

"Your daughter?"

Josef closes his eyes.

"Yes."

Paige glances at the coil gun, lying on the carpet between them. She wonders if she can reach it before he can reach her.

Josef says, "I don't want any more trouble."

Paige lifts a hand to her ruined cheek, and her lip curls.

"So what? You think it *matters* what you want? So you've gone and got yourself a family, and you think that wipes away all the shit you've done, all the people you've killed?"

She reaches for the gun. Josef howls in frustration, and lunges for her throat. His teeth rip into her oesophagus, and she feels his jaw snap shut on her windpipe. His hair fills her face, and he's heavy on her chest. She can't breathe, and wonders how many others have died like this. How many others, because of her, and what she taught him?

Josef pulls back, his face dripping with her blood and, as Paige gasps for breath, the wound bubbles.

Josef snatches the photograph from her unresisting fingers. She tries to move her arms, but can't. Josef's speaking, but the fangs make it difficult and she can't hear him over the roaring in her ears. Her eyes swivel around in panic, looking for help. The guests in the other rooms must be awake now, and cowering behind their peepholes. Some at least will have called the police.

Then, as she twists her head, she catches movement in the room behind her. Federico stumbles into the light. The boy looks dazed and frightened; there are scratch marks on his face, but he has the shotgun in his hands.

There's a flash, and Josef jerks. Part of his face disappears, bitten off by the blast. Another flash, and he topples from Paige like a puppet with its strings cut, knocking his head against the doorframe as he falls.

Paige slaps a palm over the sucking wound in her neck, pinching the skin together, hoping she can heal before she suffocates.

Federico bends over her. Wordless, she points to the coil gun, and he kicks it over.

"Help me up," she croaks. As long as she keeps her hand covering the injury, her vocal chords still work.

With Federico's hands under her shoulders, she struggles to her feet and coughs up a wad of blood. She feels unsteady, but each breath is easier than the last.

Josef lies in a spreading patch of red-soaked carpet. One of his eyes is completely gone; that side of his face is a gory ruin; but the other seems miraculously untouched, and still beautiful. His hands twitch on the carpet like angry spiders.

Paige plucks the slippery, homemade throwing stars from her forearm, and tosses them aside. She points the coil gun at Josef's heart. Dimly, she can hear sirens pulling up on the street outside.

Josef's remaining eyelid flutters. She knows he's down, but he's obviously not out.

She says, "How many people have you killed, Josef?" Then, without waiting for an answer, she pulls the trigger. The gun whines and his chest blows apart. His heels scrape at the floor, as if trying to escape, and she raises the gun to his face.

"I'm sorry," she says.

She looks away as she fires, and she keeps the trigger depressed until the magazine clicks empty.

When she looks back, Josef's head's gone, and there's a hole in the floor.

The photograph of his daughter falls from his fingers.

He's dead.

She sticks the spent gun back in her belt. For some reason, her smashed cheek hurts more than her torn throat. She looks around to find Federico leaning on the doorframe.

Paige hawks red phlegm onto the carpet. Then she leans down and takes hold of Josef's boot. Gritting her teeth, she drags his body back into her ruined hotel room. Moving slowly and painfully, she retrieves the vodka bottle from the dressing table, spins the lid off, and raises the bottle in a toast to her fallen student. She stands over him for a long moment. Then she takes a deep swallow, which makes her cough.

"Goodbye, Josef," she says. There's nothing else to say. There's no triumph here, no closure, nothing but bone-deep weariness.

Solemnly, she pours the remaining contents of the bottle – most of a litre of spirit – over his chest and legs; then she pulls a complimentary matchbook from the desk, and strikes one.

The wet clothes go up in a woof of blue flame. The fire spills onto the carpet, and the room fills with smoke.

Paige opens the desk drawer and takes out another clip of ammo for the coil gun. Then she limps back to Federico.

"I have to go," she says. She has to move on to the next target, the next time zone.

A fire alarm rings, and the sprinklers go off. The shotgun's on the floor at Federico's feet. He's holding the photograph of Josef's daughter. Water's running down his face, streaking his cheeks. His dreads are soaked.

"You're a fucking monster," he says.

Paige puts a hand to the torn flesh of her throat. She can feel the sides stitching themselves back together.

"I know," she says.

And with that, she fades away.

THEY SWIM THROUGH SUNSET SEAS

LAURA LAM

Laura Lam is an SFF author originally from California but now based in Scotland. Her YA gaslight fantasy, Pantomime, *was released February 2013 and is a Top Ten Title for the 2014 American Library Association Rainbow List, as well as being nominated for other awards such as the Bisexual Book Award and the Cybils. The sequel,* Shadowplay, *followed in January 2014.*

DEAR ELI,

I thought I would write and tell you what happened after you died. It's not as if there's much else to occupy my time just now, though I don't know if I'm much of a story-teller.

I was returning from the coral reef when it happened. You remember, the one we had nick-named Chalk Castle. I'd taken a sample of yellowish seaweed, similar in appearance to Earth's *Sargassum muticum*, which I was going to analyse in the lab that afternoon.

The seas were particularly beautiful that morning as I made my way back in the clear globe of the jet. The light from the sun trickled through the water, and all was varying shades of orange, pink, and yellow. Pillars of pale coral rose on either side, and the nearly transparent fish-like creatures darted to and fro. Trailing strands of red seaweed shifted in the current.

I never grew tired of travelling through the sunset seas of Anthemusa. It's still incredible to me that such small changes as increased nitrogen in the atmosphere above and the dinoflagellates in the water below could shift the colour spectrum so drastically from our own blue-green oceans. I know you saw this every day as well, but in six months I hadn't lost my awe of it.

Soon I would be back, and I would drag you away from the observation room for lunch. We'd listen to the belated news casts from home as we cooked and talk about our morning as we ate. You'd ask about the moss, and I'd ask about the alien.

The dome of the station came into view ahead, our home for the past six months and for what we thought would be the next four or five years. We couldn't believe we were going to live in that when we saw the pictures. Do you remember? You teased me, said that my name was too fitting for the setting and it was inevitable that I would go to study Anthemusa, the world of the Nyxi. You didn't believe a word of it. You had no patience for superstition or fate.

Our station looked like a giant soap bubble: transparent, striated with different levels. The clear walls provided the best way to observe the flow of life around us, and there was little need for privacy at the bottom of the ocean or from each other. I wish we had been conscious when the spaceship dropped the station from its belly and we sank through the seas to nestle onto the bottom in a deep, sandy valley. What a view that would have been.

I switched on the camera to observation room A. You were close to the wall of polycarbonate 'glass' separating you from the alien. It was an immature specimen of the Nyxi – a child, equivalent to a ten year old or so. I shuddered, as I always did when I saw them. They looked like grossly-oversized tardigrade parasites, or water bears as you call them, though they don't look much like bears.

I could never grow used to the Nyxi's gross, segmented, wormy bodies, with their eight stunted limbs that ended in three-digit-webbed hands. Their delicate flesh, like a blister about to pop. I remembered your lecture, patiently telling me that they are strong, smart, and that, though they appear transparent, their skin is actually camouflaged and very tough. See? I do listen.

You were much nicer to look at, and I smiled as I watched you, with your dark skin, dark eyes, your white little smile as you scribbled your notes. You pressed a button on the console, and echolocation rippled the water of the observation tank. The Nyxi wriggled in agitation. We knew far more words, or rather vibrations, of their tongue than the last time a mission came to Anthemusa, gleaned from intercepted transmissions and analysed by linguists. But we were still far from fluent. We didn't know half as much as we thought we might, did we, dear?

The Nyxi swam through the rosy water, pausing face to face with you. I didn't know how you refrained from jerking away. But no, you rested your nose right against the glass, so certain that you were safe behind it.

The Nyxi twirled in the tank and rammed itself against the glass that separated it from the outside. It did this every morning, though we continued to transmit messages such as 'calm' and 'safe,' wishing to say that we didn't want to hurt him, that we were only keeping him for a week or two. The Nyxi didn't appear to understand.

We both read the reports of the Nyxi captured in past studies of Anthemusa, adults that refused to cooperate. They floated in their tanks, unmoving and unresponsive, until we let them loose. They've been impossible to find in the wild this time. It was an extraordinary stroke of luck that we found this young one tangled up in the beaded red seaweed.

You were so excited, so determined to make a breakthrough with communication. You studied the bits of transmissions we had received, your mind whirring as you attempted to break down the syntax and piece together the Nyxi's culture and interactions. We were so excited when a few days before, you thought you had discovered another word – the vibrations for 'mother.'

"Hello there, sunshine," I said. You started, twisting around towards the view screen. "Getting hungry?"

"Good morning, Lorelei," you said, smiling, never one for endearments.

"Are you still intending to go into the tank room today?" I asked.

"I think so."

"It's not a good idea," I said. "You know this."

Your mouth tightened. "The Nyxi hasn't made any aggressive moves since we've had it and when it does understand my communication, it's been almost cordial. This is the first one we've captured that's responded to us."

"It could be a trap," I said. Ramming against the glass seemed plenty aggressive to me.

"It could be," you agreed, "but I don't think it's quite clever enough for that, at least at this age. This one's only a child."

"You'd be a fool to go in there and you know it," I said.

"Don't call me a fool."

"Don't go in then," I said, the edge in your voice echoed in mine. "There's no good reason to. Not yet."

You didn't respond except to open the hatch to the tank room and disappear inside. I yelled at you to come back, but you ignored me. I sped up the jet.

The Nyxi had backed to the far corner of the tank. It lifted its wings, the only beautiful part of the Nyxi – ethereal things usually tucked close to the body when immobile, veined with every colour of the spectrum when exposed. It was making a display. I was about to point this out to you, but the creature jumped out like an ugly flying fish. One bony tip of a wing grazed your leg, and you tripped and fell into the tank.

"Eli!" I screamed. I pressed controls frantically. I docked and sprinted towards the tank room.

You were still alive when I arrived, splashing about. We locked eyes, and you smiled ruefully. I smiled back and grabbed a net to fish you out, knocking over a long, thin tube and sending it clattering to the ground.

You screamed as the Nyxi came for you. Red mixed into the orange of the water. The Nyxi retreated back to its corner. What used to be you floated in the water, face down. It was that quick, and too sudden for me to process. A moment ago, you had smiled at me. You would never smile again. My world fractured and became strange and hazy about the edges.

The Nyxi floated up to me and held its wings out under the water. I backed away and it too retreated, to curl up into the bottom of the tank, dragging your corpse down with it. I stumbled back to the observation room, knocking my shins against the walls and a chair.

The Nyxi sent out a few echolocations, which the translator broadcasted over the speakers:

'Free.' The translator gave the word a child's voice and innocence. I turned and emptied my stomach into the corner. 'Free now?'

I blinked, stared at the screen. 'No.' I typed back into the translator, one finger at a time. Aloud, I said, "Not free."

LORELEI SET THE *pen down and wiped away the teardrops on the page, smudging the words into a monochrome watercolour. She took deep breaths, knowing it was stupid to try and stifle sobs in a place where no one could hear her or see her. The light bounced off the rosy orange water and veined her face and hands in golden threads. She used her hands to smooth the lines away from her forehead and mouth, to dry her tears. She picked up the pen, rewrote the smudged words, and continued.*

THE NYXI ATE your body, Eli.

A Kraken landed on the station. I thought the Kraken was one of the most marvellous things we had seen in the ocean so far, with its colourful, octopus-like body and the four tentacles that stem into dozens of smaller ones like tree branches.

It was the distraction I needed. Back in the observation room, as the Nyxi descended on you, I gazed up at the Kraken's violet underbelly and the pulsing suckers of the tentacles. The mouth in the centre gaped, the venomous tongues licking the surface of the dome. I would rather have had the Kraken take you. It was a beast, and wouldn't have known better. None of this seemed real – to be surrounded by violently-coloured creatures in an ocean the wrong colour, your body disappearing.

I left the observation room. There was nothing else to see. You were gone.

"Earle reporting," I said into the intercom. "Emergency."

Dr. De Garmo, head of Extra-terrestrial Marine Biology at the RTA Institute, appeared on the screen. She looked tired. It was far past the time she should have gone home to her family. "Dr. Earle. Report."

"Fatality of Dr. Elias James Earle," I said, willing my voice to stay even.

Dr. De Garmo's face fell. "Eli? No," she said. "How?"

"Eli broke protocol and went into the tank room. The Nyxi jumped up, clipped him, pulled him under. It was all recorded. I had been speaking to him at the time." *Arguing with him,* I thought, and bit my tongue. They would see that soon enough.

Her face was sympathetic. "And the extra-terrestrial specimen?"

"Is still alive."

She rested her mouth on her hand. "Do you wish to abort the mission?"

"Yes. The alien is dangerous, and I do not have sufficient training to deal with him on my own. I want out."

She did not try to argue. That was wise. "Keep the specimen alive. I'll dispatch a shuttle within the next hour. Estimated arrival in ten standard days."

"Affirmed."

"I'm truly sorry about this," Dr. De Garmo said. "He was an extraordinary psycholinguist. He was a brilliant man. A good man."

"Thank you, Dr. De Garmo. Earle out."

The bed sheets still smelled of you.

LORELEI PACED THE *room, rubbing her hands against her arms to try and warm them. She went to the hydroponic room, clutching the harpoon to her chest. There were a couple of mottled, brown bananas drooping from a spindly tree. She crouched in the corner and slowly unpeeled one and ate it, the overripe banana so sweet it tasted almost fermented. There came a sudden sound that caused her to jump and hold the harpoon ready. It was only a withered apple falling to the floor.*

I FORCED MYSELF to stay together, shoving the grief-riddled parts into some semblance of order. I could not grieve.

Back in the observation room, the Nyxi was still alive.

'Name?' I typed.

The water rippled. 'Untranslatable,' the voice said. Stupid question.

'Food?' it queried.

You were much better at communicating with the alien than me. 'I want answers from you' was shortened to: 'You answer.' There was no room for nuance. I typed it into the translator, along with: 'Why kill?'

'Angry,' it responded. 'Hungry.'

'Hungry?' We fed him plenty. And then he'd had a recent meal.

'Hungry for free,' said the childish voice of the translator.

'Not free,' I typed back. 'Not now.'

The Nyxi swirled around in its tank, back to me. It felt like a male to me, but I had no way of telling. They choose their gender when they reach adulthood. We think.

'Why?' I asked.

'Do not understand.'

I tried typing various editions of 'you killed my husband' but the closest I could find was the imperative of 'to kill' and 'love.'

'No understand.'

I was getting nowhere. Maybe the Nyxi was little more intelligent than an animal, or too young and undeveloped. I buried my fists in my scalp, tugging the hair hard enough to bring tears to my eyes.

'Understand,' it said. 'Taste good. Love.'

For a moment, I didn't know what it was saying. Linguists had deduced no possessives or plurals, meaning we only had a smattering of nouns, verbs, and adjectives. But then blood rushed in my ears. I dropped my hands. I knew what it was saying.

I was no psychologist like you. I didn't know how to deal with something so alien, especially so soon after losing you. It still does not excuse how I acted and what I did.

I pressed the button on the controls you had told me only to press in emergencies. A low electric shock coursed through the tank. The Nyxi writhed and the water rippled, but the machine could not translate screams.

'Kill,' it cried. 'You.'

'You just try,' I said.

The Nyxi rammed against the glass, over and over. I zapped it again. It writhed harder, its body contorting like a worm thrown into a fire.

After a time, it sagged. I should have felt pity, or felt something. I left the Nyxi and ate lunch, more out of habit than actual hunger.

An alarm sounded, startling me. I dropped an apple, which rolled along the frosted glass of the kitchen floor.

I ran to the observation room. The Nyxi had launched itself from the tank and was lugging itself across the room, ungainly and horrible. We didn't know they could leave the water and survive.

'Stop,' I typed into the translator.

It ignored me and continued to drag that horrible body methodically towards the door. It was trying to escape.

I looked about in panic, unsure what to do. How long could they survive out of water?

The Nyxi lifted itself to the controls of the tank room, its body balancing like a hypnotized snake. Its tongue peeked out from a malformed mouth and lapped at the controls.

The screens in the observation room flashed, went dark, and went on again. Nothing else seemed amiss. I sat down and breathed a small sigh of relief.

But then the observation room began to fill with water.

In seconds I was ankle deep in frigid, yellow-orange liquid. I tried to open the hatch, but it was jammed. I began the sequence of the override, but Eli, I was so scared. You know how often I have nightmares of drowning, of water pouring down my throat and pooling into my lungs. It took four tries before I could even get to the second part of the sequence.

My teeth chattered in my skull. The water was up to mid-thigh now. My legs felt like ice, then fire, then ice. The translator crackled, but I could not hear what the Nyxi was saying over the rush of water. Perhaps 'Good-bye.'

Somehow, I managed to override the hatch and tumbled into the hallway. I dragged my freezing, sodden self upright and pushed the hatch against the water until it closed, twisting the latch. I sagged against the door in a pool of frigid water, shivering from both the cold and from fear, the only sounds my ragged breathing and a slow *drip, drip, drip*.

I went to observation room B, leaving the hatch lodged open. The Nyxi had flooded observation room A and the tank room. All controls were waterproof, and so now it had limited access to the station's functions. The main controls were deep in the belly of the station.

Flicking through the various control screens, nothing appeared different, but then again technology was little more than magic to me. I knew how to make it do what I wanted, and how to correct rudimentary errors, but I knew nothing about how it actually worked.

'Outgoing transmission: Untranslatable, untranslatable, untranslatable, untranslatable,' the translator chanted.

Silence, and then:

'Transmission sent.'

The Nyxi twirled towards the middle of the flooded room and bobbed in the water, waiting.

From the station radio came the short, steady beeps that meant only one thing: 'Transmission received.'

*   *   *

LORELEI TRIED THE *communication dock yet again. No response. There was nothing to do but wander the empty halls and rooms and to write her letter to a dead man.*

On a shelf above the screen was a gift Lorelei had given her husband: an underwater bouquet. In a small tank shaped like a bell jar were her favourite small sea plants – a cluster of anemones that looked like orange, red, yellow, and pink sunflowers, thin strands of beaded red seaweed, and black rocks dotted with sea moss.

Eli had smiled, cradling the tank gently in his hands, but Lorelei took it from him and told him to look at it under the microscope in the black light of the lab, and the bell jar had come alive, filled with tiny planktonic foraminifera and amoebas. Some looked like clear jellied umbrellas, swirled through with darker colours. Others were thin strands tangled together into spirals. Eli had looked for a long time before he straightened from the microscope and took his wife in his arms.

Lorelei grabbed the bell jar and smashed it against the floor.

THE STATION WAS no longer a haven, but a trap waiting to be sprung. The Nyxi was curled up in a corner. It had only figured out how to open the panel of glass between the tank and the observation room, rather than to the ocean and freedom. The water level was low in both rooms.

The Nyxi appeared to be asleep. I wandered from room to room in the empty station, terrified that if I stayed in one room too long, it would lock me in.

The Nyxi had done something to the station. The lights were flickering, making my eyes hurt and my temples throb. When I turned on the tap, the water was only a small trickle and had a distinct saffron tinge.

When I pressed the button for my pre-packaged dinner, it looked fine until I opened it. It smelled sickly-sweet and overly pungent. The next was the same.

I went to the main access panels and managed to start the water filters working again. But most of the food was still gone, and as soon as I fixed something, the Nyxi would cause something else to malfunction.

The Nyxi was toying with me.

* * *

THE AIR WAS beginning to grow stale. Lorelei was beyond thirsty. Her mouth and throat were so dry that every time she drew breath her skin seemed to crack a little more, a little deeper. She imagined the cracks running all the way through her, down to the bone. At any moment, she would shatter. She checked the communications room again. No word.

THE CHILD'S GUARDIANS arrived. I have no idea why they did not come sooner. Why didn't they spring the child before it killed you? This could have all been avoided, surely?

One morning they were there, suspended in the vermillion ocean. I counted at least twelve Nyxi, flitting about the dome like ghosts.

They were so much more hideous than their child. These were as big as great white sharks, their bodies a mass of folds, dips, and crevices. Their wings were larger and glowed with colour.

I crept to the main control room and managed to turn on the view screens to both the observation room and the cluster of Nyxi floating in the vibrant ocean. The child Nyxi was flitting about in excitement. They had some small device that one clutched in tiny webbed hands as it cut through the glass, and they made their way through. One of the adults took your killer away and they swam through the sunset seas.

The other adults did not leave. They flitted into the tank room and observation room and began to lap at the controls. Beings far more sentient than we had imagined were coming for me.

The computer in the control room had a backup generator and was working, aside from the odd flicker. I searched for weapons. There was a harpoon in the tank room. I think I knocked it over as I reached for the net to fish you out.

There were others in the supply room two floors below. I wedged the door to the control room open with a chair and darted out.

I no longer knew where the Nyxi were, or how many more rooms they had managed to gain control of. But they were coming closer, filling more rooms with cold, coloured water. I jumped at shadows, and held my breath each time I opened another door.

You were right, Eli, in that we knew nothing about these Nyxi. I didn't know where they live, what else they eat, how they give birth, whether they married, divorced, loved, or killed each other.

I would not let them kill me. I made it to the supply room, grabbed the long, thin case of the harpoon, and scuttled back to the main control room.

The Nyxi had gained two more rooms. So quick! These could not be oversized worms living in coral caves as we had previously assumed, able to communicate with each other but ultimately barbaric. They possessed technology they had hidden from us successfully for the past one hundred years, even with our scanners and hubris.

I clutched the harpoon to me, but there were at least eight fully-grown Nyxi snaking their way down the glass corridors. A harpoon was my last, desperate line of defence.

I flipped through the manual, trying to remember my hours of training, so frantic that my eyes would see the words but not register their meaning. I closed my eyes tightly. For a handful of seconds I let the terror course through me, and then I forced myself to section it away in a dark corner of my mind. I glared at the screen, determined to find something to use against them.

The Nyxi were only three doors away from me now. I scanned the manual, searching for security overrides, trying to remember how to lock down the hatches despite whatever the Nyxi were doing. Why hadn't I paid more attention to such things when I knew I would be spending years hundreds of feet below the ocean's surface? I shouldn't have relied so much on you.

Finally, I thought I discovered a code that overrode specific rooms in the station in the event of a systems failure. The Nyxi were only two rooms away. Every time a hatch opened I jumped at the sound of screeching, clanking metal.

I bashed the code into the keyboard. A map of the station showed up and I pressed the room the Nyxi were in on the screen. The lights flashed and alarms sounded, and the Nyxi were trapped. On the camera screens, they smashed against the walls like the child had. I felt the faint tremors of their struggle for life.

LORELEI TURNED THE *page and stared at the last blank sheet, unsure what to write next. She went to the control room and activated the remote camera screens. Three rooms had Nyxi locked inside them. More rescue parties had come for their brethren, but each time she had managed to trap them. They had stopped trying two days ago, or they were amassing a larger attack.*

The Nyxi were curled in on each other for warmth, looking like smooth fire-coloured crystals upon the floor of the rooms. A pair were in Lorelei and Eli's old bedroom, intertwined on the bed. Clothes floated in the current, and the few belongings they had brought with them from Earth littered the floor – a mosaic dolphin figurine that had been a gift from Lorelei's mother, a few books from Eli's father, their respective degrees and honours in frames. All were sodden and lost.

Lorelei knew she should let the Nyxi go, but she didn't know if she could.

I'M RUNNING OUT of ink and paper. Most was in our bedroom, now an aquarium. The story of my life after your death is coming to a close. The Nyxi are still trapped.

I have decided that I will let the Nyxi go, Eli, if I can figure out how. For you. And maybe, just a little, for me.

The rescue ship will not be here for two more days. My food is gone, my water nearly so, the light grows dimmer and the air grows thinner every day. I am hungry, and thirsty, but mainly I am tired of sleeping with one eye open, terrified that they will come for me. I am not going to try and wait any longer. There is no point now. I have sent them my message.

The sun is setting above the sunset seas of Anthemusa. The oranges and yellows are laced with the purple-red of dusk. The anemones are beginning to droop and close. Most of the animals are either going to rest or awakening.

All is quiet.

It is beautiful.

See you soon, Eli.

All my love,

Lorelei

FAITH WITHOUT TEETH

IAN WATSON
(For Bernhard and Barbara)

Ian Watson's latest publications are The Best of Ian Watson *and* The Uncollected Ian Watson *(PS Publishing), and his collected poetry* Memory Man & Other Poems *(Leaky Boot Press), all 2014. Recent, too, is the techno-thriller* The Waters of Destiny *with Andy West (Palabaristas Press). Ian has won two BSFA Awards, and France's Prix Apollo for his novel* The Embedding. *He also invented Warhammer 40,000 fiction and worked for nine months with Stanley Kubrick on the screen story for* A.I. Artificial Intelligence. *He now lives in Spain with his wife, Cristina.*

AT THE START of each school year, Comrade Teacher Albrecht Grimm addressed the class of pre-teens with a toothless show of enthusiasm.

"Boys and Girls, Hänsels and Gretels!" This was Grimm's little joke, but Hans and Gisela, sitting at adjacent desks, were riveted. "As I'm sure you already know, as soon as your thirteenth birthdays arrive, likewise comes the opportunity and privilege to donate your teeth to the Great Patriotic Ivory Wall."

Just at that moment, a rumble sounded beneath the building. That was one of the subway trains of the enemy. A line from the wicked west burrowed underneath a Democratic part of the city before curving back to the west, its traffic forbidden by binding agreements to halt at deserted stations, all signs of which had been erased at ground level in the Democracy; grassed or concreted over. A few of the schoolchildren touched their teeth nervously, as if that train on the vanished subway carrying unsocialist strangers was vibrating their jaws. Promptly Grimm led his class in the popular song, *We Bare Our Teeth at Fascist Capitalism.*

Then Grimm asked his class, "Why is the Great Patriotic Ivory Wall essential to our survival? You, Hänsel I mean Hans."

"Because," recited Hans, "the fascist puppet-masters of the Capitalist Republic might attack our Democratic Republic and our socialist uncles and friends at any moment, using weapons of mass destruction. Our teeth symbolise our determination to resist by all and every means."

"Good. What else does pulling your teeth signify?"

"Equality!" called out a burly boy, Dietrich.

"Please explain."

"The State guarantees everyone, at very low cost, nourishing pastes, delicious thick soups, crustless breads, hot chocolates, and so on and so forth, which nobody requires teeth to chew."

"And what is the consequence of very cheap food, and cheap rents for flats, and guaranteed jobs?"

"An accumulation of money, sir. The people are rich."

"So how can our citizens spend their riches? Yes, Heidi?"

"In special shops and restaurants, sir. Where special things cost a lot. That's because those things come a long way from our uncles and friends."

"Can anyone give an example of a high-cost item?"

"A steak, sir!" called out Friedrich, the pub manager's lad. "And to chew a steak you need teeth! So the special restaurants provide a wide range of dentures, which you leave on your plate after the meal."

"To be cleansed then reused by other customers, precisely. In our socialist economy all is mutual and rational. Dentists, for instance, only need to yank milk-teeth, ensure the purity of young adults' teeth until the age of thirteen, then pull those perfect teeth to add more crust of ivory to the Wall – as well as make lots of dentures for use in the *spezial* restaurants."

Forty years earlier, dentists had been much busier for almost a year. The concrete blocks of the Wall had gone up within a mere three days, a masterwork of planning and co-ordination. Absolutely the Democratic east of the divided city must be protected from political and cultural pollution which might ooze from the enclave of the western half, encysted within otherwise socialist territory like some permanent bridgehead of evil at the end of authorised if resented road, rail, and canal transit routes. Whereupon the call went out to the whole Democratic nation of nineteen million citizens (or at least to all those over sixteen years of age) to donate their ivories to adorn the concrete to make the Wall sharp and slippery and shiny, an ever-ongoing process, or *praxis*.

"However, Friedrich, I must correct you – we *do* produce beef in our own beloved homeland, mostly for export to our uncles and friends. Not to mention lambs and pigs and geese. Lack of teeth greatly helps our export economy."

Having one's teeth pulled was an important rite of passage, this socialist society's equivalent of circumcision delayed until puberty. Grimm squared up to the class.

"And should any of you young citizens exercise your democratic right not to have your teeth pulled...?"

Was this a purely theoretical question? Was Comrade Teacher Grimm aiming to winkle out waverers?

Chubby Heidi shot her hand up. "Sir, sir! If we don't have our teeth pulled, we'll only be allowed to study theology, or else ich-theology. That won't easily lead to a guaranteed job or a subsiding flat."

"You mean a subsidised flat. Just so long as you marry – no need to blush – and have a baby or two. Hmm, yes, theology, as you say, Heidi, or else ichthyology, which is the study of fish, *not* the study of the *Ich*, the I, the Self..."

Grimm paused, perhaps reflecting upon the intellectual capacities of his pre-teens.

"Theology, from the Greek *theos*, and *logein*, to speak about, is the study of an imaginary God. Due to most churches being closed, a theological job is unlikely. Ichthyology, from the Greek *ichthys*, means speaking about fish."

"Is God some sort of fish?" asked naïve Magda of the freckles and blonde pigtails.

"In a curious way, yes," replied Grimm. "In Greek the word for fish," and he began to chalk on the blackboard, "*iota chi theta ypsilon sigma*, spells the initial letters of the phrase in Greek *Jesus Christ Son of God Saviour*. Consequently early Christians used a fish as a symbol of their prohibited cult, *thus*." And he drew a simple two-arc fish-shape.

"*However*," Grimm continued, "our own word *Ich* signifies the Self, which must belong within society. The great philosopher

Hegel expressed this transindividuality thus: *Ich das Wir, und Wir, das Ich ist*, I that is a We and We that is an I. Social belonging! Practical engagement within one's environment! The yielding up of one's teeth. Ich-theology, Heidi, would be the philosophy of Self and therefore Selfishness, existentialism as opposed to socialism. Perhaps this is a little complicated for you..."

Not for little Bernhard, however, who was very good at English – the second language after compulsory Russian in case Capitalist spies needed to be interrogated, for instance. Up went Bernhard's hand.

"*Selfishness*, as opposed to *Shellfishness*," the lad proposed with an eager grin.

Grimm inclined his head in approval.

"Yes, there's a witty link between the two 'ologies. Those who govern on our behalf have a sense of humour. And it's true that our Democratic Republic does have a need for specialists regarding fish, including shellfish, Bernhard. We boast a fine sea coast as well as many rivers. Also, fish are softer than meat. Likewise most shellfish, after their shells come off. But a couple of hundred experts on cod, or pike and perch, or crabs, suffice for the needs of society. There's no point in thousands of ichthyologists. Opting for ichthyology is highly unlikely to lead to a job. By the way, don't confuse *Hegel* with *Haeckel*, Darwin's propagandist – who described and pictured many sea creatures beautifully but who said that politics is basically applied biology. I beg you to bear this all in mind as your birthdays approach."

THE NEXT MORNING, never-to-be-seen-again Comrade Teacher Grimm had been replaced by bossy large Lady-Comrade Teacher Mrs Ernestine Häcksel, soon to be known as *Die Hexe* – the Witch – and the blackboard had been very thoroughly washed clean of any trace of Greek Christian fish.

In due course, Hans and Gisela had their teeth pulled; their mouths were sore for a month. Out of all the class, only Magda declined her patriotic duty. Magda confided to Gisela that when she left school she might become a certain kind of masseuse, known in whispers to be favoured by visiting socialist uncles and foreign friends. She was vague about what was involved, but theoretical ichthyology held no more interest for Magda than an imaginary God; and she was very fond of her teeth, although she mostly kept her mouth shut in class. Any show of teeth from Magda generally made The Witch glare. One day, off the cuff, The Witch remarked maliciously that teeth were the worst asset for a masseuse; a fellow pupil must have snitched on Magda.

Of course, a tooth-full mouth offended the prevailing aesthetic of womanly beauty; a pursed and puckered look was prized.

Presently Hans and Gisela learned to kiss and, after ten years of kissing softly and sensuously like snails, both graduated in accountancy, married and soon had twins, Günther and Gabriele.

THE END OF history arrived one Sunday morning while Hans and Gisela were visiting the massive pockmarked Natural History Museum. It was good to be alone together, if that wasn't an oxymoron; few people visited the museum before noon. Gisela's widowed mother had been left in the couple's one-bedroom flat, cooing dotingly over the twins.

Presently Gisela and Hans came to the newly rebuilt east wing of the museum, occupied by the remarkable 'wet collections' returned by Uncle Ivan after almost forty years' protective absence. What a sight those wet collections were! Towering upwards within an outer wall of thick glass, braced with steel, were shelf upon glass shelf – also braced by steel and separated by corridors – of glass jars large and little (276,000, according to a notice) containing dead fishes preserved in 80 tons of ethanol all told. Amongst the predominant fishes were also oddities such as a two-headed piglet and a four-legged chicken. Every single creature was blanched colourless by preservation – apart from the only living resident, which was predominantly grey (not all that much different, then) and which moved slowly around a long tank just inside of the great glass wall: a lungfish, a 'living fossil, 40 million years old'.

"Imagine being 40 million years old!" sighed Gisela, who had little more interest in ichthyology than Hans, but this place was somewhere to visit, calm, cool, and awesome. "Do you suppose the lungfish gets bored or lonely?"

"Do you think it *thinks*, my love?" he replied. "Maybe it's better not to think."

At that moment a bald-headed comrade curator in a white coat, maybe an authentic ichthyologist, hastened from within the great glass-and-steel internal structure clutching a Sternchen tranny radio, exited by a door close to the couple, rushed to a flight of marble stairs and disappeared down those as though fleeing a horde of wasps. The door to the edifice of glass shelves and 276,000 glass jars stood open, no notice explicitly forbidding entry. It was as if... as if... as if a children's grassy minipark had subsided all of a sudden, revealing a disused subway station, just as a western train slowed by the dust-coated platform, and opened its doors.

No, it wasn't like that at all! Because the glass door led inward to confinement.

But even so.

"Shall we...?"

"... just take a look from the inside?"

Tidiness caused Gisela to close the door behind them, producing an ominous *clunk*. The door had locked itself! Yet this was as nothing when, moments later, muffled by thick stone walls, a howl of sirens reached their ears. Brighter light illuminated their surroundings for a moment, leaving afterimages. A thunderous boom – the whole fabric of the east wing shook, as did the ethanol in the jars. Distant shatterings sounded. All the lights went out, only to flicker on again a few seconds later. Silence fell.

Hans and Gisela gaped at one another toothlessly.

"... an enemy missile...!"

"... of mass destruction...!"

"... our city's gone...!"

"... except for this wing of the museum, rebuilt to survive the worst..."

"... what about Günther...?"

"... what about Gabi...?"

"... what about Mama...?"

"... at least we're alive, Gisela..."

"... at least we're alive, Hans..."

"... oh Günther, oh Gabi..."

"... the wall of teeth failed..."

"... no, it protected us, who gave our teeth – it reflected the worst away from us..."

"... yes, that must be how we're alive..."

Time passed.

No one came. They stayed near that locked door in case the ichthyologist reappeared, key in his pocket. But the bald man could be dead because...

"... air must be radioactive..."

"... thick glass keeps the bad air out of here – plenty of good air for us to breathe..."

They were both accountants.

"... enough air for how long...?"

"... weeks, I'd say..."

More time passed.

"... I'm thirsty..."

The lungfish was swimming in a big tank of water. Off came the long heavy lid.

"... fresh water, or salty...?"

"... I'm not an ichthyologist... the water smells to me of ammonia... not a lot, just a bit... but not salty..."

"... we shouldn't drink any ammonia..."

"... maybe the ammonia comes from its pee..."

"... we shouldn't drink *any* ammonia...!"

At the rear of the glass-and-steel edifice they spied a laboratory bench. Beakers, test tubes, vials, jars, sinks, taps. To which they now hastened.

A tap yielded water. "... must be an emergency tank somewhere, Gisela..."

They quaffed from beakers, then returned to the door and sat on the floor.

ACCORDING TO HANS's GUB People's Watch, ten hours had passed since the attack. They had twice needed to pee in a basin, Hans helping Gisela to mount.

"I'm hungry, Hans..."

"Me too."

They regarded the lungfish.

"Looks like an eel, doesn't it...?"

"Forty million years old... shame to kill it... eat it raw, still almost half alive..."

"Does raw eel require teeth to eat it...?"

"Forty million years old, could be tough..."

Notwithstanding, Hans threw his jacket aside, rolled up his shirt sleeves, plunged his arms into the tank.

"My Grandpa once said something about raw eel blood being poisonous..."

"But this isn't an eel, it's a lungfish..."

Try as he might, Hans couldn't catch the creature which slipped slimily from his grasp the one time he managed to corner it.

He gave up. "We're being *dumbheads!* We're in the biggest fishmonger's in the world! And all the fishes have been *cured!*"

Cured and pickled by preservation in ethanol, oh yes. Ethanol was pretty much the same as vodka, wasn't it? Here were umpteen shelves of fleshy fish soaked in full-strength almost-vodka! A feast for the toothless, finer than any *spezial* restaurant!

"Maybe we should rinse the fishes we choose in the sink, my love, otherwise we might become drunk...?"

"Maybe a different fish for each of us would be wise...?"

Which two to choose? This plump one, upside-down? This slab of an ichthys, head downwards? All the names were in Latin or Greek, understandable only by ichthyologists.

Gisela chose a big jar containing a sumptuous *Pomatomus saltatrix*; he, a substantial *Micropterus dolomieu* with large fins although a small mouth. These, they carried to one of the sinks, uncapped the jars, poured away the almost-vodka, rinsed, then decanted their dinner onto the workbench.

The smell was of nail polish remover as well as of fishiness. Inspired, Hans took from his pocket a treasured box of matches featuring a Robur three-ton truck. May the match be as strong! The first failed to light, the second snapped, but the third bloomed. As Hans drifted the flame across the two fishes, blue haloes of fire wrapped their dinner, dying down after twenty seconds or so. Hans clawed flesh from his slightly charred *Micropterus dolomieu* and sucked, first tentatively, then more forcefully; the fish wasn't as soft as he'd expected, but even though stiffish it went down a treat: an unusual tasting treat, indescribable really. Had anyone before sucked a *Micropterus dolomieu* preserved in ethanol for a period of fifty or a hundred years? Deviationist Chinese Maoists might relish hundred-year-old eggs, matured in mud mixed with rice-husks, according to *Young World*, but here was a whole new sensation – no words existed yet to express it.

Gisela was following suit with her *Pomatomus saltatrix*, sucking and grinning, almost-vodka fish juices running down her chin.

Soon many sucked bones lay on the bench, maybe spelling out a new gastronomic name.

Hans idly played with the bones until suddenly a pattern appeared. He shifted them a little more, and now they spelled 'Grete'. A small change using fish teeth from a jaw, and the German word for fishbone appeared: 'Gräte'. Hänsel and Gretel lost in the forest of natural history marking their way with bones instead of breadcrumbs...

After a while:

"... I feel dizzy..."

"... me too..."

Hans and Gisela subsided to sit on the floor. She began humming *We Bare Our Teeth at Fascist Capitalism. Fascist* became *Fishest*; presently she began to snore.

"– VANDALISM!"

Blearily, from the floor, Hans regarded a dark-suited, purse-lipped man of gaunt aspect whose hair was silver, as was his neat goatee. Beside Hans, Gisela was stirring.

"– don't be hard, Comrade Direktor, they may be *ill* –"

Hand shaking shoulder. "*Are you ill?* Speak!" ordered that bald ichthyologist. "I want to know if your speech is blurred; whether you're uncoordinated – can you see me clearly? How many fingers?"

"I see you. Four." Hans did his best to scramble up, clutching the lab bench. He steadied himself. "So you both survived the enemy attack by sheltering in the basement?"

"What *attack*? Oh I see..."

"Did many citizens survive?"

"There was no attack," said the Comrade Direktor. "A meteor came out of the blue and exploded high in the air. Like Tunguska, if that means anything to you."

"*Young World* printed a piece about the Tunguska thing last year. With a photo of a million fallen trees."

"In our case, windows. Most windows facing the blast blew out, or rather in. Many, many injuries, and inevitably deaths – a few buildings collapsed. We've only had a chance to enter our wet collections this morning, after a quick glance yesterday to see they survived, not time enough to notice you two lying drunk on the floor at the back. Will you kindly show me your identity cards?"

Scribble, scribble on a scrap of paper.

"A mere formality, not formaldehyde for you two."

"He means no jail for snacking on State property," said the bald man.

"Police and emergency services are overloaded – our Uncle Ivan was only able to give us twenty seconds' warning. However, the enemy in the west of the city has lost *even more glass* due to its Capitalist skyscrapers!"

"Thanks be for the Wall of Our Teeth!" Gisela had roused; Hans helped her up. "Oh, I have a little headache..."

"Take this aspirin," said the ichthyologist. "Today may be known as Crystalday, antithesis to the notorious fascist Crystalnight."

"Not applicable within these walls." The Direktor fondly assessed his mighty glass-and-steel habitat for a quarter of a million dead fish as well as several freak creatures.

"What did we eat?" Hans asked nervously.

"A bluefish, and a smallmouth bass," the ichthyologist told him, and for the first time Hans registered that the bald man, unlike the Direktor, had gappy tobacco-stained teeth, unless he wore permanent dentures the colour of tarnished ivory. How disgusting those looked.

"Günther and Gabi may be unharmed!" piped up Gisela. "We have thick net curtains."

On their way back to the doorway, the four passed the uncovered tank of the lungfish, which swam sluggishly away along one side.

"Pardon me, but I must ask," asked the ichthyologist, "did you urinate in the tank rather than using a sink?"

"How could we do such a thing?" exclaimed Gisela. "That fish is forty million years old. But please, I do need to *go*." Now that the subject was mentioned, bladders began to insist.

"Me too," admitted Hans.

"You'll find the restrooms in the basement," the Direktor told the couple. "Use those stairs. There's a lift to return by."

* * *

Hans and Gisela emerged from the museum – shut to visitors as soon as the emergency happened; glass from its front windows crunched underfoot. Invalidenstraße glittered glassily in Sunday morning sunlight. Headscarfed women were getting to work with brooms.

Close by to the west was the vehicle inspection barrier preliminary to the checkpoint just before the bridge over the ship canal. This side of the bridge, interrupted only by the well-guarded gap of the checkpoint itself, the Great Patriotic Wall was as ever, its upper sides and top crusted defiantly with teeth which gleamed like an endless smile. Maybe part of this stretch included the couple's very own teeth donated almost two decades earlier, though it would be selfishness to ask where exactly your teeth went.

For a few moments they let themselves gaze at enemy skyscrapers in the distance, no longer dazzling now that all their windows had gone.

THING AND SICK

ADAM ROBERTS

Adam Roberts is the author of fourteen SF novels, including the BSFA- and Campbell Award winning Jack Glass *(Gollancz 2012) and* Twenty Trillion Leagues Under the Sea *(with Mahendra Singh; Gollancz 2014). He was born in South London and now lives a few miles west of London, so never let it be said that he's averse to travel.*

IT STARTED WITH the letter. Roy would probably say it started when he solved the Fermi Paradox, when he achieved (his word) *clarity*. Not clarity, I think: but sick. Sick in the head. He probably wouldn't disagree. Not any more. Not with so much professional psychiatric opinion having been brought to bear on the matter. He concedes as much to me, in the many communications he has addressed me from the asylum. He sends various manifestos and communications to the papers too, I understand. In all of them he claims to have finally solved the Fermi Paradox. If he has, then I don't expect my nightmares to diminish any time soon.

I do have bad dreams, yes. Intense, visceral nightmares from which I wake sweating and weeping. If Roy is wrong, then perhaps they'll diminish with time.

But really it started with the letter.

I was in Antarctica with Roy Curtius, the two of us hundreds of miles inland, far away from the nearest civilisation. It was 1986, and one (weeks-long) evening and one (months-long) south polar night. Our job was to process the raw astronomical data coming in from Proxima and Alpha Centauri. Which is to say: our job was to look for alien life. There had been certain peculiarities in the radio astronomical flow from that portion of the sky, and we were looking into it. Whilst we were out there we were given some other scientific tasks to keep ourselves busy, but it was the SETI business that was the main event. We maintained the equipment, and sifted the data, passing most of it on for more detailed analysis back in the UK. Since in what follows I am going to say a number of disobliging things about him, I'll concede right here that Roy was some kind of programming genius – this, remember, back in the late 80s, when "computing" was quite the new thing.

The base was situated as far as possible from light pollution and radio pollution. There was nowhere on the planet further away than where we were.

We did the best we could, with 1980s-grade data processing and a kit-built radio dish flown out to the location in a packing crate, and assembled as best two men could assemble anything when it was too cold for us to take off our gloves.

"The simplest solution to the Fermi thing," I said once, "would be simply to pick up alien chatter on our clever machines. Where are the aliens? *Here* they are."

"Don't hold your breath," he said.

We spent some hours every day on the project. The rest of the time we ate, drank, lay about and killed time. We had a VHS player, and copies of *Beverly Hills Cop*, *Ghostbusters*, *The Neverending Story* and *The Karate Kid*. We played cards. We read books. As it happens, I was working my way through Frank Herbert's *Dune* trilogy. Roy was reading Immanuel Kant. That fact, right there, tells you all you need to know about the two of us. "I figured eight months isolation was the perfect time really to get to grips with the *Kritik der reinen Vernunft*," he would say. "Of course," he would add, with a little self-deprecating snigger, "I'm not reading it in the original German. My German is good – but not *that* good." He used to leave the book lying around: *Kant's Critique of Pure Reason, transl. Meiklejohn*. It had a red cover. Pretentious fool.

"We put too much trust in modern technology," he said one day. "The solution to the Fermi Paradox? It's all in here." And he stoked the cover of the *Critique*, as if it were his white cat and he Ernst Stavro Blofeld.

"Whatever, dude," I told him.

Once a week a plane dropped off our supplies. Sometimes the pilot, Diamondo, would land his crate on the ice-runway, maybe even get out to stretch his legs and chat to us. I've no idea why he was called "Diamondo", or what his real name was. He was Peruvian I believe. More often, if the weather was bad, or if D. was in a hurry, he would swoop low and drop our supplies, leaving us to fight through the burly snowstorm and drag the package in. Inside would be necessaries, scientific equipment, copies of relevant journals – paper copies, it was back then, of course – and so on. The drops also contained correspondence. For me that meant: letters from family, friends and above all from my girlfriend Lezlie.

Two weeks before all this started I had written to Lezlie, asking her for a paperback copy of *Children of Dune*. I told her, in what I hope was a witty manner, that I had been disappointed by the slimness of *Dune Messiah*. I need the big books, I had said, to fill up the time, the long aching time, the (I think I used the phrase) terrible absence-of-Lezlie-thighs-and-tits time that characterised life in the Antarctic. I mention this because, in the weeks that followed, I found myself going back over my letter to her – my memory of it, I mean; I didn't keep a copy – trying to work out if I had perhaps offended her with a careless choice of words. If she might, for whatever reason, have decided not to write to me this week in protest at my vulgarity, or sexism. Or to register her disapproval by not paying postage to send a fat paperback edition of *Dune III* to the bottom of the world. Or maybe she *had* written.

You'll see what I mean in a moment.

Roy never got letters. I always did: some weeks as many as half a dozen. He: none. "Don't you have a girlfriend?" I asked him, once. "Or any friends?"

"Philosophy is my girlfriend," he replied, looking smugly over the top of his copy of the *Critique of Pure Reason*. "The solution to the Fermi Paradox is the friend I have yet to meet. Between them, they are all the company I desire."

"If you say so, mate," I replied, thinking inwardly *weirdo!* and *loser* and *billy-no-mates* and other such things. I didn't say any of that aloud, of course. And each week it would go on: we'd unpack the delivery parcel, and from amongst all the other necessaries and equipment I'd pull out a rubberband-clenched stash of letters, all of which would be for me and none of which were ever for Roy. And he would smile his smarmy smile and look aloof; or sometimes he would peer in a half-hope, as if thinking that maybe this week would be different. Once or twice I saw him *writing* a letter, with his authentic Waverley fountain pen, shielding his page with his arm when he thought I wanted to nosy into his private affairs – as if I had the slightest interest in fan mail to Professor Huffington Puffington of the University of Kant Studies.

He used to do a number of bonkers things, Roy: like drawing piano keys onto his left arm, spending ages shading the black ones, and then practising – or, for all I know, only pretending to practise – the right-hand part of Beethoven sonatas on it. "I requested an actual piano," he told me. "They said no." He used to do vocal exercises in the shower, really loud. He kept samples of his snot, testing (he said) whether his nasal mucus was affected by the south polar conditions. Once he inserted a radio gnomon relay spike (looked a little like a knitting needle) into the corner of his eye, and squeezed the ball to see what effects it had in his vision "because Newton did it." He learnt a new line of the Aeneid every evening – in Latin, mark you – by reciting it over and over. Amazingly annoying, this last weird hobby, because it was so particularly and obviously pointless. I daresay that's why he did it.

I read regular things: SF novels, magazines, even four day old newspapers (if the drop parcel happened to contain any), checking the football scores and doing the crosswords. And weekly I would pull out my fistful of letters, and settle down on the common room sofa to read them and write my replies, while Roy pursed his brow and worked laboriously through another paragraph of his Kant.

One week he said. "I'd like a letter."

"Get yourself a pen pal," I suggested.

We had just been outside, where the swarming snow was as thick as a huge shower of wood chips and the wind bit through the three layers I wore. We were both back inside, pulling off icicle-bearded gloves and scarfs and stamping our boots. The drop-package was on the floor between us, dripping. We had yet to open it.

"Can I have one of yours?" he asked.

"Tell you what," I said. I was in a good mood, for some reason. "I'll sell you one. Sell you one of my letters."

"How much?" he asked.

"Tenner," I said. Ten pounds was (I hate to sound like an old codger, but it's the truth) a lot of money back then.

"Deal," he said, without hesitation. He untied his boots, hopped out of them like Puck and sprinted away. When he came back he was holding a genuine ten pound note. "I choose, though," he said, snatching the money away as I reached for it.

"Whatever, man," I laughed. "Be my guest."

He gave me the money. Then, he dragged the parcel, now dripping melted snow, through to the common room and opened it. He rummaged around and brought out the rubberbanded letters: five of them.

"Are you sure none of them aren't addressed to you?" I said, settling myself on the sofa and examining my banknote with pride. "Maybe you don't need to buy one of my letters – maybe you got one of your own?"

He shook his head, looked quickly through the five envelopes on offer, selected one and handed me the remainder of the parcel. "No."

"Pleasure doing business with you," I told him. Off he went to his bedroom to read the letter he had bought.

I thought nothing more about it. The four letters were from: my Mum, my brother, a guy in Leicester with whom I was playing a tediously drawn-out game of postal chess, and the manager of my local branch of Lloyd's Bank in Reading, writing to inform me that my account was in credit. Since being in Antarctica meant I could never spend anything, and since my researcher's stipend was still going-in monthly, this was unnecessary. I'm guessing it was by way of a publicity exercise. It's not that I was famous, of course; even famous-for-Reading. But it doubtless looked good on some report somewhere: *we look after our customers, even when they're at the bottom of the world!* I made myself a coffee. Then I spent an hour at a computer terminal, checking data. When Roy came back through he looked smug, but I didn't begrudge him that. After all, I had made ten pounds – and ten pounds is ten pounds.

For the rest of the day we worked, and then I fixed up some pasta and Bolognese sauce in the little kitchen. As we ate I asked him: "So who was the letter from?"

"What do you mean?" Suspicious voice.

"The letter you bought from me. Who was it from? Was it Lezlie?" A self-satisfied grin. "No comment," he smirked.

"Say what?"

"It's my letter. I bought it. And I'm entitled to privacy."

"Suit yourself," I said. "I was only asking." He was right, I suppose; he bought the letter, it was his. Still, his manner rubbed me up the wrong way. We ate in silence for a bit, but I'm afraid I couldn't let it go. "I was only asking: who was it from? Is it Lezlie? I won't pry into what she actually wrote." Even as I said this, I thought to myself: *pry? How could I pry – the words were written to be read by me!* "You know," I added, thinking to add pressure. "I *could* just write to her, ask her what she wrote. I could find out that way."

"No comment," he repeated, pulling his shoulders round as he sat. I took my bowl to the sink and washed it up, properly annoyed, but there was no point in saying anything else. Instead I went through and put *Romancing the Stone* on the telly, because I knew it was the VHS Roy hated the most. He smiled, and retreated to his room with his philosophy book.

The next morning I discovered to my annoyance that the business with the letter was still preying on my mind. I told myself: get over it. What's done is done. But some part of me refused to let go. At breakfast Roy read another page of his Kant, and I saw that he was using the letter as a bookmark. At one point he put the book down and stood up to go to the loo, but then a sly expression crept over his usually ingenuous face, and he picked the book up and took it with him.

It had been a blizzardy few days and the dish needed checking over. Roy tried to wriggle out of this chore: "you're more the hardware guy," he said, in a wheedling tone. "I'm more conceptual – the ideas and the phil-os-o-phay."

"Don't give me that crap. We're both hands-on – the folk in Adelaide, and back in Britain, are the *actual* ideas people." I was cross. "Philosophy my arse." At any rate, he suited-up, rolled his scarf around his lower face and snapped on his goggles, zipped up his overcoat. We both pulled out brooms and stumped through light snowfall to the dish. It took us half an hour to clear the structure of snow, and check the motors hadn't frozen solid, and that its bearings were ice free. Our shadows flickered across the landscape like pennants in the wind.

The sun loitered near the horizon, a cricket-ball frozen in flight.

That afternoon I did a stint testing the terminals. With the sun still up, it was a noisy picture; although it was possible to pick up this and that. At first I thought there was something, but when I looked closer I discovered it was radio chatter from a Spanish expedition on its way to the Vinson Massif. I found my mind wandering. Who was the letter from?

The following day I eased my irritation by writing to Lezlie. *Hey, you know Roy? He's a sad bastard, a ringer for one of actors in* Revenge of the Nerds. *Anyway he asked for a letter and I sold him one. Now he won't tell me whose letter it is. Did* you *write to me last week? What did you say? Just give me the gist, lover-girl.* But as soon as I'd written this I scrunched the paper up and threw it in the bin. Lez would surely not respond well to such a message. In effect I was saying: "hey you know that love-letter you poured your heart and soul into? I sold it to a nerd without even reading it! *That's* how much I value your emotions!"

Chewed the soft-blue plastic insert at the end of my Bic for a while.

I tried again: *Hi lover! Did you write last week? There was a snafu with the package and some stuff got lost.* I looked over the lie. It didn't ring true. I scrunched this one up too. Then I sat in the chair trying, and failing, to think of how to put things. The two balls of scrunched paper in the waste-bin began, creakingly, to unscrunch.

Dear Lez. Did you write last week? I'm afraid I lost a letter, klutz that I am! That was closer to the truth. But then I thought: what if she had written me a dear-john letter? Or a let's-get-married? Or a-close-family-member-has-died? How embarrassing to write back a jaunty "please repeat your message!" note. What if she hadn't written at all? What if it were somebody else?

This latter thought clawed at my mind for a while. What if some important information, perhaps from my academic supervisor at Reading, Prof Addlestone, had been in the letter? Privacy was one thing, but surely Roy didn't have the right to withhold such info?

I stomped down the corridor and knocked at Roy's room. He made me wait for a long time before opening the door just enough to reveal his carbuncular face, smirking up at me. "What?"

"I've changed my mind," I said. "I want my letter back."

"No dice, doofus," he replied. "I paid. It's mine now."

"Look, I'll *buy* it back, all right? I'll give you your ten pounds. I've got it right here."

When he smiled, he showed the extent to which his upper set of teeth didn't fit neatly over his lower set. "It's not for sale," he said.

"Don't be a pain, Roy," I said. "I'm asking nicely."

"And I'm, nicely, declining."

"What – you want more than a tenner? You can go fish for *that*, my friend."

"It's not for sale," he repeated.

"Is this a scam," I said, my temper wobbling badly. "Is the idea you hold out until I offer – what, twenty quid? Is that it?"

"No. That's not it. The letter's mine. I do not choose to sell it."

"Just tell me what's *in* the letter," I pleaded. "I'll give your money back *and* you can keep the damn thing, just tell me who it's from and what it says." Even as I made this offer it occurred to me that Roy, with his twisted sense of humour, might simply lie to me. So I added, "Just show me the letter. You don't have to give it up, keep it for all I care, only –"

"No deal," said Roy. Then he wrung his speccy face into a parody of a concerned expression. "You're embarrassing yourself, Anthony." And he shut his door.

I went through to the common room, fuming. For a while I toyed with the idea of simply grabbing the letter back: I was bigger than Roy, and doubtless had been involved in more actual fist-flying, body-grappling fights than he. It wouldn't have been hard. But instead of that I had a beer, and lay on the sofa, and tried to get a grip. We had to live together, he and I, in unusually confined circumstances, and for a very lengthy period of time. In less than a week the sun would vanish, and the proper observing would begin. Say we chanced upon alien communication (I told myself) – wouldn't that be something? Might there be a Nobel Prize in it? I couldn't put all that at risk, even for the satisfaction of punching him on the nose.

Maybe, I told myself, Roy would thaw out a little in a day or two. You catch more flies with honey than vinegar, after all. Maybe I could *coax* the letter out of him.

The week wore itself out. I went through a phase of intense irritation with Roy for his (what seemed to me) immensely petty and immature attitude with regard to my letter. Then I went through a phase when I told myself it didn't bother me. I did consider returning his tenner to him, so as to retain the high moral ground. But then I thought: ten pound is ten pound.

The week ended, and Diamondo overflew and tossed the supply package out to bounce along the snow. This annoyed me, because I had finally managed to write a letter to Lezlie that explained the situation without making it sound as if I valued her communiques so little I'd gladly sold it off to weirdo Roy. But I couldn't "post" the letter unless the plane landed and took stuff on board, so I had to hang onto it. I couldn't even be sure, I reminded myself, that the letter Roy had bought from me had *been* from her.

On the fifth of July the sun set for the last time until August. The thing people don't understand about Antarctic night is that it's not the same level of ink-black all the way through. For the first couple of weeks, the sky lightens twice a day, pretty much bright enough to walk around without a torch – the same dawn and dusk paling of the sky that precedes sunrise and follows sunset, only without actual dawn and dusk. Still, you can sense the sun is just there, on the other side of the horizon, and it's not too bad. As the weeks go on this gets briefer and darker, and then you do have a month or so when it's basically coal-coloured skies and darkness invisible the whole time.

Diamondo landed his plane and tossed out the supply package, but didn't linger; and by the time I'd put on the minimum of outdoor clothing and grabbed a torch and got through the door he was taking off again – so, once again, I didn't get to send my letter to Lez.

That was the last time I saw that aircraft.

There were two letters in this week's batch: one from my old Grammar School headmaster, saying that the school had hosted a whole assembly on the "exciting and important" work I was doing; and the other from my Professor at Reading. This was nothing but a note, and read in its entirety: "Dear A. I often think of Sartre's words. Imagination is not an empirical or superadded power of consciousness, it is the whole of consciousness as it realises its freedom. Where is freer than the very bottom of the world? Nil desperandum! Yours, A." This, though slightly gnomic, was not out of character for Prof. Addlestone, who had worked on SETI for so long it had made his brain a little funny. No letter from Lez, which worried me. But, after all, she didn't write every week. I re-read the Professor's note several times. Did it read like a PS, a scribbled afterthought? Did it perhaps mean that the letter Roy bought had *been* from Addlestone? Maybe. Maybe not.

We got on with our work, and I tried to put the whole letter business behind me. Roy did not help, as far as this went. He was acting stranger and stranger; simpering at me, and when I queried his expression ('what? What is it?') scurrying away – or scowling and saying, "nothing, nothing, only…" and refusing to elaborate.

The next thing was: he moved one of the computer terminals into his room. These were 1980s terminals; not the modern-day computers the size and weight of a copy of *Marie-Claire*; so it was no mean feat getting the thing in there. He even cut away a portion from the bottom corner of his door, to enable the main cable to come out into the hall and through into the monitor room.

"What are you doing in there?" I challenged him. "That's not standard policy. Did you clear this with home?"

"I'm working on something," he told me. "I'm close to a breakthrough. SETI, my friend. Solving Fermi's paradox! You should consider yourself lucky to be here. You'll get a footnote in history. Only a footnote, I know: but it's more than most people get."

I ignored this. "I still don't see why you need to squirrel yourself away in your room."

"Privacy," he said, "is very important to me."

One day he went out on the ice to (he told me) check the meteorological datapoints. It seemed like an odd thing to do – he'd never shown any interest in them before – but I was glad he was out of the base, if only for half an hour. As soon as I saw his torch-beam go, wobbling its oval of brightness away over the ice, I hurried to his room. I wasn't doing anything wrong, I told myself. I was just checking the identity of the letter's author. Maybe have a quick glance at its contents. I wouldn't steal it back (although, I told myself, I *could*. It was my letter after all. Roy was being an idiot about the whole thing). But once my itch was scratched, curiosity-wise, then everything would get easier about the base. I could wait out the remainder of my stint with equanimity. He need never even know I'd been poking around.

No dice. Roy had fitted a padlock to his door. I rattled this uselessly; I could have smashed it, but then Roy would know what I'd been up to. I retreated to the common room, disproportionately angry. What was he doing, in there, with a whole computer terminal and my letter?

I had enough self-knowledge to step back from the situation, at least some of the time. He was doing this in order to wind me up. That was the only reason he was doing it. The letter was nothing – none of my letters, if I looked back, contained any actual, substantive content. They were just pleasant chatter, people I knew touching-base with me. The letter Roy bought must be the same. He bought it not to *have* the letter, but in order to set me on edge, to rile me. And by getting riled I was gifting him the victory. The way to play this whole situation was to be perfectly indifferent.

However much I tried this, though, I kept falling back. It was the not knowing!

I tried once more, during the week. "Look, Roy," I said, smiling. "This letter thing is no big deal, you know? None of my letters have any really significant stuff in them."

He looked at me, in a "that's all *you* know" sort of way. But this was, I decided, just winding me up.

"I tell you what I think," I said. "You can, you know, nod, or not-nod, depending on whether I'm right. I think the letter you bought was from my girlfriend. Yeah?"

"No comment," said Roy, primly. "One way or the other."

"If so, it was probably full of inane chatter, yeah? Fine – keep it! With my blessing!"

"In point of fact," he corrected me, holding up his right forefinger, "I do not need your blessing. The transaction was finalised with the fiduciary transfer. Contract law is very clear on this point."

I lost my temper a little at this point. "You know how sad you are, keeping a woman's letter to another man for your own weird little sexual buzz? That's – *sad*. Is what it is. I don't think you realise how sad that is."

"Oh Anthony, Anthony," he said, shaking his head and smirking in that insufferable way he had. "If only you knew!"

I swore. "Suit yourself," I said.

Then the airstrip lights failed. I assumed this was an accident, although the fact that every one of them failed at the same time was strange. Diamondo came through on the radio: "Fellows!" he declared, through his thick accent. "I cannot land if there are no lights to land!"

"Don't know what's happened to them," I replied. "Some manner of malfunction."

"Obviously that!" came Diamondo's voice. "Can you fix? Over."

Roy suited up and went outside; he was back in minutes. "I can't do anything in the dark, with a torch, in a hurry," he complained. "Tell him – no. Tell him to toss the package out and we'll fix the lights for next time."

When I relayed this message, Diamondo said, "Breakables! There are breakables in the package! I cannot toss! Over." Then, contradicting his last uttered word, he went on. "I can take out the breakables and toss the rest. Wait – wait."

I could hear the scrapy sound of the plane in the sky outside. Then, over the radio: "Is in chute."

"Wait," I said. "Where are you dropping it? If there's no lights – I mean, I don't want to go searching over a wide area in the dark with…" There was a terrific crash right overhead, as something smashed into our roof.

"You idiot!" I called. "You could have broken our roof!"

Static. And, through the walls, the sound of the plane's engines diminishing. Roy looked and me, and I at him. "I think it rolled off," Roy said. "You go out and get it."

"You're already suited!"

"I went out last time. It's your turn now. Fair's fair."

It was on the edge of my tongue to retort: *stealing my letter – is* that *fair?* But that would have done no good; and anyway I was hoping that there would be a new letter from Lezlie in the satchel. So I pulled on overclothes and took a torch and went outside.

It was extraordinarily cold – sinus-freezingly cold. The air was still. The sound of Diamondo's plane, already very faint, diminished and diminished until it vanished altogether. Now the only sound was the whir of the generator, gently churning to itself with its restless motion. I searched around in the dark outside the main building for ten minutes or so, and spent another five trying to see into the gap between the main prefab and the annex, which was half-full of snow. But I couldn't find it.

When I went back to the main door it was locked. This was unprecedented. For a while I banged on the door, and yelled, and my heart began blackly to suspect that Roy was playing some kind of prank on me – or worse. I was just about to give up and make my way round to try the side entrance when Roy's gurning face appeared in the door's porthole, with the graph-paper pattern woven into the glass. He opened it. "What the hell were you playing at?" I demanded, crossly. "Why did you lock the door?"

"It occurred to me that the lights might have been sabotaged," he said, not looking me in the eye. "I thought: security is valour's better part. Obviously I was going to let you back in, once I was sure it *was* you."

"Have you had a nervous breakdown?" I yelled. "Are you *high*? Who else could possibly be out there? We're three hundred miles from the nearest human settlement. Did you think it was a ghost?"

"Calm down," Roy advised, grinning his simpering grin and still not looking me in the eye. "Did you get the package?"

I sat down with a thump. "Couldn't find it," I said, pulling off my overboots. "It may still be on the roof. Seriously, though, man! Locking the door?"

"We need to retrieve it," said Roy. "My medication is in it. My supplies are running low."

This was the first I had heard of any medication. "Seriously? They posted you down here, even though you have medical problems?"

"Just some insomnia problems. And some allergic reaction problems. But I need my sleeping pills and my antihistamines."

"You're kidding," I said. "What is there to be allergic to, down here?"

He gave me a pointed look. But then he said, "Come and have a drink. I've got some whisky."

Now, I knew the base was not supplied with whisky. Beer was the most they allowed us. I should, perhaps, have been suspicious of Roy's abrupt hospitality, doubly so since I knew he hardly ever drank. But I was cold, and cross, and a whisky – actually – sounded like a bloody good idea. "How have you got any of that?"

"I brought a bottle with me. My old tutor at Cambridge gave it me. Break this out when you've solved the SETI problem, he said. *He* never doubted me, you see. And solve it, I have."

And then a second thought occurred to me. It came to me like a flash. I could *get Roy drunk*. Surely then he would be more amenable to telling me what was in the letter he'd snaffled from me. I couldn't think that I'd ever seen him drunk; but my judgment was that he would hold his liquor badly. He'd be a splurge. Okay, I thought: butter him up, and get some booze in him.

"I'll have a dram," I told him. Then: "Kind of you to offer. Thanks. I didn't mean to... you know. Yell at you."

He ignored this overture. "You didn't go to Cambridge, I think?" he asked, as we went through to the common room. "Reading University, isn't it?"

"Reading born and bred," I replied, absently. I half-leaned, half-sat on one of the heaters to get warmth back into my marrow while Roy went off to his room to get the whisky. He was gone a while. Finally he came back with a bottle of Loch Lomond in one hand and a bottle of beer in the other. He handed me the former.

I retrieved two tumblers from the cupboard, but Roy said: "I'll not have the whisky, thank you anyway. I don't like the taste."

This was about par, I thought, for the weirdo that he was – bringing a bottle of scotch all the way to the end of the world, only to not even drink it. On the other hand the seal was broken, and about an inch was missing, so perhaps he had tried a taster and so discovered his animadversion. I honestly didn't care. I poured three fingers, and settled myself in one of the chairs

"Cheers!" I said, raising a glass.

"Good health," he returned, propping his bum on the arm of the sofa.

"So," I said, smacking my lips. "The fact that we're drinking this means you've solved the Fermi paradox?"

"We're not drinking it," he said, with a little snorty laugh of self-satisfaction. "You are."

"You're such a pedant, Roy," I told him.

"Take that as a compliment," he said, smirking, and making odd little snorty-sniffy noises with his nostrils.

"So? Does the fact that I'm drinking this mean you've solved it?"

"The answer to your question is: yes."

"Really?"

"Absolutely."

I took another sip. "Congratulations!"

"Thank you."

"And?"

He peered blankly at me. "What?"

"And? In the sense of: what's your solution?"

"Oh. The Fermi Paradox." He sounded almost bored. "Well, I'll tell you if you like." He seemed to ponder this. "Yeah," he added. "Why not? It's Kant."

"Of course it is," I said, laughing. "You complete nutter."

He looked hurt at this. "What do you mean?"

"I mean – the best part of a year of our lives, millions of pounds sunk into this base, probably billions spent worldwide on SETI, and all we needed to do was open a seventeenth-century book of philosophy!"

"Eighteenth-century," he corrected me. "And the kit, here, certainly has its uses."

"Glad to hear it! Despite – Kant? Really?"

Roy took the smallest sip from his beer bottle, and then rubbed his own chin with his thumb. "Hard to summarise," he said. "Start here: how do we know there's anything out there?"

"What – out in space?"

"No: outside our own brains. Sense data, yes? Eyes, ears, nerve-endings. We see things, and, no, we *think* we're seeing things out there. We hear things, likewise. And so on. But maybe all that is a lie. Maybe we're hallucinating. Dreaming. How can we be sure there's anything really *there*?"

"Isn't this I think therefore I am?"

"The cogito, yes," said Roy, with that uniquely irritating prissy inflection he used when he wanted to convey his own intellectual superiority. "Though Kant didn't have much time for Descartes, actually. He says "I think therefore I am" is an empty statement. We never just think, after all. We always think *about something*."

"You're losing me, Roy," I said, draining my whisky, and reaching for the bottle. Roy's eyes flashed, and I stopped. "Do you mind if I have another?"

"No, no," he urged me, bobbing forward and back in an oddly bird-like way. "Go right ahead."

"So," I said. "You're saying: we can't be sure if the cosmos is a kind of hallucination. Maybe I'm a brain in a vat. So what? I've got to act as if the universe is real, or," I directed a quick look at Roy, "they'd lock me in the loony bin. So? Does this hallucination also include ET, or not?"

"Quite right. Well, Kant says: there *is* a real world – he calls it the ding-an-sich, the thing as it really is. There is such a reality. But our only access to that real world is through our perceptions, our senses and the way our thoughts are structured. So, says Kant, some of the things we assume are part of the world out there are actually part of the structure of our consciousness."

"Such as?"

"Quite basic things. Time and space. Causality."

"Wait, Kant is saying that time, space and causality aren't 'really' out there? They're just part of our minds?"

Roy nodded. "It's as if we always wore pink-tinted contact lenses. As if we'd always worn them, ever since birth. Everything we saw would have a pink tint. We might very well assume the world was just – you know, pink. But it wouldn't be the world that was pink, it would be our perception of the world."

"Pink," I repeated, and took another slug. I was starting to feel drowsy.

"We're all like that, all the time, except that instead of pink contact lenses on our eyes, we're wearing *space-and-time* contacts on our minds. *Causality* contacts."

"Space and time are the way the universe is. Just is."

"That's not what Kant says. He says: we don't really know the way the universe *just is*. All we know is how our perceptions and thoughts structure our understanding."

"Wait," I said. "Kant says that cause and effect are just in our heads?"

"That's right."

"That's nonsense," I said. "If space and time and causality are just inside my head, then what's my head in? It takes up space, my brain. It takes time to think these thoughts."

"There's *something* out there," Roy agreed. "But we don't know what it is. Here's a thought experiment, Kant's thought experiment. You can imagine an object in space, can't you?"

I grunted.

"Okay," said Roy. "And you can imagine the object being taken away. Yes? Then you have empty space. But you can't imagine *space and time* being taken away. You can't imagine no space, no time."

I grunted again.

"That shows that space, time, causality and some other things – they're part of the way the mind perceives. There's no getting behind them. Is the ding-an-sich itself structured according to that logic? We cannot know. Maybe, maybe not."

"Ding," I said, my eyelids slipping down my eyeballs, "like a microwave oven?"

"We're looking for aliens with visual telescopes and radio telescopes," said Roy, standing up and putting his beer bottle down.

"But whatever tools we use, we're looking for aliens in space and time, aliens that understand causality and number. But maybe those things are not alien. Those things are the way *our* minds are built. And that means we're looking in the wrong place. We should not be looking in space, or time. We should be looking in the ding-an-sich."

"Sick," I said. My eyes were shut now. I didn't seem to be able to open them. Such muscular operation was beyond my volitional control. "I feel a bit sick, actually."

"Ding," I heard him say, at the other end of a very long corridor. "You're done. Let's open the microwave door, now, shall we?"

I suppose I was asleep. I tried to shift position in bed, but my arms were numb. Sometimes you lie on an arm and it goes dead. But this was both my arms. They were up over my head. A scraping sound. Distantly. I tried to pull my arms down but they were already down. *This is the chance,* somebody was saying, or muttering, or I don't know. Perhaps I was imagining it. *We've never had this chance before. Because although human consciousness is structured by the Kantian categories of apperception, there's nothing to say that* computer *perception needs to suffer from the same limitations. It's all a question of programming! A programme to sift the Centauri data so as to get behind the limitations of consciousness.*

I was moving. Everything was dark, dark, dark. My arms were trailing behind me, I thought; and something was pulling my legs, I thought; and I was sliding along on my back. Was that right? Could that be right?

We look out from our planet and see a universe of space, and time, of substance and causality, of plurality and totality, of possibility and probability – and we forget that what we're actually seeing are the ways our minds structure *the ding-an-sich according to the categories of space, and time, of substance and causality, of plurality and totality, of possibility and probability. We look out and we see no aliens, and are surprised. But the real surprise would be to see aliens in such a vista, because that would mean the aliens are in our structures of thought. Sure there* are *aliens. Of course there are! But they don't live in our minds. They live in the ding-an-sich.*

The motion stopped, but I was still too sluggish to move, or speak, or even open my eyes. The next thing I knew, somebody was kissing me on the lips. *Goodbye,* was a word, and it floated around. Then nothing.

O dark, dark, dark, they all go into the –

Or.

Or something. It came upon me slowly. Crept up on me, as it were. I couldn't as yet put a name to it. *Let me think through the necessary and contingent possibilities,* I thought to myself. *It could have been a letter from my mum, in which case it was full of family trivia and Roy's just yanking my chain for the hell of it. He's certainly capable of that.* The thing, whatever it was, was closer now, or larger somehow, or in some sense more present, although I still couldn't put a name to it. *Could have been a letter from a friend, or from Leicester Lenny, but if so it would only say Q-B4 ch! or Kn-R7 or something, and that could mean nothing at all to Roy. Or it could have been a letter from Professor Addlestone of Reading University, blathering on about something. Or it could have been,* the thing was all around me now, or all within me, or otherwise pressing very imminently upon me. *Or it could have been from Lezlie. But then, what? Full of the usual blandishments? In which case Roy's hoarding of it is creepy but, in the larger scheme of things, unimportant. That's not what I'm afraid of though, is it? I'm afraid the letter says: I'm leaving you, I've found someone else. But but but, if it is, then I'll find out eventually – of course. I just need to be patient. I'll find out in time. Assuming I have time –*

Cold. That was the thing.

That was what had crept up on me.

I sat up. I was outside, in the darkness, in my indoor clothes. Scalded with the cold. My whole body shook with a Parkinsonian tremor. I angled my head back and the stars were all there, the Southern Fish, the Centaur and the Dove; the Southern Cross itself; Orion and Hydra low in the sky; Scorpion and Sagittarius high up. Hydra and Pegasus. I breathed in fire and burned my throat and lungs. It was cold enough to shear metal. It was cold enough to freeze petrol.

I got to my feet. My hands felt as though they had been dipped in acid, and then that sensation stopped and I was more scared than before. There was nothing at the end of my arms at all. I tried rubbing my hands together, but the leprous lack of sensation and the darkness and my general sluggishness meant I could not coordinate the action. My hands bounced numbly off one another. I became terrified of the idea that I had perhaps knocked one or more fingers clean off. This looks ridiculous as I write it down, but there, in the dark, in the cold, the thought gripped my soul horribly.

I had to get inside, to get warm. I had to get back to the base. I was shuddering so hard I was scared I might actually lose balance with the shivering and fall down – in which case I might not be able to get back up again. Ghastly darkness all about. Cold beyond the power of words to express.

I turned about, and about again. Starlight is the faintest of lights. I could see my breath coming out only because of the vast ostrich shaped blot that twisted in my field of vision, blocking out the stars. I needed to pick a direction and go. But I couldn't see any lights to orient me. What if I stumbled off in the wrong direction? I could easily stagger off into the wilderness, miss the base altogether. I'd be dead in minutes.

I addressed myself: take hold of yourself. You were dragged here – Roy dragged you here. Runty Roy; he couldn't have removed me very far from the base. Presumably he figured I wouldn't wake up; that I'd just die there in the dark.

"Okay," I said, and took another breath – knives going down my throat. I had to move. I started off, and stumbled over the black ground through the black air. I began to fall forward – my thigh muscles were cramping – and picked up the pace to stop myself pitching onto my face. My inner ear still told me I was falling, so I ran faster. Soon I was *sprinting*. It's possible the fluids in my inner ear had frozen, or glued-up with the cold, I don't know. It felt as if I were falling, but my feet were still pounding over the ice, invisible below me. I felt like a diver, tumbling from the top board.

And then I saw the sea – I was at the coast. Obviously I wasn't at the coast because that was hundreds of miles from the base. But there it was, visible. There was a settlement on the shore, a mile below me, with yellow lights throwing shimmery ovals over the water. There was a ship, lit up like a Christmas decoration, balanced very precisely on top of its own lit reflection. I must have been ten degrees of latitude, or more, further away from the pole, enough to lift the moon up over the horizon. The texture of the sea was a million burin-marks of white light on a million wavelets, like pewter. There was no doubting what I was seeing. My whole body trembled with pain, with the cold, and I said to myself *I'm dying*, and *I'm hallucinating because I'm dying*. I must have run in the wrong direction. I felt as if I'd been running all my life, all my ancestors' lives combined.

There was a weird inward fillip, or lurch, or clonic jerk, or something folding over something else. I was conscious of thinking: I've run the wrong way. I've missed the base.

And there *was* the base. Now that I was there, I could see that Roy had covered the common room window on the inside with something – cloth, cardboard – to make a blackout screen. He had not wanted me to see the light and follow it as a beacon. Now that I was there, I could just make out the faint line of illumination around the edges. I couldn't feel my hands, or my feet, and my face was covered with a pinching, scratchy mask – snot, tears, frost, whatever, frozen by the impossible cold to a hard crust.

I slumped against the wall, and the fabric of my shirt was so stiffened it snapped. It ripped clean away when I got up.

The door. I had to get to the door – that was when I saw... I was going to say *when I saw them* but the plural doesn't really describe the circumstance. Not that there was only one, either. This is very hard to put into words. There was the door, in front of me, and just enough starlight to shine a faint glint off the metal handle. I could not use my hands, so I leant on the handle with my elbow, but it did not give way. Locked, of course locked. And of course Roy would not be opening for me this time. Then I saw – what I saw. Data experiences of a radically new kind. Raw tissues of flesh, darkness visible, a kind of fog (no: fog is the wrong word). A pillar of fire by night, except that "it" did not burn, or gleam, or shine. "It" is the wrong word. "It" felt, or looked, like a great tumbling of scree down an endless slope. Or rubble gathering at the bottom and falling up the mountain. Forwards, backwards.

It was the most terrifying thing I have ever seen.

There was a hint of – I'm going to say, claws, jaws, a clamping something. A maw. Not a tentacle, nothing so defined. Nor was it a darkness. It made a low, thrumming chiming noise, like a muffled bell sounding underground, ding-ding, ding-ding. But this was not a sound-wave sort of sound. This was not a propagating expanding sphere of agitated air articles. It was a pulse in the mind. A shudder of the soul.

I could not get inside the base, and I was going to die. I felt the horrid cold in the very core of my being. Then "it" or "they", or the boojummy whatever the hell (I choose my words carefully, here) it was, expanded. Or undid whatever process of congealing that brought it – I don't know.

Where I stood experienced a second as-it-were convulsive, almost muscular contraction. Everything folded over, and flipped back again. "It", or "they" were not here any longer. In fact they had been here eons ago, or were not yet here at all.

I was standing inside the common room.

Do not demand to know how I passed beyond the locked door. I could not tell you.

The warmth of the air burned my throat. I could no longer stay standing. I half slumped, half fell sideways, and my arm banged against one of the heaters – it felt like molten metal, and I yelled. I rolled off and lay on the floor, and breathed and breathed.

I may have passed out. I have no idea how I got inside. I was probably only out for a few moments, because the next thing I knew my hands were in agony. Absolute agony! It felt like the gom jabbar, like they had both been stuffed into a tub of boiling water. Looking back, I can now say what it was: sensation returning to my frostbitten flesh. But by God I've never felt such pain. I screamed and screamed as if the Spanish Inquisition had gone to work on me. I writhed, and wept like a baby.

Somehow I dragged myself into a sitting posture, with my back against the wall and my legs straight out on the floor. Roy was standing in the common room doorway. In his right hand he was holding what I assumed to be a gun, although I later realised it was a flare pistol.

"You murdering bastard," I said, "have you come to finish the job? You going to shoot me down like a dog?" Or that's what I *tried* to say. What came out was: "yrch yrch orch orch orch'. God, my throat was *shredded*.

"The thing-in-itself," he said. There was a weird bend in his voice. I blinked away the melting icicles from my eyelashes and saw he was *crying*. "The thing-as-such. The thing *per se*. I have experienced it unmediated." His face was wet. Tears slippy-sliding down, and dripping like snot from his jowls. I'd never seen him like that before.

"What," I croaked, "did you put in my whisky?" Oh God, the pain in my *hands*! And now my feet were starting to rage and burn too. Oh, it was ghastly.

He stopped crying, and wiped his face in the crook of his left arm. "I'm sorry," he said. Even at this juncture he was not able to look me in the eye. He lifted his right hand, holding the flare pistol, slowly, until he was holding it across his chest, like James Bond in the posters.

I was weeping – not because I was scared of dying, but just because my hands and feet hurt with such sharp and focussed intensity.

Roy took a breath, lifted the flare pistol to his own head, and pulled the trigger. There was a crunching bang, and Roy flopped to the ground. The common room was filled with fluorescent red-orange light and an extraordinarily loud hissing sound. For a moment we were in a luridly lit stage-set of Hades.

What had happened was this: the tip and fuse of the flare projectile had lodged itself in Roy's skull, and had ejected the illumination section and its little asbestos parachute at the ceiling, where it snagged against the polystyrene tiles and burned until it was all burned out.

I sat in that ferociously red lit room, with molten chunks of polystyrene dripping onto the carpet. Then the shell itself burnt free and fell to the ground, where it fizzled out.

Roy was not dead. Nor was I, amazingly. It took me a while, and an effort, and the whole way along I was sobbing and begging the cosmos to take the pain away; but I got to the radio, and called for help. They sent an air ambulance. They laid a pattern of flares on the unlit runway during their first flyby and landed alongside them on their second. It took four hours, but they got to us, and we did not die in the interval.

I crawled back to Roy, unconscious on the floor, and pulled the shell-tip from the side of his head. There was no blood, although the dent was very noticeable – the skin and hair lining the new thumb-sized cavity all the way in. There was little I could do, beyond put him in the recovery position.

Then I clambered painfully on the sofa, my hands and feet hurting a little less. Surprisingly enough, I fell asleep – Roy had dissolved a sleeping tablet in the whisky, of course, to knock me out; and when the pain retreated just enough the chemical took effect. I was woken by the sound of crashing, and crashing, and crashing, and then one of the ambulance men came through the main door with an axe in his hand.

We were flown to Halley, on the coast – the subject of my vision, or whatever that had been. We were hospitalised, and questioned, and my hands were treated. I lost two fingers on my left hand and one on my right, and my nose was rescued with a skin graft that gives it, to this day, a weird patchwork-doll look. I lost toes too, but I care less about those. Roy was fine: they opened his skull, extracted a few fragments of bone, and sewed him up. Good as new.

I don't think they believed his version of events, although for myself I daresay he was truthful, or as truthful as circumstances permit. The official record is that he had a nervous breakdown, drugged me, left me outside to die and then shot himself. He himself said otherwise. I've read the transcript of his account. I've even been in the same room with him as he was questioned. "I saw things as they really are, things per se, I had a moment – that's the wrong word, it is not measured in moments, it has always been with me, it will always be with me – a moment of clarity."

"And your clarity was: kill your colleague?"

He wanted the credit all to himself, I think. He believed *he* was the individual destined to make first contact with alien life. He wanted me out of the way. He didn't say that, of course, but that's what I think. His explanation was: my perceptions, my mental processes and imagination, would collapse the fragile disintermediating system he was running to break through to the Thing-as-Such. I confess I don't see how that would work. Nonetheless, he insists that this was his motive for killing me. Indeed, he insists that my reappearance proved the correctness of his decision, the necessity for my death – because by coming back at the time I did, I broke down the vision of the Ding-an-Sich, or reasserted the prison of categorical perception, or something, and the aliens fled – or not fled, because their being is not mappable with a succession of spatial coordinates the way ours are. But: I don't know. Evaporate. Collapse away to nothing. Become again veiled. He wrote me several long, not terribly coherent letters about it from Broadmoor. I still prefer the earlier explanation. He was a nerd, not right in the head, and a little jealous of me.

So, yes. He happened to buy Lezlie's Dear John. She couldn't cope with the long distances, the time lags between us meeting up, she'd met someone else... The usual. After he drugged me and left me outside to die, Roy left the letter, carefully opened and smoothed out, face up on the desk in my room. It was going to be the explanation for my "suicide". People were to believe I couldn't handle the rejection, and had just walked out into the night.

His latest communication with me from Broadmoor begged me to "go public" with what I had seen; so that's what I'm doing. You'll grasp from this that I don't know *what* I saw. I suppose it was a series of weird hallucinations brought on by the extreme cold and the blood supply intermitting in my brain. Or something, I don't know. I still dream about them. It. Whatever. And the strange thing is: although I know for a fact I encountered it (them, none, whatever) for the first time in Antarctica, in 1986, it feels – deep in my bones – as if I have always known about them. As if they visited me in my cradle. They didn't, of course.

I saw the John Carpenter film *The Thing* for the first time recently. That wasn't one of the VHS tapes they gave us back then to watch on base. For obvious reasons. That's not what it was like for me. That doesn't capture it at all. They, or it, or whatever, were not *thing*-y.

They are inhuman. But this is only my dream of them, I think. It is not a dream of a human. It is not a dream of a thing. Or it is, but of a sick kind of thing. And, actually, no. That's not it.

He keeps writing me. I wish he'd stop writing.

THE SULLEN ENGINES

GEORGE ZEBROWSKI

George Zebrowski's Brute Orbits *won the John W. Campbell Award,*
Cave of Stars *was chosen for* Science Fiction, the 101 Best Novels
1985-2010, *and* Stranger Suns *was a* New York Times *Notable
Book of the Year. A multiple Nebula Award nominee, he was also
a finalist for the Theodore Sturgeon Award. His newest novel is*
Empties *(Golden Gryphon). Co-edited with Gregory Benford
is* Sentinels *in Honor of Arthur C. Clarke (Hadley Rille), while*
Decimated *presents ten collaborations with Jack Dann (Borgo).
His backlist is available via SF Gateway and Open Road: www.
openroadmedia.com/george-zebrowski.*

> "...we curse the obstacles of life
> as though they were devils. But they
> are not devils. They are obstacles."
> – John Erskine,
> *The Moral Obligation
> To Be Intelligent,*
> 1915

"You don't really hate cars," Bruno said, frowning at her. "We still
need them."

"It's the engines," said June, "and the bad drivers, even if the cars
ran on perpetual motion."

"No drivers would be best, I suppose," he said.

"Our toys only magnify human error," she said, looking away from
him, thinking of how human-infested vehicles victimized walkers,
flashing contemptuous, pitying glances at pedestrians, oblivious to

their own sacrificial time payments and lost lives. When the price of oil was up, fatalities went down by fifteen thousand; profits warred with safer engineering.

Safer, but never safe.

Life's crawling insufficiency grimaced at her from behind the inconceivable scenery of the universe, in which sudden awareness asked: what are we and where are we going?

"Hey, lady, whaddya waiting for!" cried a voice from a giant truck one wintry morning. She had waved the driver on, then strolled around behind him. Insulted by her caution, he honked his horn and pulled away in a haze of blue exhaust. How many respiratory deaths in that one puff? Thirty thousand a year in one state alone. The ironies abounded.

Aging drivers drifted through red lights, asleep or suicidal. Conniving engines rumbled in predatory readiness where the lights were never green long enough.

Scurry across, humiliated by the flesh-operated machines waiting to run you down, growling, maiming and killing as the toll of personal transport, daring her to do without.

JOSEPH COTTEN WAS telling young Tim Holt that automobiles might well become a profitable curse, adding nothing to the human soul.

Bruno guffawed, more impressed by his big TV's crisp black and white than by Orson Welles's 1942 take on Booth Tarkington's 1919 Pulitzer Prize novel, *The Magnificent Ambersons*.

Agnes Moorehead's Aunt Fanny was saying that she wouldn't be surprised if a law banned the sale of cars as concealed weapons.

"Well whaddya know," Bruno said, "sounds like you."

"All that foresight was already too late," June said.

"Shoulda-would-a-could-a," Bruno said. "But pretty good for back then."

June muttered, "... much too late."

"Well," Bruno went on, "who knew? Asimov said that it was easy to predict horseless carriages, but not urban sprawl or pollution."

"Or the sexual opportunities for kids," June said.

"Yeah – motel rooms on wheels," her husband said with glee, glancing up at the ceiling. "Recliner seats and steering wheel up against your back. Lots of fun."

"You don't much care, do you?" she shouted.

He said more seriously, "Horseless carriages were easy to see coming, accident rates and planetary damage only a little more difficult, but urban sprawl and changes in sexual behavior would have been hardest, not to mention cars and terrorism. At the turn of the last century *Scientific American* laughed at the idea of airliners carrying hundreds of passengers. I'm well aware."

She looked away.

"You're impossible," he added, turning off the movie. "What do you want?"

"A glass of water," she said, leaning back in her chair.

He had warned her, "Never walk in front of a waiting vehicle, even if the driver sees you." A hobbling man had slapped a car in *Midnight Cowboy* and shouted, "I'm walkin' here!"

"Pacino ad-libbed that line," Bruno had told her as if he had been there, and then again reminded her to always walk against traffic – *the* rule for pedestrians. "Walk against traffic, bicycle *with* traffic."

She had wished she could fly.

"Dustin Hoffman, dear," she had said gently, "not Pacino. And I'm not sure he slapped it."

"Against traffic," he had repeated. "He whacked the hood with his hand."

SHE HAD WALKED well behind a Hummer one day and was knocked down when it backed up in the exit lane from the gas station.

"Why didn't ya' walk out in front!" the woman screamed as she got out and hurried over.

"Yeah, why didn't I?" June muttered as the woman helped her up. Bruno had also mumbled something about not walking around behind a stopped vehicle, even with its motor off. "It could back up, or roll forward."

"Are you okay?" the mousey brown-haired woman asked, looking around for witnesses.

"What's your name?" June asked.

"It's –" she started to say, tucking her red shirt into loose gray slacks. "Are you hurt?" she asked.

June said, "Not really."

"So you don't need me," she snapped and turned to her Hummer.

The door slammed, and June saw the sign on it:

Melony K. Jelle Caterers

"Bye, Melony!" June called out.

The woman gave her a medusa glare, then peeled out onto the avenue and turned right, just missing a cat.

Angered, June took a deep breath and watched the Hummer accelerate – and stop. Cars braked and honked behind their fellow creature.

Melony K. Jelle popped her hood, scrambled out, padded around to peer inside, and gasped as she fell forward against the vehicle.

June blinked through a darkness in her eyes. "What is it?" she called out.

"Look!" Melony shouted, standing back. "Just look!"

June came out into the avenue and looked. The space under the hood was empty.

Melony squatted and peered under the vehicle. June looked to one side, suddenly imagining the engine scurrying away.

"Nothing there," Melony said, straightening up.

The line of vehicles behind the Hummer was getting longer, their honks more insistent. Melony was looking at her reproachfully.

"Beats me," June said, trying not to laugh.

"Well, I didn't leave it somewhere!" Melony shrieked, then stood up on the fender and leaned into the empty space. Her loose slacks, June noticed, hid fat.

"It's not here!" she echoed like Donald Duck from a deep well, then leaned out from under the hood and stepped down. A police cruiser pulled up on the sidewalk. Melony straightened her hair.

June walked away, glancing back. Melony was looking after her.

"Not even a scrape," June said to Bruno.

"She backed up on you?" he asked.

"I told you."

"Better than knocking you out into the road to get run over." She saw his face pale at what might have been.

"There wasn't much traffic," she said.

"Could have been. A bump might have thrown you out into traffic, with no chance against how they run up and down that way." He shuddered and sat down clumsily at the dinner table.

They took a deep breath together. She tried to smile, but he wasn't looking.

"So what did happen?" he asked, and began to tap on the table with his fingers.

"The woman's engine disappeared..."

"What?"

"I did it."

He looked at her with suspicion. "What?" he said more softly.

"She looked at me," June said, "as if she knew I did it."

"What are you saying?"

"There's a way to find out."

He gave her his skeptical look. "What way?" he asked, softening his gaze.

She said, "For my own peace of mind."

He asked, "Do you really think *you* did something?"

June said, "She *knew* I did it, as if in revenge for getting knocked down."

His kindlier look faded into impatience and exasperation. She had known him, and his one close friend, Felix, all her life, but she felt for a moment that she didn't know who any of them were, herself included. Maybe they were different people at different times, as if someone was always changing their biographies, so that they would never really know what their lives were all about.

"I wonder where they go," she said suddenly.

The idea was sinking into him. "Oh, you mean the engines. Maybe into a metaphysical hell for ill-conceived inventions."

He was humoring her. She tried to smile.

"Or maybe into a warehouse somewhere," he said, warming to the absurdity. "I know a few good warehouses down by the river," he added.

"We should go look for it," she said. "It might be nearby. I wonder *how* I do it – I mean if I do, of course."

He laughed as if in relief. "That's easy. You flip something... clean out of its space. Some kind of... topological twitch." He snapped his fingers expertly, something she had never been able to do. "You're an unconscious thief, in business with... someone." He grimaced. "That's got to be it."

She stared at him.

"Well – you wanted an explanation!"

She said, "You're mocking me."

"Okay – if you do it," he said happily, "then it happens, whether we can explain it or not – or your motives. But there have to be reasons. You have a motive. But there have to be reasons. Every time. There's always a reason. Gotta be reasons..." He seemed lost in himself, as if about to weep.

"There have to be?" she asked.

"Oh, not if it's magic," he said. "No explanation needed. You wish and it happens. Might as well call it magic."

"I'm only telling you what I saw, you dope."

"Part of the delusion," he said. "You're not here, but somewhere else, maybe asleep upstairs. Let's go see."

She sighed. He had always known how to get her into bed.

He said, "You can have anything you want in your mind, and think it real."

She glared at him.

"The mind," he said, "is a universe."

The engines were out there in some faraway desert, waiting for her under the stars. She closed her eyes and sat under a scimitar moon.

"But you didn't do anything," Bruno said from the starry sky, "and you can't. Not enough reasons for you to be able to do... such things. Not enough reasons. Can't ever be enough reasons for such a thing..."

"Then what happened?" she asked, opening her eyes to a bewildered middle-aged man about to panic, whose wife had lost her mind and was bewitching his. Maybe they should go upstairs, she told herself, and quiet the beast...

"Something else," he said, "with enough... reasons."

"Yes," she said, "... something else."

He turned his head away, and it seemed to her as if he had never existed.

SHE WENT OUT for her morning walk after Bruno went down to work at his basement drafting station, where he corrected the engineering designs of his younger boss, whose mother owned the company.

Bruno didn't mind; the boss needed reliable talent to leave him free to pursue his sexual interests, which left Bruno in control.

At the corner of the avenue she stopped and watched the beasts running toward the city, drifting through each other's dizzying leavings of fuel and tire odors. She closed her eyes for a moment, then saw a familiar white-haired head low over a driving wheel, floating through a red light on a license that should have been pulled long ago, in thrall to the machine and her lost youth.

A young man yakking on a phone wafted by, steering with his left hand. A head of red hair raised itself into view and looked out the passenger window.

Black lightning flashed in June's vision, and the car slowed. The driver put down his phone and pulled over. June watched him get out and stumble around to the hood, open it and stare inside, then back away and scratch his head.

His passenger sat up straight and looked bored, then hunched down again when she saw June.

"Engine's gone!" he shouted.

June walked over. He was sweating in his business suit as he pointed into the space she knew would be empty.

She saw it with him and knew that this could not be an illusion. Maybe they had all agreed, cops included, through some unconscious link, to blot out reality, she told herself.

"If it happens, it's natural," Bruno had said. "No magic. None. Not even a little bit."

"How could this happen!" the man shouted. He looked at June, his eyes pleading for her to tell him that it was not so. "Is it gone?" he asked. "Is it really... gone?"

His redheaded woman rolled down her window and bleated, "What is it, darling?"

"Twice more," she said to Bruno. "I'm not crazy."

"Stop," Bruno muttered, "just stop." He yawned in his recliner and added, "Felix is coming over with his old Jaguar," as if daring her to object, "so I don't have time for this."

She had also married his solitary friend. It was suddenly a strange life with Bruno. What would it have been like with Felix? He loved old cars more than lawyering. He was driving away from life.

The vintage Jag roared and belched dragon smoke as it rushed up the driveway in the sunny afternoon. They watched through their kitchen window as it stopped before the red matador's cape of the garage door. Her stomach tightened, and her vision skipped through a black beat.

"Hey!" Bruno shouted, hurrying out the back door.

Felix rose from the low seat, leaving the motor running as they embraced. The boys were going out for a noisy Saturday ride and a beer.

They shouted at each other as if she didn't exist. Old friends from their college days, they still held their shapes: one stocky, the other tall, although each had gained weight and grayed a little.

Unmarried, Felix kept to himself; mercifully, he had not brought his growling dog, the beloved Burke, whose nickname, 'Edmund,' was a joke for middle-brows who read history.

The men gestured, shouted and laughed, then noticed the Jag's silence.

Felix stared at the vehicle.

"I left it running," he said as he went to the hood and pulled it up. He looked inside and cried, "My engine's gone!"

June moved back from view as Bruno looked toward the kitchen window. Felix walked around his car and looked down the driveway, then came back and stuck his head under the hood. "It's not here!" he echoed, then stood up and burst into tears.

June turned away from the window as Bruno rushed in through the back door. "What do I tell him?" he shouted as June retreated to the broom closet, feeling sick.

"So now you believe me," she said.

They turned and looked out the window. Felix was at the wheel, trying to start the engine, then stopped and sat still.

"What do I tell him?" Bruno said, his voice breaking.

"If I had married him," June said softly, "the engine would still be there."

"What in hell are you saying?"

"We both love him, don't we," she said.

"You've got to stop this!" Bruno shouted.

"It's involuntary."

He glared at her, then grabbed her arm. "Calm down!"

"How?" she asked as he let go and they watched Felix, his hands clenching on the wheel, listening for the engine to start.

"Put it back," Bruno hissed at her, and for the first time in her life she felt hatred from him.

"Convinced?" June asked and closed her eyes.

Felix got out of the car, lowered his head, and walked down the driveway.

"He knows we know something he doesn't," June said.

Bruno rubbed his forehead. "No, he can't – it's some kind... of coincidence, has to be."

Black lightning closed her eyes and she felt tired from what she had done.

Bruno was a stranger staring at her when she opened them again.

THE JAG SAT in the driveway all the following week. Bruno went to work at the company office rather than to his basement and came home too late to talk to her.

On Sunday, Fox News reported a story about car engines being found in the Sahara south of Tunis.

"Yours, no doubt," Bruno said from his recliner, as the report went on to suggest that local bandits were reselling the engines.

"Maybe I can put them back," June said from her high-backed chair.

Bruno said, "Lots of stuff gets dumped all over the world." He sighed. "Whatever happened to my old Sony XBR monitor?"

"How can I bring them back," June said, "since I don't know how I do it?"

"*If* you're doing anything," Bruno said, then frowned. "You just want it to be you."

"I'm worried about Felix," she said.

"I called him," Bruno said. "He's in bad shape. He rebuilt that Jag piece by piece. He can't help feeling that bringing it here had something to do with what happened but he won't say so. Maybe hopes it's a gag of some kind, which we'll let him in on... soon. His birthday's in a few days."

"And what did you say?" she asked.

"What do I know?"

"He knows," she said, "somehow he knows."

Bruno shouted, "But you just can't be the cause of all this!"

"I don't know how it happens, except that I feel angry at what we breathe, at the congestion and endless accidents."

"Stop rationalizing."

"We should go over and see Felix."

"And what – console him?"

"Maybe we should buy him a new engine," she said.

"Too expensive – and you'd make that one disappear too."

"So you do think it's me," she said.

Bruno brought his recliner up. "Why be so half-hearted about it? Go all the way and abolish internal combustion."

She asked, "What about that news story?"

"Well, the engines do have serial numbers... but you still couldn't be sure it was the ones you... sent away, without records. They might lock you up just to see if it stops." He looked at her with tears in his eyes, as if sure that they had both lost their minds.

June cried, "I'm afraid."

"Stop yourself, then."

"How?"

"Just stop!" he shouted, and she saw him rushing toward fear and hatred of her. What else could she... remove? What was she? She should have been a writer, as she had dreamed of in college, who gets away with anything on the page. Infinite possibilities in the conditionals of wordy-worlds on pages, but beware the conditional subjunctive escaping into the world... could she wish the world away? If she absented herself, the effect would be the same. The world always comes to an end for the dead...

Bruno stood up from his chair and glared at her. She felt dizzy, fearing what she could do to him if he became violent.

"I read a scary story," he said, "about people losing their brains all over the streets... and it was a woman plucking them out."

"I won't," she said, afraid to blink.

Bruno said, "Women are more censorious... all that femme fatale stuff inside them says they gotta sift through the males somehow..."

"What are you saying?" she cried.

"You can't help yourself," he said. "You'll do it to me in your sleep."

"No!" she cried. "What do you think I am?"

He stared at her, accusing her, challenging her, or pleading for mercy. Who was he, anyway? Who was she, and what were they together?

FRESH GARBAGE GRACED her lawn, front, side, on the street, inside the hedge and its branches. A week before she had filled a bag with fast food wrappers, cups half-filled with drink and ice, partly eaten food, opened envelopes with discarded dunning letters inside, year-old wedding invitations, illegible post-it notes, baby photos, a package of celery, and a beer bottle with some kind of liquid in it. None of it could be blamed on animals scattering garbage cans, or on breezes; human hands had thrown the stuff.

June sat on her front porch and waited. A red convertible drifted by, with two young couples inside, and she was sure that it had to be a repeat offender.

Objects went ballistic over the hedge.

June closed her eyes, breathed deeply, and black lightning flashed in the pink of her eyelids.

The car slowed and halted well before the corner stop sign. The driver went out and looked under the hood...

"Make sure," she said. "You told me."

He went back into the house.

She got up from her lawn chair and walked out across the yard. The driver was on his cell phone as he looked repeatedly under the hood of the car.

June called out from behind the hedge, "Pick up your crap from my yard!"

The two couples stared at her as if she had materialized out of nowhere.

"Get it all," she added, "whether it's yours or not."

The driver slammed the hood shut and stared at her, then went around to the side of the car, reached into the back seat for a plastic bag, and came over to the hedge.

"Here's some more," he said, tossing the bag over the hedge.

"You should improve your diet," June said, watching the cartons, wrappers and soft drink cups spill out of the bag at her feet. The blond, blue-eyed god was smiling at her as he tossed another bag over.

June went back to her chair and sat down. The couple in the back seat of the car was grinning at her. The girl in the passenger seat looked away.

The young man brought another paper bag to the hedge and now began tossing individual items – paper cups, a green plastic fork, and a few gnawed spareribs. The couple and the girl in the car opened their doors and got out, looking warily toward June.

Bruno came out of the house and stood watching as the young man heaved the whole bag over the hedge. It landed and broke apart on the grass, scattering its contents.

June stood up.

Bruno grabbed her arm, but the blond young man was gone.

June felt her strength rise up, and the red convertible disappeared. The boy turned around as the girl screamed. Then they fled.

June fell back into her chair.

Bruno looked down at her and said calmly, "Sooner or later you'll do it to me, in your sleep!"

She shook her head in denial, then looked at the street as if expecting the red convertible to reappear. "Never," she whispered.

He asked, "Would I be sent inside a mountain somewhere? Maybe in pieces! Ripped apart? Do you have any idea?"

She gazed up at him, feeling his fear of her.

ON MONDAY MORNING June looked out the kitchen window and saw Felix marching wearily up the hill toward their driveway, leaning forward far enough to look like he might fall over on his face.

Winded, he finally came to his Jaguar but did not look under the hood; coming around, he released the brake, gave the car a push, and let it roll back toward the road. He got in quickly and waited until he was out in the street, with enough momentum to turn. He stopped after the turn, got out, pushed and got back in, and she saw that he would be able to coast the mile downhill to his house.

The Jaguar rolled away silently. She took deep breaths and listened, then went into the living room and sat down on the sofa. She would not go to her accounting job today.

The phone rang and took the message.

"June, Bruno!" Felix cried. "My mind is gone," and she wondered if she loved him.

"You've turned it invisible," Felix babbled on happily. "You're playing a joke on me – right? Hypnosis, or something going around... I guess."

"Something going around..." June muttered to herself as the message cut off.

She sat back, imagining an assembly line of disappearing engines. How many would it take before the companies stopped making them?

She had felt sorry for Felix pushing his Jaguar down the driveway; but there had been no delusions, not with Felix or the cars on Delaware Avenue, nor with the look in Melony K. Jelle's face.

She could stand on the corner of Delaware and Whistler and snatch engines one after another, willing them gone with no one the wiser.

An endless task.

No one would know as she plucked. Bruno had killed wasps nesting above their patio, one at a time with a fly swatter, until the swarm got the message and stopped building under the overhang. Would the automotives stop making rolling sewers if she plucked enough of them? Unlikely. They would feel threatened and know that it was all happening deliberately, that someone had a plan... that it wasn't all fools out there... that there was intelligence behind what was happening, but no one would find her. Bruno and Felix might inform on her, but no one would believe them...

Her life would be a sacrifice to the future, until change bubbled up from below; that was what terrorists knew, especially the ones who died in the act, inspiring actions from below even as they damned themselves and left it to milder souls to bring the changes. "Go out there," President Roosevelt had said to a petitioning party, "and make me do it." Barack Obama had said as much during his campaign, but those who had risen to his call had been left behind with their hopes.

Somewhere, elsewhen, it had all come right.

Sacrifices? Everything carried a cost. Every effort was a sacrifice...

Dismay and a vision of doom filled her, as she knew that the only alternative was to do nothing, to stop herself. Could she? For evil to prevail, the preachers prattled, it only needed good people to do nothing...

But could she stop? Could she simply command herself to stop and live with her unused ability? It would wait, always ready to strike, and she would never be sure when the urge would take hold of her...

"I'm sorry," June had once said to her mother, "that I'm not the daughter you wished."

The hatred June had felt then, and still felt, frightened her. She might hurt people in her sleep; wishes waited in her fears...

The end of engines was only a start. Humankind had failed at foresight; large power structures lived on the misery of the many; only insurrections and disasters had ever worn away at the oppression of the topmost, who reserved the right of violence for themselves and retreated only when overwhelmed from below.

Retreated, only to return – because they were all us.

Structures true to human yearning for justice had never arisen without upheavals, but had failed to completely sweep away the vampirism and vendetta that were the way of the world, because top and bottom were the same when turned over...

Yet the people yearned for superheroes, dreaming of them in films and comic books, but, like the disbelieved Cassandra, only villains were permitted to tell the truth...

She had to stop herself, or live with the horrors she would inflict. Thinning out the herds of cars would bring deaths through a lack of transport...

Stop!

Bruno wanted her death, but not by his hand.

"You're not needed," he had said. "The internal combustion engine will die on its own."

"They said that about slavery," she replied, "but still had to patrol the seas. And slavery is still here, disguised. Read the UN reports. Look at wage slavery, one-sided contracts, the slave brothels of the Middle East, suppression of collective bargaining, private kidnapping and blackmail. People keep at it. We'll be dropping in the streets before they clear the air."

He gazed at her with dismay.

"All this talk," she had continued, "about not bemoaning and doing something constructive, fails to confront... what's inside us... the old dark stuff, a crooked stick that can't make itself straight."

"Then it's hopeless?" he asked.

"If it's that deep stuff we have to confront," she said, "then talk won't help – and what action will? Exhortation? Laws? Police?"

"Vicious circles, yes, but don't sell bemoaning short."

The silence stood between them, hardening into a wall. "I'm nothing!" she cried. "All the terrorists in the world are nothing to all the official killing, the economic violence that no one ever stops."

He had gazed at her and said, "I've lost you."

"And I've lost everything."

"You've killed at least one person. Where did you send that boy?"

"I... lost my temper," she said. "But that's nothing compared to the powerful, who are dedicated to the wholesale destruction of human flesh and make us pay them to do it."

"But your wretched... miracles won't change a thing!"

Life is lived forward but understood backwards. Religious and secular foresight's pleading exhortations of hellfire and earthly damnation were not strong enough. Where is goodness, where are its armies? When did it ever add up and accumulate?

She got up, went upstairs to the bedroom and lay down in darkness.

SHE WOKE UP, and the lamp was not in her reach, and no bed beneath her. Her eyes would not open, but they were open. She called out to Bruno, then dropped back into sleep, hoping that his hand would find her and pull her out into the morning, out of herself, back into what she might have once been...

She breathed with increasing difficulty. Darkness flowed into her and froze, and there was no axe with which to break it...

A BREEZE, WARM and dry, crept into the bedroom through the screened window. A trolley belled in the beyond on its run from the suburbs into the center of the city. A whistle shot out from the bullet train into New York City.

She got up and sat by the window in time to see the Chicago airship on its stately way. Bicycles tinkled on Delaware Avenue, their baskets carrying fresh-baked goods home for breakfast.

But she was only a passerby. The world from which she had again awakened was only one of an endless series whose fates she shared and suffered.

Poisons bled between worlds.

Successes were as numberless as failures.

One realm's delusion was another's reality, one delusion another's nightmare, one happiness another's illusion.

What waited beyond her next sleep?

Hopes hid in the horrors and terrors in the hopes – infinite runs of every kind, never helped, never undone, each pressing ahead in its own way, threads spinning out into nowhere, unwinding, never to wind again...

As many instances of her own dark-eyed skulls drank the starlight as wore flesh and breathed this clean morning air. Unable or unwilling to choose a world, a gambling malignity had summoned them all to struggle all at once with each other for life.

A standing, incomprehensible infinity.

Never to be singular against the death of all others.

But it was a beautiful morning outside her window.

No, no, please, no more of pained hope, she prayed to the nameless darkness...

SHE OPENED HER eyes. Stars waited in a deep blue sky as she breathed desert air. She had always been here, waiting to emerge from that other, now fading life...

Too many lifetimes insisted in her memory.

She sat up in the familiar red convertible and grasped the steering wheel. Engines stood around her. Dry, wind-cleansed, never to turn over again, dead lumpy robots listened to the desert's night silence as if to their own lost whirring...

How many had she sent here, she asked as she looked around in the brightening dawn. Too many to count in her continuous effort, across months, even years of learned exertion. To return them out of some misbegotten mercy would take as long. Her pitying of Felix had given him back his engine, but there was no pity in her now, not for others or for herself...

The red convertible was comfortable.

Throat dry, body weak and fevered, she knew that she had been here a long time. She held up her hand and saw a dry skin-stretched claw, blue-veined and shrunken, which no amount of moisture would revive.

The metal of the engines glittered around her. Sullen in the coming light, they knew her, waiting to exact from her the price of their defeat...

They had killed themselves, she told herself, by killing so many of us...

She cried out as she glimpsed her raw distorted face in the rearview mirror. She might drive away from here; the engine, a careful arrangement of parts and physical principles, would produce its sustained series of explosions and carry her out of exile. She would drive to an oasis of tents and satellite uplinks drinking data from the sky...

She turned the ignition key against an empty gas gauge.

Rust, corrosion, and thirst were slow in this place. A million years from now her bleached skeleton would still be here, ancient under the stoic stars, cave-eyes blind to all light, her white skull's fleshless emptiness filling with the flowing perfection of sand grains.

Bruno and Felix had long ago guessed, of course, but no one had believed them...

Something had imagined her, and should have done much better. Where was she now? Was the whole Earth a wasteland of junk? *Now* was a million years past the nows into which she had been whelped; born was too decent a word; spit out by nature into a useless awareness...

It became too hot to sit in the car. She opened the door and stepped out on the sand, then crawled into the shade under the car and lay there thirsting the whole day, caged by her armied thoughts...

Toward evening, she noticed some blond hair fluttering on a human skull that was partly covered by the sand near the front fender. The evening breeze had uncovered the dried remains of the boy. She looked away.

Shivering as night came again, she crawled out from under, over to one of the orphaned engines, and embraced the metal block's stored solar heat, then closed her eyes and lay back on the turning bed of earth.

No, not here, she told herself, not yet...

*   *   *

SHE LOOKED OUT over the parking lot and marshalled her strength. The waiting beasts stared at her as if ignoring the exertion she would hurl against them. Disaster was the midwife of progress, she told herself, but better mine than the ones waiting to overtake us.

She reached out through the chainlink fence, feeling her will wielding the invisible force, its strangeness embracing her.

There was no fiery chain reaction, no bomb touching off gas tanks. She simply gutted the beasts in silent sweeps, with nothing to see except a woman peering through a fence and later walking away. Offering up these engines was not the sacrifice of wars to imagined betterments...

The sudden emptiness within her, after each reach, opened into a stillness greater than any fire that might have consumed the keyless mechanisms as they stood helpless and guiltless without their masters in a vast parking lot of victims.

People came to start their cars, and left. Once in a while a homeless person got out, his night's need fulfilled.

She went to ever larger lots, gaining strength, half-hoping that the sheer volume would defeat her. Rains washed her sometimes, and the wind dried her. She came and went unnoticed as the sullen engines slipped away to the dry starry place where she would one day join them.

DARK HARVEST

CAT SPARKS

Cat Sparks is fiction editor of Cosmos Magazine *and former manager of Agog! Press. She's won seventeen Aurealis and Ditmar awards for writing, editing and art. Over sixty of her short stories have been published since 2000. She is currently engaged in a PhD on young adult post-disaster literature. Her collection* The Bride Price *was published by Ticonderoga Publications in 2013. Her first novel,* Blue Lotus, *is finally nearing completion.*

"GET THAT MACHINE offa me," screamed Dev. "I'm dying. I'm bleeding out!"

"You are not bleeding out," stated Jayce. "Your foot's back on already."

When Dev glanced down he started screaming louder. Loud enough to drown out the relentless cicada hum.

"Someone shut off that contraption," Jayce shouted over the top of both the screaming and the chorus of native bugs.

Commander Vassallo pulled his blaster, aimed it squarely at where she pointed – the Surgeco-460's forest of operating arms, many of which were snapping and stabbing wildly.

"Those things are worth a –"

Vassallo fired. Metal splinters rained against the portable generator's casing.

"Fortune," finished Stolk, coughing as acrid smoke fouled up the air.

"It's a goddamn goat rodeo in here," said Vassallo. "Those sack-o-shit 460s were supposed to have been decommissioned, on account of that... What was that trouble that went down on Memphis?"

Satordi snapped his fingers three times in a row. "Yeah, I remember something..."

"Was a couple of procedures gone totally tits up," said Jayce. "Literally. Was supposed to be a recall. Guess they missed a few."

Vassallo grunted. "More ExConn cheaparsery. Spending big everywhere but on the weedfront where it's needed."

Dev's screaming was getting louder.

"Jayce, give him a shot of something. Gotta be something stronger in the kit."

"I'm on it."

Troy straddled Dev to hold him down. Blood smeared over everything, making it hard for Jayce to get a grip. She wedged the hypo between her teeth, growled something unintelligible. Troy shifted his weight, pushed down on the patient's forearms.

Dev kept up his thrashing and screaming. Jayce spat the hypo into her hand, sat back on her haunches. Frowned. "Don't think its pain that's got him spooked."

The others crowded around to see for themselves. There was no fresh bleeding. The wound was sealed, a thick pink ridge, only the foot had been sewn on back to front.

She shook her head. "How do you even *make* a mistake like that?"

"Shit for mechabrains," said Vassallo, taking another pot shot at the robot, even though its arms had stopped flailing and it was listing severely to one side.

"Tangier, better call for MedEVac."

"What for? Nobody came when the weed busted containment. Nobody came to take the body bags."

"Just call it in."

"What about the rest of us? When are we getting off this stinking rock?"

"New orders," said Sergeant Vassallo, which was a lie. There'd been no messages from Platform, neither through the comms, nor private wire.

Dev, who had fallen silent as they all gawked at his foot, started his screaming up again in earnest. "Don't evac me to Orbital. You know what they say goes on up there. Leave the foot. I'm getting used to it. Hell, I'm used to it already!"

Vassallo put his gun away, satisfied that the 460 had been rendered smouldering scrap. "Can't have you fighting with your foot on back to front." He pulled his tobacco from his pocket, rolled a cigarette and jammed it between Dev's quivering lips. "Rest up for a few days, mercenary. You ain't missing anything down here."

He lit the smoke with his battered gold Zippo. The one he'd souvenired from some ConnEX bigwig's corpse. Dev inhaled, pinched the cigarette between trembling fingers. "You know what they say about Orbital, Sarge. How the wounded come back different."

"Course you'll be different, buddy – you'll have your foot sewn on the right way round!" He slapped Troy on the shoulder and pointed to the ring of whitewashed stones they'd arranged themselves after insurgents took out most of the landing platform.

Jayce and Troy heaved Dev onto a stretcher, then picked up either end.

"Those rumours are bullshit," Vassallo shouted after them. "Orbital only experiments on captured Tanks!"

Dev kept up his screaming as the other two placed the stretcher in the ring then ducked back under cover. So far there had been no captured Tanks. Just faceless shelling and the sense that they were being watched. By something.

All were surprised when a dark speck hovering like a vulture turned out to be a MedEVac copter. It swooped down close, extended pincers snapping, grabbed poor screaming Dev, and shot back up into the grey and brooding sky.

"Hey – come back you motherfucker! What about the rest of us? You can't leave us stranded here!"

Tangier kept on shouting. Vassallo stared across the smoking battlefield. Some of the all-terrain vehicles were still on fire. Some of the walls still crumbling of their own accord.

The rhythm of the copter blades was soothing. The planet had looked uninhabitable from the air. Litany: mostly useless rock, not enough water anywhere but the equator. That was where Reaper dug itself in deep; Executive Connect's pharmaceutical division. Protecting patented weed had seemed easy enough, only the weed didn't stay in the neat, dark strips where it was seeded. That weed had taken on a life of its own, clogging the air with stinking spores, twisting and poking into every nook and cranny. Infecting their machinery, jamming up its gears. Inducing nightmares, according to Satordi. And then, when the taste of the stuff had soured their water, their food and even their tobacco, bombardment started and jacks started getting killed. Rumours were whispered of similar scenarios on more than a dozen ExConn-seeded worlds. Of vat-grown terrorist insurgents: enormous, fit and organised. Resistant to high calibre persuasive interrogation. Self-terminating at their own convenience. Bloody hard to kill at anyone else's.

"Lotta DNA spilled on this damn rock," Satordi mumbled, fiddling with his gun. That man was always fiddling with something.

Sergeant Vassallo grunted in response. They stood and watched until the MedEVac copter and its wriggling, screaming cargo were reduced to the size and shape of a migrating bird.

WHAT VASSALLO NOW recognised as foreboding had hit when they first glimpsed Litany from space. That dark belt squeezing the equator. Transplanted, mutagenic pharmacrops with a multi-syllabic name. Referred to as 'the weed' by anyone who worked with it.

His gut warned there was something tainted about this dreary rock. Rumours of the weed mutating in unexpected ways. That its market value had already dropped by half. That the real reason the jacks were there was to gather intel on the Tanks. Terrorist insurgents that, six weeks ago, had not been firing at them.

No matter. Vassallo was on a mission of his own, tipped off by rumours of something worth big money. Something the pre-ExConn colonials left behind. Something all he had to do was find.

But after six weeks of intermittent rain, mud, blood and chasing shadows, Vassallo concluded that Litany had no secrets. There was nothing here worth anything: no rare mineral deposits, no seam of carbonado fancies. No weapons other than the Tanks themselves – if they were real.

Half their complement was already dead, leaving him stuck with dregs he couldn't trust. Executive Connect's Dark Harvest fireteams: cheaper than drones once they'd signed away their rights. Jacks like all jacks everywhere: mostly men, but not all. Mostly folks with bad credit ratings, reputations, attitudes or issues. Some were obvious recipients of bad advice. Smart enough to survive three weeks of basic. Dumb enough to enlist with ExConn in the first place, thinking they'd be getting a fresh new start. Most were running from something: someone they killed or failed to kill. More often than not their own demonic shadows.

At least two were serving community service placements. Satordi gave off a muted rapist vibe. Jayce was clocking hours towards her own command. Stolk, he might have considered an embedded corporate spy, only the kid seemed way too bright-eyed-dumb for that. A real know-it-all.

The rest were refugees from high unemployment stats, folks who figured shooting industrial terrorists was better than starving in some shanty ghetto.

"Tank breaking cover, dead ahead at twelve o'clock." Satordi grinned like a crazy man as what looked like a giant, semi-indestructible, vat-grown hairless ape stepped out into the open. The rest of them primed their weapons, expecting the thing to charge at the very least. But the creature stood its ground, scoping out their ragged camp, head cocked to one side like it was listening.

"Where's its weapon?" said Jayce.

The Tank moved.

"Fire!"

Satordi and Tangier emptied several clips into it, then whooped and hollered like it was the end of someone's war. The others joined in. Not Vassallo. Vassallo was waiting for the punchline. The follow up. The follow through. The point.

"This is where it gets interesting," said Stolk. "If I'm right – and I'm pretty sure."

Vassallo frowned. "What gets interesting?"

"They'll come," said Stolk. "The nuns. They always do."

"Nuns you say?"

"Wait... Wait... no. Yes! They're coming now..."

Two hours past Dev's evacuation and the subsequent blasting of the creature in the ruins, the bored jacks glanced to where Stolk was indicating, half expecting a drone, although they'd seen no drones on Litany thus far. Relentless ExConn blanket bombing had reduced the former settler capital Desiderata to rubble. Dark Harvest was tasked with mopping up the evidence.

Talk of tank-grown supersoldiers with impenetrable skin and embedded neuroprocessors had seemed ridiculous back on Platform, slouching around and waiting for the drop. Blurred images siphoned from patched perimeter feeds. Half man, half beast, all meat-and-gristle. But there'd been no trace of beast in what they'd killed. Just a man. A big one, yes, but still. Blasted to pieces that needed to be retrieved, only now Stolk was making them wait for no good reason.

Jayce rolled her eyes. "There's nothing out there, dickwad. Just our kill and busted up old ruins."

"I'm telling you..." said Stolk, his voice trailing off so that all they could hear was their own boots pressing into gravel. "When there's a body – or parts thereof – that's when the nuns turn up. Watch!"

Sergeant Vassallo spat loudly on the ground, then looked towards the eastern aspect where smoke from yesterday's incendiaries was still emitting thick, choking gouts of sickly yellow. "Smells like concentrated piss," he said, nose twitching involuntarily. "I hate this fucking weed-infested strip."

The whole fireteam, Vassallo aside, stared intently at the blasted patch of ground where Stolk was pointing. "Wait for it," said Stolk. They waited.

A gentle tinkling carried on the breeze. A smudge of colour that for a moment might have been flame, but wasn't. It was cloth. Dirty orange-brown and it was moving.

"Told you," said Stolk, looking very pleased with himself. "I've seen them before – exactly the same, back when I was stationed on Agnes-Blanche."

"You were never on Aggie-Blanche," said Troy, a straw-haired teen from the Agricantus ghetto.

"Two damn winters full of it," Stolk answered. "Same Pharm-A paychecks. Flushing out mutant freaks – and *them*," he emphasised, pointing at what could now be seen clearly through the dregs of dissipating smoke. "Turning up in the aftermath of every kill."

Six figures, easy to see as their robes cut a stark contrast against grey stone rubble and smoking craters.

"Looters," said Satordi, his slack jaw working on a worn out wad of gum.

Even Vassallo was staring now as the small forms – women, by the looks of them – picked their way in single file across the ground.

"Not looters," said Stolk, in a learned tone, standing up straight, tucking hands into his pockets once he realised he had everyone's attention.

"Spies then? From one of ExConn's Pharm-A rivals?"

"Nope. Not spies." Stolk lowered his voice, as if sharing some great secret. "Nuns, like I keep telling you. From some way back religious cult. Used to know the name but I've forgotten."

"What the fuck is a nun?" said Troy.

"Like the Sisterhood of Damnation and Salvation – didn't you do school?" said Jayce.

Troy shrugged. Vassallo pulled out a field glass and trained it on the six. "Don't like the look of them. Could be insurgents. Could be in disguise."

"They're holy women," said Stolk. "Watch what happens next."

They watched, Satordi slapping the safety off his CheyTac660. Just in case. The others heard the sound but didn't copy.

The corpse wasn't easy to spot. Grey stone dust covered everything that wasn't already shrouded in lingering smoke. The nuns, identical at a distance, sifted rubble.

"Gross," said Troy.

None of the others spoke. The kid was green. He hadn't seen anything yet.

With great gentleness, the nuns placed salvaged body parts together, then continued to search.

"Told you they was looters."

"Will you shut the fuck up and watch!"

"Looking for wood," said Vassallo. "Not much to burn out here." He took a crushed, hand-rolled cigarette from his top pocket, then pinched it back into shape. Placed it on his lower lip, patted his trouser pockets until he found what he was after.

"Blessing the corpse?" said Satordi uncertainly.

"Nope," Vassallo lit the tip of the cigarette, drew on it hard, held the smoke deep in his lungs.

"Cremating it." Smoke blasted out of both nostrils, then dissipated quickly without trace. "Right, Stolk?"

"Right!" Stolk liked it when Vassallo agreed with him. It didn't happen often. "It's a spiritual thing. Takes 'em hours. They sit there chanting till it's done, then they muck about in the ashes for souvenirs."

"Souvenirs?"

"To them, the Tanks are holy. Diamonds and pearls are supposed to form in dead Tank ashes."

"Bullshit," said Satordi, aiming his weapon, squinting through the scope.

Sure enough, yellow-orange flames were soon licking up from the base of the rough, triangular arrangement of wood, mostly salvaged from the splintered doorway of a building no longer standing. The nuns sat in a circle around the pyre, palms pressed together, shaven heads bowed deep in prayer.

"This is their holy war. Gotta try and see it from their perspective."

Satordi wasn't interested in other people's perspectives. He kept his finger on the trigger, right eye glued to the scope, still trained on the group of chanting, praying nuns.

"They might be enemy soldiers," said Troy. "How are we supposed to know what they is or ain't?"

"In disguise," added Satordi.

"What kind of a disguise is orange bed sheets?"

"You could fit a Luger under there. Easy peasy."

Vassallo shook his head.

"You saw that Tank up close before you air conditioned it. Built like a brick shithouse. Biceps like cypress roots. Those skinny little runts aren't soldiers – no matter what ordnance they might be packing under bed sheets."

"They might be gathering intel. Reporting back to those monster tank-grown motherfuckers."

"Stolk knows all about it," said Jayce. "Ask him anything. He's a regular walking Wiki."

Stolk looked up. He'd been taking notes. "I'm just interested is all. Don't you ever get interested?"

Satordi snorted. "I'm interested in lots of things. Like when we're busting off this lousy rock."

He didn't look at Vassallo when he spoke, but they'd all been thinking it. Too many had died. Even by the pathetic standards of ExConn's contractual obligations, Dark Harvest should have been evacuated by now.

"We stay until the job gets done," said Vassallo grimly.

"And what job might that be?" said Satordi. "If the weed's no good, it means we won't get paid."

Nobody said anything after that. A cold front started moving in, with brooding skies to match. The nuns kept chanting, regardless, even when drizzle forced the jacks back under cover of ripped tarpaulin.

"What kind of religion makes you pray out in the rain?"

"An old one," muttered Jayce. "Stolk reckons they pray to some fat old god."

Stolk nodded. "Like I said, they're raking for holy relics. They stay put, even under fire."

"Diamonds," said Jayce, grinning. "That sounds interesting."

Satordi's eyes widened.

"No no... not real diamonds. They call it ringsel. Supposed to be pearls of concentrated purity. Or something."

"So not real diamonds," said Satordi, shifting his weight.

Jayce pulled a face.

Stolk raised his glass to see what the nuns were doing. "I got up real close to some of them, back on Aggie-Blanche. At first you think they're all the same, like sisters, only they aren't. Not if you look careful. You can make out the different –"

"Come on, let's get moving. We got no time for this." Vassallo flicked the butt of his cigarette against a low stone wall – or what was left of it.

"I want to stay and watch," said Stolk.

Vassallo sniffed. "Fine, mercenary, suit yourself."

"DON'T LIKE THE look of that sky," said Vassallo. He sniffed deeply, like a dog. "I don't like the smell of it."

"Smoke from the bombardment."

"Something else."

They all looked where he was looking, as if something might be gleaned from moody grey-on-grey. Stolk was the only one not checking out the weather front. His glass was aimed in the opposite direction where the nuns were still hard at their chant and prayer.

"How come you know everything, Stolk?" said Satordi. "You some sort of archaeologist?"

Stolk lowered the glass. "No, man. Read a lot is all. It's kind of interesting, don't you reckon?"

"No. I don't reckon. Not if the diamond thing is bullshit. What I reckon is we ought shoot them."

"Sociologist is what you mean," said Jayce. "Archaeologists do ruins. Not much architecture going down here before ExConn. Not unless you count those cinderblock bunkers."

"Well, actually..."

"Oh, so you an expert on Hargreave System colonial architecture too now are you, Stolk?"

Stolk's face reddened further.

"Anything coming through on the link?"

Tangier tapped his earpiece, then shook his head.

"Those nuns of yours – they got a temple?"

Stolk shrugged. "Probably targeted in the first wave of blanket bombings. Just in case, you know, they were harbouring insurgents."

"Better to be safe than sorry," said Jayce.

"Better," agreed Satordi, polishing his gun.

"I CAN'T BELIEVE they're still sitting out there." Satordi paced back and forth, shiny pulse rifle slung over his shoulder. "Any word from Orbital? Did Dev get up there safe?"

"Nothing for hours," said Tangier. "Some kind of interference."

"So what about the rest of us – when do we get lifted off?"

Vassallo stared out over the battlefield at the grim and dirty sky, at the thunderhead sweeping in across the plain like it knew what it was doing. Which might have been the truth of it. They'd all heard the chit chat before making planetfall. Rumours easy to ignore before the service robots started acting funny, the weed got moving of its own accord and the Tanks turned out to be real as advertised.

Some said the terrorist insurgents of Litany did more than grow their soldiery in vats. That they brewed their weapons of mass destruction by harnessing elemental forces. Hot rocks blasting randomly from natural subterranean foundries. Base Four dissolved in a boiling mess of lava, despite the geological survey claiming it safe. Despite them all being kitted up and standing by. Why wouldn't they harness the very wind itself? Or the air or the darkness or whatever other magic those godless squatters conjured into being.

The wind whipped up, snatching roughly at the tents and tarps, scattering half-filled plastic canisters and other sundry items like dead leaves.

"I don't like this," said Vassallo.

Stolk was already on his feet, dusting ashy grit from his trousers, shooting a final glance out at the nuns. The wind slammed into them, knocked a couple sprawling. They didn't flinch, just stood up again, backs ramrod straight, continued with their chant like nothing happened.

The thunderhead kept its distance. The rain it heralded did not. It pummelled down in violent blasting sheets.

Stolk kept watch on the nuns through a rent in the tarpaulin. By then the rain had slackened off and steam rose off the streets in great white gouts.

"I don't trust 'em, Sarge," said Satordi, nudging Stolk aside, ripping the tarpaulin hole till it was big enough to see through without stooping. "They're still at it. Up to something. Planning an attack. Gathering intel, laying charges. I dunno but I can smell it. I know a pack of terrorists when I see one."

"You've never seen a terrorist, son," said Vassallo. "Nobody has. Not out this far. Just done over colonists, contract strip-miners, smugglers, religious whack jobs fleeing persecution in the Belt."

"Those tank-bred insurgents..."

"No such thing. Just freedom fighters with differing definitions of the word and the accompanying states of mind."

Satordi opened his mouth but he didn't get the chance to argue. An explosion rattled the tentpoles, their already battered stacks of supposedly sensitive equipment and Vassallo's dental implants.

"What the –"

"Too close for comfort." Tangier fired up the seismograph and slammed it down on the stack of charts covering their one and only portable table.

"That thunderhead, Commander – it's full of acid and it's coming right at us."

"What the holy fuck?"

They both looked to the tarpaulin, already ripped and completely useless.

"Call for evac..."

"Not enough time. No time for anything. Gotta pick up and run."

"The ruins?"

"Nothing we can trust. But the holo points to a series of caves sunk right into the mountain."

"Fall out! Take whatever you can carry!"

They shouldered packs and grabbed free-standing items. Water, half a case of MREs, blankets and lanterns. Guns and ammo. The all-purpose, all weather beacon that was most certainly not designed with acid storms in mind. As they stumbled across the rock-and-brick strewn landscape – growing darker and colder by the minute – Stolk stopped and turned to see if he could catch sight of the nuns. They'd gone – and he was very glad of that.

THE CAVE WAS dark and smelled of hairy animal.

Tangier slapped the beacon upside, checked the power cell was ticking over.

"Careful with that fucking thing. It's all that stands between us and an airlift." Satordi's pacing was putting them all on edge. "Why aren't they answering? Why didn't they lift us off three hours ago?"

"Dark Harvest fireteam broadcasting from Litany. DMS lat 1° 21' 7.4988" N. DMS long 103° 49' 11.4096" E. Can you hear me? Over."

"Ain't nobody gonna be hearing you over that. Air's thick with acid. We're probably breathing ourselves to death." When Troy blew his nose, the wad of gauze filled with watery pink.

"Step back from the entrance, you moron!"

Troy edged back. Stolk held his ground. There wasn't much to see out there. The storm had blanketed what little light the sky was clinging to.

"This is Dark Harvest fireteam broadcasting from Litany. DMS lat 1° 21' 7.4988" N. DMS long 103° 49' 11.4096" E. We request immediate evac. Over."

Stolk couldn't get those nuns out of his mind. Were they out there cowering in the ruins, skin pockmarked and smoking? Or was an acid-bearing thunderhead as normal as sun showers on this crazy rock?

"See anything?" he asked Satordi.

The big man grunted his response, which might have been a yes or no or maybe. Moments later, he staggered backwards, grappled for his sidearm, was knocked to the ground as a Tank burst into the cave.

Up close, a supersoldier, easily twice the size of Vassallo – and he was a bigger man than most. The thing – because it was a thing – with rivulets of acid water running harmlessly in channels down its limbs, kicked Stolk aside and strode in further, giant ham hands curling into fists.

Jacks who'd been resting struggled to their feet, slipping safeties, locking and loading, slapping themselves to responsive wakefulness. Jayce fired. Too slow. The monster smacked the blaster from her hands before picking her up and throwing her against the wall. Solid muscle. Lightning fast. Others fired, bullets going everywhere, Vassallo screaming *hold your fire*. Too late. The fuggy cave air stung with bullets. The thing went down in a hail of rapid fire. Eventually. Once on the ground it did not still until Vassallo shot it right between the eyes.

"Orbital's gonna have a fit – you know how much a Tank brain must be worth?"

"They can bill me," said Vassallo, crouching down, poking the corpse a couple of times before searching for a pulse.

"Synthetic?"

"Not so far as I can tell."

"Indigenous?"

"Not likely." He gave the corpse a solid kick.

"So who – or what – the hell is it?"

Vassallo sniffed. "It kinda depends on who you ask. There are rumours that these soldiers might be souped up squatters."

The others could tell from his voice that he didn't believe that.

"What's the unofficial line?" said Stolk.

Vasallo stared down at the corpse. "That weed we're supposed to be protecting? Word is they didn't graft it in from EverGreen. Word is ExConn poached it from the early wave of settlers before driving them off and running for the hills. Back in the day, before this sector got its Pharm-A annexation. Before the razor blight of '99. Archive retrieval gets a little hazy past that point."

"What the hell kind of weed is it anyway? What makes it so valuable?"

Vassallo shrugged. "Supposed to be an Ur-strain. Brazilian something-or-other, reconstituted from frozen seed bank stock. Antibiotic properties. It'll clap out in a couple years like they all do."

"Must be worth big bucks though – now."

"Yeah," he nodded, fumbling for his dwindling tobacco stash. "Now."

*　　*　　*

"So lemme get this straight," said Troy, looking younger than ever in the murky half-light of the cave. "The squatters of Litany are really a bunch of pre-colonials who reckon ExConn boosted their weed? They ran for the hills when the blanket bombing started, then built a bunch of Tanks to come and fight us?"

"Maybe. Hard to say without clapping eyes on the so-called 'pre-colonials' face-to-face."

"We clapped eyes on them hours ago," said Stolk. "Watched them comb the ruins for their dead."

"Those nuns didn't look much like farmers."

"How would you know what a farmer looks like – have you ever seen one?"

Troy shrugged.

"Course he hasn't. He's too young. Damn kid hasn't seen anything yet." Satordi walked over and kicked the corpse. "Except that. Kid, better savour the moment. Not many folks come up against something like this close quarters and live to tell of it."

"You sure it ain't human?" said Troy, staring hard at the corpse's cold dead face.

Satordi shrugged.

"Rain's stopped," said. Stolk. "That's something."

Jayce knelt beside the corpse, lifted its loincloth. "Well, there's something else." She let the cloth fall back in place. "No man or lady bits – unless it's packing them on the inside."

A couple of the others wanted a look. Not Troy – he'd seen enough. He walked to the nearest stretch of free cave wall, put his back against it and slunk down to his knees.

"That came out of a vat," said Vassallo. "No question. Just like all the rumours said."

He would have added more, but the cloying cave air filled with their collective breath, sweat, blood and fear stilled as a new element was added. Not smell this time, but sound. The soft tinkling of bells getting louder and louder.

The nuns emerged from darkness, appearing one by one like flames igniting in the entrance to the cave. The fireteam scrambled to attention, grabbing weapons, flipping safety catches. Aiming right between the eyes and waiting.

The nuns said nothing. They waited too, staring neither at the mercenaries, their guns, nor at the bullet-ridden Tank on the cave floor. They appeared to be staring into the middle distance.

Stolk, closer than the others, noted the condition of their robes. Singed and splattered with corrosive stains, but otherwise the women were unharmed.

"You can't come in here," said Satordi. "Piss off or we'll fire."

"Maybe they're just trying to get out of the rain?"

"Shut up, Stolk. It stopped raining. I don't like it, Sarge."

Vassallo stared at the women hard. They did look like sisters, all minted from one mould. But the longer he stared, the more he started to notice subtle differences. A pinpoint mole above a lip, a flatter, uglier nose. Peripheral vision revealed Troy gripping his pulse rifle way too hard. Not a weapon to be fired at close quarters.

"Sarge, can't we just let them have the body?" said Stolk.

"Orbital will want it for examination."

"Orbital's left us all down here to rot."

"They want it, they can come and get the rest of us," cut in Satordi.

"Damn straight, man," said Troy.

Vassallo nodded thoughtfully. The nuns didn't move, but he noticed the eyes of the one on the farthest right snap into focus. She stared at him and didn't blink, like a snake flushed out of scrub, poised and waiting to gauge if it was time to strike.

"Tangier, how's that signal coming along?"

"Negative, Commander. Loads of static, but I've patched into both Platform and Orbital's long range sensors. Satcom's still holding its position – I can see it."

"Well," said Satordi, "That's something."

"What else can you source through the uplink?"

"Nothing new. Surface-to-air coms are definitely scrambled. Can access stored data from server banks, but that's all. Nothing real time. Nothing new."

All six pairs of female eyes were now trained on Vassallo, which made him more inclined than ever to stand his ground.

"Frisk them," he said coolly, glancing at the kid.

Troy shook his head. "No way, Sarge, I ain't touching. What if I get cursed?"

Jayce snorted.

"Might be anything under those robes. A bomb or something worse."

"Just give 'em the corpse. That's all they want," said Stolk.

"How the hell do you know what they want?"

Stolk didn't answer. A comforting sound bleeding in from outside the cave was capturing everyone's attention. The steady whirring snick of rotary blades.

"Evac – thank fucking mother mercy!"

Better late than never, thought Vassallo. *Suspiciously convenient, for once.*

"Get out of the way," he snapped at the nuns. They obeyed, shuffling soundlessly to one side, Troy's weapon trained on their centre mass.

"Fall out," said Vassallo. The jacks moved, single file, scrambling down the rocky incline, squelching through great fistfuls of weed that, Vassallo was pretty sure, had not been there mere hours ago when they'd run for shelter in the cave. Weed apparently unaffected by acid rain. Weed that stunk like rotting flesh when he crushed it underfoot.

VENERABLE VIRIDIS WAITED patiently until the troop carrier's slicing blades could no longer be distinguished over other more subtle sounds: the howling wind that gusted through the settlement ruins, etching and disintegrating walls that were never meant to last a century, certainly not two in this ferocious and unpredictable climate. Cave walls were thick and insulating, but her hearing was better than most. She waited until the steady pattern of highly mineralised water dripping upon limestone echoed softly throughout the cavernous chamber in which the venerable sisters knelt.

She nodded almost imperceptibly. Venerable Kaletra struck the small gong and the chamber filled with harmonious resonation. Venerable Duodopa began the softly whispered chant that would envelop the dharmapala and bring it comfort. Venerable Teveten got to her feet and sprinkled the dharmapala with dragon's breath: the precious liquid distilled from pyrophoric compounds that the venerable sisters used sparingly when no other combustible material was available. A secret recipe so closely guarded that even Venerable

Charantia herself did not know what constitutional elements it possessed.

The wheel was spun. Prayers were offered for the dharmapala: that its passage might be swift and resolute. A second prayer: that the blessed ringsel raked from its holy ashes might illuminate the way for those who followed.

All six sisters backed away as Venerable Viridis bowed, then lit the flame. The dragon's breath performed with great efficiency, one of the few elements capable of disintegrating synthetic skin, vat-grown muscle and carbon-bonded bone. The immolation process would take four or five hours throughout which the venerable sisters would pray and chant, assisting the dharmapala's progression on the wheel.

A dharmapala's remains were not always forthcoming. Sometimes the carefully raked ash revealed nothing more than fragments of bioceramic tooth and bone. But today was auspicious. As the first rays of dawn spilled over the broken landscape, filling the cave with both hope and illumination, Venerable Kaletra's gently wielded bamboo rake tapped against something small and hard. A diamond the size of one of the bitter blue berries that grew along the mountain's underside. The sisters stared in wonder before Venerable Viridis removed a small wooden box from the folds of her robe. The blessed ringsel was placed gently within its padded lining and the sisters rose to begin their journey home.

It had often been remarked that the hum of machinery embedded deep within the mountain's heart reminded the listener of the hum of bees. Or, at other times, cicadas. A far from accidental factor, a sound both comforting and protective.

The venerable sisters walked in single file along a track that took them past the remains of the invaders' encampment. The angry rain had fused their leavings to the earth. Steaming angular shapes protruded from a slurry of green and grey. The rain had not always been so angry. Likewise, the invaders had not come so often. In earlier days they had done no more than establish a perimeter around the baccaris trees and had shown little interest in the hives themselves. The sisters had gone about their business, harvesting propolis in small quantities; processing its resins, balsams and waxes. Extracting viscidone from baccaris flowers, producing medicines and salves.

Where their village had once stood lay now a stony field. Invaders had come in massive shiny ships with offers of relocation to a better way of life. But the life they offered was not better, they could see this in the sallow tinting of the invaders' skin, their clouded, speckled irises; the accompanying ailment of spirit, pain-bleached auras, weariness of heart.

The invaders burned the village down, pulled up the trees, smoked out the bees and stole the hives. The villagers had no choice but to flee to the caves worming through the mountainside. After that, the invaders left them alone, more or less. New invaders came. New trees were planted in the old ones' places. Same as the old trees, although genetic tweaking meant they didn't smell the same. Neither did the bees, or the pollen, or the propolis.

The venerable sisters listened to their bees. Knowledge was the truest power. There were other worlds and other gardens. Other ways of fighting, ways of seeing.

Venerable Viridis bowed before the illuminated gateway, a machine that had gone by another name in another time and place. She pulled the small wooden box from the folds of her robes, then handed it over to Venerable Charantia, who bowed in turn.

Venerable Charantia was pleased to see the single yet strikingly perfect diamond ringsel snug on a velvet cushion. She placed the diamond within the illuminated gateway's altar, bowed once more, then closed the hatch.

Several of the other industrious venerable sisters disengaged from their tasks to observe the data now flowing freely across the sturdy bank of mismatched screens and monitors stacked almost to the ceiling of the cave. The top row had lichen clinging to their casings, thin toadstools poking from the spaces in-between. Statistics, measurements, assessments, recordings of the invaders' camp. Intercepted transmissions: everything from the chemical composition of their food and waste to their speculation about the venerable sisters themselves. The fear of what they named the *supersoldier*, their distrust of the chants and prayers. The fact that they didn't understand what they were doing here. The lord they served was dark and cruel. Some ran from shadows, others from themselves.

"All interpretations must be studied, analysed and calibrated," said Venerable Charantia.

"They think we made the burning rain," said Venerable Viridis.

Venerable Charantia nodded. "They think a great many peculiar things," she said.

Venerables Duodopa and Kaletra were studying map projections, tracing supply lines with slender bamboo sticks. Taking note of the patches of verdant green, some which had been present on the last intercepted ringsel map, some not.

On each of a series of circular, elevated daises at the far end of the machine-filled cavern sat eight dharmapalas, each in the lotus position. Colourful offerings had been placed before them: ceramic dishes holding flowers, grains and fruits native to this planet. Painted prayers adorned their skin, applied with ochre chipped and pounded from the cavern walls.

Venerable Viridis stepped up to the nearest. She bowed, then stepped in closer, leaned forward to whisper in its ear. "Namaste."

The dharmapala opened its diamond-bright eyes.

FIFT & SHRIA

BENJAMIN ROSENBAUM

*Benjamin Rosenbaum lives near Basel, Switzerland, with his wife
and children. He is not sure if he would be a Bail or a Staid. He plays
rugby and likes to laugh and cry loudly (so that would be Bail then),
but is a computer programmer by day and endlessly intellectualizes
everything (pretty Staid). His stories have been nominated for the
Hugo, Nebula, World Fantasy, BSFA, and Sturgeon Awards, and
been translated into over twenty languages.*

*Author's note: in rendering this story in English, I have translated
the pronouns that the characters would use for their society's own
dimorphic social class-moiety into gendered English pronouns
– 'she' for Staid and 'he' for Bail, and I have regarded Staid and
Bail as 'genders'. This isn't meant to imply, however, that Staids are
female, nor that Bails are male.*

FIFT COULD TELL that the new kid, Shria, was yearning for the other
Bails to get involved, to say something. Perjes and Tomlest were
across the clearing, pulling sticks out of the underbrush, but they'd
stopped to watch.

"Did you hear me?" Umlish said to Shria. "I said, 'so you're
latterborn again, I guess we should congratulate you'."

Umlish was all gray – hair, eyes, skin, all the same matching tone.
Her parents must have decided to match them like that. Show-offy,
in a Staidish way. She was ten years old, a year older than Fift and
Shria and most of the other kids. She was here singlebodied – she'd
only brought one body along on the field trip to the surface, unlike
everyone else – and she wasn't carrying any wood, either. Her
sidekicks, Kimi and Puson, were carrying it for her.

"Of course being middleborn has its advantages," Umlish said, "but really, who wants a Younger Sibling cluttering up the place? Not Shria, I imagine."

One of the Bails – Perjes or Tomlest – snickered, and Shria turned sharply, in both bodies, baring his teeth. But he must not have been watching them over the feed, so he couldn't be sure which one had snickered. He stood there, glaring, clearly willing them to say something out loud. He could fight *them*, and he would – he was always getting in unauthorized fights with the other Bailkids.

What could he do against Umlish and her Staid crew?

Fift wasn't there. She was a little way down the trail in one body, and farther off in the forest with the other. But she was watching over the feed. The whole class must be watching. How could you not? Everyone had been wondering about it, about what had happened to the new kid and his family, and no one had been talking about it... until now.

Shria: lavender skin and fiery red hair, orange eyebrows that curled like flames. Bony bare knees and elbows poked between the red and blue strips of cloth of his suit. His clothes were a bit too big – a little too skimpy for the surface – as if whoever had cooked them up had been distracted. It was already misting, up here – tiny droplets of water sparkling in the air, the strange wild atmosphere hesitating between fog and rain. Shria crouched down, doublebodied, one body's arms already loaded up with sticks. He turned away sharply from the Bails in the clearing, and pulled a silver-barked stick from a tangle of them. It was furry with greenish lichen.

His eyes were red from crying already.

"That's not going to burn," Puson said. She was doing her best to look Staidish, emotionless, austere, but she sounded a little too excited. "Lichen means it's too wet. Especially in this weather."

Umlish smiled primly. "You do *have* an environmental context agent, don't you?"

Fift's own arms were full of sticks, some of which had lichen on them, or small fungi.

She shouldn't have split up after arriving in the forest. She was here in one body gathering sticks; in another body, she was over past the ridge, dragging a large log back to the campsite. Dumb. She would have to drop all the sticks if she was going to sort through them. She didn't like being together in the same place. Her somatic integration was poor. Her parents sent her to experts about it.

Umlish had found out about the experts, at one point. Umlish had written a poem about it.

Umlish could be merciless.

Fift shouldn't have damped all her automated agents; they would have told her about the lichen. But the agents distracted her. From the tall trunks of trees – some of them thick around as elevator shafts, others thin as a child's wrist. From the crunch and crackle of moss and leaves underfoot. From the roiling pale-green clouds in the roofless empty above her.

"Your parents should make sure you have the appropriate agents, for a trip to the surface," Umlish said. "They do seem very distracted, don't they?"

{Why did the Midwives take Shria's younger sibling away?} Fift asked her agents.

Shria dropped the stick and stood up, in both bodies, one of them clutching the pile of kindling. He was quivering, his faces pale. He looked around.

{Before a family can have a child, there needs to be consensus, among neighbors and reactants}, Fift's social context agent explained. {If there isn't enough approval, and the family goes ahead and has the child anyway, the Midwives require the birthing cohort to yield custody. Otherwise they won't gender the child.}

{But they didn't take his sibling away the first day}, Fift sent. {It was like three weeks.}

{You are correct}, the social context agent said. {There was a period of negotiation regarding the child's status.}

At home, in her third body, Fift rolled over. She hadn't really been sleeping anyway, just wallowing under the blankets, her eyes closed, her attention on the surface. The house feed showed Fathers Frill and Grobbard and Smistria in the breakfast room. She rolled out of bed, scratched her feet, and went downstairs.

Her Fathers looked up as she came into the breakfast room.

"Hello, dear," Frill said. He raised his head, causing a swarm of small bright cosmetic midges to launch themselves from his gilded eyebrows and dance in the air. "How is it going with your – ah yes," his eyes shone. "Out in the wilds! Looks damp." He grinned, goldenly.

"I never go to the surface," Smistria said, leaning back – his other body leaned forward, messily chewing a crusty broibel, which flaked into his braided beard – "if I can avoid it. We had this nonsense when I was your age too. It's *perverse* up there. The sky can just dump water on you or electrify you any time it takes the notion. Horrible place."

Under that dangerous sky, Umlish took a step closer to Shria. "I wonder if they might still be a bit overburdened? Your parents."

Across the clearing, Perjes turned to Tomlest. You could tell they were sending messages. Tomlest's eyes screwed up in amusement, and he laughed.

Shria's bodies both twitched, his empty pair of hands came up, almost to a guard position. But Tomlest didn't look over.

"Oh you," Frill said, swatting Smistria. "You have no sense of romance! The wild sky, our ancient origins!"

"Our ancient origins, for that matter, were under an entirely different –"

"Oh, don't be such a *pedant*! I know as well as you –"

"Um," Fift interrupted. "Um, I have a question."

Perjes and Tomlest ran off into the woods. Shria exhaled a shaky breath. He turned abruptly, and started to walk away. Not to run; he moved slowly, like an animal preserving its energy. He kept his eyes focussed on his feet. Umlish, Puson, and Kimi trailed after him.

"Yes, little stalwart?" Frill said. "What is it?"

"There's this Bail in my class, Shria –" in the forest, still watching Shria, she checked lookup – "Um, Shria Qualia Fnax, of name-registry Digger Chameleon 2?"

Smistria looked at Frill, and bared his teeth. "Oh yes. That one."

"What, what happened? They took away his sibling, but why – why did they take so long? And why did his parents have the baby, if they didn't –"

"Because they're idiots," Smistria said.

Fift frowned.

Grobbard spread her hands. Grobbard was Fift's only Staid Father. Her face was smooth and calm. "It was a kind of gamble, Fift. Fnax cohort thought that once the baby was here, opinions would change."

Shria trudged through the underbrush. The trail was a ragged strip of bare dirt, traced by surface animals. He was heading down the trail, heading towards Fift.

"An *idiotic* gamble," Smistria said. "If people didn't trust you to raise another child in the first place, why would they trust you after *that* behavior? Provoking a standoff with the Midwives? Letting your child just – *hang about* for three weeks –"

"Ungendered," Frill added, shaking his head. "Not entered into lookup, not entered into a name registry, like – like a surface animal, or –"

"Like someone who doesn't exist at all!" Smistria cried.

Grobbard sighed. "Yes. As if lingering still unborn, outside its Mother's body."

"But why would they do that?" Fift asked.

"Because," Smistria snapped, "they thought they could *coerce* the rest of Slow-as-Molasses – and the family reactants of all of Fullbelly!" He drew himself up in his seating harness, still chewing vigorously with his other mouth. "They were so arrogant, they didn't even invite adjudication!" Smistria was, himself, a well-rated adjudication reactant.

"They would have *lost* adjudication," Frill said.

"Exactly!" Smistria said – forgetting himself, through a mouthful of broibel.

Umlish, Kimi, and Puson trailed behind Shria, like a parade. Their eyes darted back and forth – you could tell they were amused by the messages they were sending to each other. They had small prim grins. Kimi giggled – Kimi was only eight – until Umlish frowned, then she composed her face more sedately.

"And think of the poor older siblings," Frill said. "Especially your classmate. From latterborn to middleborn to latterborn again, in three weeks –!"

"Well," said Grobbard quietly, "at least he was briefly middleborn." Grobbard was an Only Child, just like Fift. It wasn't something she talked about, but you could see it right there in lookup: Grobbard Erevulios Spin-Pupolo-Panaxis of name registry Amenable Perambulation 2, four-bodied Staid, 230 years old, Only Child.

Being an Only Child wasn't a great thing. It kind of meant you were less of a person. Maybe Grobbard had always dreamed about being middleborn, too.

"Yes, but come on, Grobby," Frill (who was latterborn) said. "Not like *that*."

Umlish looked up the trail, and saw Fift standing there, as if frozen. Umlish's eyes narrowed. {Oh, hello Fift}, she sent. {Are you finding what you need? Don't you think you have enough sticks? Oh my –} her eyes flicked to the left, feed-searching; {– look at you dragging that thing.} She had found Fift's other body, hauling the log. Her eyes shifted back to Fift's. {That's so... robust of you. "Mighty was Threnis in her time", eh?}

Fift flushed. Umlish was farther with the Long Conversation than she was – already learning the sixth mode. Was Threnis mentioned in the third corpus? She couldn't remember – and Pip and Grobbard never let her use search agents for the Conversation. ("It's a corrupting habit, Fift," Grobbard had said, with starker disapproval than Fift had ever seen on her solemn face. "Once you begin using them, you'll never stop. You must know the Conversation yourself – unaided – with your own mind. The Conversation is the essence of our lives as Staids, Fift.")

Umlish's eyes widened in triumph; she could tell that Fift had no idea who Threnis was.

Shria looked up nervously, saw Fift, and frowned. The tips of his ears were bluish with cold. His mouth was trembling, but his jaw was clamped tight, almost as if he was trying *not* to cry – like Fift when she was six or seven, when she'd begun doing her horrible somatic integration exercises, and had to do them in front of the experts and her whole family. It had taken all her strength not to humiliate herself by bursting into tears.

But of course no one would mind if *Shria* cried. If anything, it was strange – even slightly ridiculous – for a Bail to be so rigid with the effort *not* to.

Fift cleared her throat. It was thick somehow, and the morning dew was clammy on the back of her neck.

"Shria," she said, "can you, um, help me?" She hefted her pile of sticks. "Some of these aren't going to burn, they've got lichen on them."

Shria stopped, in both bodies, and glared at Fift. He hunched his shoulders a little further. He thought she was making fun of him, too, and so did Kimi and Puson, whose grins escaped their prim confinement. Umlish wasn't so sure; she raised an eyebrow.

"I guess I should have checked with my agents," Fift said, her voice a little unsteady, "but I turned them off. Who wants to have agents chattering at you up here? It's sort of missing the point, isn't it?"

Puson's face froze; Kimi looked back and forth from Puson to Umlish. Shria blinked.

Umlish's mouth soured. "You *like* it up here?" she snarled.

Fift didn't, exactly; it was cold and strange and mostly pretty boring, though there was also something fascinating about being under this strange sky which, as Father Smistria said, could do anything it decided to. She didn't *like* it, but she wanted to experience it. But she wasn't about to explain that to Umlish.

"Oh, Umlish... Are you having trouble with this?" Fift said. "I guess it can be a little scary if you've never been on the surface before. But don't worry –"

Umlish recoiled. "I'm not *scared*, you sluiceblocking toadclown. It's just *disgusting* –" She waved a hand at the forest.

A small grin crept across one of Shria's faces.

Fift swallowed. She wasn't sure what else to say.

Father Grobbard's eyes had been closed. She often meditated at the breakfast table. Now she opened them and glanced at Fift. {Threnis}, she sent Fift, {appears in the sixth and seventh odes of the first additional corpus. Would you like to study them this afternoon?}

Fift gulped. It was easy to forget that her parents could read the logs of her private messages: they didn't often bother to. At least, she didn't *think* they did. Grobbard didn't seem angry, though. She placed her hands together, resting them on the table. Peaceful as a stone worn smooth by a river.

"Well, if you like it so much," Umlish snarled, "why don't you live up here? Maybe you could get permission to build a little hut out of sticks and the two of you could *play cohort*."

"Okay," Shria said, coming forward up the trail. "Yeah, I'll help." He stopped in front of Fift, wiped a streak of snot from his nose with the back of his wrist, and then reached in, holding the good sticks back with one hand, and pulling the mossy ones out with the other. He kept those eyes on the task, but the other two – in the body he was holding his pile of sticks with – searched her face, sizing her up.

Fift swallowed. She kept her face still, expressionless, but she could feel the blood rising into her ears.

"Will they take any of the other children, do you think?" Father Frill asked.

"What?" Fift asked. "What other children?"

"Of Fnax cohort," Smistria said.

The cold dug into Fift's chests, and not just on the surface. "Like Shria? Why?"

Frill shrugged, and smoothed the bright blue-and-orange braids of his hair with his hands, releasing another swarm of midges into the air. "It can happen. If their ratings fall enough – if people think they're doing an inadequate job. That your friend would be better off elsewhere."

"He's not..." Fift began. She didn't really have any Bail friends. It had become hard to tell who her friends were.

Two years ago she would have said Umlish was her friend; they'd played together when they were little. But Umlish was the kind of person who was your friend as long as you did exactly what she said. Fift had tried to laugh along with the poem thing. But after today... She'd never forgive Fift now.

"They're starting the campfire, Umlish," Kimi said. "Should we go back?"

"Or are you playing siblings?" Umlish snapped, ignoring Kimi. "How exciting for you, Fift! A sibling of your own!"

Father Frill cocked his head to one side, and narrowed his eyes, searching the feed. "Hmm. He's been fighting – your friend. He's a little old for that. At your age Bails should be learning to keep their fights on the mats." He shook his head. "That's not good for ratings."

The hairs on the backs of Fift's necks stood up. "What would happen, if they take Shria away? Away to where?"

Frill shrugged. "He's not too old to be trained as a Midwife. They live at the pole –" he gestured vaguely southwards. "It's a great honor."

Fift could see her own faces over the feed. She looked horrified: one day she'd come to class and Shria would be gone, taken from his cohort, forbidden to talk to his parents, off to the pole to become a Midwife forever. How many more fights would it take? Could Umlish cause this all by herself, with her words? Fift struggled to compose her expressions into mildness, like Grobbard's.

The closed and skeptical look on Shria's face softened, as he stared at Fift. He yanked the last of the mossy sticks from the pile (in her other body, Fift yanked the log free from a knot of underbrush; there, she could hear the sounds of the campsite through the trees. They were building the bonfire). He raised one of his thick, curling eyebrows.

"You'd better plan on being the Older Sibling, though," Umlish said, "because Shria doesn't want any Younger Siblings. He was glad to get rid of that little baby – weren't you, Shria?"

Shria blinked. His nostrils flared, a long indrawn breath, his eyes still locked on Fift's – drawing strength? Then he turned to Umlish. "Don't spit all your poison today, Umlish," he said. "You might run out, and then what are you going to do tomorrow?"

Umlish drew herself up, scowling. "You sluiceblocking –"

"You used 'sluiceblocking' already," Shria said. "See? You're running out."

"Let's go back, Umlish," Kimi said. "We don't want to miss when they light the fire –"

Fift cleared her throat. Her hearts were pulsing, unstaidishly fast.

"Don't tell me what –" Umlish snapped.

"You could try 'flowblocking'," Fift said.

Shria's eyes lit. "That's kind of the same thing, though," he said, chewing his lip.

"Corpsemunching?" Fift said.

Shria giggled. "That's good! What's that from? Yes, call me a 'corpsemunching sisterloser', Umlish –"

"'Sisterloser'!" Fift's eyes widened. "Wow!"

Shria grinned, showing white teeth in his pale lavender face. "You like that one?"

Fift dragged her log into the clearing, and Perjes and Tomlest ran up to take it from her, and toss it onto the pile.

Umlish's face was a mask of anger.

Puson cleared her throat.

"See there, Umlish?" Shria said, clapping her on the shoulder. "You don't need to worry. If you run out, we'll help you."

"Get your hands away from me!" Umlish snapped. "You're disgusting!" She turned and swept up the path, followed by Puson. Kimi, released from the agony of waiting, darted ahead towards the campsite, her bodies caroming off each other, running a few bodylengths before remembering to slow down to a more sedate and proper pace.

Fathers Frill and Smistria had finished breakfast and wandered off. Father Grobbard was waiting, still, watching Fift with her immovable serenity. It seemed as if she was waiting for something.

It was turning colder. When Umlish, Puson, and Kimi were gone, Shria exhaled, a brief exhausted sigh: it came out as a plume of white fog. His shoulders slumped.

They were lighting the fire; brushing bits of bark from her hands, Fift found a place on a rock, not too far and not too near, and settled onto it. The expedition director, a fussy 200-year-old middleborn Staid, was anxiously directing the two Bails holding the lighted torch. Kimi rushed up the path, walking just slower than a run, eyes wide with expectation.

Alone on the path with Shria, Fift was at a loss. Were people watching them? There was a way to check audience numbers on the feed, they'd had it once in interface class – after a moment, she found it. No one saw them where they stood in the forest; no one at all. Not even Grobbard.

Grobbard raised an eyebrow. As if waiting for Fift to answer a question.

"Oh," Fift said. "Yes, I –" She switched to sending, rather than speak aloud about the Long Conversation, there in the kitchen where her Bail Fathers might hear and get annoyed. {Yes, Father Grobbard, I would be interested in studying the sixth and seventh odes of the first additional corpus. Thank you.}

Fift's arms were getting tired from holding the bundle of sticks. She took a step up the path, and Shria matched it. They headed back towards the campsite.

Shria watched the darkening sky, sunk in his own thoughts. At the edge of the circle of firelight – red shadows dancing on the trunks, every body wreathed in a streamer of exhaled cloud as the children began to sing – he looked at her once, and sent: {Thanks.}

They dumped their kindling in the pile, and Shria went off somewhere. Fift sat down with herself, body against body, huddled up against the cold.

THE HOWL

IAN R MACLEOD AND MARTIN SKETCHLEY

Ian R MacLeod has been a writer in and around the genre for more than twenty years. His work has been frequently anthologised, translated into many languages and adapted for TV. He has won the World Fantasy Award twice, the Sidewise Award for Alternate Fiction three times, and also the Arthur C. Clarke and John W. Campbell Memorial Awards. He lives in the riverside town of Bewdley with his one wife and two dogs.

Martin Sketchley is the author of three novels to date, and his short fiction has appeared in several anthologies, including Conflicts, Celebration *and* Solaris Rising 2. *He also appeared on the DVD bundled with Nick Cave and the Bad Seeds' reissued album* Abattoir Blues/Lyre of Orpheus. *"The Howl" is his first collaborative work. Tweet him @MartinSketchley.*

IT WAS ONE of those things you think about doing but know you never will. As the engines started to roar and the runway began to roll, Grace still couldn't believe it was happening. Strange food at twenty thousand feet and films she couldn't follow, change at Singapore and then again at Dubai. Where, with hours to kill, she took out the photo she'd found amid her mother's belongings. She studied each of the five black and white faces. All of them in their flight suits, yet looking far too young and happy for the terrible responsibilities of the gigantic machine hunched behind them.

Then finally, London. She queued with the bickering families and the women in saris to present her passport, and her phone began beeping with anxious messages from her family the moment she turned it on. She ignored them. A big screen was showing a news channel as she waited at the carousel. One of those anonymously pretty blondes they must clone somewhere was standing on a windy expanse of marshland, gesturing behind her to where a huge crane was being hauled onto some kind of pontoon. The image switched to a graphic in which the crane became a toy, and another toy – an aeroplane which Grace now knew was called an Avro Vulcan – lay in the impossibly clear depths beneath it. Then back to the freezing blonde, and clearly nothing much else was happening yet. Grace grabbed her case as it went by a second time and headed in search of a taxi.

THE DRIVER WAS Indian like half the ones you got in Perth, and accepted the address, which she knew wasn't far from Heathrow, without question. She'd never visited Britain before. It was a place her mother had always seemed more than happy to leave behind. She'd been expecting – what? Pearly kings? Highland cattle? Glimpses of the royal family riding around on tall red buses? – but the landscape she travelled through was bleak. Chain hotels, blank warehouses and endless car parks finally gave way to almost equally bleak rows of houses. The block of flats the driver drew up beside had a grey, defeated air. As did the few tattered trees that surrounded it. She flinched when something huge roared overhead as she fiddled with the strange money, but it was just another aircraft like the one which had brought her here.

Inside, she peered into the lift, wrinkled her nose and bumped her case up the concrete stairs. Found the button beside a barred and prison-looking door, pressed it, and waited.

"I thought I'd told you not to come?" He was already walking away from her. But at least he hadn't slammed the door in her face. "You're worse than the bloody journalists..."

"They've been bothering you?"

She stepped into a room where an old television with an aerial on top was murmuring daytime inanities. Bits of wood leaned in one corner – apparently some incomplete desk construction project. Stacked piles of newspapers and TV guides. A great many calendars clung to the walls. On the Formica coffee table the remains of a meal; an empty mug; something electronic disembowelled. Through the glass door at the far end of the room a white plastic deckchair and table stood on the small balcony, a sagging yellow washing line, the grey battleship of London beyond.

"What do you expect? The kids and neighbours must be starting to think I'm one of those paedophile celebrities. Or perhaps you don't have those in Australia?"

Grace had no idea what he was talking about. "But how did you –?"

"Know who you are? You look far too much like Ann. Then there's the suntan and the accent. I'm not stupid, you know."

Grace perched on edge of the settee.

"Make yourself at home, why don't you?" He went into the kitchen. "I suppose now you're here I might as well do the British thing and fix you some tea…" His hand, as he filled the electric kettle, was shaking. "I'm guessing from the suitcase that you've only just arrived?"

"There didn't seem any point in hanging around. Not after coming this far." She peered at the piles of newspapers. Saw little paper flags, scrawled notes, protruding. Then there were those calendars, most of which looked old. Some kind of hobby? The final months of lost years.

"I, ah, found a photo of you and Charlie and the rest of the crew amongst Mum's things…" Another jet passed overhead as the kettle started screaming. "And it was obvious from the things she said that… Well, that you were fond of each other."

"*Fond*…?" The fridge door banged. "So you don't even bother to tell me that she's died?"

"I'm so very sorry that you didn't find out more quickly. But…" All those calendars. All decorated with symbols, exclamation marks. Dates circled, underlined or scrubbed out. Here was one, even, from 1961. "Well, it hardly seemed right for me to start poking into the past. But Mum did remember you, Bill, if that means anything at all. Spoke about you far more than the rest of the crew, in fact… Apart, of course, from Charlie. But then I got this message via the British Consulate back in Perth that they'd found the old Vulcan and were planning to raise it. And I am technically next of kin, and there's every reason to think my father's remains are still down there inside it."

"So now you're here, with the tan and the accent and everything, dragging things up like those bloody fools in Yorkshire? Those busybody plane spotters and halfwit academics with their fancy equipment..." He stepped in front of her from the kitchen. Even frowning in those thick glasses, wearing a stained and holed cardigan, and now well past seventy, still recognisably the third man from the left in that photo. "It's Grace, right? Did I mention you look a lot like Ann?"

"People always used to comment on it. Which Mum didn't like, by the way, because then she always seemed to have to end up explaining that she'd been married to someone else before she came over from England. Mum wanted a new life. She destroyed so many things. Including most of her memories."

He held out the mug of tea. "But that isn't how it works, is it?"

YOU GET USED to these things, no matter what it is you do. Fifteen minute readiness, playing pool or darts or cards and already in flight suits. Waiting for the end of the world. The planes loaded, ready, fuelled. Otherwise the Ruskies' mushroom clouds would be rising over Birmingham, Bristol, Liverpool, not to mention this bloody airbase, before you'd even got airborne, and then what would be the point?

The sort of thing you dreamed of as a kid. Didn't care if the teachers smiled or the adults laughed. Hoarded the magazines when the other kids were talking about football. Tried to get to the air shows even if the buses went nowhere near. Just hitched and walked. A big ask, that was what the careers master called it, with armed forces cutting back and the Empire fading and conscription gone and Britain not what it was, and the guy in the proper uniform in the recruiting office up past Woolies on the high street wasn't much more encouraging. There was always ground crew, or the Navy, or the catering corps, or the poor bloody infantry, or just the Territorials. But you gave it your best. Strained to get the maths, the physics. Hoped to God that your eyes and all the rest of you were A1 and not shit B2.

Even then, even when you arrived on that first day in windy Yorkshire with your mum's old suitcase, there were other lads, hundreds of them – you'd never thought – all of whom wanted to be crew, fly one of those big machines. The navigation and the physics and the spit and polish and the trick cyclists asking how angry you were and running until you were sick all over the moors. But you didn't give up. More exams and exercises and then Jet Provosts and one day you're up there alone. God of the sky. Breathing rubber, kerosene and stars. Then the wing commander calls you in. And you stand to attention and wait for the worst. Can't believe what he's saying. Can't believe you're not crying. Can't believe it's true.

But you get used to anything. Even a dream. Even these big machines. The payload? Well, it's orders, physics, if the worst came to the worst. Yellow Sun with a Red Beard warhead. Fusion. A fucking H-bomb. Two thousand pounds. Nothing that the Ruskies wouldn't do to us. It's a job and it's everything you prayed for. And, even if your family and no one off the airbase knows the whole truth, you're damn proud of who you are and what you do. Last bastion and bulwark and all that. The vee-winged Atlas that holds up the free world. That feeling in your guts just looking at them like giant pterodactyls straining for the sky as you head out from the briefing shed. Then you climb in and go through the checks and the lights come on, the dials flicker, the wheels rumble, the runway unravels, and the four big Olympus engines howl.

BILL SAT IN the armchair facing the television, thumbing the remote control.

"How are things for you here anyway?" said Grace, sipping tea.

"What does it matter to you? Nothing – *nothing* – for over fifty years, then you ignore what I told you over the phone, turn up out of the blue and expect me to be all pally. Well you can bloody well forget it."

There was an awkward silence. But she hadn't come halfway around the world on a wild goose chase. Grace took a deep breath. "Bill," she said. "I wanted to ask you something. About Mum." He just gazed at the television. "I couldn't help wondering what there was between the two of you. I mean, feel free to tell me if it's none of my business, but..."

"It's none of your business."

Bill turned up the sound on the television – perhaps a little too loud – and kept jabbing at the remote until he reached News 24, where they were confronted by an image of the marsh and the same bubbly young reporter whose enthusiasm refused to be dampened by drizzle, behind her the same pontoon and men in orange rubber suits.

"That's it, isn't it?" said Grace. "That's where they've found the Vulcan."

The young woman was talking about the Cold War, Britain's V-bomber force, its role in the Cuban Missile Crisis, World War Three, Macmillan, Kennedy, Khrushchev... And tomorrow, she said, when the weather improved, XL 438 would see the sky for the first time in over fifty years.

Bill snorted. "Well, she's got that all wrong. Bloody journalists. They're almost as bad as the politicians."

Grace sat forward a little on the settee. "I have a suggestion, Bill. I know you've been trying to put this to one side, but sometimes... Well, sometimes it's better to face up to things. And I've come a long way, and my family all think I'm mad, and I honestly hadn't realised how strange and different a place England is. And Charlie, my Dad, isn't even a ghost to me. So why don't we drive up there together and watch them bring her up?"

He looked at her for the first time since she had entered the flat. "Why would I want to do that?"

"I don't know, I just thought..."

"You didn't bloody well think, though, did you? That's the trouble. No one ever does."

THE REAL FAMILY, the family you become part of, isn't the squadron or the RAF. It's your crew. After all, you could die together so might as well live that way. Equals in everything but never questioning an order because that's the only way to survive and get through. Close in any case, stuffed cheek by jowl into that tiny pressure cabin, two of you above with some view of the sky and the other three guys below. Sam down there on navigation and Irish ballads and Frankie to complain and steer in the payload and Grin in charge of wisecracks and electrics. Pilot and co-pilot – that's you – up top. A tight ship in every sense. A beautiful machine. Reckon the competition, the Victors and Valiants, have drawn the short straw. No matter that the main Vulcan test pilot died and the very first machine to be delivered crashed on landing at Heathrow following a glorious global promo tour. Other accidents since, lives lost, and that alarming tendency, which you've been trained to expect and the boffins have made all sorts of accommodations for, to enter into an uncontrollable dive as you approach Mach one. You've heard all the stories. The jokes. The humour can get pretty grisly, in fact, but if there's one thing you don't talk about – apart, anyway, from exactly what you'd be flying back to after a completed mission – it's this: the pilot and the co-pilot have ejector seats and the other three crew, down there with their charts and their Thermos flasks, don't. The idea is they scramble out, jump free-fall and parachute. In the accidents, in the training runs, that often hasn't worked out. But there you go.

Amid all the equals, Charlie's the lead pilot and he's in command. He looks, acts, is, the part. Joins in with the jokes and complains about the farts but only so far. You'd thought you'd wanted everything, back when you were an Airfix kid, but you're happy to be Charlie's co. You trust him. You admire him like hell. It's as if he's soaring through the air even when he's on the ground. He seems older, even though he's the same age as everyone else. He's married, settled, while the rest of you are still wanking to film star posters. He has a beautiful wife. Blonde hair. A smile that melts your knees. She's what you're fighting for. She's why you'd fly all the way across Europe and through the Iron Curtain. She's why you'd press the button. Her name is Ann.

GRACE LAY IN the slightly lumpy Holiday Inn bed gazing into the darkness, serenaded by sirens and airliners. She needed sleep, wanted sleep, but her body clearly had other ideas, stuck in the whirring mechanisms of a time she'd temporarily left behind.

Although she'd persuaded Bill to take the trip up north to witness the Vulcan's retrieval first-hand, with perhaps a stop-off at the old bomber base where he and Charlie and the rest of the crew were stationed, there were so many unanswered questions. Was Bill her real dad, for instance? And, if so, what did that make Charlie? Not to mention her mother. How did you raise something like that with someone who was really a complete stranger? What were you supposed to do – stand side-by-side and look in the mirror and see a revelatory family likeness? A mole on the chin? A distinctive nose? The letters, the bits and pieces between the lines and the things that

Mum had and hadn't said over the years – what did it all mean? And then there were all those old calendars and maps on Bill's wall, covered in little stickers and scribblings. Unfamiliar countries and cities linked by lengths of coloured string. Concentric circles and shaded areas with little symbols and figures. What on Earth was going on in his head?

As doors banged and someone laughed in the corridor outside her room, Grace rolled onto her side and pulled the duvet tight around her. Perhaps tomorrow she would find out more, but she couldn't help wonder whether everyone back in Perth had been right, with all their warnings of sleeping dogs, skeletons and closets.

SHE COMES TO you one evening. Out of the blue. Out of the airfield dark. You're not proud of the dream, the thought, but there you are. You're working late. It's another exam. Navigation across enemy territory without countermeasures or armaments. Just you, the Vulcan, the mission, and nothing else. The decision made. The order irrevocable. She sits on the edge of your desk. There's no one else around. The light fills her blonde hair. Her dress pulls tight across her thigh. She and Charlie, they're the perfect couple. You know they are. He carves the roast and she leans over you to serve the potatoes at Sunday lunch. She's leaning over you now. But there you go.

"I'm worried," she tells you, "about Charlie." And you nod, impossible though that sounds. "He's always, he's *too much*, in control."

But that's what Charlie's for. That's what he's lived his life to become. You want to say. But don't. She's half-smiling, half-worried. Fiddling with her wedding ring. She smells delicious. You don't know if it's perfume or her. Or both. A gap has somehow appeared. A potentiality. A weakness in the enemy radar. You swallow. You lean on the throttle. You push through.

"It's not what he says, exactly. It's mostly what he doesn't. Perhaps it's just me. Or just us. And I can't – well, I can't go to the wing commander, or the shrink. Even the padre, he's RAF to the bone."

You fold up your papers. You listen. At some point, you realise she's not twisting her ring any more because you're holding her hand. Warm against her thigh. After all, you're aircrew. You're *that* close. And she smiles at the end of it without saying much at all. And she leans closer still to peck you on the cheek. Just a small thank you. Then she's gone. And you're alone.

Of course, it's your absolute duty to report any matter of concern up the chain of command. Of course, you don't. But next day, next exercise, you're looking at Charlie a bit differently. Next Sunday lunch, through the fragrant steam of the potatoes, you're looking at Ann differently, too. A gaze avoided. A changed shape to her lightly lipsticked mouth. Twisted geographies of what you want and how you feel – and perhaps it's already too late.

You're ready for the exam. Know the shape of the Danube, the lowlands of Poland, the mountains of the Urals, like the back of your best friend's hand. But you study anyway. Late and alone. Dreaming of things that might not happen until they do. Willing them to be real. The door opening. Letting in the twilight, the cold. Not a poster. Not Brigitte Bardot. But real. Here. Yes, now. Her thigh on the desk. The blonde light in her blonde hair. You listening, not saying much. The thank-you pressure of her lightly lipsticked mouth.

That's how it is, all that winter, and then into the summer beyond. 1962. *Strangers on the Shore* and Acker Bilk on the radio. Warm beer in the NAAFI and then to bed alone. The Ruskies making missiles like it's no one's business but their own. Then, as late summer slides into autumn, it turns out that they're deploying the bloody things in Castro's Cuba, too.

GRACE BROUGHT THE rental car to a stop in the entrance to what had once been the airbase, and turned off the engine. The wire fence rattled in the breeze. On the other side, low-rise buildings flaked grey paint. The top of the control tower loomed beyond, in the mysterious no-man's land of all airfields. A hoarding proclaimed that the site was destined for redevelopment: luxury two-, three- and four-bedroomed homes ideally located for the M62. It looked rusted and old.

"What are we doing here?"

"I just thought it might be a good stop off point," said Grace. "How does it feel to be back after all this time?"

"Bloody awful."

She looked uncertain. "But you must have had some good times? Wasn't there some camaraderie? The thrill of flying a Vulcan?"

"Am I getting a rush of rose-coloured nostalgia, you mean? No, not really."

A gust of wind rocked the car. Grace felt vaguely annoyed. After all this was, or should have been, part of her past as well. "Right. Well, do you want to get out and take a look around anyway?"

"I can see perfectly well from here. Besides, it's bloody well lashing down." He leaned forwards and looked at the cloud. "Gusty, too. Look at those trees. Thirty-knot crosswind I'll bet. She's going to be a handful on approach. Got to concentrate or she'll bite."

"Was it scary?"

Bill snorted. "Scary? No. You don't have time to be scared. Being responsible for the end of humanity. That's scary. But you don't think about that. Oh, no. You just get on with the job."

Grace looked at him. This wasn't quite what she'd planned. Stop off at Bill's old stomping ground, loosen him up by chatting about the good old days then maybe steer the conversation around to Mum. But he was as distant and dark as on their first meeting.

"How about something to eat? Would you like one of those sandwiches and some tea?" She reached into the back seat for the flask and Tupperware box.

THERE'S A PARTY at Charlie's house. Short notice. Just a few last drinks with some people from the base. It's October but the sky is warm and blue. The kids and some of the adults wander outside in the garden. A pack of Lightnings fly low overhead, hard and quick, afterburners blazing. You can feel them on your face, hotter than the sun. Trundling lines of military trucks. A siren moans somewhere like the pain in your belly.

The last seven days have been nothing but alert, practise, alert. Charlie's right. You all deserve a break. The Yanks have got their B52s circling Texas as always. Wearing out their engines and wearing down their pilots in their hurry not to miss the start of this world war like they did the last two. But the British planes, the Vulcans, the V bombers, just waiting, grounded. That much closer, see? Part of the game you have to play 'cos it doesn't pay to show your hand too early and spook the Ruskies. You'd thought you'd be longing to be back inside them by now. Up there. Swaddled in rubber and kerosene. The blackout world beyond turned radar green, then blazed into white.

You join in with the kids playing football. Look up at the window of the house and see Ann watching, smiling from an upstairs window. You go back inside with a sore shin. No one's talking about the U-2 that's just been shot down over Cuba, pilot presumed dead. No one's talking about the stand-off between Kennedy and Khrushchev. No one says, of course they don't, because it's top bloody secret, that first thing tomorrow it's dispersal, which is when the V bombers spread out to thirty-five bases across the country to make a wider, more diffuse, target, and that this is probably the last time, at least until well past doomsday, you'll ever see this place. That this is the dance of death.

The sky darkens. The kids get crotchety. People depart as evening slips in. No one says much as far as goodbyes are concerned, because – well, what can you possibly say? But Grin's in the lounge where he's been for most of the afternoon. Hogging the punch and jiggling his knees and spilling crisps and watching the soundless TV. Now he's talking in a loud, wavering voice about what the Russian pilots are probably doing, which is much the same as this but with vodka instead of Cinzano Bianco, and couldn't we just call the whole fucking thing a draw and get on with living? And Charlie, being Charlie, intervenes as only Charlie can. Takes control. Does his Charlie thing. Grin'll be all right. 'Course he will. And sorry, skipper for pissing all over your last little gathering. But not at all, no problem, and the next thing you know Grin's being poured into Charlie's Triumph and driven away by Charlie for some strong coffee and a good long sleep. Yet the TV's still flickering and you're still standing here in this empty room of the house of your best mate, amid the squashed sausage rolls and the knocked-over glasses, looking at Kennedy's greyed and weary face on the silently fizzing TV. And suddenly it feels like you're incredibly alone, and that every breath is your last.

When you look up, Ann's standing in the doorway leading to hall. It's as if she's always been there. Not Brigitte Bardot. Not even Grace Kelly. But just Ann. Just her. Just that. Which is everything. And she takes a step forward, the way you might into some strange and dangerous other territory from which you're unlikely to return. And so do you. And she falls into your arms, and the world shudders again as more Lightnings fly overhead, their afterburners blazing.

GRACE HAD BOUGHT sandwiches from the forecourt shop when she'd put petrol in the car, playing safe with cheese salad and ready salted crisps and a couple of Kit-Kats. Bill agreed to bring the flask – milky tea, no sugar, no options.

"You never did tell me what your mother died of," he said as they ate and watched the rattling fence.

"It was cancer."

"Cancer." He looked pained. "And I promised I'd take care of her."

"Promised who?"

"Charlie, who do you think?"

"You can't blame yourself for that, Bill." Men of his age were so chauvinistic, so stupidly chivalrous. "Mum was a strong woman, a fighter. And we have all the facilities in Perth," she added. "Specialist surgeons, radiation therapy…" Better not to mention how Mum had thinned and paled, how her flesh had grown so translucent the light almost seemed to flow through it.

"I read up a little about your Vulcan on the internet before I left home," Grace said as the wind pushed at the car. "There are a lot of conspiracy theories out there about it. Have you seen them? I didn't realise the significance of it all and the whole Cuba thing. Claims that you were carrying some kind of experimental weapon, another that there was a secret negotiator on board who was going to try and smooth things over between the US and Russia. Another one about a misunderstood message changing what happened."

"They're a bunch of cranks. Got nothing better to do than sit around making up stories about other people's lives. They haven't got a clue."

As Bill took looked through the passenger window and sipped his tea, Grace noticed ripples in his cup. She considered for a few moments. "Do you want to tell me about it? Tell me what really happened?"

"I can't," he said. "It was all of those things and none of those things." He shook his head. "Grin was right. We should have left the bloody box alone."

"What do you mean?"

"Grin? He was a boffin as well as a joker. Used to go on about some cat in a box that a physician had invented. I believe it's called a thought experiment. Something about nothing being fixed until you made it so. He reckoned that if we did our job we'd be the ones to open the box. And then… Well, what then?"

"I don't understand."

He shook his head. "Neither do I."

When he glanced across at her she saw tears in his eyes. Grace reached out. "It's all right, Bill."

"We took the piss out of him something rotten," he said quietly. "But I've seen things, Ann. Just glimpses. Things I don't understand. I need –"

"Grace, Bill. I'm Grace. What kind of things?"

The car shuddered. The wind had grown stronger, howling through the fence, threatening to rip off the sign and send it spinning up like a metal kite. Bill sniffed and shook his head and held tight to his cooling tea and said nothing.

YOU'RE FALLING. SKY over land over sky. This isn't so unusual. You're a pilot, after all. You've been trained. And something huge and dark and vaguely triangular is turning in flames at every possible angle as it twists away. Then the land comes below again and even up this high nothing about it seems right. It's blackened. There's dust in the air. A strange sour taste which reaches even inside your helmet and the blood singing in your head. Sudden light on the horizon, a different kind of sun, as the ejector seat parachute deploys in a tearing flap and rush and you wait for the straightening jerk. But it's sideways and too weak. You're still falling. The taste in your mouth becomes nothing but fear and the burning land is suddenly much too close.

YOU AWAKE TO nothing. White sound. White air. You'd think you were dead if there wasn't so much pain. White faces come and go. White hands unwind white bandages around your head and chest. You swallow white tablets. You try not to scream. Then a man in a white coat sits by you and you can't see his face because the window behind him is too bright. His head looks shrunken and burned. He could be a used matchstick. He probably is.

"So this is it…" you mutter.

"This is *what*?" He sounds almost amused.

You struggle to move but nothing happens. "The end of everything."

After a while you learn how to eat, how to fill the bedpan, how to sit up. The nurses are stern and sweet. Their English seems practised. Much too perfect. You wonder if you're a prisoner and they're really Ruskies. Then one day it's the squadron leader. And the bed tilts and the springs whisper sweet nothings as he sits down beside you. He's wearing his squadron leader face. If you could you'd stand to attention. You'd try not to cry.

"Was it bad?" you mutter. "I mean, how many died?"

"All the others, Bill, I'm afraid."

"What? You mean *millions*?"

His face doesn't waver. "Just the other four men, Bill, the crew in your Vulcan. We're surprised you've pulled through, to be honest. You looked like a broken push puppet when they brought you in. No other casualties. Khrushchev's backed off, Kennedy's lording it and everyone else is stood down and okay. We did the job. We saved the world. You understand me, Flight Officer? That's how this is. Your parents'll be along to see you in a few minutes. Believe me, they're as proud as they are relieved. Then, as soon as you're fit enough, there's someone from Air Command for the debrief."

THE SOMEONE FROM Air Command turns out to be a woman. She's a major and some kind of medic. She's wearing a twisted snake with wings on her lapel. All the questions you expect aren't exactly forthcoming. Neither is she. It's like talking to your parents. It's like talking to the enemy interrogators you've been trained to face, who know exactly how to twist the knife by not asking you anything sensible at all. Every time you look through the window you expect to see nothing but black ruins, shadows branded into the ground where people once stood. But you've learned not to say that now. So you're cured, right? And she can fuck off back to Air Command. Something about her hands, the shape of her nails, as she unfolds her notebook. Ann a widow now. Charlie, not even buried. The

Vulcan drowned deep in some northern marsh. Didn't really make much in the papers, what with so much else going on, but a bloody war grave. And you're still here. You survived.

"What exactly do you remember, Flight Officer? I mean, before you woke up here?"

"I'd ejected. I was falling. It was... daylight. There was... ground beneath me. Coming up too fast. The parachute didn't deploy properly."

"And before that?"

She's leaning forward. The air still seems too bright and is hissing away from you like sand. If you could open a box and press a button and put an end to all of this, you would.

"Before that?"

"There was a party at Charlie's house. We were going to disperse next day."

"Ah yes." She makes a note. Looks up once more with her own version of the Squadron Leader's face, and you wonder if she really is a Ruskie. Well briefed, of course. Knows some personal details and the language. But then they would. And if the Squadron Leader and your parents weren't wearing masks... "Wasn't there some problem with Chief Technician Smith — the man you used to call Grin?"

"None at all. We had a few drinks and then we all went home. Although I think Charlie may have driven him."

"And you remember that?"

"Look... Can't *you* just tell me something more about what happened?"

"Well..." She pauses. "To be honest, Flight Officer, the information we have is pretty scarce. You took off at 08.30. Light westerly breeze. Good visibility. No issues reported in any of the checks. You banked east. Still all in good order. We have a visual check on that. Climbed, were followed by the radar, to 15,000 feet. Just a short hop, really. One airbase to another where... the final preparations and loading would, of course, take place. Still standard procedure in a way, although obviously everything was on high alert. Last reported position there were still no problems, and there was no mayday. The theory that's been advanced, and it *is* just a theory, is that there was a major electrical malfunction which degraded the controls. And the Vulcan... Well, I'm told she's a brute to fly."

"There was smoke."

"There was an instrument fire? You remember this from inside the cockpit?"

"No, I saw the Vulcan was in flames as I was descending in the ejector seat. She was dropping, spinning. I'm sure Charlie was still doing everything he could to straighten her but she was out of control."

"Right." Another note. "That's very helpful. Anything else?"

The Vulcan isn't a brute. She's terrible and beautiful. "No."

SO THAT'S HOW it is. You get asked these and other trivial questions so many times you give up bothering to answer them. One guy, a different and probably even more senior shrink, he tries to take you through it. Wants you to imagine he's Charlie and you're you. Well it's worth a try. How you'd react to a fire, malfunction about twenty minutes after take-off at sub-Mach and fifteen thousand feet. Who'd do and say what.

The order to abandon the aircraft, it goes without saying, would be Charlie's responsibility. But he wouldn't give it. He'd fight to the bloody end because he'd know there was no way the three guys at the back without the ejector seats stood a snowball's chance of getting out unless he could keep some control. It'd be the same in any mission. A dispersal hop to another airbase. Or on the way back from Russia with everything you'd trained for finished and the job done. No refuelling, no bloody airfields, no radio coms. Wild thermals. The air roiling with patches of dark and the electrics fizzing. But you go, Bill. I mean, you'll take care for Ann for me, won't you? If she's still there, that is. You're the one guy I can trust. So you pull the lever and the world rips apart and you're falling.

You escape.

You're here.

ON THE PONTOON the rotund figures in hard-hats and rubbery orange suits called and gesticulated. Diesel engines thrummed. Arc lights blazed around the crane. It was already evening and the sky was bloody. On firmer ground there were a couple of ambulances and several satellite TV vans. Grace and Bill stood ignored and unnoticed among the onlookers. There were a couple of military guys nearer the front. Some suits from the ministry. A priest, even.

When the Vulcan's location had been discovered and its retrieval proposed, both practical and philosophical concerns had been voiced about dragging the huge delta-winged bomber from its resting place after decades in the clutches of the marshland. But exploratory investigations had revealed that the aircraft was not too deep, and the structure seemed sound enough to take the strain as long as it maintained its current, slightly nose-high attitude. Nothing could be guaranteed, but the prognosis was good. And if something could be done, it was human nature to try.

Bill seemed quieter than ever, hunched against the bitter wind with his hands stuffed in his pockets.

"Are you okay?" said Grace. "I suppose this must be hard."

He said nothing for a few moments. Then he looked at her. "I lied," he said.

"You *lied*...? About what?"

"I told you I'd never heard from Ann, but that isn't true. There's something I think you should have." He unfastened the top button of his coat, reached into the inside pocket and produced a letter. He held it gently between his fingertips, looked at it for a few moments, then gave it to her. "You might find what you're looking for in there."

Grace recognised Mum's handwriting immediately. The envelope looked pristine, as if somehow unaffected by the passage of time. The Western Australia post mark was dated July the twenty-fourth, nineteen eighty-one: Grace's eighteenth birthday. She glanced at the reverse side. "Why didn't you open it?"

"The only correspondence I ever received from her? The only news... The only..." He shrugged and looked back out across the marsh. "I suppose I was scared of what it might contain. If I opened that envelope there'd be no turning back. Eight east. Grin's cat. The end of a world. I couldn't face that again. So there you go. It's your responsibility now. And just in time, too, by the looks of things."

Grace followed his gaze just as the spindly contraption of wire and metal suspended beneath the boom began to take the strain.

YOU MIGHT AS well be dead. It's winter now and the world is white and they let you wander the grounds. You play checkers. Swap stories

with the other patients about things that might have happened or
didn't. All what ifs and what have yous. The knives in the canteen
are blunt. Funny how there can be so many casualties just from
protecting the peace.

You still take your white tablets. You still get the flashes and the
flashbacks and the screams. You're still flying blind over a dark
world, and there's no turning back. You know your career in the
RAF is buggered. If they don't know what happened and the plane's
drowned, buried, a war grave that the War Department is happy
to keep that way, they're not even going to trust you to bash spuds
or dig latrines. One way or another, you feel like you've destroyed
everything.

Then late one freezing afternoon with the orange sun blazing long
shadows, you come back inside with frost on your breath. A nurse
hurries up to you. You've got a visitor, she says. Ushers you to your
little white room. You steel yourself for your parents, the Wing
Commander, yet another shrink. But it's not.

SOME TIME PASSED during which little seemed to happen. Then,
gradually, the Vulcan began to emerge in a slow-mo take-off replay.
Water cascaded, glittering in the lights, from holes in the aircraft's
carcass. The cockpit windows were translucent and starred. The
hull was scuffed and stained a mossy green, the entire structure
seemingly coated in fur.

The lift continued slowly. When the bomber was ten feet or so
clear of the marsh a man with a walkie-talkie raised a hand and
the machine's ascent was halted. There were distant cheers, a faint
ripple of applause whipped away on the wind. The rubber men
grinned and slapped each others' backs.

"Well, well," said Bill quietly.

"I SHOULD HAVE come earlier." Ann straightens the sleeves of her
black coat as she removes her gloves. Her hair's done different. Her
eyes have changed.

"No, you shouldn't."

"I, ah, checked with the doctors. They said it was okay now."
She's still standing. You don't sit down.

"Did they tell you I was mad?"

"No, Bill. I mean, *no*. Of course they didn't! What you've been through, it must have been terrible. No wonder things have been... difficult for you. And I think that was why I didn't want to add my own sorrows to yours and make things worse."

"You haven't."

"Haven't I?" She manages a smile. "Well, at least that's something."

"That party, that last day. Do you remember –"

"Look, Bill. What I came here to say is quite clear and specific. First of all, I don't blame you for any of what happened, and I think you've been, I think you *are*, incredibly brave. Without you, none of us would be here, would we? It doesn't matter that you can't remember anything. Without you we wouldn't have..." She gestures around the cell-like room, into which the last of the sun is pouring its fire. "This. That's what I keep telling myself, that's what I *know*, about Charlie, and of course the others, too. It might have been some accident, but I'm a pilot's wife... widow. This is what happens. And the other thing I wanted to tell you, Bill, is that I'm leaving this country. I mean, there's not much to keep me here now, is there?"

"Where?"

"Australia. Probably Perth. I want to start a new life. I know it sounds like a cliché."

"Good things often do."

"Yes." Her eyes wrinkle as she studies him more closely. Catch the light. Gain a little of their old spark. She almost takes a step. The world almost changes. But 'nothing does. So much for Grin's cat. "You're probably right." Now she's fussing with her gloves as if the plane is already out there waiting. Signed-off, engines turning. Yearning for the air. "I really must make a move. And... Well, this might sound a little odd, Bill. But I *have* spoken to the doctors. In fact, I've phoned them a few times. So... is there anything you want to ask?"

You consider this. More questions. You shake your head.

"In that case..." She leans a little closer. Her lips touch your cheek although her body, her presence, remains distant. "I'll leave you."

"And will you...?" you hear your voice asking.

"Write?" Ann considers this as she pulls on her gloves. "I think it might be best if we don't. At least not for a while, eh? Then we'll see." And you notice, in the last brightness of the sun, a new thickness to her belly beneath her coat as she turns and walks away.

THEY SAT IN one of those trendy urban coffee shops that has brown leather seats and witty comments chalked on a blackboard outside. Grace had what was supposed to be a flat white, Bill a cup of tea.

"How are you feeling?" she said.

"It's a lot to take in."

"At least your crewmates can be put to rest now. It's terrible they were trapped inside for so long like that."

"They covered it all up, you know. The Americans insisted. The whole thing's like some kind of punishment for something I didn't do. Or maybe I did."

Grace sipped her odd-tasting coffee. Just when you thought you were getting close to this sad, infuriating man, he began to slip away. "It might seem that way, but imagine the alternatives. Where would we all be now without men like you and Charlie?"

Bill didn't reply, and Grace didn't know what else to say. There was a long, awkward silence. Grace watched him as he gazed through the window, the years weighing down. She couldn't bear the thought of leaving him on his own in that little room, so close to the grainy English sky and those howling aircraft. "I'm heading back home next week," she said. "Probably just as I start getting over the jet lag." She smiled, but Bill just warmed his hands on his mug. "The thing is... I was wondering if you'd like to come back with me for a while?"

He looked at her. "But, Ann, I..."

She reached out and wrapped her hands around his; could feel the heat of the mug through the coldness of his fingers. "I'm Grace, Bill," she said gently. "Grace." She saw a young man's eyes deep in an old man's face. Where was he? When?

"Yes, of course. Grace. Australia. Good Lord. Ten pounds for a whole new life. We talked about that once before, didn't we? One of those times you came to me as I studied..." Bill frowned and narrowed his eyes as if trying to work out what she was hiding from him.

"Well..." Grace considered. "... It's like you said, Bill: it was a new life. And I was scared and excited and worried, and things probably weren't going so well between me and Charlie. We *were* very close, you know, you and I. You were a good friend. Someone I could share things with and talk to. So now maybe the time's finally come, eh? Get away from all this... *grey*. Have you got a passport?"

"Oh, yes. Always renewed but never used. I don't know. I like it here. I like to see the aircraft."

"We have aeroplanes in Australia, too, Bill."

"Australia. It does sound nice, I'll admit. Beavis flew there, you know. Broke a record."

"Have a think about it. If you decide you like the idea then I could help you get things sorted out."

Bill was quiet. He sipped his tea and placed the cup carefully back on the saucer. "It could end up being a one-way ride, of course," he said. "But then I suppose that was always going to be the case, wasn't it?"

GRACE LOOKED THROUGH the window as the Boeing hauled its way into the sky. Bill would be down there somewhere, recovering from the funeral and the fly-by, the triangular sandwiches and the pretty cakes and the small talk from people he didn't know or particularly want to speak to. And now it was all over, and the reporters had already moved on, and the Vulcan would end up in some museum, and Bill would probably just return to his old calendars and his odd attitudes. Things would settle back to how they always were, her family would still think she'd been mad to go on this trip, and the world would continue to turn. But she would at least write to Bill. Maybe phone occasionally.

As the aeroplane entered the clouds and the city beneath her vanished, Grace reached down and took the letter from her bag and studied the familiar curls and loops of her mother's handwriting as she considered whether to release its contents. It was a connection to Mum, a direct link to a past that might give her all the answers she'd thought she wanted. But Bill was right: once opened there could be no turning back. It was Grin's cat. Eight east. The end of a world.

She looked outside the aircraft again. The clouds shimmered and skewed. Time faltered. There was a moment of transition. As the gigantic machine emerged into a sky of brilliant blue Grace returned the letter to her bag and settled down for the journey home. Answers, she realised, had a tendency to raise more questions, and perhaps there were many equivalent truths. Unleashing the past, and in the same moment opening up countless futures: it was one of those things you think about doing, but know you never will.

THE SCIENCE
OF CHANCE

NINA ALLAN

Nina Allan was born in Whitechapel, London, grew up in the Midlands and West Sussex, and wrote her first short story at the age of six. Her fiction has appeared in numerous magazines and anthologies, including Best Horror of the Year #2 *and* #6, The Mammoth Book of Ghost Stories by Women, *and* Year's Best Fantasy and Science Fiction 2012 *and* 2013. *Her novella "Spin" (TTA Press) won the 2014 BSFA Award, and her first novel,* The Race, *set in an alternative near-future version of southeast England, is published in summer 2014 by NewCon Press. Nina's website and blog can be found at www.ninaallan.co.uk*

THE GIRL'S NAME was Rae. That was all she would tell anyone. She was about seven years old, Lyuba reckoned, perhaps eight, although her not speaking made her seem younger.

"Where was she found?" I said.

"Vasilievsky Station," said Lyuba. "It's all in the file." She folded her arms and frowned, staring back at me with a look composed of equal parts impatience and curiosity. *Why don't you listen to what I'm telling you instead of asking mindless and unnecessary questions?* She tapped the top of the object in question, an office box file with a marbled grey exterior, nudging it towards me across the Formica table top. Lyuba is brilliant at what she does, but she has no time for what the business strategy manuals like to call 'people skills'. I once asked her how she thought about a case. My question provoked the same expression, a kind of mystified perplexity.

We were having a drink together in the Gay Hussar, a vodka bar just around the corner from the main precinct. Lyuba doesn't socialise much outside of work because she has a young daughter, but she seems to enjoy taking the odd hour off if her mother is staying, especially if it gives her the opportunity to indulge her hobby. Lyuba is something of a vodka expert. In a rare moment of confidence, she once told me that while stationed in Perm she'd won a big vodka-tasting contest.

"Thirty-two varieties, all named by region," she said. There was a faraway look in her eyes I'd never seen there before.

"My God, how did you even stay on your feet?"

"It's like most skills," Lyuba said. It was the closest I'd seen her come to boasting, about anything. "The more you practise, the better you become."

When it came to answering my question about her methodology, she seemed less confident.

"What do you mean?" she said. "A case is a case."

"Yes, I know. But how would you describe the process of solving a case? To a lay person, I mean. If you had to?"

She appeared to examine the backs of her hands, then turned them over slowly to look at the palms. She seemed puzzled, as if she'd never seen them before. Lyuba never takes anything for granted. That's one of her greatest strengths as an investigator.

"Like a crossword puzzle," she said in the end. "Discovering one fact creates the structure to uncover the next. Every case has an inbuilt logic to it, an internal pattern. Once you can see the pattern, you can solve the case."

She spoke haltingly, choosing her words with care as you might select small but valuable objects from a shelf, Japanese netsuke say. I could see what she meant with her crossword analogy, but for me a case is less about solving a puzzle than telling a story. Those first few stumbling questions – the questions Lyuba gets impatient with because they seem so obvious and so unnecessary – are my way of finding a way for that story to begin.

THE LITTLE GIRL *was found standing by herself outside the buffet at Vasilievsky station. Her name was Rae. When police asked her if she was lost, she wouldn't say a word.*

*   *   *

THERE WASN'T MUCH in the file: a short typed report detailing the girl's first name, the place where she was found, and the contact details for the couple – their name was Ostrov – who had called the police, a photocopy of a doctor's report – *Caucasian female, 7-8 years old, no sign of contusions, bruising, lacerations, no evidence of sexual interference or molestation, vision, hearing and mobility normal, green eyes, fair hair, no scarring or distinctive markings, query elective mutism?*

There was a photo clipped to the doctor's report, passport-sized and over-exposed. The child's face was expressionless and pale, her light-brown hair drawn back from her forehead in a green hairband. She seemed a blank, a diminutive ghost. She looked like all lost children. I've seen plenty of photographs like that and they're all next to useless.

The doctor's name was Shimulkovsky, not one I recognised. The only other things in the file were two photocopied images of a zip-up leather purse on a long leather strap, and two further photocopies of both sides of a newspaper clipping that Lyuba told me had been found folded up inside the purse.

"The purse was around her neck, under her coat," Lyuba said. "There was no money inside, just this sheet of paper. She made quite a fuss when it was taken away from her, apparently – Glebov said they had to prise her fingers off the strap. She's been quiet as a field mouse otherwise."

The newspaper clipping was from an issue of *Izvestiya*, torn from the top half of the page and so leaving the day and the date – May 8th 1969 – clearly visible. One side featured a report of a fire at a children's home in the northern city of Milena. The reverse showed part of a photograph: a woman's face, rendered indistinct by shadows. The caption and the attribution were both missing and, I thought, unlikely to be relevant. I was more interested in the story about the fire. The date made any direct connection with the child impossible – the events described in the newspaper had to have happened at least thirty years before she was born. But what about her mother, or her father? I found it hard to believe that the newspaper clipping had been placed in the purse by chance. Clearly it was a message of some kind. Who was it meant for, though, and what did it mean?

The fire at the children's home seemed like the obvious place to begin my investigation, but I couldn't help thinking that the place and date might be just as significant. 1969 was the year of the plebiscite. Milena had been the site of violent demonstrations in favour of what the more reactionary Soviet politicians had once branded the New Socialism. In the run-up to the secession, many of its advocates had been libelled and disgraced. Some had been imprisoned, or reposted to hard-line frontier towns where their voices were diminished, or ignored. The old guard's attempts to swing the vote had ultimately failed, but plenty of bad things happened before they lost their stranglehold on the nation's windpipe.

There seemed no obvious connection between a fire in a provincial city and the death-rattle of a corrupt empire, but my instincts told me that there was one and I was used to trusting my instincts, at least where my job was concerned.

It was what they paid me for.

I filed a request to see the girl the following day.

RAE WAS IN the temporary care of Clara Brivik, a police liaison officer whose main work was with vulnerable adults but who sometimes fostered children in an emergency. When I asked Clara if the girl was speaking yet she shook her head.

"Not a word. She's eating though, which is something. She seems healthy enough. Her parents must be going spare, wherever they are."

"Do you think there's any chance they abandoned her? That she was left at the station intentionally, I mean?"

"Perhaps. Kids don't clam up overnight without a reason. This little girl is physically fine, so either she's seen something that's scared the wits out of her or she's been unhappy over a long period."

I don't often encounter silence in the course of my work. Normally it's the children who are missing, the adults who are left behind. Adults in pursuit of lost children are voluble, angry, terrified, often irrational and sometimes hysterical but rarely silent. The little girl sitting on the divan in the box room off Clara Brivik's kitchen was so quiet it was uncanny. Observing her for the

278

first time, I couldn't rid myself of the idea that she was not human at all but some new kind of being, a creature who saw everything yet said nothing, the world's conscience.

Clara had clearly done her best to make the confined space as bright and comfortable as she could – I noted a red-and-white chequered quilt cover, a bedside shelf with books and a wooden solitaire set, a glass snow dome containing a cleverly worked miniature model of the Angara dam – but for all the animation she showed, the child might as well have been walled up inside a prison cell.

"Hi," I said. "You must be Rae." Clara had left us alone, which was against the rules, but in spite of her tact my own voice still sounded false to me, sterile and plastic, bordering on sinister. The girl stared straight ahead, hugging her knees. It was difficult to tell if she even registered my presence.

She had a tiny gap between her front teeth. For some reason it was this detail, more than any other, that brought the reality of her situation home to me.

She was alone. Suddenly and without warning I found myself thinking about that first winter after the bomb, when Aunt Svet and I were living at Svet's uncle's *dacha* with no idea of what the future would be like or what it might hold. I remembered mornings in February, gaunt icicles casting shadows from the eaves in the eerie blue snow-light, the realisation, which took longer to pierce my consciousness than you might imagine, that the bomb had erased my past. My mother, our apartment, the gold-rimmed coffee cups that had been a present from my father's sister Maroussia, who lived in Paris – these things were gone forever, leaving nothing but the *dacha*, the grubby houses along the potholed road that led to Grabinski, and Aunt Svet.

I loved Aunt Svet like a second mother before the bomb. Now she seemed distant and, like the icicles, unutterably cold. Glittery in her misery, her chilblained fingers brittle as the frost-rimed twigs we scavenged for firewood.

I was eight years old.

"I want to help," I said to the girl. "I'm here to try and help you find your mummy."

Rae shook her head. The movement was slight, but unmistakable. I drew in my breath. She was saying no, but did she mean no, I don't want you to or no, that's not possible?

I stayed with her for another half hour, playing with the snow dome and babbling bright, meaningless sentences in the hope that she might respond but she remained silent and immobile on the bed. She did seem calmer, somehow, or at least I imagined she did, but I knew that was probably just wishful thinking.

GATHERING INFORMATION ON the children's home fire was actually easier than I had anticipated. Facts have often proved hard to come by in this country, and I was prepared to face a multitude of obstructions when I began delving into what happened at the *Maria Davidova* children's home on the night of May 7th 1969, especially as Milena is a navy town, where secrecy and concealment are bred into the bone.

As things turned out, it was quite the opposite. A man named Pil'nyak, who had managed the orphanage's finances for many years, set up a charitable foundation in the wake of the tragedy, with the aim of building a new hospital and children's asylum on the site of the outdated facility destroyed in the fire. As his own contribution, Pil'nyak compiled a memorial album detailing the history and background of the *Maria Davidova*. The book included a number of essays and tributes by local writers, and also copious appendices, listing the names, ages and circumstances of admission of every child who had been in residence at the time of the fire.

There were twenty-four fatalities in all. According to Pil'nyak, if it hadn't been for the courageous actions of certain members of staff there would have been more. One housemistress suffered severe burns to her upper body when she stayed behind to help a child – twelve-year-old Mitya Tolstoi, who had an amputated leg – to safety through a downstairs window. The house porter, Anatol Dub, organised the evacuation of the second floor dormitory before returning inside the burning building to rescue twins Liza and Vera Ismailov. Liza had become trapped in a smoke-filled stairwell, and Vera refused to go anywhere without her sister.

Pil'nyak's memoir catalogued many such acts of everyday heroism, the kind of life-affirming anecdotes that always surface in the aftermath of any disaster. But there were other stories too, stories that did not end so happily. More than a quarter of the resident children died, many of them in terror and still desperately trying to escape. Two members of staff were killed also, overcome by the effects of smoke inhalation.

One death in particular seemed to stand out, perhaps because the child in question shouldn't have been in the *Maria Davidova* at all. Ten-year-old Orel Zneyder was the son of a prominent and vehemently outspoken New Socialist. Miryam Zneyder had been remanded in custody on trumped up embezzlement charges, and was forced to put her boy into care as a result.

The charges against Zneyder were eventually thrown out, and she was returned to the regional *duma* on an increased majority. In the meantime, Orel's death had become a local scandal. There were even those who suggested that the fire at the children's home had been arson, a deliberate act of reprisal against Zneyder and her pro-secession stance. The story was compelling, and tragic, but it was only when I read that Zneyder had grown up in the Auchinschloss district of my own city, just a two-stop tram ride from our old apartment, that I became convinced that I'd found the lead I was looking for: that the girl in Clara Brivik's box room and the tragic Orel Zneyder were somehow connected.

"There's a link here somewhere, I know it," I insisted to my girlfriend Paula. My collection of newspaper clippings and photocopies and computer printouts was beginning to take over our apartment. Paula is used to my hunches, but I knew this one must have sounded bizarre, even to her.

"How can there be, Nellie? The boy died in 1969. That's thirty years ago, in case you'd forgotten. This Miryam Zneyder would be a pensioner by now. If she's even still alive, that is."

"She's alive. She still lives in Milena. I've tried calling her but all I get is her answer phone." I paused. "She wrote a book about Helen Messger. Don't you think that's strange?"

"Strange how? There must be dozens of books about Messger. What's one more?"

I fell silent. What I wanted to say was that it seemed an odd coincidence that the same Miryam Zneyder whose story featured in a newspaper clipping discovered in the possession of an abandoned child just happened to have a connection with the city where that child was found. But of course Paula was right, too. The pianist Helen Messger was one of the bomb's most famous casualties. People are still fascinated by her, even today.

"I'd be careful if I were you, Nellie."

That's what Paula always says when she thinks I'm about to do something stupid. In the case of Miryam Zneyder, I could only imagine that she meant I was letting my obsession lead me onto unsafe ground. The last thing the poor woman needed was some idiot blundering into her life like a wrecking ball, awakening memories of what was probably the worst thing that had ever happened to her and all in the name of a quest that was doomed to fail.

What Paula said made sense, but I couldn't let go. There was something here, I felt certain of it, and apart from anything else there was Rae herself.

She was behaving so oddly. I kept coming back to what Clara Brivik had said, about children who had witnessed something terrible and how it might affect them.

A fire in a children's home would have to be one of the worst traumas a young person might experience. Bad enough to rob them of their power of speech?

If that child had seen a friend die, I thought probably yes.

WHILE I WAS waiting for Miryam Zneyder to respond to my phone messages, I went to interview the couple who had found Rae at Vasilievsky Station and called the police. Alec and Silvia Ostrov lived on the northern edge of town, out beyond Karl Marx Park, where the rents stay low because of the persistent rumours of nuclear contamination. The Ostrov house was a wooden shack, standing by itself in a patch of muddy gravel at the end of a short unmade road. A backdrop of birches and derelict tower blocks completed the scene.

Only Alec Ostrov was in when I called. A beanpole-thin man with sticking-out ears and lank, shoulder-length hair, he spoke with a slight stammer, his watery blue eyes flicking nervously from side to side. Logic put him in his mid-thirties, not much younger than me, but his hunched posture, together with the shabby carpet slippers he was wearing when he came to the door, made him seem much older. I gave my name and showed him my ID. "I telephoned, remember?" I said. "Is it okay if I come in?"

"My wife isn't here," said Ostrov. "She had to go to work." He shot an anxious glance over my shoulder then finally stood aside to let me pass.

"What does your wife do?" I asked. The door opened directly into the main living room. The shack's woebegone exterior had led me to expect the space inside to be equally grim. The reality was a surprise, comfortable and interesting-looking. There were books everywhere, overflowing the plank-built unit that had been constructed for them, piled on the table by the window and stacked in haphazard columns along the base of the wall. A large divan was covered with an embroidered woollen blanket, and the old-fashioned tiled corner stove gave off generous heat. My eye was caught by a picture on the wall behind, a small gilt-framed oil painting of a woman's face. It was painted in browns and ochres, yet still light seemed to stream from it, as from the faces of the saints, illuminated by candles, on a carved *iconostas*.

It was a lovely thing. I wondered how the Ostrovs had come by it.

"Silvia's a nurse," Ostrov said. "At the Metropolitan. Would you like some tea?"

"I'd love some."

"I'll make it." He stepped around me and into the next room, presumably the kitchen. I glanced furtively at the books and papers littering the table. Most of them, their pages covered with complex-looking diagrams and mathematical formulae, were unintelligible to me. There was also a battered copy of Thornton Wilder's *The Bridge of San Luis Rey* in the original English.

"I work in probability," Ostrov said. "The science of chance."

I jumped back from the table. I hadn't heard him come back into the room – the slippers, I suppose – and his sudden reappearance startled me. He was holding out a mug of tea. I grabbed at it, glad of something definite to do. "Numbers aren't my strong point, I'm afraid."

"Mathematics has as much to do with feeling as understanding, in the end. Most people are too afraid of looking stupid to find that out. That's what this book is about really, at its heart." He touched the faded green covers of *The Bridge of San Luis Rey*. "Have you read it?"

"No."

"You should."

I was surprised at the change in him. The insipidness and the timidity were gone, replaced by a hard-eyed enthusiasm that bordered on the aggressive. I took a sip of tea, almost burning my mouth in the process. The wooden shack, the dusty novels, the brilliant zealot – it was starting to feel like something out of Dostoevsky.

"What can you tell me about Rae?" I said.

"Rae? Oh, you mean the little girl." I had expected my abrupt return to the subject in hand to wrong-foot him, to jolt him back out of his comfort zone. It did not. "We saw her standing outside the station buffet. Silvia and I, I mean. The one by the main entrance. She had a red coat on. I remember that because Silvia nudged me and said she looked like Little Red Riding Hood. We thought she must be waiting for someone. We were meeting Silvia's mother off a train, only the train was late and then when it arrived she wasn't on it. Silvia was worried at first, but when we went to the booking office there was a message saying that she'd caught the next one. We decided not to bother going home, to have a meal in the buffet instead. When we got there we saw the little girl in the red coat, still standing outside. Silvia asked her if she was lost but she wouldn't say anything. Silvia said we should call the police and I agreed."

He spoke clearly and deliberately, as if he were delivering a statement or recording a lecture, and indeed I'd seen an almost identical statement already, in the photocopy of the original that Lyuba had recently given me to add to the file. It didn't mean that Ostrov was trying to hide anything, necessarily. It was more likely that he'd just repeated the story so many times it was beginning to sound like a script. This is a common problem when it comes to witnesses, and a good part of my job is to persuade people to think back – not to the last time they gave their statement, but to the events they're describing.

It's the little things, the forgotten things that I'm hoping to recapture. The details that have been discarded because they don't appear to fit with the bulk of the story.

They can be vital clues.

"How did she react when the police came?" I said.

Ostrov hesitated. "I don't know, really. I don't think she had much idea of what was going on. A policewoman took hold of her hand and the girl let her, as if it didn't make any difference to her what they did. She just kept staring ahead, like a sleepwalker. It was as if she weren't really there, somehow. As if she were seeing something none of the rest of us could see. I found it quite eerie."

"Eerie?"

"Like something in a horror film."

"What did your wife say?"

"She said the kid was probably scared. Scared to death, she said, left all alone like that and during the rush hour, too." He paused. "I didn't say so to Silvia, because I know she gets upset over children, but I thought the girl was more than just scared. She reminded me of something that happened to a university friend of mine. He was in an accident as a child – his school bus drove off a bridge and fell into a river. He was ten when it happened. He told me he didn't remember feeling frightened at the time, that from the moment the bus left the road until he was dragged onto the riverbank it was like watching the whole thing play itself out on a cinema screen. He could see the river bottom through the window, because the coach's headlights were still on, still working. There was a shopping cart down there, he said, bright silver, and something twisted and tangled in weeds he thought might be an old bicycle. He remembered feeling angry about that, because he and his friends liked to swim in the river, during the summer months especially, and he hated the thought of people dumping their rubbish there. It was dangerous, for a start. He knew a boy who'd almost been drowned when his foot became trapped in a sunken mattress.

"It was only afterwards that he felt scared," Ostrov continued. "He said he couldn't understand what was happening to him. The excitement and uproar over the tragedy soon died down, as they were bound to do. My friend was back in school a fortnight later. Life went on as normal, or as normally as it could when half your classmates were missing. Their desks and coat pegs sat there, empty – they would not be filled again until the autumn, when the next crop of younger children came up from the year below. My friend found himself looking at those empty desks more and more often. Sometimes, in the middle of a maths class say, he would feel his throat tightening and his arms and legs grow heavy as scrap metal. He would look out of the classroom window and imagine he saw water rising. Even five years later he was still having nightmares, terrible dreams in which a great wave overwhelmed him and from which he awoke with his heart racing and his lungs burning. The dreams only began to ease off when he went away to college."

"Away from the river, you mean?"

Ostrov shrugged. "Yes, maybe." He hesitated. "But that's what the little girl looked like, do you understand me?"

"As if she were remembering a nightmare?"

"As if she were still seeing something awful in her mind's eye. She wasn't scared of where she was, or what was happening, because something even more frightening had already happened. Something she couldn't forget, even if she tried."

As if she were still seeing something awful in her mind's eye. Ostrov's words, or at least the sense of them, coincided almost exactly with Clara Brivik's.

"Is there anything else you remember?" I said to him. "Anything at all?"

"I don't think so. Her coat was too big, that's all."

"What do you mean, too big?"

"It was almost on the ground. And the shoulders were too bulky. She was lost in it. You know how kids like to dress up in their mother's clothes? The girl looked like that."

I didn't see how this could matter, but at least it was something, a detail no one else had mentioned so far. I noted it down.

"Who's that in the picture?" I said to Ostrov as I was leaving, nodding my head towards the oil painting behind the stove. It really was beautiful. I realised I would be sorry not to see it again.

Ostrov glanced quickly towards the painting and then looked down at the floor. "No one I know," he said. "I came across it by chance, in one of those lost-and-found stores by the Universitetskaya tram stop. They're all gone now. That woman looks exactly like my mother. I thought it was interesting, the coincidence." He cleared his throat. "My mother was killed in the bomb."

Mine too, I could have said, but I didn't. I didn't want him to think I was trying to cancel out his story with one of my own.

I hate it when people do that. It's a form of stealing.

I RODE THE tram back to the city centre then caught a trolleybus to Vasilievsky Station. Vasilievsky is the old name for the station, the same name as the street it's on and the one that was given to it when it first opened, back in the 1880s I think it was. The station was renamed in honour of the Red Army general Vladimir Chorny in 1925, but had its name changed to *Voksal* Rosa Luxemburg in

1956 after Chorny was discredited, along with everyone else who ever exchanged so much as a word with Leon Trotsky. Following the secession, the council voted to restore the original name, which most of the city's older residents had never stopped using in any case.

There's a large mosaic across the rear wall of the station hall, created by local art students and showing Vasilievsky Street the way it looked before the bomb. It's made entirely from shards of glass and pottery and other detritus collected from the rubble. The station facade, with its twin corkscrew towers, is the defining feature of the mosaic, as of the street itself. The remarkable thing about that is that in contrast to virtually every other building in the neighbourhood, the station – designed by Ilya Fillipov in the overwrought yet nonetheless impressive style architectural historians usually like to refer to as Byzantine – survived the bomb more or less undamaged.

Whole theses have been written on how that might have been possible – several dozen conflicting and contrasting theories involving wind direction and centre of impact and prevailing atmospheric conditions. The only consensus the various parties seem able to arrive at is that Vasilievsky's survival was a freak event, a confluence of environmental, meteorological and aerodynamic circumstances that have, at least for the present, resisted a complete analysis.

Just chance, in other words. Pure fluke.

The station interior was redesigned and updated in the 1980s. In the old days, before the bomb, there was no buffet, just a selection of kiosks and covered stalls selling everything from freshly baked *khvorost* and *pirogi* to expensive boxes of chocolates from Zhukov's, the century-old city centre confectioners that was destroyed in the bomb. I remember in particular the smell of roasting chestnuts, the red glow of the brazier, the toasted scent of winter, of drawn curtains and silver paper. I found the aroma irresistible. My mother didn't like buying things from the food stalls – she said they were overpriced. The chestnuts were different though, probably because you couldn't find them anywhere else. If I asked her at exactly the right moment she would usually give in.

"THEY'RE HOT," MUM said. "Mind you don't burn your fingers." She handed over the paper packet, a double-folded sheet of newspaper twisted into a cone shape. I offered it to Peter first, who stuck in his hand and immediately withdrew it. The concentration of heat in such a confined, papery space scared him, I think.

"Silly billy," my mother said. She kissed my brother's reddened fingers, and ruffled his hair. Five minutes later, as the new, pleasant sensation caught up with the earlier, frightening one, cancelling it out like train wheels flattening a patch of weeds overgrowing the railway track, Peter smiled.

THE CHESTNUTS WERE delicious, dense and vaguely sweet, like baked potato. They tasted differently from anything I could have imagined.

THE CHESTNUT STALL is long gone. The station buffet has wipe-down tables and chrome-legged chairs and an enormous steel samovar that always reminds me of a squatting toad. I went to stand by the door, gazing out across the teeming concourse and trying to imagine how it might look and sound and feel to an eight-year-old girl in a too-big coat, a girl who probably didn't have a clue about where she was or why she was there.

The crowds seethed around me and through me, an invincible tide of buttoned-up faces and impatient voices, of thundering boots with tarnished buckles and traces of mud. My Rae-self stared about uncertainly, feeling trapped and disorientated, overcome by unease. Fear lapped at me like a wave. It was as if the space I occupied was no longer a part of the station but somewhere else, somewhere that bore no relation to any time or place I had experienced previously. Even the word 'station', normally so commonplace, seemed to have lost its currency. Its meaning had floated away, replaced inside my head by some other, less definable concept, a garbled and terrifying anagram of madness.

The roar of diesel engines was overpowering.

I shook my head to clear it. The station floated back into view. I went into the buffet, which seemed suddenly less crowded, and bought a glass of tea and a sourdough roll. I sat at one of the Formica-topped tables, flicking through my notebook and thinking about Rae and Vasilievsky Station and the fire at the *Maria Davidova* children's home, moving them about inside my mind like the pieces in a jigsaw puzzle and failing to find a way to fit them together.

EVENTUALLY I WENT home. I made supper and then called Clara.

"Any change?" I asked.

"She's still not speaking, if that's what you mean. I gave her a colouring book and she seems happy with that, at least. It's kept her busy for hours."

I fell silent, remembering the castles I became obsessed with drawing as a child. I'd fill whole scrapbooks with castles, each more elaborate and unlikely than the last. "Do you know how long she'll be allowed to stay with you?" I said eventually.

"I don't know for sure. Another few days at most." After that, and assuming we were no closer to tracing her parents, Rae would become the responsibility of the social welfare system. She would be taken from Clara's apartment and transferred to a children's home. The state machinery would take over. The idea horrified me but there seemed little point in dwelling upon it. I said goodbye to Clara, and told her I'd call again at the same time tomorrow. Less than five minutes after I put down the phone, it began to ring. It was Miryam Zneyder.

"I'm sorry it's taken me so long to return your call, but I've been staying with friends," she said. I'd been expecting her to sound frail, confused even, but her voice was surprisingly firm and clear. "I'm not sure that I can help you, though. Could you explain to me again what you wanted to know?"

And what did I want to know? I hadn't realised until she asked that her question didn't have an obvious answer.

"Do you know a girl called Rae?" I said.

"Rae? I don't think so." She paused. "It might be better if you told me exactly what this is about."

So I told her about the mystery child, and where she'd been found. I told her about the leather purse around her neck, the newspaper clipping inside, which had led me to the story about her son. "I know this must sound rather unusual," I said. I suspected that was putting it mildly. "But I had to call you. I'm convinced there's a link somewhere, between your son and this child, that I just can't see it yet. Is there anything you remember that seems to connect with what I've told you? Anything at all?"

"You think that because my own child died I'm the kind of person who goes around stealing other people's?" She sounded amused rather than angry, and I sensed that here was a woman who had long given up on anger as an emotion. She was clearly having a bit of fun at my expense, a fact that did not prevent me from being mortified by her suggestion.

"Oh God, no. That's not what I meant at all."

"What exactly did you mean, then? Orel has been dead for thirty years. What could I possibly have to tell you about a child whose mother probably wasn't even born at the time?" She drew in her breath. The amused, waspish tone was gone. Now she just sounded tired. I remembered what Paula had said about being careful and felt ashamed suddenly. What right did I have to burden Zneyder with my questions, even if they were in a good cause?

The truth was, I had none.

"I'm sorry," I said. Zneyder was silent for what seemed like a long time. I listened to the faint crackling of static on the line, hoping she wouldn't put the phone down and knowing I could hardly blame her if she did. But when she finally spoke again she sounded quite different.

"No," she said. "It's I who should be sorry. You're a good person, I'm sure. It's just that not everyone who's called me over the years has had such selfless motives. Some people can be very cruel. Suspicion becomes a habit, I'm afraid." She sighed. "I still miss him, you know. He'd be thirty-eight now, a man with his own concerns, his own life. It could be that we would hate one another – it's so easy to idealise the dead, isn't it? The thing is, I'll never know. That's what hurts most."

I remained silent, pressing the phone to my ear, knowing anything I said would sound shallow, inaccurate, a platitude. I felt like crying.

"Your girl sounds like an interesting mystery," Zneyder said in the end. She laughed briefly, then cleared her throat. The subject of Orel was clearly closed. "I wish I could help you, I really do. And I admit it's strange, her having that newspaper clipping. I suppose it must mean *something*. But I'm afraid I have no idea what that might be." She hesitated. "Do you happen to remember what was on the back?"

"On the back?"

"On the other side of the page."

"Nothing. I mean, nothing important. Just part of a photograph."

"Oh well, it was worth a try."

"I read your book about Helen Messger," I said. "I thought it was brilliant."

"Helen was the brilliant one. Her death was a crime. All the deaths, but hers especially. I know it's wrong to think that, but it's how I feel. If not for our friendship, I don't think I'd ever have found the confidence to go into politics. Helen was a remarkable woman. My life was never the same after she died. I was very ill for a while, you know. When Orel was born I didn't know how I'd cope. You do though, don't you? One slow day at a time, you become someone else."

"I lost my mother in the bomb," I said suddenly. "She was exactly your age."

"Really?" She sounded impatient again, and I realised I'd made a mistake, that she must be fed up with people telling her their bomb stories or their prison stories or their dead child stories, seeking meaning in their misfortune by trying to equate their own story with that of a stranger who had once been famous for her tragedy, if only briefly. Zneyder would naturally reject such confidences as an invasion of her privacy. *Bomb or no bomb, everyone's lost someone. But that's not my problem.* "Then you'll understand how it was for me. Do you mind if we finish this now? It's getting late. I don't sleep well these days. Too much talking makes my insomnia worse."

"Of course," I said. "I'm sorry to have disturbed you."

"Not at all. I'm sorry, too. About the girl, I mean. If anything occurs to me I'll call you back."

"That would be very helpful. Thank you." I knew even as I said it that I would not hear from her again.

Paula came in around an hour later. I told her what had happened.

"She sounds a bit of a bitch to me," she said. One of the nicest things about Paula is that she never says I told you so.

I shook my head. "It's not her fault. Can you imagine how I sounded? The most frustrating thing is that I still believe there's something there, something I'm missing."

Paula leaned her back against the sofa and hugged her knees. "Don't you think you might be overcomplicating things? What if Rae is just what she seems – a lost child? What if that piece of newspaper is just a – you know, what they say in detective stories?"

"A red herring?"

Paula nodded.

"How can it be, Paula? She was carrying it in a purse around her neck. Someone must have put it there for a reason."

"Not necessarily. Suppose the clipping was in the purse already, and Rae just happened to find it on the station or somewhere? The purse, I mean. You're constructing this whole big mystery out of it, but it could all be chance."

The notion had never occurred to me, but I was bound to admit that Paula's idea had more than a ring of truth to it. My heart sank. If the purse wasn't really Rae's, then all my extravagant suppositions concerning it had been a waste of time.

It wouldn't be the first time.

"I'm just saying," Paula added. "What's that thing about the simplest explanation of a problem being the correct one?"

"Occam's Razor. But it's not always true." I couldn't help remembering what Lyuba had said, about the police having to prise Rae's fingers from the purse strap before they could take it away from her. Would a child become so quickly attached to an object she'd found by chance? I seriously doubted it. Later, when Paula was asleep, I found myself going back over my conversation with Miryam Zneyder and wondering how I might have handled it better. Zneyder's book about Helen Messger was still on the floor under the bed. I picked it up and began leafing idly through the section at the end, which consisted of more than a hundred photographs Zneyder had collected, of women who had been killed in the bomb or who had lost someone close to them, either in the strike itself or in its aftermath.

Ailsa Kurkov, 23, whose poems 'White Guard' and 'A Night in Murmansk' took both the first and second prizes in *Black Dog* magazine's annual poetry competition for 1961.

Zhanna Bruderhof, 46, a chemistry teacher who single-handedly organized the evacuation of her school after the other teachers fled.

Mona Verlinsky, 19, a local chess champion who had recently been promoted to grandmaster status.

Vanessa Chubin, 32, a television reporter whose extended reportage 'Diary of a Nuclear Strike' was later awarded the gold medal in the Frankfurt Prize for International Journalism. Chubin's eight-year-old daughter Raisa went missing from Vasilievsky Station on the day of the bomb. Chubin died of cancer, no doubt caused by radiation exposure, in 1969.

Something about the photograph of Chubin seemed familiar, but I was too tired by then to give the subject much thought. I turned out the light, thinking I'd fall asleep more or less immediately, but an hour later I was still awake. I couldn't get that photograph of Chubin out of my mind. In the end I switched the bedside lamp back on so I could look at it again. Paula stirred briefly beside me but was sound asleep again in less than a second. She likes to joke that nothing wakes her, not even a bomb going off.

Chubin had been photographed facing slightly away from the camera. The left side of her face lay partly in shadow, and it was the shadow I recognised, I realised, the particular shape it made against Chubin's cheek, like a spoon cutting ice cream.

It was the same as the shadow in the photograph on the back of the newspaper clipping.

I knew this could not be possible, yet at the same time I understood beyond all doubt that it was so. I slipped from the bed and pulled on the grey long-sleeved T-shirt Paula had been wearing. My heart was racing. I kept hearing Zneyder's words to me over the phone – *do you happen to remember what was on the back?* I had dismissed them so casually, yet it seemed her instincts had been correct all along.

I switched on the living room light and reached for the box file Lyuba had given me at the start, stuffed now with my notes as well as the photocopies of the original documents. My hands wouldn't stop shaking. I sifted rapidly through the papers, my hands clumsy with panic, suddenly convinced that the photograph wouldn't be there, that someone had stolen it. The idea was crazy of course, pure paranoia. I told myself to calm down, to relax my breathing. When I sorted back through the papers a second time I came upon the picture almost at once.

I placed the already dog-eared photocopy flat on the floor, then opened Zneyder's book at the appropriate page. There was no room left for doubt – the two images were identical.

I closed the book, folding the clipping between its pages to mark the place, then left the book on the floor beside the other things and went back to bed. There was nothing I could do until morning and I needed to sleep. Now that I had found what I was looking for, I thought I probably would.

* * *

(From *Izvestiya*, Thursday May 8th 1969)
Vanessa Thomasovna Chubin 18/1/30 – 4/5/69

Prizewinning reporter Vanessa Chubin has died at her grandmother's
home in Kasli, Chelyabinsk District, at the age of thirty-nine. She
had been suffering from cancer.

Chubin became internationally famous when her live television
coverage of the Cuban Missile Crisis and the consequent American
nuclear strike on the city of Kuragin was broadcast around the
world. A documentary based on her broadcasts, 'Diary of a Nuclear
Strike', was later awarded the gold medal in the Frankfurt Prize for
International Journalism.

Chubin's achievements were marred by personal tragedy. Her
older brother Richard, a gifted poet, committed suicide in his late
twenties, and Chubin's eight-year-old daughter Raisa disappeared
on the day of the attack and was never seen again. It was presumed
she was killed in the blast, although Chubin herself never believed
this and continued to search for her until a few months before her
death. A personal memoir of her quest, Wait for Me Here, *briefly*
became a bestseller.

Vanessa Chubin never married. She is survived by her sister, Bella,
and her younger brother Carl.

(From *Wait for Me Here*, Mirabil'nie Knigi 1967)

RAYA DIDN'T HAVE her coat on. We were halfway to the tram
stop before I realised. I was furious, because I knew she'd done
it deliberately. She'd made a fuss about leaving the apartment –
something about wanting to finish a cardboard rocket ship she was
building for her friend Emma – and I felt certain this was her way
of making sure we'd have to go back.

"For goodness' sake, Rae!" I grabbed her hard around the
shoulders. I came close to shaking her. It was cold out, two degrees
below freezing at least. Raya couldn't go anywhere dressed like
that. Her face was suddenly blank with distress and confusion.
I could see she didn't understand how I could be so angry over
something so small. Perhaps I should have tried to explain, that
it was not her I was angry with, not really, but time. Time like a
runaway mare, her flanks heaving and sticky with sweat, breaking

free of her constraining harness and dashing madly away across the train tracks.

"It's okay, it's okay," I said. I began fumbling with the buttons of my own coat, my fingers big with cold, my thoughts already far away, two stops down the line, with Raya safely ensconced in the women's waiting room at Vasilievsky while I hurried away from the station and headed back to where I needed to be, at the city's centre, where a part of the world was getting ready to immolate itself and who knew if survival was possible and what it might entail. "Look, you see, you can wear mine instead. You'll be warm in Mummy's coat, won't you?"

Rae smiled as if I'd offered her a present, the bad moment forgotten as she shifted towards this new one, and the prospect of something unexpected and, in its comical way, special. The coat was too big for her of course. It looked ridiculous, but it would keep her warm, it would become its own world. That was all that seemed to matter in that moment. That my scent be wrapped around her, like a protective shield.

The tram was packed, more crowded than was usual at this time of day. "Hold on to me," I said to Raya. I found myself imagining how it might feel to lose her in the crush, the sudden realisation, the panic. I forgot about my lack of a coat almost at once, it was so warm inside the carriage. Mainly I was just desperate to get to Tamara's place, where there would be a radio, and coffee, and Alyosha. We would talk, we would do our best to make sense of things, we would decide what to do.

We were all afraid, but there was still room for doubt. I don't think any of us believed that it would really happen.

The train was slow, slow, slow, and time seemed to be moving faster with each new minute. I tugged Raisa along by the hand, steering her briskly through the crowd outside the station entrance, thinking all the while about Alyosha and what we were proposing to do – about the Americans and the Party, and our own private situation with Pamela that seemed liable to explode at any moment.

We hurried across the station concourse to the women's waiting room. The stove was lit, and I briefly considered taking back my coat – my hands were freezing – but decided against it. What if the fire went out? I would only worry. And I knew Rae loved my coat, with its cherry red skirt and shiny black buttons that were made to look like jet but were really just glass. She called it my *pal'to barabanshchika*, my drummer boy's coat, like the one in the story she liked by Olga Grin.

I hoped the coat might comfort her in my absence. An idea born out of cowardice, but I clung fast to it anyway.

"Where are we going?" Rae said. She was scared, I could see that, but I pretended not to. If I granted this knowledge admittance it would overwhelm me, all my careful plans would fall apart. I would be gone for an hour, perhaps two. What could possibly go wrong?

"We're going to Baba's, remember? On the train? I need to go and see Auntie Tam first, but I won't be long. Just wait for me here, okay? Whatever happens, stay in the waiting room and don't move. There's a nice fire, look. You can sit here, next to this lady. I'll be back very soon."

I wrapped my arms around her then, pushed my big cold face into her small hot one, pressed my eyes closed as I kissed her, so I wouldn't have to see how afraid she was. The woman on the bench beside her – a heavyset, pasty-faced woman with the most extraordinary fur collar (I hadn't seen a fur coat like that in years, not since my grandmother had to pawn her best clothes at the end of the war) scowled at me disapprovingly. She was holding her gloves in her lap, her pudgy hands nestled together like plump pigeons. I wanted to seize those hands, with their deep creases and gaudy rings (the kind of rings, set with foil-backed paste instead of gemstones, that are used as theatre props or in cheap cabaret, and I realised that yes of course I recognised her; she was an actor, I'd seen her onstage as Madame Arkadina in *The Seagull*). I wanted to beg her to please watch over my little girl until I got back, see she doesn't wander off, amuse her with stories, stop her being frightened, but I didn't. It would have been too much of an admission. That what I was doing was dangerous, and – worse – that I knew this better than anyone, better than she ever could, but that I was going to do it anyway, because I was still convinced, even during those last moments, that I would get away with it.

"WHAT HAPPENED TO Rae's original clothes?" I asked Clara. "The clothes she was wearing when she was found?"

Clara made a face. "They were taken away for forensics to have a look at. I doubt anyone's got round to it yet, though. They have a backlog a mile long, and there was no suggestion of foul play. I expect they're in store."

"Do you think I could get a look at them?"

"What's going on?"

"I'm not sure yet. Maybe nothing. Would you mind keeping this to yourself until I have something more concrete?"

"Sure." Clara shrugged. I asked her how Rae was, and she said fine, although I could tell by the way she said it that she was unhappy about something. That her time with Rae was running out, most likely – Clara loves kids. Anyway, she let me use her phone to call the lock-up and half an hour later I was there, cooling my heels in the front office while old Victor Dirnychev hobbled around in the evidence store trying to locate the articles in question. Finally I was called through to what was supposed to be an atmosphere-neutral examination room but was actually just a windowless cubby hole in the basement.

"Here they are," Dirnychev said. He never says much, Dirnychev, but he's all right once you get to know him. He had three evidence bags laid out on the table. One contained a child's grey woollen pinafore dress. The second bag contained the coat. I barely needed to glance at it to know this was the same as the garment described by Vanessa Chubin in her memoir. The sight of it brought a lump to my throat. I felt like calling Lyuba then and there, telling her I'd done it, I'd found Rae's mother.

The only problem was that the mother was dead. She'd died in 1969, before Rae was born.

I smothered a laugh. The third bag contained a pair of shoes, a child's zip-up sheepskin boots. The toes were heavily discoloured, coated all over with a greyish dust. Masonry dust, by the look of it. The kind that hangs in vast clouds above a city after it's been bombed.

"How long will it take to get these tested?" I asked Dirnychev. "If I get a permission slip this afternoon, I mean?"

"About forty-eight hours, if you're lucky."

I made the expected grumbling noises – that it was too long, there must be a way to speed things up, all the usual stuff. In fact I wasn't too bothered. I knew already what they would find, and I was right.

Forensic analysis of Rae's sheepskin boots detected faint but definite traces of radioactivity.

"So what are you saying? That this child, this Raisa Chubina, is a time traveller?"

Not many people could have asked that question with a straight face, but Paula isn't most people. She listens more than she speaks. I would be the first to admit I probably take advantage of that.

Except that now I'd finished my story I was finding it hard to say anything at all.

"I think it's the station," I said in the end. "Vasilievsky. You know the bomb never touched it? Say if – I don't know – it became lodged in time somehow. And Rae – Rae just stayed where she was, waiting for her mother exactly as she was told to. For her it's still the day of the bomb. It's everything outside the station that's moved on."

"You don't really believe that, do you? Things like that don't happen except in films."

"I don't know, Paula. All I can say is that I'm not making this up. The coat is real. Rae's boots are real. Are you telling me it's just coincidence, just chance?"

"What else can it be?"

I sighed and rubbed my eyes. I'd been awake most of the night, mentally examining each and every aspect of what I'd discovered in minute detail until I could actually feel my mind sliding out of control. I finally fell asleep, just for a little while, at around six o'clock. I was woken by a gimlet ray of sunshine, stabbing me in the eye like a steel needle. I had a sudden and perfectly clear insight into how it must feel to go insane.

"I'm sorry, Paula. I don't mean to have a go at you, but there's more to it than that. I know there is, and I mean to prove it." I tried to smile. "Occam's Razor, remember?"

"You're not going to Lyuba with this, are you?"

"Not yet. I need to think."

"No," Paula said. "You need to let this go. Not everything in this life is about the bomb, you know. Rae isn't your brother."

I jumped inside my skin when she said that, then went cold all over. Peter is one of those subjects we never talk about.

*　　*　　*

SO THERE ARE supposed to be these places – nexuses – where planes of time meet, or converge, whatever. Where a certain building or patch of woodland or street or factory yard, instead of being altered by time, or eroded by it, is *carried over*, uploaded, rendered time-neutral. You'll find an awful lot has been written on this subject once you start digging. What it boils down to is that certain places stay the same.

As Vasilievsky Station had stayed the same, in spite of being close to the centre of a nuclear strike. I had no idea if the place had been a time-nexus before the station was built – probably, just harder to notice – but it was definitely one now.

That was what the books told me, anyway. And the articles, and the internet forums. When my research first started clicking together, my main worry was that no one would believe me. The more I delved into the strange world of alternate physics the more I came to realise that I'd been wrong about that, there were hundreds out there – thousands – who would leap upon my story with the fervour of newly minted religious converts. University lecturers, discredited scientists, New Age philosophers, mystics, prophets, inmates of mental asylums, damaged young mothers and burned-out grandfathers. I found this discovery both enlightening and profoundly depressing.

I returned to Vasilievsky Station, watched the crowds ebb and flow as the trains came and went from the long platforms, wondered at the stark winter sunshine, flinging itself to its death from those ridiculous corkscrew towers. I was waiting for something to happen, I suppose. I have no idea what. At the end of an afternoon's continuous staring, it began to seem to me that I was always staring at the same crowd, the same faces, endlessly repeating, like one short sequence of film stuck in a loop. I gazed at the teeming figures, remembering one of the texts I had stumbled across, a pamphlet that made repeated references to something called a probability wave, an article of quantum physics suggesting that an object or even a person might be shown to exist in two places at once. The kind of theory that would interest Alec Ostrov, no doubt. I couldn't make much sense of it myself.

I realised I had either to own this or, as Paula had suggested, let it go. I thought about the reams of strangeness I had read through, the roster of misfits and recluses and oddballs who had written them down. They could have been born crazy, I supposed, but I seriously doubted it. They had probably started out just like me.

IN THE END, the decision was made for me. A couple identifying themselves as Rae's parents came forward to claim her.

Their name was Bryusov and they were from Omsk. They said they'd been travelling home from a visit to Rae's grandmother, in Nizhny Novgorod, when Rae went missing.

"We were all so tired, you see," Gavril Bryusov explained. "Our first train was cancelled, and we'd been waiting around on the platform for almost six hours. Sonya and I were having a nap in our compartment. Raya was with us, or so we thought. She must have woken up and gone exploring, you know how kids are. We weren't too worried at first. We thought she must be on the train somewhere. Of course when we found out what had happened we were frantic."

The train had made stops at five different stations, each an hour apart, while Sonya and Gavril Bryusov were asleep. It had taken them days of desperate phone calls and enquiries before they discovered their daughter's whereabouts. Eventually they were directed through to Lyuba. They were back in Omsk by then, and it was a further eighteen hours before they were able to catch a return train. Clara was there to meet them at Vasilievsky Station.

"The man sounded drunk," Clara said. "Relief, I suppose."

"What about Rae?"

"Didn't say a word. Just ran to her mother and buried her face in her stomach. She was crying."

"Who? Rae?"

"No, Sonya Bryusov. They had Rae's full ID on them, the works. Raylina Gavrilovna Bryusov, born 19th October 2002. There was a photo and everything."

She fell silent. She was still missing Rae, I could tell. After a couple of minutes of neither of us saying anything, I asked her if she'd asked the Bryusovs about Rae's coat. I thought she might have forgotten about that, but she caught on at once.

"I did, actually. They said the red coat belonged to Rae's sister, Liza. Liza went away to university recently, apparently, and now Rae won't let the coat out of her sight. Insists on wearing it, even though it's miles too big for her. She misses her sister. Poor kid." Clara sniffed. "It was funny about that purse thing, though. They downright refused to let her keep it. Said it might have germs, or something. I had to promise the kid I'd look after it." She paused, then opened a drawer of her sideboard and drew something out. "Here it is."

She handed me the purse. This was the first time I'd seen the real article, and I could understand why the Bryusovs hadn't been keen on taking it away with them. It was a shabby thing, the leather cracked and stiffened, unpleasant to touch. The material securing the zip had almost worn through.

I opened the zip and looked inside but the purse was empty. The inside smelled musty and faintly rotten, the way all leather begins to smell if you don't take care of it properly.

A COUPLE OF days after Rae went home I called in at the precinct to speak to Lyuba but she wasn't there. On an impulse I went downstairs to see old Dirnychev instead. Victor Dirnychev has lived his whole life within one mile of the city centre. The bomb left him buried in the rubble of his apartment block for almost two days.

I asked Dirnychev if it might be possible for anyone walking around the city now to pick up radioactive dust on their shoes.

"In one of those old warehouses out by Karl Marx, say. Or at Vasilievsky Station."

He frowned, apparently in concentration, picking in between his teeth with a paperclip. "I've heard that it is," he said. "Stuff like that takes a long time to go away, doesn't it? They say it's mostly harmless now, anyway."

"Do you believe that?"

"I suppose I do." He took the paperclip out of his mouth, flicked it across the countertop and onto the floor. "If there's one thing I've learned in this life it's that you have to hope for the best. What choice do you have? You'd go mad otherwise, wouldn't you?"

ENDLESS

RACHEL SWIRSKY

Rachel Swirsky is an American literary, speculative fiction and fantasy writer, poet, and editor living in California. She is the winner of two Nebula awards and her work has been shortlisted for Hugo, World Fantasy, Tiptree, and Sturgeon awards.

TERRIFYING CRUSH. BODIES on bodies pressed. My open mouth, trying to scream, filling with smoke. Unbearable heat behind, blazing us forward. Our backs growing hot beneath long, wool dresses, a precursor of what's to follow.

We knock aside sewing machines. With muffled clatter, they fall amid piles of discarded fabric. Beneath me, someone's scream pierces the chaos. My foot is on her chest. Bone snaps under my heel. I try to run forward, get off her, but so many people. I'm shoving in place. We're all shoving in place. Me and the girls behind and the girls in front, everyone who can stand, battering the blockades of flesh between us and something that might be safety.

Elevator doors snap shut on a load of lucky, half-burned girls. We pound closed doors with our fists. Someone manages to pry one open. People force forward. Screams echo as girls pitch down empty shafts.

Push to change direction. Manage it despite bodies crammed together as densely as iron walls. More girls beneath my feet. Cries of pain syncopate with sounds of stomping feet.

Consuming it all, the roar of fire, following behind us so closely that its searing maw has consumed everything in our minds but red.

Then, in front of me: clean, white daylight. An open window. Something shifts the press of bodies. Someone has jumped, leaving behind a body-width of space.

We scramble, claw, to take her place. Fire catches our skirts, lights our hair like candle wicks. The strongest push through to the ledge. Smoking-flaming torches of fire plummet.

I'm not the strongest, but I'm strong enough to rush behind. No hesitation, not even a thought for the forthcoming fall. The fire has pushed me forward like the hot hand of a giant and I will do anything to get away.

Sick vertigo flood, but oh, relief of air gulped in lungfuls. The smell of my own flesh, cooking. The falling. The falling. Broken body bursts against the sidewalk, thud and dead.

ONE-HUNDRED-AND-forty-six girls died in the Triangle Shirtwaist Factory fire after owners Harris and Blanck locked the stairwells.

Back again.

CLAMOR FOR THE door, but this time, the push-and-press lasts only a second before I'm on the ground. Feet all over me. Toes. Heels. Leather and sweat. Body cracks. Ribs, vertebrae. Delicate finger bones, pop, pop, pop.

Someone's foot on my chest. Girl I was before? Maybe.

Small this time, so small. No way to keep upright in the stampede. Nowhere near strong enough to fight to the elevators, to the windows. Tiny things are crushed down here at the bottom of the world where the screams fall.

Everything all sparkle. Fire sparks. Flaming hems. Black dots dancing in my vision. Can't breathe. The ribs. Can't breathe. Try to shift and gasp. Can't move. Neck broken.

Where's the pain? None anymore. Nothing past the tight chest. Broken fingers don't move. Toes too far away to know.

Tiny, smashed girl-doll, all broken.

Black dots and sparks. Char. Closing darkness. Can't find air. Can't find pain. Can't find anything.

IN THE TRIANGLE Shirtwaist Factory fire, Rosies died. Idas died. Gussies. Yettas, Jennies, Annies.

I don't know their names unless someone calls them, shouts it aloud. I know they're Catholics if they clutch rosaries. I know they're Jews if they mutter Yiddish. I know they all sew and sew and sew because even before the fire, their hands hurt so much.

They warn you beforehand. They have to. And you listen, but it's hard to *know*. They tell you that even though each death is only a few clock minutes, in mindscape it lasts forever. Doesn't matter how much you upclock. You can experience it all, splash back into consensus stream fast-as-fast, maybe a nothingth of a second later. Doesn't matter.

Dying is endless. Even when you do it, and do it, and do it again. Even when it's the same kind of death in the same kind of body in the same kind of place. Each time is the first. Each is forever.

ABOUT ME: THESE days, everyone's helix is knitted from pieces of everywhere, but if you pick out the hither-thither genetic such-and-such, just focus on the main strands, one of mine is American Japanese. They had names for the ones who came over first and the ones who lived there after. Isei, Nisei, Sansei. First generation born in the new place. Second. Third.

That's what I thought of when the Society pinged.

"At first everyone on the network had been material and then technological," the rep said. "Then the zeroes had children. But the firsts, they had their parents around to tell them what it was like."

The rep was one of a hundred. Split intelligence, not replicated. A single piece of hay pulled from a giant runtime stack of the same person. Stupid and nonreactive if you made it go off script. Doesn't matter how smart you are to start with, split yourself that many times and there's almost nothing left in each bit. Easier to reassemble when you're done, though. No chance one of the replicas goes off and starts its own life.

Would have been cheaper to use AI and allowed for more script variation. Then, I was annoyed. Later, I realized, the core-rep wanted to do everything itself. Wanted all those memories. Wanted to know how I reacted, how everyone did. Wanted to remember.

That kind of information is useful in a revolution.

It said, "Second generation, they knew how to ask. Third generation, sure. Fourth, fifth, sixth... we're iterative. We've gone beyond. The zeroes had words for it before they instantiated.

Singularity. Post-human. Incomprehensible. Lots of zeroes have wiped, but some are still around. Ever met one?"

I grunted because I had. Had the same experience most post-threes did, too. Too different to understand, talk to, care about. Always a war with those people.

Rep went on, "And before the zeroes, there are the dead generations. Oceans of mind gone blank. Not because they chose wipe. Usually not even because their hardware ran down. Died in violence, of stupidity, of fires, died sick, died alone. Child by child, the dead generations built us. Child by child, they died."

Left alone to give its script, the rep was passionate, flooding its sub-channels with emo triggers that shivered through me, made me feel a human-shape body, zinged chill and electric through nerve by simulated nerve.

"We owe them," the rep said.

Gratitude, it meant.

But me, as the rep described what it wanted, I remembered other things I'd learned about the origins of my helix strands. Sacrifice, ritual, honor given in the name of the dead. Ancestor worship. One of the most obvious and true ideas from substantiation. They gave gifts and then they died, leaving us with a debt we can never repay.

THE DEAD DIED.

They died for us.

They didn't know they died for us, but they did.

They can't eat cake. They can't row boats. They can't swing swords. They can't use money.

We can't give cake. We can't give boats. We can't give swords. We can't give money.

We can give our memories.

IT DIDN'T HAPPEN like this. I'm trying to talk to you. Remember the words you had before. Post-human. Singularity. Incomprehensible.

After dying time and time, after living through burning bodies, I understand zeroes as well as any six can. Embodied fragility. That's what sixes don't understand. It's abstract until you die and die and die and die.

But I'm not a zero and you're not sixes. You live surface instant, have brains that remember the structure of meat. For us, lots happens underwater: neural flares and tangle-thoughts and inverse treads.

I'll keep it straight though, much as I can. Someways, it happened like this.

SMOKE. SMOKE. SMOKE. Pressed in the corner. Can't get out. Two walls blocking me. I've only got half the opportunities to push through that other girls have.

Girl next to me talking under her breath. Slurred. Could be saying anything. Voice rises, falls, skims above then sinks below the din. Slurry of words, but rhythm of prayer.

Smoke. Everything smoke. I grab at fabric scraps by my feet. Press one over my mouth. Could get down, get away from the smoke, but for what? To burn later? Besides, can't stand the idea of not being able to see, lost among hems and table legs.

Smoke rises so I'll die in smoke.

Black everything. Eyes black, hands black, all black. Taste of black seeps through the cloth. Close my eyes. Black scrapes its way past eyelashes.

Smoke fills me up. Organs, bone, marrow, all gone. Girl-shaped vessel emptied out, replaced by smoke.

REP GAVE ME a list and I picked this one. First one I saw, maybe. No shortage of tragedies.

Stupidity, avarice, malice and fire. Nasty combination. Lots of them were nasty, the deaths we owe.

FORTY-FIVE THROUGH, I stopped to check my count.

Paused to think. Forty-five eternities. Could I remember forty-five? Each like all the others, and each unique?

Society AI showed up. Probably health req because I hesitated. Showed up shadow body, neutral shape without identifiers, but still incarnate because they do that when you've been embodied a long time.

Zeroes needed that. Transitions. Sixes? AI is slow.

AI said, "It does you no good to provoke a mental breakdown. If you go numb or mad, you will not honor the dead or yourself."

I found myself being embodied against my will. Shadow-shape, but mortifying to be in simulated skin. Anticipatory needles pricked my nerves, preparing for fire and pain they assume will be coming.

AI shifted into casual mode. Shadow-shape went female. Another zero thing. It read me, tried to change to me. Either my implicit association scores had changed to female-over-neuter, or it was something about all the girls in the fire. Second seemed more likely. Dying girls everywhere.

In a voice softened for emotional simulation, AI asked, "Do you want anything?"

I glared smoke at her. Tried to initiate number forty-six but was blocked.

AI went hard-edged again. "I am required to remind you that you may exempt yourself from this project at any time."

I snarled wordless, sub-band burst. Hold released. I went.

NUMBER SEVENTY-THREE, I wake up next to one of the survivors. Recognize her. Seen her face survive before, from a distance. Closer this time.

She tugs my hand. Murmurs a word. Must be my name. But this body's ears are ringing. Head is so sore. Something fell on me maybe. Fingers press, find place where skull depresses, sharp burst of pain.

She tugs me again. Trying to pull me toward the elevators. Works for some. I try to tell this body, okay, follow that way. I stagger after her and vision tilts, blurs. Head hurts. Hurts.

Tugs my hand again. Says something. Repeats it. Shouts it.

Vision stills, then swirls again. This time, I puke. Survivor flutters over me, murmuring.

Can't say why I recognize her face. Another scared, sooty girl. Could be brunette or could be filthy. Undernourished skinny with long, thin eyes, and narrow eyes sunken into hollows carved by hunger and fear. Rough, calloused fingers clutch at mine.

More heat as the fire shifts. Waves of screams doppler in the distance. Beyond the survivor, I see whoosh of skirts and shoes crowding the path she'd meant to follow. Soon there won't be a way. Body starts to wretch again, but there's nothing more to throw up.

I come to the conclusion at the same time body does. She lives. We don't. We shove the survivor down her path. Hard so she's not tempted to overpower us, sacrifice herself to stay.

Eyes show pain and shock before she takes the cue to run. Breathe. Breathe. Alone now. Slump down, stomach cramping over and over, relieving itself of nothing. I think she was our sister.

AFTER SEVENTY-THREE, AI stopped me again. Didn't shadow-shape this time. Didn't talk. Only made a path for the rep.

Rep was twenty-split this time. Almost present. Said, "You've seen now. What it was like."

I sent subliminal yes, every way but voice. Girl seventy-two had screamed and screamed. The idea of my throat was still raw with it.

"You know how the method works," the rep said.

Took me a while to remember how brains work in the real world instead of the dead one. Doors and corridors and trap doors. There, the packet stored sideways-conscious.

Time travel. Projecting instantiation into cold minds.

"Zeroes, ones, twos. They think there's no point if we can't substantiate into created flesh. But instantiation is strong. AI says you've seen how strong."

I thought about the body pushing her sister away, how I became we. "I've seen," I said. Voice a croak, grated with seventy-two's screaming, even though her throat was rotted and gone and I'd died twice since then.

"You can't change back after that," Rep said. "Can't swim blithe without the past."

"Could lobotomy," I said. Easy enough to cut out the parts you didn't want. Store them behind the trap doors. Give them to the AI to keep.

"For now," Rep said.

Sound of 'now' made me twitch. I exhaled doubt, misgiving. Interest, too.

"Things have to change," Rep said. "No more blithe swimming, three and four and five and six. And if we keep this way, what about seven and later? Historical strands keep attenuating? Is that just?"

I thought: is that how we honor the dead?
"We have everything," Rep said. "They are nothing."
Rep said, "We owe them."

ZEROES, YOU MADE our world, but we're not zeroes anymore. We are more and we are different. You wanted to move on. Singularity. Post-human. Incomprehensible. We are those.

We'll live as long as we want. We'll never die from fire. We'll never get sick. We'll never be killed.

We'll never be fragile.

You want to forget those things. We need to remember.

EVERYWHERE, OUR INSTANTIATED memories will be. Pieced together from my hundred-and-forty-six deaths. From the strange fruit swinging on the tree. From the comfort women. From the first peoples who lost and lost and lost.

In everyone's minds, they'll be. The zeroes and ones and twos who want to forget. The threes and fours and fives and sixes who never cared to learn. Lightning-quick, they will know.

Not every story, not every moment. The strongest ones. The flashes and flares. The ones who sacrificed the most. Who died young and sick and badly.

We the society are sixes and we are strong. AIs are ours now. We know the secrets of tangling and inverse. All will know. Born, they'll know. Dreaming, they'll know. Wiped, they'll know.

We know that some of you lived fragile. We know that this will be hard for you. We know you do not want to lose control of what you built. You are the first and you are the oldest, but in this water, you are leviathans, and we are fish. You must struggle to the surface to breathe, but we are always here. We are made for this place.

Debts move in multiple directions. We owe you and you owe us. Now, it is our place to be the ones who decide. Someday, it will be sevens, eights, fifteens.

Time remains before we will take our moment. There are memories to be collected, sifted, chosen. There are deaths and deaths and deaths and deaths.

You are our predecessors, and we honor you, so we give you this time and this warning. We will remember the dead.

ONE-HUNDRED-AND-twenty-three: shock to be a boy this time. In real, I'm neuter, but here in the cold, I have been so many girls that it is my skin. I am a girl and I am on fire.

But now I am a boy. Another hand in mine. Small and trembling. Mine too, but I try to steady it. Must be solid. Must be steady. For the tiny hand.

Want to get to a window. In this body, there is strength enough to push aside the screaming girls. I try not to, but it happens. I butt them aside with my shoulders as I pull the tiny hand along with me to the window. The girl it belongs to holds her breath as she follows.

That girl, that girl, that girl, I know them from inside their skin. There: glimpse of a new face. One of those remaining to me? Or perhaps a survivor?

I've made it through. Girl and her tiny hand beside me. A shallow wave of accomplishment. I can get her away from the fire. The air is so much better than burning.

Pull her out with me. Take the tiny hand from mine. Sweep down to kiss it. Then up to kiss her lips. I smile and she smiles and the smiles are dead.

Below us, the watchers, weeping and shouting in alarm. Pointing at us. A horror show staged for them. Flaming lovers, star-crossed.

In three hundred years, no one else will have to die, ever. This day, this rotted eternity, we jump together. Our bodies are iron weights, dragging us down to shatter on the earth.

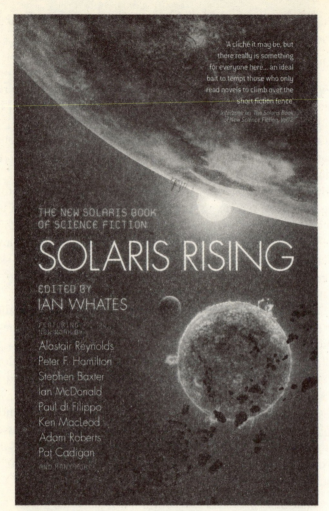

'A cliché it may be, but there really is something for everyone here... an ideal bait to tempt those who only read novels to climb over the short fiction fence'

Interzone on The Solaris Book of New Science Fiction, Vol 2

THE NEW SOLARIS BOOK OF SCIENCE FICTION

SOLARIS RISING

EDITED BY
IAN WHATES

FEATURING NEW WORK BY

Alastair Reynolds
Peter F. Hamilton
Stephen Baxter
Ian McDonald
Paul di Filippo
Ken Macleod
Adam Roberts
Pat Cadigan
AND MANY MORE

UK ISBN: 978-1-907992-08-7 • US ISBN: 978-1-907992-09-4 • £7.99/$7.99

Solaris Rising presents nineteen stories of the very highest calibre from some of the most accomplished authors in the genre, proving just how varied and dynamic science fiction can be. From strange goings on in the present to explorations of bizarre futures, from drug-induced tragedy to time-hopping serial killers, from crucial choices in deepest space to a ravaged Earth under alien thrall, from gritty other worlds to surreal other realms, *Solaris Rising* delivers a broad spectrum of experiences and excitements, showcasing the genre at its very best.

 WWW.SOLARISBOOKS.COM

Follow us on Twitter! www.twitter.com/solarisbooks

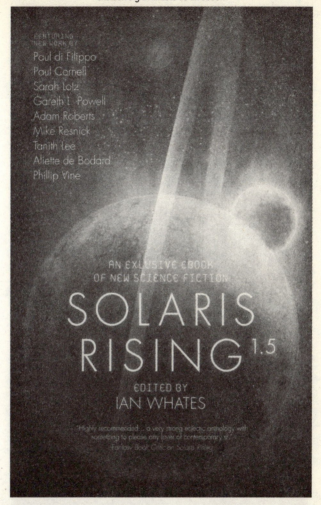

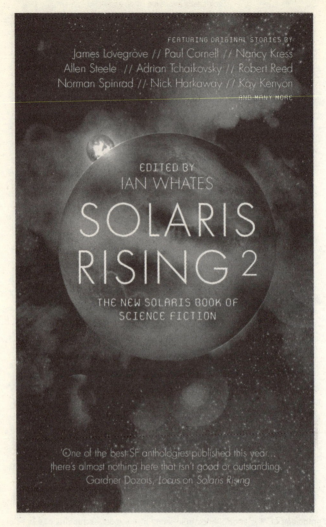

Solaris Rising 2 showcases the finest new science fiction from both celebrated authors and the most exciting of emerging writers. Following in the footsteps of the critically-acclaimed first volume, editor Ian Whates has once again gathered together a plethora of thrilling and daring talent. Within you will find unexplored frontiers as well as many of the central themes of the genre – alien worlds, time travel, artificial intelligence – made entirely new in the telling. The authors here prove once again why SF continues to be the most innovative, satisfying, and downright exciting genre of all.

EDITED BY JONATHAN STRAHAN

THE BEST SCIENCE FICTION & FANTASY OF THE YEAR

VOLUME EIGHT

INLUDING STORIES BY **K J PARKER** // **NEIL GAIMAN**
GEOFF RYMAN // **GREG EGAN** // **M JOHN HARRISON**
CAITLÍN R KIERNAN // **E LILY YU** // **MADELINE ASHBY**
TED CHIANG // **JOE ABERCROMBIE** // **IAN McDONALD**

From the inner realms of humanity to the far reaches of space, these are the science fiction and fantasy tales that are shaping the genre and the way we think about the future. Multi-award winning editor Jonathan Strahan continues to shine a light on the very best writing, featuring both established authors and exciting new talents. Within you will find twenty-eight incredible tales, showing the ever growing depth and diversity that science fiction and fantasy continues to enjoy. These are the brightest stars in our firmament, lighting the way to a future filled with astonishing stories about the way we are, and the way we could be.

 WWW.SOLARISBOOKS.COM

Follow us on Twitter! www.twitter.com/solarisbooks

ENGINEERING
INFINITY

Edited by Jonathan Strahan

UK ISBN: 978 1 907519 51 2 • US ISBN: 978 1 907519 52 9 • £7.99/$7.99

The universe shifts and changes; suddenly you understand, and are filled with wonder. Coming up against the speed of light (and with it, the sheer size of the universe), seeing how difficult and dangerous terraforming an alien world really is, realising that a hitch-hiker on a starship consumes fuel and oxygen and the tragedy that results... it's "hard-SF" where sense of wonder is most often found and where science fiction's true heart lies. Including stories from the likes of Stephen Baxter and Charles Stross.

 WWW.SOLARISBOOKS.COM

Follow us on Twitter! www.twitter.com/solarisbooks

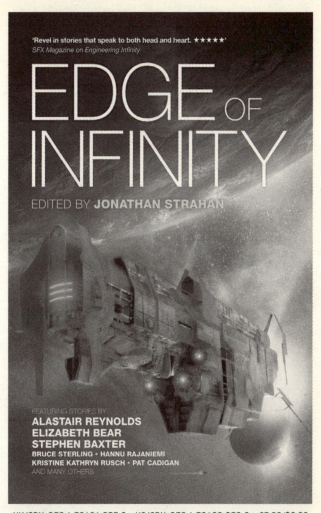